The Tiny Things Are Heavier

The

Tiny

Things

Are

Heavier

A Novel

ESTHER IFESINACHI OKONKWO

BLOOMSBURY PUBLISHING

NEW YORK · LONDON · OXFORD · NEW DELHI · SYDNEY

BLOOMSBURY PUBLISHING
Bloomsbury Publishing Inc.
1359 Broadway, New York, NY 10018, USA
50 Bedford Square, London, WC1B 3DP, UK
Bloomsbury Publishing Ireland Limited,
29 Earlsfort Terrace, Dublin 2, D02 AY28, Ireland

BLOOMSBURY, BLOOMSBURY PUBLISHING, and the Diana logo are trademarks
of Bloomsbury Publishing Plc

First published in the United States 2025

ISBN: HB: 978-1-63973-410-8; EBOOK: 978-1-63973-411-5

LIBRARY OF CONGRESS CATALOGING-IN-PUBLICATION DATA IS AVAILABLE

2 4 6 8 10 9 7 5 3 1

Typeset by Westchester Publishing Services
Printed in the United States at Lakeside Book Company

To find out more about our authors and books visit
www.bloomsbury.com and sign up for our newsletters.

Bloomsbury books may be purchased for business or promotional use.
For information on bulk purchases please contact Macmillan Corporate
and Premium Sales Department at specialmarkets@macmillan.com.
For product safety–related questions contact productsafety@bloomsbury.com.

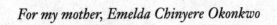

For my mother, Emelda Chinyere Okonkwo

For whom is it well, for whom is it well?
There is no one for whom it is well.

—CHINUA ACHEBE, *THINGS FALL APART*

Part One

S ommy notices his legs first, hairy and stumpy, the part not covered by his tan-colored shorts. He's standing by the airport's exit, watching a woman on tiptoes, a piece of cardboard held above her head. His name is Bayo, Sommy's new roommate. She'd imagined him to be taller. Over the phone, he sounded like a big man, a kind of gushing boisterousness about him. And he'd once told her, unprompted, that he ate twelve bananas in one sitting. About her now are people walking slowly, clasping passport booklets, sandwich bags, phones, their luggage skidding behind them. Nothing like the mad crowd at the airport in Chicago, where she'd first landed, that avalanche of people sweeping past with speed, a terse, cosmopolitan sheen to them.

Bayo still hasn't noticed her, though she's standing right next to him. His gaze is fixed on the woman holding the cardboard.

She taps his shoulder.

He turns. "Sommy?"

His tight eyes inspect her quickly, and relax, as if in approval. He slides his phone in his pocket, grabs the bag to her left.

A short static tumble from the airport speakers, and then a flight announcement.

"Hope I didn't keep you waiting," she says.

"Not at all," he whispers, and smiles, a secret smile, motioning his head toward the woman with the cardboard. Sommy's close enough now to read the writing on the cardboard. It reads: WELCOME HOME MY LYING SNIVELING CHEATING HUSBAND. Sommy studies the woman, dressed sanely, in a short floral dress and black ballet shoes. Her skin, clear and plump, contrasts sharply with the red circles around her eyes. She's looking to the sharp corner Sommy had turned when she descended the escalator. The airport crowd doesn't pay the woman any substantial attention. They throw glances her way and look on ahead, as if, like Sommy, they feel the spectacle to be too naked, too private.

Bayo, satisfied that Sommy's seen what he wants her to see, tugs her bag behind him and walks out of the airport, into Iowa's blinding heat.

Sommy walks behind Bayo, tugging at the strap of the duffel bag hanging on her shoulder, watching his sloping, one-sided walk, each step forceful, announcing itself: the walk of a short man, a man who's had to stretch himself to be heard. She imagines that in secondary school his classmates called him "small stout." The thought amuses her, and she rubs her eyes until she no longer feels like laughing.

He turns to her now, his eyes wide with mischief. "I wish we stayed to watch the entire drama."

She nods, forms a strained smile. Strange, she thinks, this desire of his to bask in another's misfortune.

"You are tired, abi?" he says. "Sorry, the drive is not that far. You will soon rest."

She swipes beads of sweat from her forehead. She did not anticipate the heat. She's always associated America with the cold.

They walk on ahead. The air smells clean. The sky, clear like an overshined glass. Unlike Lagos's gray sky and fogged air. It occurs to her then that she's indeed landed. She is in America. She wants to throw her arms around Bayo, say to him: "We are here, we are here." But it passes, the giddiness, as swiftly as it came.

Bayo forces her bag into the car boot. When she tries to lift the other bag beside her, he says, "No, no, let me carry it for you," and then grins.

Soon they are driving past vast expanses of greenery, trees and grasses, past large billboards bearing names of unfamiliar brands—Blue Moon, State Farm, Wells Fargo—and past several road construction sites, streetlights, and the occasional pedestrian.

"Yes," Bayo says, as though able to read her thoughts. "America fine die. Too beautiful. See as everywhere clean. Everything just set."

She nods, smiles. He's a talker, this one. He'd been talking since the car engine spurted to life. He'd described the apartment they'd rented. Small, neat, very modern, he said. He'd given her details about the generous classmate of his who'd allowed him to borrow his car just three days after they met, and about the new white church he'd attended the day before, just a stone's throw from their apartment, where he'd met another generous American who'd offered to give him some used furniture. He told her about his two-day flight from Lagos a week ago. He'd spent the night in Doha, at a hotel inside the airport. He'd been unable to sleep, anxious about missing his connecting flight, and even when he decided to sleep, sleep wouldn't come, and usually, he would watch porn, masturbate, you know, to release the anxiety, but he couldn't watch porn in Doha, because Sharia Law and all. He didn't know how they would know he was watching porn. But what if they had a server that alerted some officials when someone logged into Pornhub? Of the woman with cardboard at the airport, he said that he understood the spectacle. "She wants validation," he'd said. She wants someone to walk up to her and say they are sorry. Isn't that what people seek on social media when they share intimate details of their life? He said he would have gone up to the woman, told her, "Madam, that man—he's not worth it. Chin up. Move on," but he doesn't feel as free here, in America, to just approach people, even when they seem to beg for the attention. "Any small thing someone would just call police for you," he'd said. And, he added, with this whole Me Too movement thing, he's especially careful with women these days. He looked at Sommy briefly and took his gaze back to the road. He believes women, of course. He said this loudly, as if prompted by something he'd glimpsed on her face. But he's also aware that not everyone says the truth about a matter. In short, he'd said, it's a little condescending to believe that women always say the truth. Women are human beings, and human beings lie. He nodded, agreeing with himself, or perhaps proud of having said what he believes to be profound. He then threw her glances so quick and beckoning that she, too, began to nod. Though what she wanted to do was sigh. Bayo often tweeted in support of Nigerian feminist Twitter. She viewed his tweets as progressive but sensed in them a kind of lazy posturing, as if he believed misogyny, at least an active performance of it, beneath him, primitive. She feels validated now.

When she asked if she could connect to his mobile hot spot, she'd expected a simple yes or no, but he launched into a tirade about the plan the phone company had made him buy. With this plan, he could not connect to any device.

Sommy, tired, aching from the twenty-four-hour trip, responded to most of these with a long, exclamatory "That's effed," or "Nice," or a nod or several, depending on what response she thought he was anticipating. But she's not interested in conversing with him. She wants to call her brother, Mezie. She'd called him from the airport in Chicago, and then immediately when she landed in Iowa and could connect to the airport's Wi-Fi, but he did not pick up. She's not surprised. Since his attempt, he's stilled himself to her. She imagines that he is lying on his bed now, staring at the ceiling. Or seated in the sitting room, eating. She wants to tell him about the woman at the airport. She wonders how he would react. Years ago, she would have been able to guess. She isn't so sure anymore.

Now Bayo asks, "So you say you grew up in Ojo?"

"Yea, Iba Estate."

"Some of my guys live in Ojo," he says. "I used to visit there often. In short, there was one time I almost started dating a babe living there."

"Nice."

"The girl was bigger than me, so I just respected myself and left her."

"That's effed."

"We were not on the same level at all. She fine die and the guys chasing her were plenty. I don't mean, like, normal guys. I mean men, those big-bellied men with plenty cash to throw around."

Sommy shrugs, looks out the car window. The houses about are squat, modest, most of them painted a dull white, fenced with short wooden planks, bright gardens, and one or two gleaming cars parked in their driveways. Trees sandwich houses, stand beside them like body-guards. They pass a gas station, a McDonalds, and a Chinese restaurant.

"That's our house," Bayo says, pointing to the middle flat of a gray apartment building.

"Nice," Sommy says.

"Right? I like it. Very small and cute. Like a button."

He turns off the car, looks at himself in the rearview mirror before stepping out.

Sommy stands in her empty room, by the window, looking out at the tall apartment building on the other side of the matted green lawn. Bayo has chosen the bigger of the two rooms. She'd taken a quick look into his room while she stood in the sitting room inspecting the apartment. It's twice the size of hers and he's already furnished it with a bed, a reading table, and a tall lamp. He's also occupied the only storage room in the house. He's lined his shoes on the floor and stacked his empty bags and boxes by the wall. She'd not expected him to take the smaller room. She would have done the same if she were in his position. But he has no right to occupy the storage room. She paid exactly half the rent, and she deserves exactly half the space. She thinks of how hastily she'd agreed to their roommate-ship, how when he'd commented under her slightly viral tweets about getting admitted into James Crowley University's English department on a full ride, her senses numb with joy, her happiness concentrated and total, that everything everyone told her then was fortified with honey, with possibility. Me too, he'd written. Congrats to us! He'd then sent her a direct message, and soon they were looking for an apartment on Craigslist together. He found the apartment, and took charge of everything, corresponding with the landlord, getting a cosigner since they did not have social security numbers. She'd sent him her share of the deposit and rent in naira, and he'd changed it to dollars, and paid it into someone's account, who paid it into the landlord's account. All this she'd been grateful for. But now she understands that it had been about him all along, his need to establish ownership. She wants to march to him, demand that he removes his things from the storage room, or maybe give her half the space, but he opens the door then, and saunters in.

"Settling in, I see," he says, looking overly satisfied, standing there, a sly smile on his face, like he's just wanked himself off.

"My room is bigger," he says. "But I like yours more, you know. The window is bigger and lets in more sunlight."

"So why didn't you take it instead?"

"I wanted you to have more sunlight." He grins. "Have you heard of SAD?"

"Nope."

"Seasonal Affective Disorder. Iowa is horrible in the winter. I mean, it is one of the coldest and gloomiest places in America in the winter after Alaska and Alabama. So shit gets real quick, and you can get depressed from the lack of sunlight. So the more sunlight you can get in the summer, the better for you." He pauses, walks to the window, stands. He turns to her after a short while. "Imagine saying to someone, I am sad from SAD? Isn't that funny?" He watches her face, looking for signs of amusement. He then laughs.

She lowers herself to the ground and opens her boxes, hoping to signal that she's done entertaining him. She unfolds the plain gray bedsheet she's had since her days in undergrad. She eyes the room, searches for the best place to lay the bedsheet, to pass the night. She knows she needs Bayo, needs him to drive her to the store where she can get a new mattress and phone, a desk and a chair, needs the knowledge of the town he's glimpsed since his arrival a week ago. But she's going to do without it. She's going to stay on her own. She won't even ask him to clear the storage space. She will not feign a friendliness she doesn't feel. She dislikes the boy—it is as simple as that. He talks too much. He has a large and loud self, an unmitigated energy. He seems to her the kind of roommate who will be oblivious to boundaries, who will touch her things, eat her food without permission, sit on her bed, and maybe even use her body sponge.

"It feels good to have someone I know around," he says, after he's emptied out his laughter. "These past days have been weird. I have felt very alone. Not in a depressing way or anything. I don't have depression or any of that stuff. But I kept thinking about how strange it was that I did not really know anyone around. If something happened to me, no one in this whole state would feel obligated to get in a car and come to my aid. It wasn't a terrifying thought or anything. It was just strange."

She turns to him. "But we don't know each other."

"Huh?"

"We are strangers to each other."

"Oh," he says, pressing a wrist to the wall.

She turns her attention back to her open boxes.

After a moment of silence, he says, "Let me leave you to unpack."

"Thanks," she says. She doesn't turn to look at him.

Alone now, she sits on the floor, her back to the wall. She pulls her phone from the pocket of her jeans. In Lagos, the time is about six A.M. She imagines that Mezie is asleep. Before she left for the airport, they'd exchanged hasty goodbyes. She stood by his bedroom door, and he sat on the bed, near the window, shirtless, his bony back slightly curved. "Safe journey," he said. "Take care," she replied. She'd wanted to say more, but nothing came to mind. That she was leaving him two weeks after his attempt was all she could think, and she was certain that it was all he could think. The woman at the airport, holding the cardboard, comes to mind now. Sommy understands the impulse to allow strangers to gawk at one's pain. Since Mezie's attempt, she's found herself, at odd times, wanting to stop strangers to tell them that the force holding her life has been blitzed, and she's now without a center.

It's the shock, she should have said to Bayo, when he implied that the woman only sought attention. It's feeling yourself to be steady in a thing, and then having it become so suddenly a figment. There's the urge to call Mezie again now, to go to Bayo's room and ask if she can use his phone. But she waits instead for morning, when she's able to walk to the mall, to the AT&T shop.

James Crowley University is interwoven in the city's center. It has buildings scattered about, sitting side by side with the city's businesses: restaurants, grocery stores, banks, boutiques. It is nothing like what Sommy knows of universities. It has no fences, no large, looming signpost signaling an entrance to the school's premises. The English building is located near the bus station, and like all the other school buildings, it has the glassy, clinical finish of modern constructions. It could pass for a bank, or the branch of a software company. Sommy finds this slightly disappointing. She expected buildings modeled like castles. It is what *Legally Blonde* and *Good Will Hunting* promised her. Still, she feels sharp moments of awe while walking around the campus, past the polite shops around it—their front yards, furnished with tables and chairs and umbrellas, spilling out to the road, their menu lists, featuring their Happy Hour discount, written on dwarf blackboards in different colors of chalk—past the sprinklings of white students sauntering up and down the sidewalks in shorts, crop tops, T-shirts, sneakers, past the groups of four or five laying on long patches of grass, half-naked, their books and baskets filled with snacks and cans of beer set in front of them.

On these walks, she's sometimes attacked by an eerie sense that she's sneaked into the country, that there's been a mess with the school administration and the embassy personnel and the border officers, and that mess has landed her here. It would make sense if Amara, her best friend, were in this position—Amara has long dreamt of schooling in America, as had Mezie. He'd always clutched the American dream to his chest, even before it became a matter of survival for him.

When Sommy had gotten her admission letter to James Crowley while Mezie was still in Oslo, she'd imagined that on these walks she would call him, and they would spend long minutes arguing about which was better—Iowa City or Oslo. She imagined that he would brag about Oslo as he usually did. "This place is chassis," he'd said to her around the first week of his arrival in Norway, his voice cracking with hope.

But she's been unable to reach Mezie in the two weeks since her arrival. She'd sent him a message on WhatsApp as soon as she got her new AT&T sim card, called several times, all to no avail. When she complained to her mother, she'd said to give him time, and so had Patrick, Mezie's closest friend. Sommy decided to do so. She stopped calling and texting, and she's now taken to eating away her sadness.

Today, after her solemn walk around the campus, she picks up a bunch of ripe plantains at the co-op a few minutes from the house. Her plan is to deep fry them and have them with egg sauce. But, as she stands in the apartment kitchen, the brown paper bag of plantains in hand, she's certain that a meal of fried plantains and egg sauce will not numb her feeling of dread, so she goes to Bayo, who is prostrate on the sitting room couch watching the television, a YouTube video on cryptocurrency, and asks if she can use his phone.

"For what?" he says, voice shrouded in mockery.

"I want to call my brother," she says.

"And you can't use your phone?"

She opens her mouth, and then closes it. "It's fine," she says. "I don't want it anymore."

"Take joor," he says, handing her the phone. "Small play, and you are hyperventilating."

In the past week, they've developed a pattern of interaction, one where he meets her irritation with the amused resignation of an adult watching a child throw a tantrum.

She takes the phone, dials Mezie's phone number.

"Can you turn down the volume?" she asks.

"Yes, my madam," he teases.

She rolls her eyes, places the phone to her ear. Her irritation with Bayo is unfair, she knows. He is mostly nice. But his buoyancy unsettles her curated atmosphere of gloom. He sings in the shower. He watches YouTube videos titled different variations of "How to Grow Money in Thirty Days." He spends long hours on the phone with his numerous Lagos friends, laughing and laughing. She always fights the urge to kick down his door and ask, "What is funny? Why are you disturbing me?"

The phone rings, but Mezie doesn't pick up. She tries again and again, until Bayo says, "If I'm the one you are calling like that, I'll vex o. Why person go call me five times? When I no dey owe you money?"

"Bayo, please, just shut up."

"Sorry o! Madam caller."

She tosses the phone at him, and he strains to catch it. "If you spoil my phone, you will buy a new one."

"Just let me know if he calls back."

"No 'Thank you'?" He picks up the TV remote, turns up the volume. "This girl, you are very rude."

"Shut up."

"Why body dey always bite you?"

She ignores him, walks to the kitchen, pulls out the plantains from the bag and holds them under the gushing tap.

Bayo comes behind her, asks, "You want to fry plantain?"

"Obviously."

"Fry for me."

"I've heard," she says.

He shakes her shoulders limply, says, "My guy, my guy."

"Bayo, remove your dirty hands from my shoulders."

"Please ehnn," he says. "I like my plantains fried, fried. Deep golden brown. I didn't say burn it o. Just fry it well."

She walks to the cupboard, throws it open, and pulls out a chopping board. Mezie probably saw Bayo's area code and decided not to pick up. She dabs the plantains dry with a handful of paper towels. She wonders if she's overreacting, catastrophizing. If all Mezie needs is time. Time to heal. She wonders, too, if all there is to this panic of hers is guilt—the guilt of leaving him behind.

Bayo leans on the countertop, his face near her arm, and asks if she plans on attending the meeting organized by the Black Graduate Students Org later that evening. At the International Students Orientation a few days ago, a group of girls had walked up to them and handed them flyers for the event.

"No," she says.

"Why?"

"I just don't feel like it."

He stands upright, frowns. "I am not trying to fight or anything," he says. His shirt hangs around his neck like a rope, and he tugs at it. "And I don't necessarily have anything against angry and moody, but is this your constant state of being? I'm just asking because when we used to talk on the phone in Lagos, you were chiller."

"Maybe it's because you were less annoying then," she says.

He laughs. "Just follow me to the meeting. You did not come to this country to lock yourself up in your room."

She's now slicing the plantains into oval slabs. "You know what will make me chiller? Turning down the volume of the TV whenever you want to watch those nonsense crypto videos."

"It will be fun," he says, ignoring her. "I don't want to go alone."

She pauses now to look at him. At the International Student's Orientation, he'd glided through the crowd of new students with ease, introducing himself, drawing laughter, while she stood in the corner near the projector, watching. He'd come to her, urged her to network. "Some of the people in this room might be able to help you one day," he said. She envied his razor-sharp intentions. Like an ambitious farmer at the start of the planting season, he's planting early. She, on the other hand, is stuck back home, always reaching toward it, to Mezie, unable to see what's in front or ahead.

"I've heard," she says to Bayo now. She'll go with him.

"And you will not go and hide like you did at the orientation lunch?"

"Bayo, please, be going."

Later, from the sitting room, over the high TV volume, Bayo yells, "We leave at seven, so start getting ready at six! I know how you girls are with your makeup!"

On their way to the BGSO gathering, as they walk past a Kum & Go store, Bayo turns to her and says, "How is this even a real name?"

Sommy studies it for a while and breaks into laughter. "Your mind is just dirty."

"Seriously," Bayo says. "The other day I saw a mechanic shop. Guess what it was named?" He watches her expectantly, and then laughs. "Dick Servicing. That's the name. I almost died of laughter. I'm sure they choose these names on purpose."

At the restaurant, Sommy walks in shyly. The crowd before her is intimidating. About thirty black people, seated round a long table, chatting, laughing. The restaurant is Italian, coated in blue lights, and the severe waiters are in white shirts and navy-blue pants. Classical music plays in the background.

Sommy sits next to Bayo, who seems to have none of her anxiety, and who leans over the table now to say hi to a thin dark-skinned girl with short hair and eyebrows dyed a blistering blonde.

"I'm glad you could make it," the girl says.

The girl had been amongst the group handing out fliers at the orientation lunch. Sommy remembers being struck by the color of her hair and brows, thinking the decision to appear radically different so brave. It's a virtue Sommy does not possess. Her instinct is to assimilate, to disappear.

Bayo introduces them. The girl's name is Kayla.

"Sommy," Kayla says. "I like your name."

Sommy tells her that her full name is Somkelechukwu. Kayla attempts to pronounce it. Her version sounds like the name of a rare flower. "Sumkelchoku." Bayo laughs, and Sommy laughs. Kayla laughs, too, says, "Oh my god, oh my god, I'm terrible."

"You tried," Bayo says, a sudden American accent surfacing. "Don't mind us."

He's seated cross-legged, looking prim in his light-blue T-shirt and plain black pants. He so easily could have been one of the boys in her childhood estate, with whom she attended secondary school. They were the *almost* kids, the kids who had just enough to escape the categorization of poor street kids. They had roofs over their heads, even if the roofs sometimes leaked. They ate rice and beans, even if without eggs and fried plantains. They attended secondary schools with libraries, even if the libraries were empty of books. They lived amongst thieves and cultists, but also amongst teachers and civil servants. They were the kids who could switch from a British accent to an American one, who, during morning assemblies, argued over whether Beyoncé was a better dancer than Ciara. They were the kids who could make it. They were the chameleon kids. They did not reek of poverty. You had to come a little closer to smell it.

She feels a deep affinity to Bayo in the moment, as she watches him flirt with Kayla. Back home, he and Sommy wouldn't even be seated so close. Bayo would look at her from afar, and conclude that she's out of his league, already at the age where every conversation is somehow steered toward getting married or having kids. He'd think her a woman for an older man. And she would look at him and think him a small boy looking to play around. But here, they are more. They not only share a home, but they also share a peculiar childhood. He could have been one of Mezie's secondary school classmates, boys who gathered in their sitting room after school to watch football replays. It is something, she thinks. She's on his side. She suddenly wants him to win Kayla's attention, so she compliments Kayla's blouse, a silky black thing, and then adds, "I've been admiring your hair color by the way."

Kayla smiles, turns her head here and there, showing off the curved carvings on each side. "Thank you so much!"

"I told her the same thing," Bayo says. "The color really fits her."

"You are too much!" Kayla exclaims.

The boy sitting next to Bayo, to whom Sommy has paid no attention until now, turns to Bayo, asks if they are Nigerian. He is deep-dark-skinned like Kayla, with the sharp jawbones of West Africans. Bayo says they are Nigerian, the boy says he's Gambian, and his name is Michael. He then asks why he sees Nigerians everywhere. Most of the Africans he met at the orientation lunch are Nigerian. Sommy cannot tell if there's humor in his voice, so she's silent. Bayo spreads his hands nonchalantly but says nothing.

The table clatters now with chattering, none of which Sommy can make out. In the air is the sense of excited anticipation. She'd felt it at the orientation, where they were made to sit and listen to different people give lectures on acclimatizing to the American condition. How to make friends. How to open a bank account. How to avoid scam calls from fake car dealers. Everyone had the bright-eyedness that comes with the first day of school, the ambience thick with prospect. It's the same way now, and in her spirit is a fight to allow herself to feel it.

Bayo asks if she'd like a drink, and Sommy says she'll have what he's having.

Kayla says to her, "Try the pomegranate cocktail. It's amazing."

Michael leans over and says to Bayo that he thinks the rivalry between Burna Boy and Wizkid is pointless. Everyone knows that Burna is the real artiste, he says, Fela reincarnated. He then swerves into a harangue about Nigerians and their exceptionalism.

"Name one Gambian artiste you know."

"I don't know any," Bayo says.

"Just one artiste."

Bayo guffaws. Sommy and Kayla exchange a knowing look. Michael, irritated now, turns his attention to the end of the table, where a stout, freckled girl is speaking. The word PRESIDENT lays crested on a pinstripe on her breast pocket, underneath it her name, NIA. She speaks with her shoulders high up, and with a practiced fake smile Sommy recognizes well—in secondary school, all the girl prefects wore that smile.

"We have some new members in our midst," Nia says. "I won't do the embarrassing thing of asking them to introduce themselves. But I do want to take questions if anyone has any."

Michael raises his hand. "Where can one buy good weed in this city?"

The table shuffles, a few snorts of laughter.

"What?" Michael says. "No one here smokes weed?"

"It's illegal," Nia says, smiling curtly. "Now let's ask questions I can actually answer."

Michael raises his hand again. "How does the organization navigate our differences? I'm asking this because I'm hoping this is not some 'black power, one people' organization."

"Do you mind rephrasing your question, um, Mm . . . Michael?"

Bayo pinches his nose as if to refrain from laughter. Kayla has her hands over her face. Sommy clears her throat intermittently. It's the only thing keeping her from coming undone with laughter.

"Does the organization recognize our differences?" Michael continues, slowly, emphasizing each word. "Yes, we are all black, but we are still different, with different histories, cultures." He turns to Sommy, nodding, seeking support. Sommy turns away. Her eyes are teary from swallowing her laughter.

Michael continues: "I just want to be sure that the group understands that we are all different and we see things differently. Also hoping that one culture will not impose on the others. For instance, I hope that our next meeting can be held in an African restaurant." He looks around. "I think it's important that we take this seriously, and not go about acting like our colonizers and enslavers."

"Oh," Nia says. "We will look into that."

"Great," Michael says, relaxing, smiling.

He turns to Sommy, opens his mouth to speak, and she says sharply: "Excuse me. Restroom."

He grunts, moves his attention back to the table.

Sommy walks outside, finds a dark spot by the hotel entrance. Behind a red Toyota, and alone, she buries her face in her palm and laughs quietly for a long time, hiccupping, snorting, and it comes to her that in the past half hour, she's not thought about Mezie. The guilt dampens her, and she straightens herself, pauses, looks about the open space, which has the character of a courtyard. The ground is paved. Stores and restaurants surround it, creating the impression of a fortress. Bright light beams from poles and everything appears bathed in a clear yellow. People stand in small groups smoking, chatting. On the bench a few steps to her right, a couple sits, their faces so near each other. She takes her gaze to the city library, which stands beside a water sprinkler, and around which two white kids run, laughing, splashing. The library is closed now, but light breaks through its glass walls. She's wanted to go there since her arrival. Get a library card. Browse through its aisles. Feel like a member of the living. She's determined now to do so. Uncloak this suffocating sorrow. Mezie did not die, did he? And for all she knows, he could be hanging out with Patrick now, sharing a beer.

She walks a bit to get a better view of the water sprinkler, so she can watch the kids. One of the kids, noticing her, pauses, beats his hands to wrench off water, and then runs toward her. He looks to be about four or five. His short dark hair lies flat on his head like a wet cloth. He stops right in front of her and says something she can't hear, so she squats, says, "What's your name?"

"Liam!" he screams.

His teeth are so tiny, little white bricks, and it amuses her. Kids amuse her. Everything so small and crackling with potential. Until recently she'd wanted kids of her own. Mezie's attempt has obliterated that desire.

"You are very handsome, Liam," she says now.

"I know," Liam says, bouncing as if high on sugar. "And I'm also smart. And I'm also strong." He flexes his bony arms. "And I'm Superman."

"You are," Sommy says.

"And I'm kind and I'm patient."

"You are!"

The boy tells Sommy to say that she, too, is smart and kind and patient. He says, "It's good for your confidence."

"How do you know what confidence is?" Sommy says. "You are, like, four."

She recognizes that he's an affirmed child, a child whose parents read parenting books and attended parenting seminars. She's never met an intentional parent. All her friends have parents who wing it. Her own parents winged it. Children for them were necessities, and the one aim was to keep them alive. Feed, clothe, and shelter them. Whatever happened inside, in the mind, in the spirit, was left to chance.

She's laughing with Liam when a woman appears, her face hard as a rock. She doesn't look at Sommy, nor does she say a word to her. She pulls the boy away. "Silly," she says to him, her voice stiff with contempt. She's clearly the mother. They share the same blue-black hair, the same pointy nose. Liam begins to cry. Sommy remains in the squat position, her laughter stuck in her throat, too embarrassed to stand and meet the gaze of any one of the people about watching. She has it in mind now to run after the woman and demand an apology. But an apology for what, really? This is the sort of insult that Amara would accuse her of bringing upon herself. "If you weren't doing *nice nice*," Amara would say, "no one would see space to insult you." Or perhaps, she's thinking now, this is the nature of microaggressions. The "micro" part of it being its imperceptibility, its dismissibility. If she tells this story to someone, they could argue that the woman was simply trying to take her kid away from a stranger, a mother's instinct. But what about the contempt in her voice, the curve of her elbow, as if trying to build a wall between them? Sommy thinks now that she would rather a big insult than a small insult. She can burnish and display a big insult. "Look what that idiot did to me," she can say, and then feel good for having borne it all with grace. A small insult, a passive insult—of what use is that? It pinches and stings but commands no real attention. She would rather that this woman had spat in her face, snarled some disgusting slur at her.

Sommy stands with much effort and starts to head back to the restaurant. She's not even angry at the woman, she thinks. She's numb, and she knows it has something to do with the heft of the pain she's experienced in the past weeks. Everything now pales in comparison. Everything feels like a joke. A scared, mean woman cannot pull any meaningful emotion from her. She's watched her brother almost die, watched him vomit and shit blood, dragged all six feet seven inches of him down their staircase and into their father's old Volvo, watched his body straighten like a stick and then go limp like a rope. She's seen things, she thinks. She's seen shege.

"Hey," someone says from behind her now.

She turns, startled, clutching her purse. "Sorry?"

Before her is an anxious-looking man, somewhere in his late twenties, average height, and very light-skinned. Full, curly hair. Black, but mixed with something. White? Brown?

"I'm sorry to walk up to you this way," he says, taking off his glasses to reveal dull-brown eyes. "I was watching you from over there." He points to the bench by the water sprinkler. "And I saw." He says "saw" emphatically. "And I just wanted to say that I think that was fucked up. I don't want you walking around with that interaction in your mind, and I thought it might make you feel better to know that you have a witness."

He has on a black T-shirt and a pair of shorts, and against his very light skin, the dark T-shirt looks even darker.

"Thank you," Sommy says, smiling. "That's thoughtful of you."

He stretches his hand for a handshake and says his name is Bryan.

She hesitates, stares at his lean hand, his clean pink nails, the beaded bracelet on his wrist, and then takes the handshake. "Sommy," she replies. "Nice to meet you."

There's a moment of awkward silence. They both smile stiffly, waiting for the other person to steer the conversation, so Sommy says, "Thanks again for saying something."

He nods, says, "You are welcome."

She unclasps her hand from his and continues on her way back to the restaurant.

At the restaurant, Sommy tells Bayo about the woman, and then Bryan.

"Which one is witness again?" Bayo says, irritated. He hands her the pomegranate cocktail. The crowd has thinned. A few people sit about, talking even louder than before, loosened by alcohol. The light has grown dimmer, the music lower.

"I thought it was sweet," she says.

"I don't know," Bayo says. "It feels too self-righteous. Too 'Look at me I'm a sensitive person.'"

Sommy laughs, takes a sip from the cocktail. "You have a point."

She thinks now that Mezie would say the exact thing about Bryan, a man who wears his goodness on his sleeve. "With people like this," Mezie would say, "you never see it coming." She wonders if it is perhaps a matter of socialization, for men to be so weary of displays of kindness. Kindness that is muted, mangled by feigned or real disdain, sure. But kindness that announces itself as kindness? It seems excessive to them.

Sommy asks about Kayla.

"You won't believe she let that fool, Michael, drive her home."

"Jesus, it's a lie."

"I swear. I don't understand women."

Sommy smiles affectionately and flicks the edge of his collar. "She's a real mumu. Don't mind her."

They both finish their drinks and head home.

The semester begins snaillike. Syllabuses are read, expectations are laid out. At the reading-writing center, where she's assigned to work ten hours a week, no one signs up the first week. She sits there five times a week for two hours, watching the other consultants click away on their laptops. Back when she received her admission letter, she spent long hours dreaming of doing exactly what she's doing, walking down the formidable hallways of the department, clutching large classics, her face serious and learned. She was even going to get into coffee. She was going to be one of those people whose days did not begin until they had a sip of coffee. America was going to wash away her former self, her lazy self, her waiting-around-for-magic self. She was going to be renewed. But she's here, walking the hallways, clutching the books, and even drinking coffee she buys from the café a few blocks down from the departmental building, yet she feels unrenewed, like she's filled with mold and cobwebs.

Bayo's demeanor is a mirror opposite. She comes home to find him with his nose buried in a book, his head so filled with ideas. "I did not come to America to count NEPA poles," he tells her. He has plans. He's already started looking at summer internships, started eyeing jobs for when he graduates. He has responsibilities, he tells her. He wants his sister to come to America for university. He wants his brother to comfortably pursue his graphic design dreams. He wants to buy his mother a house.

It's how Mezie always laid out his plans. Growing up, he'd been so certain that he was going to be somebody, and that was how he said it—"I am going to be somebody." He was obsessed with autobiographies, especially those of famous athletes. He spoke to her of drive, ambition, excellence. He always had plans: plans to develop a gaming app, plans to start a real estate business, plans to become a shoe designer. His interests were disparate, his goal singular: wealth. And he talked about a near utopic future, where she, Sommy, would know no lack.

"I won't buy a house on Banana Island," he'd say dreamily. "I think it's stupid to buy a house just because of its location and nothing else. Plus, Ikoyi and Lekki will be under water in a few years, so I don't see the point."

She liked listening to him dream. He spoke with such certitude and criticality that she, too, began to dream with him. She dreamt of his Ikeja mansion, with a pool and a gym, and a simpering gateman. She dreamt of his G-Wagon, black and glossy. Mostly, she dreamt of him bursting with accomplishment, his swagger shining, his heart at rest.

She did not need to dream for herself. Her path was laid out for her. When she was about ten years old, her mother declared that Sommy would be an English teacher. Even then, Sommy could sense that this decision had nothing to do with her abilities. Being a teacher was, to her mother, a thing to do alongside the primary identities of a woman— wife, mother. Sommy sauntered into her mother's ideal future with a glacial smoothness. After graduating with a BA in English literature, she taught English language for a year at a public secondary school during her National Youth Service. There, she quickly realized that she hated teaching, the monotony of it, planning lesson notes, grading assignments, attending staff meetings.

The part of the job Sommy liked most was her daily banter with her favorite students, the overly ambitious ones, serious with schoolwork, ever ready with questions for her. She loved entertaining them, teasing them. She loved that they were still at the age where they were allowed amorphous ambitions—*I want to be a scientist, an astronaut, a rich man!* they exclaimed. And it sustained her, this part of the job, until she completed her service year, and decided to do something else, to find what she liked. She applied to all the jobs she was qualified for: at a bank as a cashier, at a pharmacy as a receptionist, at an oil and gas company as a marketer. She wrote the tests, went for the interviews, but the rejections piled, and each time, she told herself it was okay. It was okay because Mezie was abroad, working, and his dreams would materialize, and just being near his glory would be enough. Of course, there remained the pinching thought that she'd not learnt to dream, to love something, that she'd subconsciously held on to the unspoken promise that if she played her part, stayed in school, graduated, avoided getting pregnant, she'd somehow get what she wants from life: safety, ease. And she'd done it all, even if with cold impassivity. Mezie's deportation, and then his attempt, revealed her fragility. There was no glory to share in. She stood now at the bottom of something deep, waiting to be pulled out.

She knows better than to tell Bayo to slow down, to unburden himself. Like Mezie, he's defined himself around these responsibilities. It's what makes him *somebody*. Without this pursuit, he'll become Mezie after his return, zombielike Mezie, looking for a way out.

So, just like she'd done with her brother, she sits and listens to Bayo talk and plan and dream. She doesn't say to him that the pursuit of the saving wand is martyrdom. She doesn't say, "What if you fail?" or "What if you think you've failed?"

The semester cranks up in the third week. All her three professors assign a full book a week, alongside essays. She can't keep up. She's always behind. She thinks, surely, the professors had at some point attended graduate school, and understand the impossibility of the tasks they dish out and do not expect them to be all shimmery with knowledge and comments during class. But she's wrong. Her classmates raise their hands during class discussions and speak eloquently about biopolitics and postmodernism and deconstruction. They use words like "Anthropocene" and "phenomenology." They reference Foucault and Derrida and Latour. They stand in the hallway and talk about books they've read, books she's never heard about, and essays by this critic or that critic in the *New Yorker* and the *Atlantic*. It doesn't exactly look pleasant, these conversations they have in the hallway about books and essays. It seems always like a contest of literacy, all of them trying to outshine the next person. If someone mentions Tolstoy, the next person mentions Dostoevsky, and the other person then reaches further down history to excavate an older Russian, say Pushkin. They go round and round until somehow, they arrive back in the twenty-first century, where this critic has written a not-so-refined essay on the latest successful commercial novel.

"The essay reads like a Goodreads review," someone would scoff.

"No one brings rigor to critical analysis anymore," another would add.

Around the fifth week of the semester, Sommy finds herself wanting desperately to be part of this club. It's why she left home. To do something with herself. To find her passion. She wants, too, to reference Russian writers as though she's read them all her life. She wants it to be worthy of the sacrifice of leaving Mezie behind. So she starts to raise her hand in all her classes, especially in the theory class. She picks up the gestures of the smart, speaking fast and with a pinched expression. She makes passionate hand movements—she read somewhere that it creates the appearance of intelligence, in the same way that a pair of glasses does. She learns to always quote a different theorist, whether or not their purported theory relates to the discussion at hand, and to make sure to start every contribution with "It's interesting how," or "What I found interesting is." It's how many of her smart classmates begin their contributions, with the word "interesting" sandwiched somewhere in their first phrases.

She also makes sure to read every text carefully, and then search for their summaries on YouTube. She practices her delivery in front of her Samsung camera. She goes to the Goodwill nearby and buys two of each of these: short skirt, long-sleeved crop top, plain T-shirt, jeans, tights, and boots; and two pairs of fake designer sunglasses for some edge.

Once, in a class discussion about Nietzsche's *On the Genealogy of Morality*, she vaguely strings together a Toni Morrison quote on goodness, something related to the human tendency to stand in awe of evil.

"It's telling," she says to the class. "Nobody does a documentary about good people. Like everyday good people. It's always the serial killers."

The professor nods thoughtfully, and then goes on to link Sommy's point to an earlier Foucault reading. Sommy's pleased with herself, and she rides this. Her hand is always up in class, and sometimes, when she speaks, she feels the sun wriggling past the blinds, past the heads of her classmates, and pouring all over her, a great beam of bright light.

But on one densely hot afternoon, while the class sits discussing the Kantian Sublime, Sommy, feeling moved to speak, repeats one of Kant's arguments. She says that she'd enjoyed reading Kant, that she found his anxious repetition and overemphasis endearing and thought of him as a man interested in having his arguments understood, and not revered. To her, it's the most eloquent of her class contributions, and after she's done speaking, she takes a sip of water from her bottle, infusing in every movement the elegance of a world-class orator. It's after she's placed the bottle on the table that a chubby-faced brunette says, "I think what Sommy is trying to say is that Kant's distinction of the beautiful and the sublime is vague." The girl nods as she speaks, senselessly chewing the bottom of her pen. The classroom sizzles with murmurs of agreement, and a minute passes before Sommy says, "I didn't know that this was a translation class. Glad that someone here speaks *African*." It's what she wishes she'd done with the water-sprinkler woman. She wishes she'd spoken up. The class goes on as usual, the professor saying nothing in reply, the brunette biting her pen even harder.

Sommy's show comes to an end after this episode. Usually, after someone says their contribution, another classmate breathes thoughtfully, and then says: "Just to go off on said person's point . . ." But after her exchange with the brunette, none of her classmates go off on her points. She's not referenced, or rebuffed, or translated, even.

The mood in this class colors her experience in her other classes. In her Transnational Feminism class, she feels a new urge to say something to the contrary, an itch to create disruption, to unsettle. It's a smaller class than the theory class, about eight students who, each Tuesday afternoon, sit around a circular table discussing poverty and war and patriarchy in what they refer to as "countries in the Global South," a term that Sommy learns is the nicer synonym of "Third World." The professor, an Indian American woman, stern, always dressed in too-large monochromatic suits, accompanies every lecture with slides of poor women hunched over firewood, stirring pots, sleeping babies secured on their curved backs with swaths of clothing, or women in groups, clay pots balanced on their heads, walking down untarred roads. The heat and sweat from these slides seem to seep through the screen, swirl in the cold, brightly lit classroom. Until the incident with the brunette, she did not give much thought to the steely discrepancy between what she sees on the screen and what she sees right before her. But now, sore from what she considers a small insult from the brunette, this discrepancy traps a caustic fume inside her so that when she makes her contributions, there's the almost insuppressible need to resist concurrence.

It's the same in Modern Loneliness, her favorite of all three classes, where she'd taken a small comfort in the stories of loneliness her classmates shared. They all felt isolated. Why? They couldn't say. Social media, they postulated. The rise of diet culture, productivity culture, the "Do better, be better" culture. They blamed capitalism and racism and neoliberalism. They blamed poverty. They blamed the president of the university and the president of the United States. They blamed the United Nations and the Red Cross. Sommy left every class feeling guiltless, able to pin her roving, acrid sadness to an external cause. But when the nadir arrives, it eclipses everything, and even in this class, where she had formerly felt solidarity, she wants to scream; she wants to say, "Everyone, shut up, shut up, please, shut up."

She stops raising her hand in all her classes, stops caring about looking edgy, about her boots, and short skirts, and sunglasses. All day, she craves sleep, and even that is sometimes difficult to achieve, so she takes to masturbating furiously. It nudges her to sleep, the sad, barely there orgasms, and sometimes she jerks awake, certain that a supernatural wind has defied the science of time and space and has brought Mezie's voice to her.

Bayo notices her renewed despair, and he forces her to another BGSO meeting. This time she's even more subdued than before. It's a larger, noisier group than the first meeting, and Sommy looks on at them with envy. She wants to join them. She wants to make and laugh at jokes. She wants to hug freely. But it's caught up with her, the feeling, which she had tried to suspend with flinging herself into schoolwork, that she's not meant to be here, that she ought to be with Mezie, nurturing him back to life, and that the only way to redeem herself now is to speak to him, ask for forgiveness.

"You've been sitting here alone," Kayla says from behind. "It's called a mixer for a reason."

Kayla's obviously had a little too much to drink. Her eyeliner is smudged, and the strap of her black dress hangs loosely on her bicep. When she takes the seat beside Sommy, Sommy tugs the strap back on and takes away the drink.

"I think you should stop drinking," Sommy says, placing it on the table.

"I think you should get yourself a drink," Kayla says, and grabs the glass.

Just then, the president, Nia, walks up to them, puts her arms around Kayla, and says, "She's a drunk."

"She's a prude," Kayla says of Nia.

And the three girls begin to laugh. The crowd is getting thicker. The room smells dully of smoke.

Kayla asks Sommy if she's met Nia.

"I did see Michael give her hell at the last meeting," Sommy says.

"That Michael," Nia says. "He's a curious character."

"'Does the organization recognize our differences?'" Kayla says, bouncing her head sideways, an attempt at mimicking Michael.

Sommy throws her head backward, attempts her own caricature. "Where can I buy weed around here?" She broadens her shoulders, widens her eyes. "I don't care that it's illegal, and I'm seated in a crowded restaurant, I'll just ask my stupid questions anyway."

Kayla's wiping tears from her eyes. "Girl, you're killing me."

Nia, too, is laughing, and then she says, "But you did fuck him, didn't you?"

Kayla pauses, places the glass on the table. Her face closes like folded paper, now blank when it had, a few seconds ago, been agape, cheerful.

"Hey, come on," Nia says, throws an arm around Kayla. "I'm not judging. What matters is that it was good." She winks at Sommy as though they both understand something about Kayla that no one else does. It's a look friends give each other.

Kayla fights weakly to escape Nia's grasp. Nia's holding on tight, pressing quick kisses all over her face. Kayla begins to laugh, and playfully punches Nia. She then turns to Sommy, says, "Michael is many things, but what he's not is bad in bed."

They laugh in unison again. Sommy thinks that Kayla would get along with Amara. They possess the same disposition, quick to anger and quick to mercy.

Nia unclasps from Kayla and takes the seat next to Sommy. She asks if Sommy's liking graduate school.

"No," Sommy says, with exaggerated despair.

Kayla high-fives her. "Girl, preach. School is a scam."

Sommy wants to tell them all about the brunette incident, but she's slightly embarrassed at her reaction to it, the quickness with which she'd collapsed, regressing into herself like a small, slow animal. She also doesn't want to pollute the air, which is growing even more jubilant. The crowd is mixing. The girls, who had earlier sat in groups just like them, have split, coupling with the boys flapping about in sexual excitement. It never fails to happen, Sommy thinks, this mating game. In all gatherings, at all times, sex exists as a magnet, attracting or repelling people.

Sommy complains instead about the workload. Kayla asks if she misses home.

"Of course," Sommy says, and smiles.

Kayla curves her red lips. "Listen, we've got you, okay? Nia and I've got you."

She's drunk still but Sommy can tell that Kayla means it. She wants to laugh away the moment because it's who she is: displays of earnestness discomfit her. She can only sit here feeling deeply that she must embrace this new life, that she must stretch out her hand to meet what and who stretches theirs toward her. For a moment she's certain that this is what must happen, so she asks Nia and Kayla to join her for coffee the next day.

"I'll show up with a hangover," Kayla says. "But I'll show up."

"Looking forward," Nia says.

Sommy's conviction wanes after this, and she decides to reach out to Mezie one last time. She excuses herself and walks out of the restaurant. Outside, she sits on a bench, and sends a Facebook message to Elin, Mezie's Norwegian girlfriend. She's put it off for a while now. To her mind it's the most pathetic of all her attempts. She does not like Elin, and for slippery reasons. It started with a picture Mezie had posted of them seated on their couch in their apartment in Oslo. In the picture, Mezie has his arms around Elin, and he's smiling stiffly. Sommy had studied the picture for a long time, thinking it seemed off: Elin was laughing; Mezie wasn't. Mezie had by then been in Norway for four years, slithering around the country with expired papers, and Sommy knew that Elin knew, and that Elin had the power to change that. She could marry Mezie, make his stay legal. Sommy hated the thought of that. She hated not only that Elin had that power but also that Elin knew that she had that power, and that there existed the possibility that Elin might entertain the impulse to emphasize that power. Perhaps speak to Mezie poorly because she knew he needed her. These thoughts riled her, and Elin became a symbol of Mezie's helplessness. When Mezie called and said, "They are deporting me," it was Elin's smug face that came to Sommy first. It was Elin she blamed. It was Elin she wanted to slap. But now, she'll talk to Elin, beg, roll on the floor, eat shit, even, if Elin could at least get Mezie to talk to her.

Elin replies immediately with a message of her phone number. WhatsApp? she writes. Sommy adds Elin's number and is about to dial it when someone takes the seat beside her. She doesn't turn to look at the person, but she's irritated. There are other empty benches in the space this person could've taken, but they chose to sit so closely beside her. She thinks now that the restaurant's front yard propels chaos toward her. It was first the water-sprinkler woman. She makes to leave, when the person leans over and says, "Hey."

She turns. It's Bryan, the witness. She laughs.

"I thought you were about to rob me," she says.

He puts his hands in the air. "I tried to not be creepy this time."

"You did not do a very good job with that," she says. "I'm a Lago-sian. If anyone I don't know comes five inches near me, my alarm goes off."

"Lagos? Nigeria?" he says, eyes narrowing.

"Yes, I'm Nigerian."

He folds his arms and relaxes into the bench. The move is so hilariously Nigerian, his leaning back in disbelief, that when he says that he's Nigerian, too, "kind of, sort of," she grins and says, "I don't doubt it one bit."

She asks if both his parents are Nigerian. It's a cautious gesture. He looks obviously biracial, but you never know.

He says his father is the Nigerian. He's never met the man, though, he adds quickly.

"Oh," she says, because it's not the sort of thing a person says to a stranger: "I do not know my father."

He smiles weakly at her.

"Is that your look of pity?" he says, laughing.

She straightens her jaw. "No, no."

"I imagine you have a great relationship with your dad," he says. "It's always the ones with the best dads who clutch their chests when I tell them."

"You've imagined correctly. My dad is a good man."

He makes a face, says, "I'm jealous."

She laughs, "I can share him with you."

"I'll take you up on that offer."

She asks if he's Igbo, and before he replies, adds, "The full cheeks give you away."

He cups his cheeks, laughing. "You are right, actually. My mother says my father is Igbo. I actually have an Igbo name. Obinna."

She wants to correct his pronunciation of "Obinna," but she hesitates, and it occurs to her that he's probably never heard the name pronounced correctly. It saddens her that he walks around the world with a name he cannot pronounce.

He asks what she's always doing hanging around outside the restaurant. She asks what he's always doing hanging around. She says it with sass, like she would if she were flirting with a Nigerian. It's automatic, the wry sultriness of her voice, that nodding-and-smiling thing she does when she's shy. She can't say whether he's flirting back. If he were a *real* Nigerian, she would know for sure. She'd notice the schmaltziness in his expressions, the overeagerness. Amara says that Nigerian men wear their ashawo like a rainbow jacket. If they like you, it's as obvious as a lightning bolt. She knows nothing about American men. Her undercooked notion is that they sit and wait for women to chase them.

"The library," he says. "I work here until late."

"You work at the library?"

"I mean, I'm a writer. I'm working on a novel."

"Oh nice," she says. "Do you have published works?"

He says he doesn't. He's "emerging," he says, fingers making air quotes. He says he's still pursuing an MFA in creative writing. She tells him she's a graduate student in the literature department.

He says, "That's really cool. We have so much in common already." His voice is clearly laden with hope. It's obvious that he wants something more. She throbs inwardly at the thought of this. She looks at him full-on in the face now. There's a restfulness that wasn't there in their last meeting, and it's like a burnish, forcing forth the sharp edges of his beauty. In their first meeting, she'd thought him attractive in the conventional sense, light-skinned, curly-haired, devastatingly square-jawed, and he'd lingered in her mind because of this, drawn as she was to the conventional. But, under the yellow light pouring from the lamp above them, she sees clearly and is drawn, too, to his unconventionality, the roundness of his nose, his pert ears, the almost imperceptible way his eyeballs misalign when he squints.

He asks what her focus is. She says, "Romantic Love. In Igbo literature." And then adds, with a discomfiting laugh, "Not that I'm looking for it in my own life."

He pauses for a moment, his eyes thoughtful. "Interesting," he says. "Smart, too. Love is such an organizing energy in our world, and one would think that there'd be more academic work done on it, but that isn't the case."

"So true," she says. "I guess us literature folks don't think it a serious enough subject."

"If you really think about it, it's an intimidating and inconsistent concept. It's almost futile to speak intelligently about it."

She doesn't want him to stop talking, so she asks if he believes it's really a thing, love. Not just the manifestation of brain chemicals and societal conditioning, but something more, something spiritual.

"I think so. But I generally refuse to think too much about it. I don't want to demystify it. Like poetry, for instance. I love to read poems. I'll never write them seriously. I'll never publish a poem. I don't want to know how they work. I just want to feel them."

She takes her gaze to the people walking out of the restaurant now, and says, with a low, regretful voice, that she has to go. Her roommate might start to worry about her.

He looks into her eyes, a clear intent in his expression, and says, "Sommy." A pause: he wants her to know that it's been six weeks, but he remembers her name. "Would you like to grab coffee with me tomorrow?"

She hesitates from the sheer anomaly of it all. She's usually had to grow on men. A slow, often complicated formation of a relationship, where she's cynical about a man's intentions for her, and he, too, sensing her resistance, remains unserious and teasing, until months, maybe even years pass, and they both realize that they are enmeshed in something profound and undefined. This one, clear-eyed and straightforward, is rare for her.

"I'll grab coffee with you on Wednesday," she says. "My friends and I are already hanging tomorrow."

She likes the sound of "my friends and I." She likes the sound of her life filling out with chykers and friends.

"Wednesday, then," he says, bending, palms on both knees.

He takes her number while they walk to the restaurant, promises to call. At the entrance, they stand looking at each other, just like the first time they met, both of them struggling with parting words.

He finally stretches a hand for a handshake, and she takes it, says, "Do you know what I call you in my head?"

He shakes his head. "What?"

"Bryan, the witness."

His face breaks into laughter, and the sound ushers in a weeding out, a clearing right in the middle of her heart. She'll not call Elin, she decides. She'll not call Mezie. She'll stretch her hands to whomever stretches theirs to her.

The encounter with Bryan is cheerful content to share with Nia and Kayla the next day, while they sit on a high table at the quaint café snaked through with flowers. It is early afternoon. A stupendous sun bursts through the window, blinding Sommy whenever she moves her head without caution. In contrast, though, is the sky, a great sea of dismal blue, all its vigor sucked by the greedy sun.

"Do you think it's strange that he didn't text last night?" Sommy asks.

Kayla says she's sure he'll text sometime that evening to properly set up their date. Nia says she doesn't know. She thinks men untrustworthy.

"Nia is a man-hater," Kayla says.

"Oh please," Nia says, waving Kayla away.

Sommy learns that the girls are both graduate students in the mechanical engineering department. Their conversations are peppered with "lab" this, "lab" that. They think Sommy admirable. At least, Nia says, Sommy's studying something she's passionate about. She can't say why she chose to study engineering in the first place. Sommy understands Nia's assumption that literature is a subject passionate people study. It's not exactly where one pitches their tent if they plan to make money, but Sommy thinks herself an anomaly in this matter. She's not passionate about literature. She never dreamt of graduate school. In her undergraduate years, as a student in the English department, she'd been passive, sitting around, moping during lectures. Her application to James Crowley had been Amara's idea. It was how most of their former classmates were leaving the country, and it was another experiment in her search for a passion. But she doesn't say all of this to Nia and Kayla so they don't think her unserious.

Kayla says she sort of agrees with Nia. "Do not put your eggs in one basket." She pouts as though giving a lesson she's learnt through experience. "Are you on Tinder?"

Sommy says it's not her thing, meeting people online.

"I don't think it's anyone's thing," Kayla says. "But if you are going to get any action, that's the way to go."

Nia says, "That's not what I mean. Do not listen to Kayla. She's confused."

Kayla does a fake shiver and takes a sip of her Diet Coke. It's been an hour since they sat down, and Sommy's noticed how quickly and frequently Kayla's and Nia's arguments condense into hostility. Everything they say leads them to arguments: about sex, it's underratedness or it's overratedness; beauty standards, it's importance or unimportance; love, Nia thinks it rare, that you get one or two big loves, and Kayla is certain it can be found anywhere and at any time, you only had to look. The girls tug at each other's convictions with desperation. Sommy wants to tell them now, as they stare at each other with battlefield anger, that there are really no rules. When it comes to desire, there is no bringing someone to the other side. People want what they want.

Bryan ghosts her, and it's carcinogenic. The moments they spent together felt suspended from her real life, untainted by the mournfulness Mezie's attempt and silence have cemented in her, and now she feels cast away. She wonders at how tightly she's anchored herself to the fact of Mezie's existence, how because she had him, her brother, her own person, she'd never felt this clambering need to belong to someone else. And what is this need? She thinks often now of a proverb in Chinua Achebe's *Arrow of God*, a required reading in her Transnational Feminism class: "When we see an old woman stop in her dance to point again and again in the same direction we can be sure that somewhere there something happened long ago which touched the roots of her life." She's certain that, for her, Mezie's attempt is the thing that touched the roots of her life, and it is the direction she'll forever point at. Why else would this encounter with Bryan make her constantly feel like sinking to the ground in pain?

She goes on Tinder to distract herself. She meets her first date, Masoud, a PhD Student from Iran, at the same café she now frequents with Nia and Kayla.

"Glad you could make it," he says, leans in for a half hug.

She smiles. "Glad you could make it, too."

He's pale-skinned, lean, with dark hair that falls on his face. There's a sad quality to his beauty. She thinks it's his eyes, their soft glow.

"They have the best donuts," he says, as she scans the menu.

Their seats are by the window, in the corner of the shop facing the road. Her view is of a brick house with fogged windows. In front of the house, two bicycles lay slant, chained to a rack.

"I'll have those if you say so."

After they place their order, a strange silence descends. They sit, smiling awkwardly. Sommy finds this odd. They'd had interesting text exchanges, an astronomical shift from her conversations with her other Tinder matches, most of which were deadened by small talk: *What are you up to? Nice weather today, huh? Do you go here? Nigerian? Oh I used to know a Nigerian back in college.* There was usually nothing more. But he'd been different. When she told him she was Nigerian, he'd asked, *Are you Igbo? Or Yoruba? Or Hausa?* And though she could tell that he was overly proud of his knowledge of the Nigerian landscape, she'd been pleased that he'd not told her about his one colleague who is Nigerian, and she'd texted this to him. He'd sent multiple laughing emojis and said he could relate, and for a few seconds Sommy felt that they shared the intimacy of two people who understood the anatomy of a specific pain.

Sommy contemplates telling him now, as a joke, an attempt to revive that intimacy, that since they both did not order coffee, and yet had agreed to grab coffee, they perhaps have adopted the American way of asking a person on a date. It's what most of the men on Tinder tell her, *Let's grab coffee*, without asking if she likes coffee. It's what Bryan had said that evening, too, while they sat on the bench outside the restaurant. She wishes now that she'd taken Bryan's number. She would have sent him an obscenity-rich message. She would have said to him: *Who but a monster raises a person's hope only to dash it? YOU KNOW,* she could have texted him, in all caps, *YOU COULD HAVE JUST GONE ON YOUR WAY. YOU DID NOT NEED TO ASK ME FOR MY NUMBER. YOU COULD HAVE LEFT ME THE FUCK ALONE!*

She decides against the coffee joke, thinking it inappropriate to talk about her other Tinder matches on a date.

"It's awkward?" he says with a shivery chuckle.

"Yes, it is," she says, sighing loudly. "First dates are rough."

"Right?" he exclaims, and they both laugh.

Their laughter cracks them open, and they slide into an easy conversation. He tells her of an ex-girlfriend back home, the love of his life until recently. The distance had torn them apart, and he can't seem to find anything close here. He says he misses home, misses his mother, misses the food, the sharp, dusty smell of Tehran's air. Sommy tells him she understands. She has no undying romantic flame back home, but she misses her family, too. She wants to tell him about Mezie. The part about him leaving home six years ago to Norway. Getting arrested with expired papers. Getting deported. Not about the attempted suicide. Not about his refusal to speak to her after she left. But she's hesitant to open up quickly.

Their order is called, and they walk to collect it, and for a moment, Sommy imagines herself and Masoud as boyfriend and girlfriend, and it makes her feel like a person certain of their taste. When people saw them together, she thinks, the Iranian and the Nigerian, they would believe them to be truly in love. What else, if not love in its purest form, would cause two people with what she considers vast cultural backgrounds to want each other?

When they get back to the table, Sommy asks if he's ever dated a black girl. He squints, leans forward, and then says he hasn't. In America, he's mostly dated white women.

She senses, in the dip of his voice, that he finds the question unsettling, and she tries to change it, asks what he has planned for the weekend, but he lunges into a monologue about white people. They date themselves, he says. "Look around," he says. "Do you see an interracial pair here?"

Sommy looks around, perplexed, and then says, "But, sorry to ask. Aren't you white?"

He folds his lips, as if trapping expletives. "I am not white."

She studies his pale skin. "I don't get it. I don't get the race thing. Sorry." She pauses. "Aren't you white if you look white? Isn't that the point?"

"I am Arab," he says.

"But what do you tick on forms? I don't see Arab. I see White, Black, American Indian, Asian. I don't see Arab."

For the first time, he takes a sip of his mint tea. "I tick 'white' and it's crazy. I shouldn't. Why call me white when I don't have the privileges of a white person?" He scratches his head. "White people bomb my country, call me a terrorist, don't want to fuck me unless they think I'm a rich Dubai prince."

Sommy laughs at the Dubai prince part, but he doesn't join. His eyes shine with pain, and she's suddenly sorry that she's swerved their discussion into troubled waters with a stupid question about race.

"I want to date people of all races," he says with a resigned air. "And if I'm being honest with you—I feel like I can be honest with you—I'm most attracted to white skin, long hair, straight nose. But I'm not comfortable around them anymore, white women." And, as if controlled by a tricky supernatural being looking to play a jest on an unsuspicious human, Masoud tells her, in one breath, about his encounter with a blonde middle-aged white woman whom he'd met at a gas station while on a road trip to Wisconsin. They'd hit it off immediately. They liked the same books, the same movies, the same music. After standing in the aisle for a while, the woman invited him to sit in her car for a bit. He liked her very much, he says now to Sommy, and had thought that if they did not fuck, they could at least remain friends. But then she said to him, unprompted, that her son was serving in Afghanistan. She pulled from her purse a passport-sized photo of a man in his midtwenties, golden-brown hair slicked back, bright brown eyes. She brought it to his face, told him to study it, and then said: "Promise that you'll save my son if he's ever captured by ISIS."

It has been a year since the encounter, Masoud says, but it has followed him like a second shadow. He's getting a PhD. He's teaching undergrads physics. At the time, he'd published a paper on graph theory in the *European Journal of Combinatorics*. And it was still not enough. Still isn't enough.

He's silent and contemplative. There's pure anger in the whites of his eyes. He picks up a donut and begins to munch slowly, gloomily, ignoring her, as though having pondered it, he's now decided that no woman, white, black, or brown, can ever be trusted.

"I'm sorry," Sommy says, because the quiet is uneasy, not at all because she's sorry. Whatsoever pity she felt evaporated the moment he mentioned his dating preference. What then is she? The settled-for option?

Masoud doesn't reply to her apology. Sommy doesn't make another attempt. She eats her donut silently; he sips his mint tea silently. When they both stand to leave, they do not say goodbye. They give each other polite nods and walk in opposite directions.

Later that evening, she texts Kayla: My date was so bad. Like so bad it is laughable. Kayla calls immediately.

"No, he did not!" Kayla exclaims at each high point of Sommy's narration.

"I felt bad for him," Sommy says.

"You should not," Kayla says. "He's a weirdo."

"I swear," Sommy sighs. "Tinder is a weird country."

"Listen, I'm on there just to fuck. These men aren't useful for anything else."

Sommy imagines that Kayla's forehead is stretched in that way she does to emphasize her disregard. She hasn't told her about Bryan's ghosting. She's too embarrassed. At the café, she'd told Kayla and Nia of the intensity between them. She told them of how he'd come to her, declared himself a witness. She did not exactly tell them that she'd thought of him as a man she could follow, a man who could guide her. Outside of her head, it felt demeaning that stamped into her consciousness was this impulse to stand behind the imposing force of a man. So she spoke instead of his shining brilliance, and the whiff of wealth he gave off with the caramel-colored woolen sweater he had on, richly knitted, his plain chinos, his coat, heavy and dark and intimidating, the glassy clearness of his skin.

Kayla says Sommy deserves a nail appointment after all of that stress, and Sommy says, "Yes, I do," and they set up a meeting, even though Sommy worries about money sometimes, a habit derived from years of lack. She does this thing where she converts dollars to naira, especially when she goes to the store with Bayo. She'll say to Bayo: "This small crate of eggs is like two thousand naira if we convert the price. Something I'll buy for four hundred and fifty naira in Lagos. Chai!" And they'll both agree that America is expensive.

In his early years in Norway, Mezie always sent money in dollars, never kroner. Her favorite thing was sitting on the motorbike carrying her to the bank in Alaba and mentally making notes of her future expenses. Her second-favorite thing was haggling with the mallams by the decrepit Tantalizers eatery for the best exchange rate.

"You will not suffer in this life," Mezie had told her often. "As long as I'm breathing, you will not suffer."

In a way, she thinks now, his idea of suffering is much like her parents'. "You will not suffer" means "You will not go hungry or homeless." It means "I'll buy it and give to you." Their responsibility did not factor in mental suffering. When Sommy suggested to their mother that Mezie was depressed, she'd raised a hand and brought it down forcefully. This was around the first week of Mezie's return.

"What he needs is good food," her mother said. "What do you expect will happen to someone who has been eating bread for six years? Of course, that person will be depressed. If I load him with vegetable soup and yam porridge and enough okporoko, you'll see, he'll be back to his normal self."

"Mummy, Mezie's problem is not dry fish and soup."

"Somkelechukwu, biko, don't add to my problem," she'd said, her hand back up in the air.

Femi, the only one of Sommy's boyfriends who mattered, had said to her, on the night of their breakup, "You behave coldhearted," and she'd looked at him with pain, and said, "I beat Kayode and Yasin because they called you slow, and you have the mouth to call me coldhearted."

She'd indeed punched Kayode in the mouth and bit Yasin's bicep. She was fifteen, preparing to write WAEC exams.

"When I kiss you," he said, "you fold your mouth. When I tell you I love you, you laugh. When I want to hold your hand, you push me away. Now sef that I'm talking to you, you are getting angry. You are not looking in my eyes. It's not only by beating people for me. I want you to show me soft love."

"Soft love?" she'd hissed. "Femi, if you want to break up with me, break up with me. Stop all this nonsense talk."

"That's all you have to say?"

"That's all I have to say."

She was certain she was going to die after their breakup. She had loved him with the passion of a child, yet she did not beg, did not call him, did not promise to show him "soft love." She'd not learnt how to do that. No one in her family gave *soft love*. They'd fight, maybe even kill for each other, but they'd not say "I love you." Her friendship with Amara has taught her to show affection, and yet she toddles in the process.

She'd hitched herself to Mezie's hips after the breakup with Femi. It was the year after Mezie graduated secondary school, the year his rejection letters came from Yale and MIT. Sommy had followed him about, to Patrick's, where they sat on the balcony, smoking cigarettes, to the estate carpark turned football field, where she held his shirt on her lap and urged him on as he dribbled the ball, to evening mass to watch him serve, regal in his altar boy attire. He'd been her balm. And now, disappointed by Bryan, she feels an even stronger urge to talk to him, so two days after the call with Kayla, she texts Elin, asks when's a good time to call. It's not even a minute after the text when Elin's name appears on the home screen. It's a video call. Sommy still has on her bonnet and underneath it her afro, matted in its own mathematical way, lays like a sentient being. She contemplates missing the call, calling back, but she's desperate, so she picks up, and Elin's almond-shaped face covers the phone screen.

"Hi," Elin says.

"Thanks for agreeing to talk," Sommy says.

Sommy's suddenly tongue-tied, staring at Elin's green eyes, which in pictures had seemed pleasant, pleasing, but here, over the phone, are stern, skeptical.

"I'm glad you reached out," Elin says, and tucks her hair behind her ears. "How have you been? You are in Iowa, right?"

"Yes," Sommy says, shifting, resting on the couch.

"It gets cold," Elin says. "Just like here. Mezie hated it."

"So I've heard," she replies, placing her leg on the center table, by the white vase holding Bayo's cactus plant.

"You like it there? Your school? Iowa?"

For a minute Sommy thinks she heard Ohio. Elin's English is burdened by her Norwegian, and it is what, despite several corrections, Sommy's mother insists on calling Iowa—Ohio.

"It's okay, I guess," Sommy says. "Took me a bit of time to adjust but I'm adjusting."

"I'm glad that you are adjusting."

Outside the apartment hallway a door shrieks open, key bundles jangle, and then the tap, tap of footsteps. The apartment is otherwise silent.

"I'm worried, too," Elin says, cutting right to the chase. "About Mezie. He's struggling with the sudden change."

Behind Elin's face is a wooden kitchen cabinet. On the handle of the middle cabinet, a white dishcloth hangs. Above the cabinet an off-white ceiling.

"You guys talk? On the phone?"

"Yes, we do."

"Often?"

"Often, yes."

"We don't. He's refused to pick up my calls."

Elin breathes. She has on a green turtleneck, and a thin silver chain hangs around her neck. Her face is lightly made-up. She looks like she's on her way to meet someone. Sommy tries to imagine her having lunch with friends. What does she talk about? What makes her laugh? Sommy can't. Elin is alien to her, her world out of reach, in the same way Mezie's life in Norway is out of reach.

"He's embarrassed," Elin says. "He's not told me so, but I know. He's not much of a sharer. About what is going on in his life. He's not one to talk about that." She pauses, irritably picks at her lashes. "But I do know he wants to. To talk to you. He cares very much about what you think of him."

"I know he cares about me," Sommy says sharply. "He is my brother." The anger moves through her like a sliver of glass. Who is Elin to mediate them?

"Of course you do," Elin says, her face transforming, those severe green eyes now soft. "You do. It's just"—she sighs—"he's very avoidant and that's difficult to deal with. I'm trying to help."

Her anger is foolish. She did call Elin to act as mediator. Mezie has made it so that they need a mediator. How shameful, she thinks.

"It's hard being away at this time especially," Sommy says, and not feeling convinced she sounds remorseful enough, adds, "I'm sorry for sounding snappish."

Elin folds her lips contemplatively, and then says, "I know it's not exactly my place, and this might be too forward, but Mezie is an adult.

He'll be fine. He'll take care of himself. I'm saying this because I'm a worrier, too, and I worry myself to death about everyone, and sometimes I have to remind myself that I do not love the people in my life more than they love themselves. They do want to take care of themselves, and they will."

There's the puerile desire to ask Elin if trying to kill oneself is an act of love, of taking care of oneself? She doesn't know that Mezie has told Elin about his attempt. It seems very unlikely. How good it will feel to shatter this know-it-all air of hers.

"Would you please talk to him?" She's done. She doesn't want to hear any more of it. "Tell him to talk to me. I just want to know that he's fine. That's all."

"I will," Elin says.

"When you get around to talking to him about it, will you please call to update me?"

"Of course."

"One more thing," Sommy says. "How did he get caught?"

Elin says it's her fault. She'd made them travel, go to visit her sister in Sweden. It was stupid, but then again, they traveled often, to Sweden, to Amsterdam, to Holland. They visited family, friends, museums, and it was always smooth. He used the passport of another Nigerian Norwegian when traveling. Took on a new identity. For some reason this time, he was stopped and searched at the baggage reclaim area. Just randomly. There was no reason for him to be stopped. But he was. Singled out by the airport security. Taken away. And that was it.

Sommy's breath quickens. She feels reduced. Took on another identity?

"It's terrible," Elin says.

Her face is red, her eyes teary, and even through her irritation, Sommy feels the distance between them closing. Right in front of her, Elin is calcifying into a real person, not one she synthesizes through Mezie's eyes, so Sommy says to her that it isn't her fault. It's not her fault that he'd been moving around Europe with expired papers. There are a ton of people to blame, she says, but Elin isn't one of them.

"Thank you," Elin says. "I needed to hear that."

Sommy's smile this time is genuine. "Talk soon, okay?"

"Bye-bye."

Elin's face disappears from the phone. Sommy's lock screen is back. A picture of the sky she took a few weeks ago, deep purple like newly bruised skin, strokes of orange, its effect ominous. She'd been on an evening walk when she took the picture. She paused often to take in the trees, and the grasses by the sidewalk, and the sky, and the lamp-post, and she had the feeling that she was home, not home as a physical place, but home as a feeling in the body, a sparking of the senses, home as something historical, linguistically defiant. I cannot explain it, but I feel it, she thinks. It's the chronic opposite of this feeling she has thinking of an identity-less Mezie. A prelinguistic feeling of homeless-ness. To be cast out. To be rootless. It is a feeling prepackaged for her. He's felt it before, and because he's felt it, she's feeling it now. What haunts him haunts her. It's the way of love.

The force of the winter cold shrivels Sommy. She moves into herself involuntarily, a kind of innerness that sometimes stun her, all her light gone. The sky turns colorless. Roofs are covered with snow, and leaf-less trees stand about like sad people, their stalks and branches like hands raised to the sky hoping for answered prayers. The roads become dangerous, slippery things. Snow turns into ice, and ice turns into murky brown water. And some days, as she walks to class swaddled in layers, gloves, the thickest of beanies, a chunky scarf, the wind pulling at her, she halts, and thinks how awful, how fucking awful.

She starts to spend more time with Nia and Kayla. Their preferred spot, before the onslaught of snow, had been the College Green Park, where they laid on picnic blankets dissecting Kayla's often chaotic love life. Now, they meet at Kayla's studio apartment, with its low ceiling and barrage of hanging plants. They eat hot Cheetos and drink kombucha. Other times, they meet at the café, loaded with essays to write and to annotate. Sometimes, while they sit hacking into each other about this and that, Sommy's stunned by the swift molding of their friendship. They had immediately gelled. Sommy is the cool in the storm that is Nia and Kayla's relationship. When they go in on each other, as they often do, Sommy's there to say, "You people, please have small sense." Sommy often thinks that their friendship wouldn't have lasted much longer without her. Not for lack of love, but the opposite: they care too much about what the other has to say. Mostly, she thinks about how the girls have anchored her throughout the semester. Their weekly meetings, light and fluffy, make her feel a little human. She still hasn't told them about Mezie. She's noticed that the girls do not share much about their personal lives themselves. She's learnt that Americans call this type of sharing "trauma dumping."

She's not shared Mezie with Bayo, either. She imagines he'll tell her to get over it. He's often frustrated by waste. He says of some of his American friends, "All these opportunities, and some of them just let it go to waste. Doing drugs and just being useless." He'll scold her for being lukewarm, for grieving away this rare opportunity, so she says nothing. She doesn't even share anymore with Amara—Amara who knew everything, Amara, the first person she called when Mezie rang, and said, "Som, tell Mummy I'm getting deported."

Elin calls her on one of these winter days and says that Mezie doesn't want to talk.

"You told him I called you to ask to talk to him and he said he doesn't want to talk?"

"He says, and these are his own words, 'I don't want to explain myself.'"

"But—" Sommy pauses, gasps. "I don't want him to explain anything."

"He's being unreasonable."

"I just want—"

"I know. He's angry and he's taking it out on the easiest person to take it out on, and trust me, I gave him an earful about that."

"Why isn't he taking it out on you?" Sommy wants to ask, but she doesn't. She looks on pitifully at the wooden cabinet behind Elin's head.

The Friday she turns in her final papers, Sommy visits the rooftop bar with Kayla and Nia. They stand by the glass fence, looking out to the city, its high-rises resplendent with lights, the roads snaking around. Sommy's feeling a little subdued. Nia and Kayla will be leaving for home in two days, and she misses them already.

Nia is talking now about her decision to step down as president of the BGSO. She says it's a relief. She can't say what she was thinking when she chose to run in the first place.

"The whole thing will go to shit without you," Kayla says.

"It won't," Nia replies. "Michael will keep them in check."

At this, the girls laugh. Michael will always remain their inside joke. The cold is getting to Sommy. She thinks it amazing that people brace it year after year. She has a little meltdown every time she prepares to leave the apartment. It's as though she's gearing up for war, with all the accoutrements required: thermal tights and shirt, a sweater and at least two pairs of pants, double socks, her ginormous boots with the toothy soles so she doesn't slip on ice, a scarf, her beanie, and her mask, because even her face is not exempt from the onslaught. She's now keenly aware that nature doesn't necessarily center human comfort.

Kayla says that she isn't looking forward to spending time with her family this holiday. Sommy's never quite understood Kayla's family situation. She knows Kayla's from a big family, with uncles and aunties and cousins and nieces. She knows that something happened, and Kayla had been at the center of it, and that somehow, it is excavated during family gatherings. Kayla talks around it.

"You can stay with me," Sommy says. "We'll spend the holiday together."

Kayla smiles, a tired smile.

"Or you can come with me," Nia says.

A quiet look passes between the two, a look of shared private knowledge. Nia is privy to Kayla's family thing. There's a part of Sommy that wants to trade secrets: tell Kayla about Mezie, tell her that she'd told only half the truth when Kayla had asked why she isn't going home for the Christmas break. True, Sommy cannot afford the expensive flight, but there is also the question of what she'll meet at home, of Mezie, this new, vicious silence between them.

Sommy shakily brings her glass to her lips. She wants to suggest that they go inside for some heat, but she's feeling fatigued. The conversation about going home has despaired them.

They spend the rest of their short time together, silent and cold, and when Kayla drops off Sommy in front of her apartment building, she steps out of the car, walks Sommy to the staircase, and says she didn't know that it was possible to feel connected to someone from all the way across the world in such a short period of time.

"Maybe we knew each other in a former life," Sommy says.

They hug, long and tight.

Sommy's folding laundry when her mother calls. It's Christmas Day. Outside, the world is covered in slabs of snow. The air in the room is dry, and Sommy has to thumb her nostrils at intervals to draw out moisture.

"Mummy," she says, "Merry Christmas."

"Happy Christmas, nwa'm," her mother says.

Sommy can hear the swishing of things. Her mother is always in motion.

"You are well?"

They've not spoken in a while. Sommy has decided to stop calling. She's certain that her mother is a co-conspirator in whatever plot Mezie has created to alienate her, with her ready-made excuses for his behavior.

"We just came back from church," her mother says. "It was glorious. The Holy Spirit descended, I'm telling you. The new father is a true man of God. He has it. Some people just have it. Now I'm going to take a cold shower and eat. You know what we cooked today?" She pauses, and then continues. "We cooked turkey stew. Fresh turkey. Your father chopped salad things. Mezie fried plantains. I'm going to balance and eat like a king."

"Mummy, can I call you back?"

"Call me back for what? What are you doing?"

"I'm folding laundry."

"So folding clothes cannot wait?"

"I—"

"This girl, you are becoming something else." There's a pause. Swishing. Swishing. "Are you okay?"

"I'm okay. I just want to fold my laundry."

Her mother's breaths are loud, and they mesh with the sound of her shuffling. She's probably unclasping her brassiere. One hand holding the phone to her ear, the other bent behind her, reaching for the clasp, and then to her shoulders, tugging the straps, one hand at a time, and finally pulling the worn, lizard-like brassiere from under her blouse. Sommy has always hated when she does this, thought it to be deeply graceless.

"Somkelechukwu. I am your mother. You can deceive everyone. You can even deceive yourself. But you cannot deceive your mother. What is it? Tell me."

"Mummy, please, I just want to fold my clothes."

"Ohhh," her mother says, resigned. "I have done my part as a mother. I have asked. If you don't want to talk, that's your business. Me, I called to say 'Happy Christmas.' I'm having a good day. You can't spoil it for me. Bye."

The phone beeps. Sommy stares at her pile of folded laundry for a while, and then shoves it into the drawer.

She walks out to the sitting room to talk to Bayo, cheer herself up. They've been spending more time together since their outside world shuttered.

Bayo's seated on his papasan chair, curled up like a child, punching away at his phone.

He looks up at her. "Are you hungry?"

It's what they do now, plan their meals together.

"I'm not hungry," she says. "Are you?"

"If I see food, I'll eat," he says, squeezing his nose. "But I don't have one single energy to cook anything."

"Lazy boy."

"Did I ever claim hardworking to you?"

She walks over to him and slaps his knee playfully, and then takes a seat on the couch next to his chair.

He continues with his phone scrolling, and she sits in the quiet, studying him. She wants to talk to him about Mezie. She's never had male friends, so she's never exactly understood the world of men. She'd known the boy Mezie, for, as children, their lives were not all that different. The man Mezie is a puzzle.

"Why are you looking at me like that?" Bayo says.

She'd not realized he was watching her. "Like how?"

He does a circular gesture with his head, as if to describe the *how*.

"You have to have been looking at me to know that I was looking at you."

"Not true," he says, sitting upright. "People feel these things."

"How can you feel a look?"

"Argumentator," he says. "You have started again."

She rubs the arm of the chair. The sitting room, as usual, is in slight disarray. His T-shirt lies on the coffee table. A blue plastic cup sits by his foot. The throw pillows are strewn about on the wooden floor. The flower vase on the side table sits too close to the wall, not in the center of the table as it had been earlier. It used to irritate her, Bayo's ability to, in a short time, strip the room of its coordination. It doesn't anymore. She thinks it homey now.

"I'll go home in the summer," she says. "Next year."

She finds the wistfulness in her voice surprising.

"Rich woman," he teases. "That flight money is nothing to you,"

She turns to him. "Don't you miss Lagos?"

"Miss Lagos?" He drops his phone. "I guess I do. But, abeg, what am I going to do in Lagos? I came to this America for something, and I'm not going home until I get it."

"For what?"

He stares at her, skeptical. It is of course a stupid question. For money. For status. To pursue his dreams.

"Is that even a question?" he says. "To live my life. To be my best self."

She hates that she cannot feel this same enthusiasm about America. She wonders if it's because she's watched this enthusiasm wreck Mezie. His dissatisfaction in the years before he eventually left for Norway remains undiminished in her mind. So frustrated he was that he willed destruction for himself. His boss was terrible. His secondhand car broke down frequently. He spent long hours in traffic. His face swelled with stress pimples. "What kind of country is this?" he said to her often, incredulous. "Life should not be this hard." Things that had seemed inconsequential took on gravity. If the power went off, Sommy knew to expect a speech about Nigeria being the dwarf of Africa. "Giant of Africa, my foot," he'd say to their father. "A disgrace, this country." If he heard news of a robbery, Sommy knew to expect a speech about an impending civil uprising. "People are getting tired. Very soon the whole country will implode." She thinks now of the Sunday afternoon he'd called up a duwa duwa to adjust the waistline of his work trousers. The duwa duwa, a man of about fifty, with dark, dry skin, sat outside their door, running Mezie's trousers through the sewing machine. Sommy needed a skirt adjusted but was too tired to go searching for it in her heap of clothes, so she'd gone back into the apartment to have an apple. One bite in and Mezie's raging voice cut through the thick heat. When she rushed outside, she found him staring down at the duwa duwa, refusing to pay for the service.

"What is it?"

"Just look at." He brought the trousers to her face. "He made the waistline too tight and cut out the excess without waiting for me to try it on. Now he cannot amend it."

"He can sew on the excess to make it bigger."

"That's what I was trying to say to him," the man said, his voice pleading, his expression crushed.

"What do you mean by that?" Mezie boomed. "I should be wearing patch-patch? Because of what?" He flung the trousers and stormed out.

Sommy picked them up, paid the duwa duwa, and said, "Oga you sef. You would have waited for him to try it on first."

"I know," the man said. "My mind just fly leave me. I just dey think another thing."

Sommy had felt great pity for him, and she'd given him an extra hundred naira.

Inside, Mezie would not stop talking about it. He complained that the problem of Nigeria was more than its terrible leaders, it was also its people, lazy, greedy, a nonchalant attitude to work. He raged and raged until Sommy said, "All this talk because of one tailor? Please, let's hear word." He'd paused, looked at her, betrayed, and then, as he always did when under pressure, stormed out. They didn't speak for a week after that, but she carried with her a small shame at her contentment with the life around her.

"If you make some good money," she says now to Bayo, "would you go back?"

"In the blink of a fucking eye," he says.

"Really?"

"As in, sharp, sharp. Nothing like your own country."

He shifts to the end of the papasan chair, elbows atop the edges of his knees. She peeks at his belly rolls, the faint hair curling up his chest.

"You are asking questions as if you are homesick."

"Is that a bad thing?"

"No, not at all," he says. "I just—I just want you to know I'm here, whatever that means." He laughs. "For talking."

"Look at you being a sweet boy," she teases, smiles weakly at the realization that she'd been seeking this from her mother. "Thank you."

Their eyes lock. They've been looking at each other, arms, bellies, legs, but now they are looking into each other, passing a current that heats the cold air between them. It's not the first time that this look has passed between them. It's not the first time she thinks that it'd be nice to bury herself in his burly body. She stands and goes to him, and says, "Can I hold you?"

He looks at her, speechless, surprised. She scoots into the papasan chair, wraps her body around his, and breathes in the salty smell of his skin. In the moment, it's all she wants—to be held tightly, for his body to heat hers up. And they are that way for a while, until she heaves, takes her lips to his.

"Are you sure you want this?" he whispers.

She's ashamed of her desperation, but she cannot deny the calm in her body. How long has it been since she's held someone?

She nods, and he brings his mouth to hers. Every fiber in her body bends to the movement of his hand sweeping up her thighs, finding her panties, tugging. How to describe this passion? A fog of bliss? Savage and gentle at once.

"Condom," he says.

They unclasp. She feels sticky, an octopus-like feeling.

"I don't have one," she says.

"I do. Wait."

She sits, waiting for him, her gaze on the cactus plant, two yellowing cacti sprouting from dry earth. She'll water them afterward, she thinks. She's never watered them. He soon returns with three condom packs. She's still not making eye contact. The part of her that wants this demands thoughtlessness, demands that she refuse to think about the repercussions of sleeping with her roommate.

"Let's do it from the back," she says.

He nods. She crouches up the papasan chair mechanically, raises up her cotton dress. They fuck with her face close to the wall. She cannot say for how long.

It's over soon. Bayo is splayed on the floor, staring at the ceiling, breathless. The drip of a melting icicle dots the otherwise perfect silence. She stands, stares desolately at her brown cotton panties. Something about bending and picking them up instills shame. It's perhaps the many movies she's seen, in which the picture of a woman's panties on the floor signals a recently concluded illicit sexual encounter.

She heads to the bathroom. There, she splashes water on her face. Takes deep breaths. Paces. She wraps her face with a towel, and forces three strained breathes. She's stalling her return to him. What to say to him? She'd felt his passion as they made out, eager, wanting. He'd kissed her neck, her shoulder bone. Traced the length of an entire arm with his tongue. It is clear he'll demand more. But she doesn't see them together. It's something to do with "see finish." She's seen him finish. She's seen him fart and belch. He's seen her fart and belch. They are desperate and lonely in the same way. They are next door to each other. There's no mystique. She turns on the tap to mask her stalling. She leans on the wall, and a wave of fatigue hits her. She has a flashing urge to lie on the floor and sleep. She'll go to him and say that she enjoys him as a friend. "Sex will complicate things," she'll say. "And I value our friendship *very much*." Her decisiveness steadies her. She turns off the tap, hides her panties underneath her towel, slaps her afro into a somewhat neat bun, and heads to the sitting room.

Bayo is fully dressed, seated now on his papasan chair, scrolling through his phone. There's a lack of tension in his posture, and he doesn't raise his head. She takes the seat by the door and prepares for her speech. But he's still not looked at her. Her breath quickens. How does she talk to someone who won't look at her? She's thinking now that she might be the one to receive *the* speech.

"Did you see the trailer of the new Dakore movie?" he says with unusual quickness.

She tries, to no avail, to meet his eyes. "No."

"Okay. I'll send you the link. I think we should watch it."

She grabs her phone, scrolls to the trailer. She watches it, dazed, dry-tongued, and after, says, "Okay, let's put it on."

He turns on Netflix. She shifts, focuses on the screen. Had she conjured the passion in his touch? Has she gone mad? Worried her brain into delusion? But he had said, "I want you," or something like that. He had perked up at her touch. Or had he not?

They share only a few exchanges during the movie. Afterward, she enters her bedroom and locks herself in. Even when she begins to feel thirst, and then hunger, she doesn't leave. She cannot create the possibility of running into him. She cannot believe that she's, even to him, something to screw and no more.

She's unable to sleep, so she picks up her phone, opens WhatsApp, and begins typing a text to Mezie.

> Whatever you hold against me, you of all people must understand how lonely I feel here, without mummy and daddy and Amara, and to add onto these your silence, and the thought that you might go back on your promise, and I'll come home one day and you won't be there. It kills me, Mezie. I swear, it kills me. I need you to talk to me . . .

She reads the message. She thinks it mawkish. He'll hate it. He'll hate her earnestness. They did not speak nakedly about these sorts of things. She deletes it and tosses her phone under her bed.

She sleeps like she's waiting for a knock, her mind racing, her subconscious a web of worries. Then the knock comes, and she jolts awake. For a few seconds, she cannot decide if she's awake, or still trapped in a dream. The knock comes again, and she beats about the bed for the blanket, which she'd kicked off in her sleep.

The light from the sitting room hits her face when she opens the door, and she blocks it with a cupped hand.

"Bayo."

"Sorry. Did I wake you?"

"No. I was just—"

"I couldn't sleep. Can't sleep."

His unease reaches out to her like a pleading hand, and she digs into the blanket. "Is something wrong?"

"I know I acted weirdly this afternoon," he says. "It's just that I was confused. I did not know how you wanted me to act. But now I can't sleep because I didn't tell you then that I like you, that I have liked you from the first day I saw you." He swallows, takes a hand to the back of his neck. "So, I'm here to ask if you like me back. You can say no, and I'll just go into my room and act like nothing happened. I swear, nothing will be different. I just want to know if there's any chance."

She's shivering. The blanket is doing very little to ward off the cold. Or perhaps this is the shiver of relief, the manifestation of shame uncurling itself.

"Bayo," she says. "Come and sleep first."

With Bayo, her contentedness is a billowing thing. She's like a newborn swaddled in a soft cashmere blanket, returned to the tightness they know. Their lovemaking is desperate and coarse. The kindness comes afterward: she, helping him look for his socks, for instance, him smoothing her roughened hair. For reasons she can't explain, sex with him puts her in a thoughtful mood. She likes to lie in bed, her body crushed into his, and talk about whatever rises to her mind. Their conversations are usually laden with nostalgia. "Did you eat pepper snacks biscuit while growing up?" she asks. "Coconut milk biscuit? Speedy biscuit?" "Do you miss drinking zobo? Kunu? FanYogo?"

Once, while in bed, he picks up his phone and begins to play music. He starts with Styl-Plus's "Olufunmi." She closes her eyes, croons to it, and goes deep into herself to touch the part of her that existed both when she was nine and obsessed with the song, and now, twenty-five, so removed from the child she'd been. He plays Plantashun Boiz's "You and I." This he mimes to her with outstretched hands and a face contorted with play and endearment. *You and I, we're meant to be together, baby. Can't you see? That you are the only for me.* With this comes the smells and sounds of the estate of her childhood, where new music blasted from two loudspeakers mounted outside Fidelis's shop; Fidelis who sold cassettes, CDs, light bulbs, and extension cords, Fidelis who introduced them to Shakira, and Tupac, and Biggie Smalls. It was from Fidelis's speaker that Sommy learnt all of P-Square's songs by heart. She cannot remember the field in which she played hide-and-seek, suwe, ten-ten. The physicality of the memories is impossible to recall. But the smell, the sound, the feeling remains intact. These memories have the same hold as memories from the day before. They exist in a place of timelessness, in the singular shimmering thread of her spirit, where only music can take her, and because Bayo has become the channel to this spirit memory, she feels fiercely at home with him.

When they are weary of being indoors, they take walks around the neighborhood, sheathed in thermal gear and sweaters and coats and scarves. The streets are usually empty, the air frigid, the snow-plastered sidewalks slippery, the trees naked. On these walks, she learns of his mother, his sister, his only sibling, his father.

"It's weird," he tells her. "How much my parents still love each other. Like, they still kiss in public."

He tells her of his eight-year-old sister. "Sharp-mouthed," he calls her. "Too smart for her age," he adds, his voice glistening with love. He'd grown up taking care of her, and their relationship is sort of paternal. He's anxious about her, anxious for her future. Everything he does, he says, he does for her, and for his mother. He wants them to have the best.

When he talks of his father, his gentleness, the tender quality of their relationship, Sommy's reminded of her own father, a quiet man, generous with his affection but protective of his inner life. She knows very little about him, she says to Bayo of her father. His real thoughts and feelings, his life independent of her and her brother and their mother.

"Same with my dad," he says. "He hates talking about himself."

"That's not you at all," she says.

"Is that a compliment or an insult?"

"A compliment," she says, genuine, and then slips an arm into his.

Sometimes, between these conversations, he'll pause, and say something unrelated, curated to make her laugh. One time, he told her of a girl in his old neighborhood who barely knew how to read and write, but was eager to learn, so she watched a ton of American movies. Every time they conversed, and he said something hilarious, she threw her head backward and laughed long and hard, and then said, "Are you killing me?" At first, he told Sommy, he thought it was an expression she'd coined on her own, but soon he learnt that what she really meant to say was "Are you kidding me?" He didn't have the mind to correct her, and every time she said it, it took everything in him to resist ripping up with laughter. This story tickled Sommy to no end. It was something to do with the combination of the poor girl's certainty in her usage of the expression, and her eagerness to be perceived as the kind of person who said "Are you kidding me?"

They, however, do not talk about what they are, as though sensing that the discussion will unravel things best left barred. She'd not answered when he asked if she liked him, and he's not asked again, and she's content with this. When bubbles of doubt rise, her gratitude pricks them. She's been out in the cold, racked with anxiety about Mezie's silence, sore with Bryan's rejection, and has now entered a warm room. All she wants is to continue to stay warm. And warm she is. She takes as much delight in their shared background as she does in their different persons. She's amazed by how little of his past clangs into his present. He holds no grudges. Has no propensity for sad reflection. Pain goes through him as if through a sieve, with very little trapped in his veins. For him, everything is lustrous with hope. He believes nothing is owed him. He believes the simple things in life—breathing, the ability to feel thirst and have it quenched, a good night's sleep—are privileges. She wants to sink her hands into his soul and grab some of his private bliss.

On the first day of the year, Sommy thinks, everything is possible. Resolutions are made. Patterns seem breakable, new habits formable. Hope is dusted from dark, deserted places, and donned. The previous year, just a day gone, becomes the long past. In bathrooms all over, people stand in front of speckled mirrors and tell themselves, "Enough. *Enough.*" Some hunch in their beds, write down their goals for the New Year: eat healthier, exercise more, dress better, be bolder, cry less. Some, the brave ones, send the breakup text, the resignation letter, the *fuck you* message to the family WhatsApp group. And there are the others—those for whom New Year's is just another day in the long string of days that make up a person's ordinary, inglorious life. They eat, work, sleep, shit, and fuck like they do every other year. They engage in long monologues about the capitalist intention of holidays. They acknowledge their singularity, their awareness. They say to themselves: "I think for myself. I am no puppet."

Sommy, who earlier that morning had uncharacteristically chosen to be in the former group, the group of the profusely hopeful, now stands on the third floor of a giant, gray building downtown. It's Ralph's apartment, a boy in her Loneliness class, who'd sent an email to the departmental listserv a few days ago, inviting those in town to his New Year's party. Ordinarily of course, Sommy wouldn't have attended. She's learnt that when her classmates say "party," they do not mean music and dancing and laughter, they mean a gathering of people standing in groups of four and five, talking about medieval literature. But it's the New Year. She, like many others, has made resolutions. She is determined to be aggressively social. It's how she put it in her Notes app, *aggressively social*, underneath her third resolution for the year, which is to masturbate less. She's aware that this newfound hopefulness is a symptom of her new proximity to Bayo. It's impossible to spend so much time with him and not come away with the world looking a little glossier. So she's here, a glass of red wine in hand.

She exchanges brief greetings with the people she recognizes from her classes, the people who walk up to her. "Hi! Happy New Year." "I love your earrings." "It's freezing outside." "The food is great, isn't it?" "What classes are you taking this semester?" "Oh my god, can you believe it? A new year?" After they've depleted their reserve of small talk, a short silence follows, soon after which they wriggle away with excuses of needing to grab a drink, to use the bathroom, to go outside for a smoke.

After standing about for a while, swaying slightly to the music, Sommy walks into the kitchen, a wooden-floored space, with the drab, untidy semblance she's come to associate with cavalier male graduate students in the liberal arts, who are unconcerned with their appearances or those of the things in their care. The wall by the sink is spotted with crusty food. Streaks of dry liquid line the blue trash can. Some of the cupboards are missing doors, exposing hastily arranged plates and cups. There's a foul smell in the air, which Sommy suspects emanates from the musty carpet by the oven. Sommy rubs her palms together, as if to wipe away the foulness. She's come to get food, and although she's aware that the food had been ordered from a Chinese restaurant, and not prepared in the kitchen, her appetite disappears in an instant.

She's about to leave when a ring of laughter drifts in from the room by the kitchen. She follows the laughter, and settles upon a group huddled on a carpet, playing a game. Many of them she recalls running into in the hallways. They seem to her sufficiently pleasant, unbound by the alcohol, wild with the competitive spirit of games. From what she deduces, they are playing a game called Taboo, the rules of which are alien to her. A person stands in the middle of the circle, yells until a member of their group says the right word, or the boy in charge of flipping the hourglass flips the hourglass.

"It is a thing you use every day?" the girl in the middle says now.

"Toothbrush!" someone else yells.

"No," the girl says, furiously tapping a foot. "Like, when, say, you need a drink, you take that thing to the place where you can get the drink, and give it to someone in ex—no, in return for the drink."

"A dollar bill!" someone screams.

"Yes!"

Sommy recognizes the girl up next—Melinda, from the Loneliness class. Melinda yells a series of descriptions at her group, none of which leads them to the keyword.

"No, no, fuck," she says, feigning exasperation. "It's green and it grows."

"Ogres?" a tatted boy says, and she glares at him.

The hourglass-flipping boy flips the hourglass.

"Christ, guys," Melinda says. "A plant. Green? Grows? What else is the right answer but plant?"

Everyone laughs. Sommy takes a sip of wine and joins in the laughter. She notices Melinda staring at her then, her lips opened slightly, as though holding back a "Hey." Sommy likes Melinda. She's the only one in the Loneliness class who isn't a Literature major. She's getting an MFA in creative writing. In class, she's meditative and quiet, and when she does speak, her comments are percipient and sensitive. Sommy remembers now how passionately Melinda had contributed to a class discussion on loneliness and poverty after another classmate, whose name Sommy cannot now remember, had made a class contribution about his visiting Jamaica a few years ago, and his surprise at the abundance of happiness despite the pervasive poverty. In America, the boy said, everyone is obviously depressed—one can tell simply by looking at the high rate of drug use. Sommy had blinked back an eyeroll. She'd wanted to tell him about the codeine crisis in Northern Nigeria. Young boys strung out on cough syrup. But she'd decided to stop contributing to class by then, rankled still from the incident with the brunette. Melinda had cleared her throat, and in a voice shaky with perplexity, said that dismissing poverty-induced loneliness was a violent act, and that nothing makes a person lonelier than poverty. She'd then turned to the professor, said: "We've spent most of our class time drawing correlations between loneliness and the advent of social media, but very little discussing how, for instance, the lack of access to healthcare, homelessness, or hunger can cause a person to wither slowly. These are problems we have here in America, by the way."

Sommy, who'd always been surprised at the way her classmates pushed back at professors, drew in a long breath. She imagined herself speaking that way, in a rare moment of inanity, to a professor in UNIZIK, and laughter bubbled up in her throat. She'd fail the professor's course for sure, and the courses of the professors who happened to be friends with the disparaged professor. But this professor, a petite white woman with thin hair and too many freckles, had agreed with Melinda, and promised to dedicate a class to teaching about the intersection of loneliness and poverty. Stirred by this warm memory, emboldened by her New Year's resolution, she goes to sit beside Melinda. It is then she notices Bryan, the witness, hidden carefully between Melinda and the hourglass boy. He is seated on the floor, legs crossed in the lotus position.

"Sommy!" he exclaims.

Sommy smiles woodenly, breathes to unclench her stomach.

Melinda's gaze moves from Sommy to Bryan, her round face spreading in delight. "I never see you at these things," she says to Sommy. "And you've met *the* Bryan. How?" She's flushed from the alcohol. Green veins press out from the red skin of her forehead.

"We met a few months ago," Bryan says, studying Sommy's face intently.

"Yea," Sommy says. "We met in my second week in Iowa."

"Huh?" Melinda leans forward.

Sommy repeats herself.

"How wonderful," Melinda says.

Sommy smiles at her, and it's not the practiced, strained smile that she's learnt to dish out since coming to America. It's an easy smile, a grateful smile, for Melinda hasn't done that awkward thing that many of her classmates do—pretending to hear what she's said so they don't appear rude, appear to have a problem with her accent. She wipes away the smile when she turns to Bryan, replaces it with a stilted expression.

"Hey," she says sternly.

"Hey," he replies.

Sommy makes to leave, but Melinda says, "Oh no, join us, please."

She settles on the carpeted floor, beside Melinda. She laughs when everyone laughs, and is silent when everyone is silent, her stomach churning with rage—this Bryan boy, she thinks, she could slap him right now, just lean over to him and slap him until he faints—and it doesn't occur to her, until she's called upon, that she would have a turn.

"Come on, go on," Melinda says.

"I am good," Sommy says.

The group shrugs, shake their heads, clap their hands in encouragement. "Come on," they say. She hears Bryan's voice the loudest:

"Come on," he says, and she feels immediately transported to the court-yard, where they sat on that fall evening. How hard she'd fallen then, looking into his brown eyes, eyes she now thinks sleazy, manipula-tive. She cannot bear that he'll watch her stumble through this game and fall flat in defeat. But, she's determined to be aggressively social, so she stands, walks into the middle of the circle, feeling taller than usual with all of them sitting, staring up at her, with Bryan staring at her. She picks the card from the table, brings it to her face. It says *base-ball*—the words beneath: *bat, hit, catch, pitcher, stadium*. She's gotten the hang of the game. She knows she ought to make someone yell "base-ball." But is she to say the words beneath as clue? Or were they out of bounds? She grips the card tighter. The words turn blurry, a piebald blend of letters.

"A game," she says.

"Chess?" Melinda screams.

How to describe baseball? She's never watched the game. She's heard of it, read about it somewhere. But she's mostly unaware of it in the way a person can be about the things they have not even a slight interest in. Football, perhaps. Tennis, perhaps. But baseball? She looks up and catches Bryan staring at her. She looks away quickly. What was that slight frown on his face? Did he feel obligated by virtue of their shared blackness to win with her and to lose with her? Her vision focuses on the word *bat*. An image of a man swinging a bat comes to her, so she says, "A man."

"Woman?" a boy says.

The room is suddenly silent, and everything starts to move in slow motion.

"Time's up," the hourglass boy says.

Sommy walks back to her seat, bruised with shame, and she only notices that the group is clapping for her when she slumps back into her earlier position. She raises her head then, smiles shyly, thinking them all alike, with something in their faces she can't name, but understands acutely. Everything—the dangerous, crackling cold outside, the dark streets, the twinkling Christmas lights she walked past to get here—brings her to the realization that many of them, like her, have left home, too, and have found themselves in this new place, and have had to build, brick by brick, a new life. She thinks, too, of the desperation with which they throw these weekly parties. Perhaps, like her, they are running from the forlorn texture of the lives waiting for them in their one-bedroom apartments. Something once iced melts in her chest, and she feels an immense tenderness for this group. For Melinda. But not for Bryan.

They play the game through the night and it's around two A.M. when Sommy decides to leave. She's slightly drunk and cold, and maybe a little happy even, having socialized aggressively. She pulls out her phone and tries to book a ride on Uber. There are no cars in the area, so she tries Lyft. The Lyft driver is twenty minutes away. She says goodbye to Melinda, and then the group. She ignores Bryan, and walks to the sitting room door, where she stands waiting, watching people put on their coats, crouch on the floor to tie the laces of their boots, kiss each other good night. This choreography is a pleasing one. It's how she knows to spend the holiday, to be surrounded by people. She's been cooped up with Bayo all through, and she's begun to feel the seams of her sanity fray. After a minute, she checks for her ride, and it's twenty minutes away still, so she breathes out a "Fuck it," which gets a little attention from the crowd leaving, including Bryan, who walks up to her, asks if she needs a ride.

"I'm fine, thank you," she says, and because she doesn't want to appear obviously scorned, she adds that she's expecting a Lyft.

"Cancel it," he says softly.

He's an inch taller now, having put on his boots, and his bundle of clothing—purple puffer jacket and red scarf.

"I'm going to get charged."

"I'll Venmo you," he says, pulling his phone from his pocket.

She pauses for a bit, and then says, "My Venmo is Sommy Nwachukwu4."

He looks at her, surprise wrinkling his brows. He'd assumed she'd say not to worry.

"And the Lyft charge is fifteen dollars," she adds. She wants to say, "Look o'boy, I be Lagos babe, don't think you can try me and get away it," but her pidgin is terrible, and she really doesn't feel like a Lagos babe now. Her heart is sore.

He smiles, as if to tell her he's taking up the challenge. Her phone beeps. It's a Venmo alert for fifteen dollars and the message: Because I behaved irresponsibly.

The foyer is clear now. It's just the two of them standing at the corner by the rack. The room smells of beer.

She meets his eyes and holds them for a while. "Why should I trust you?"

"You don't have to trust me," he says, a hand pressed to his chest. "Give me a chance to explain."

She cancels the Lyft, and they walk out onto the snow-covered street and enter his black sedan.

"Here," he says, handing her his phone. "Punch in your address."

When they jolt out of the parking space and begin to ride down the dark street, he asks if she'd like to listen to music.

"I'm fine, thank you."

She looks out the window, at the trees salted with snow, and the quiet, dark houses. She tries to track what she feels, but she cannot lay a finger on a thing. It's tendrils of emotions.

"I'm glad I ran into you today," he says.

"It's not like you don't have my number."

He's silent, and then he says, "The day after we spoke, I left for Atlanta. My brother—he had an emergency. Took a while to sort that out, and when I got back to Iowa, I just couldn't call. I was ashamed I let so much time pass."

She shakes her foot and crumbs of snow fall onto the mat. She doesn't believe him.

"Is your brother doing okay now?"

"He's better. He's home now."

They are both silent for a while. She doesn't trust him. She'll manage her hope.

To sweep away the silence, she asks where home is.

"Glencoe, Illinois," he says.

They've stopped at an intersection, and while he's looking away, Sommy throws a full glance at him. Much of his body is covered in clothing, but his neck, thick and square, is exposed, and Sommy thinks it strong and assertive, like the trunk of a healthy tree. They drive into an alleyway, and then into the parking lot of Sommy's house.

When he's parked, she turns to him, says, "You hurt me." It's a surprise, this declaration of pain.

"I'm sorry."

She's silent.

"Coffee? Tomorrow?"

He doesn't break their gaze until she gives in, says, "Okay, coffee."

He heaves, breathes loudly. "Thank you. I'm not fucking it up this time around."

"To be sure," she says, "this is a date, right? You like me? I don't mean to be abrupt, but I don't understand the social cues here in America as clearly."

"I like you a lot," he says.

She laughs. *I like you a lot.* She last heard the sentence from Bayo, and before that in secondary school, where most relationships began with one person saying: "I like you, say your own." And the other person saying: "I like you, too."

"Coffee," she says, awash in relief, in gratitude.

As she climbs up to her apartment, she catches herself tracing the railings of the staircase. She stops, thinks it all embarrassing, but continues anyway. A good year has finally come. She only had to decide on hope and optimism and the world cracked delightfully open for her.

She meets Bryan at a café near the laundromat she frequents. It is there she finds out his age: twenty-eight; his star sign: Leo; the specific way he likes his coffee: black, no cream and no sugar. She does most of the talking on that first day at the café, and he listens to her intently, with a palm supporting his jaw, and those thick lashes of his frozen with commitment to her every word. She talks to him about school. She tells him that she finds being a student a bit of a drag. The most excited she's been in school is with the students at the reading-writing center, where she works for five hours a week. The essays the students bring in for consultation are usually great bores, but she enjoys talking to them. She likes that they are quick to come undone for her, tell her about their troubles at home, and with the people they are seeing, and with their strict teachers. She's always glad to be a listening ear, to say to them that it will be okay. About her classes, she says to Bryan that she feels no kinship with the canon her professors like to teach. She understands that it is a bit Philistine to confess this. Knowledge is knowledge. But is it, really? She tells him she thinks she might enjoy reading Woolf better if she were white.

"It's natural," he says. "We like to see ourselves in art."

"But it's myopic, right? For that to be the scope of my literary consumption?"

"I don't think that's the case with you. You aren't insisting on reading only literature written by people like you. You just want a diverse, balanced canon. Am I right?"

She nods, and sighs, and then says: "Maybe I'm being ridiculous. I can't come to someone's country and tell them to teach what I want."

He takes a sip of his coffee and says she isn't being ridiculous but doesn't say anything more.

"What kind of stuff do you write?" she asks.

He massages the side of his neck. "Life? I write about life." He squints and begins to drum a finger on the table.

There's the feeling that she's asked a stupid question and to distract from it, she leans over to bare her cleavage, but he doesn't seem to notice.

They drive to his place afterward. He wants them to chill, drink wine. Sommy's a bit nervous on the drive. She's not prepared for sex. She's not shaved. The brassiere she has on, though supportive, is old and fading. She makes a quick mental calculation: if it comes to it, she could go to the bathroom, strip first, and walk out naked. She's a little disturbed by the thought of that, too, the thought of the extra fifteen pounds she's gained over the last couple of months hanging bare for him to see, but she wants this to work.

Bryan's apartment is in the part of the city where locals live. The area is quiet, and the roads are lined with fenced duplexes. His sitting room is spacious, and sparsely furnished. There are only three pieces of furniture: a seventy-inch television, a dark-mahogany television stand, and a long brown couch. There's one piece of intentional décor, and it is a picture of an old man.

"Who's this?" she asks.

"Bernard London White. An old writer guy I like to read."

"Oh."

"Wine?" he asks.

He hands her the glass of wine and turns on the television. Soon he's sitting right next to her, and Fela is playing on YouTube.

"You like Fela?" she asks.

"Everyone likes Fela," he says.

He's bobbing his head awkwardly to the music and Sommy wonders if he really likes Fela, or if this is an attempt at impressing her, at creating mutual interest.

"I don't listen to Fela like that," she says.

"Really? What do you listen to?"

"I'm more of a slow music kind of girl. Whitney. Celine Dion. Boring, I know."

"Ahhh, I see," he says. "A romantic."

"A hopeless one," she says, rolling her eyes, smiling.

They spend the evening listening to Fela, and Whitney Houston, and Brenda Fassie. They drink wine. Once, they even stand and sway together to Whitney Houston's "I Will Always Love You." It all feels so surreal, all so perfect. By the time he drops her off at her apartment that evening, she's so swollen with want that she breaks a New Year's resolution and masturbates viciously to a dreamt-up visual of him fucking her, telling her she's his little bitch.

Over the next weeks, Sommy gathers evidence that she and Bryan are fated to be together. It is too early for this to be love, she gathers from her rigorous internet research, but she knows that it is more than a simple crush—this, what she's feeling, is fated, the destined meeting of two aligned souls.

Three times a week (Monday at five P.M., Wednesday at one P.M., Friday at seven P.M.) he comes to her apartment to pick her up, and they drive to his apartment. They mostly drink wine and listen to music, while she talks and talks. She's never talked so much in her life, never wanted, as much as she does with him, to have someone know her fully. He is intrigued by her stories about Nigeria. He likes her tales about Lagos, the people, the traffic, the hustle and bustle. It's the opposite of the quiet suburbs of Illinois, where he'd grown up. He wants to visit, he says, and she tells him about all the places she plans to take him when he does: Boma strip club in Lekki (he widens his eyes and laughs when she says this), Terra Kulture in Victoria Island to see plays, Illashe Beach for a boat cruise, Freedom Park to listen to live bands. He's surprised at the tales of corruption. "Unbelievable!" he'd exclaimed, when she told him about the clerk who'd claimed that a snake had come into the office and swallowed thirty-six million naira. She'd pulled out her phone and showed him a BBC News story on it, and he'd said, "What the actual fuck?" She tells him about corrupt politicians who hide billions of naira in walls in their mansions in Ikoyi and Victoria Island. Sometimes, he tries to solidarize, tells her of corrupt American politicians. "Corruption has levels," is always her reply, though she's glad that he leaves badmouthing Nigeria for her alone.

He tells her that all he has of his father is a picture, water-stained and creased. His father had left the country while his mother was pregnant with him. She doesn't talk much about it, his mother, but she insists that they were in love, that he remains still the love of her life.

"That must be awful."

He tells her of his stepfather and his two stepbrothers, and of growing up as the only black person in the room for most of his life up until college. He tells her of his decision to attend an HBCU for his under-graduate studies, the incredible pull, the deep yearning to be among black people during that time in his life. He tells her that it wasn't simply the feeling of wanting to disappear in the crowd, to be indistinct, though he suspects it was a part of it; it was largely a feeling he thought immanent, rising from the very depths of his soul, to belong some-where. He'd never belonged. And for a while in college, he felt it, this belonging, with his classmates and college friends. Over the years, it tapered, he says, and he's certain that it has something to do with his father, this rogue discomfort he feels constantly.

"I want to find him," he says, and his voice is strikingly sad.

Sommy tells him about Mezie, that for a while she thought him lost, and that although she might not exactly know how he, Bryan, feels—her mother and father have always been present, and she grew up surrounded by people who look like her and had never, until she arrived America, felt displaced, like the earth under her feet was eager to vomit her out—but over the past year she's experienced a piece of his fear, and she knows that it is all loneliness, as though one is sitting in a corner, watching everyone else live their lives. He tells her this is perhaps why he is a writer: he's lived most of his life sitting in a corner, watching everyone else live their lives.

He talks about the books he's read and the books he wants to write. He tells her of the novel he's been working on for seven years. "Sprawling," he calls it, a whopping seven hundred pages. He says fiction is the form where he breathes his deepest desires to life. When he desired romantic love, he wrote short stories with protagonists who chased and found love. When he desired friendship, he did the same. In his novel, his protagonist, Will, gets what he, Bryan, has sought all his life: a father. "It's a powerful thing," he says to her, this ability of his to create worlds and feel them as if they are real. He says he wants her to read the book.

When he talks about his book, he seems to swell, to be most alive, the very opposite of his demeanor when he talks about his father. Sommy is thrilled by him being thrilled, and she's grateful that he shares both parts of himself with her. But she is mostly rankled with shame, having nothing in her life she can talk about as passionately, not even her school-work, which she does grudgingly, and for a few weeks, she feigns an interest in the art of painting. She goes on YouTube and watches videos about painters and their process. She comes upon a famous abstract painter, Georgia O'Keeffe, and is struck, not by the depth of the work, since while considering abstract art, Sommy feels nothing but confu-sion, uncomfortable to comprehend an art piece in a manner far off from the creator's intention, but by what she believes to be its stark evasiveness. She knows people say that art interpretation ought to be personal, but she mostly thinks that bullshit talk. If she were in a space free of judgment, Sommy would say this: that she is uninterested in art left "open for interpretation"; that she only appreciates art that commu-nicates its intention in as clear a manner as possible; that she thinks "open to interpretation" is an artist's way of saying "I have nothing to say, nothing to give you, do all the imaginative work yourself." And perhaps, it is why she finds herself reading about abstract painters, and why she tells Bryan her painting is inspired by abstract painters like Georgia O'Keeffe, and why she goes to the art store on South Lucas and spends one third of her stipend on an easel, a set of six canvases, a brush set, acrylic paints, an apron, a palette knife, a roll of masking tape, and pencils. In the seeming confusion of these paintings, she can hide her own confusion.

Sommy sets her painting studio in the kitchen, on the dining table by the window. She finds the process painful and messy. She can't seem to stop the paint from getting on the table, on the floor, on the wall. Her triceps hurt from the brushing and her neck from having to sit upright all afternoon. The tricks she learns on YouTube seem easy at first, while she's simply seated watching them, but when she tries them herself, everything comes apart. She stops watching YouTube videos. Surely, she has something she wants to say. Surely, she can close her eyes and create something from the soul. She paints lines and circles and slant geometric shapes. She loves purple, so it is the color she reaches for the most. Canvas after canvas ends up in the trash behind the house. Sometimes, mid-painting, her brush piercing the canvas, she wonders if she's gone mad, if there's more to this than wanting to prove to Bryan that she, too, can be dedicated to something. There's the small thought that she's responding to Bryan's refusal to touch her. They've spent weeks together and nothing sexual has happened. Sometimes he leans in for a short kiss. Sometimes he holds her in a too-long hug. But that's been the limit of their physicality, and it leaves her glitching, wanting.

She's also found throwing herself into the strenuous practice of painting to be a good escape from Bayo's scratchy energy. He's been wanting to spend more time with her. He feels her distance, her new detachment. She knows she should tell him about Bryan, sever things. But she doesn't yet know how to define her relationship with Bryan. He has yet to say what they are. If she comes clean to Bayo, and Bryan continues to drag her along in their shapeless intimacy, she would have lost Bayo for nothing.

Often, she thinks of asking Bryan outright: "What are we?" And always the thought causes her a kind of unease, the same unease she feels when she comes across Instagram videos of women proposing to men. This feeling lives in a small, dank place inside of her, ego-fueled, almost maleficent.

Bryan sometimes invites her to hang out with his writer buddies, Melinda, Joel, Clark. They gather at his place on Wednesdays, after writing workshops, to drink wine, smoke cigarettes, and talk about the pieces workshopped earlier. She learns through this group that Bryan's book is out on the market. He's the only one in the group with an agent, and according to Clark, one of the only two people in their cohort of twenty-eight who might have a book sold before graduation.

Once Melinda asks how he feels about this.

"Validated," Bryan says, blowing a puff of smoke.

Joel says, "But Bryan doesn't care, does he?" He turns to Clark, his eyes slant with slyness. "When you've got rich grandparents a book deal is, for you, simple validation."

"Oh please," Clark says. "Get off Bryan's dick, okay."

The group laughs. It's a constant source of banter amongst them, Bryan's and sometimes Melinda's silence around their family money. Clark and Joel are the underdogs; Clark more so. But it is Joel always with the jabs. Sommy knows it makes Bryan uncomfortable, but it is a feeling he can't express, scared as he is to be regarded as the rich kid who is embarrassed by his wealth. Sommy is not empathetic to his plight, though she doesn't say so. She thinks it silly that he is insistent on living modestly, in his mutedly furnished fifteen-hundred-dollar-a-month apartment. When he told her he's worried people will dismiss him when they learn he hasn't suffered, at least in the material sense, she'd said, "That doesn't make any sense." He insisted that it does, that people are judgmental, especially toward the wealthy. She'd been surprised but was glad to realize that even the smartest people could lose common sense to anxiety. But then she'd wondered about his inability to see the truth, which is that people will mostly only listen to people who have real or perceived social capital. It feels unreasonable that he is awake to everything else, racism, ableism, all the phobias, but not to this.

It's on one of these Wednesdays, after the group has left, that she feels a drowning urge to ask Bryan to define their relationship. They are seated, watching *The Odyssey*, which Bryan insists is such a phenomenal cultural artifact it is downright crazy she's never seen it.

They are watching the scene with Penelope in labor, and Bryan is asking to see some of her paintings.

"I feel too self-conscious," she says.

He leans in, kisses her. "You don't have to feel that way with me."

There's a piece of lint hanging on his thick brow, and she picks it, blows it into the air. She's aware that this is the moment, the TV buzzing in the background, Bryan all tender and flushed from drinking wine, open to her. She could say to him that she's been flailing for a while now, looking for somewhere solid and comfortable to land, and she's found that with him. She could say she wants to be with him, for real, and she wants to know if he feels the same. But such rawness with a man is foreign to her, and when she opens her mouth, nothing comes out, so she leans into him and buries her face in his neck, kissing, biting gently. Her hands roam on his chest, and then skid downward, find the buckle of his belt. She senses it immediately, his body stiffening, and then an evident flinch. Something inside her braces, and she pulls away.

"I am sorry," she says.

On the TV is Odysseus at sea now.

"Hey," he says, touching the protruding bone of her wrist lightly, a small, helpless gesture, like a child with no words to explain his sadness.

She moves away from the touch, from him. She seethes. He smiles. They sit quietly, watching Odysseus hanging atop a jackstaff. The movie ends and they still don't say a thing to each other. Sommy is sore, so sore she can't move. She feels like filth. She wants to submerge herself in bleach. Filth.

"I'm going to leave now," she says, but she's still sitting, as though the wound is physical, under her feet.

His eyes start to search for his car keys.

"I'll walk," she says.

"It's a thirty-minute walk, Sommy. Come on."

"Please," she says, and she stands, picks up her wallet, and is out the door.

A few minutes into her walk, she regrets this decision. It is a particularly windy day, and she feels the cold enter the cracks in her coat. She walks gently, careful not to slip on the ice. In moments like these, she is wont to catastrophize, to create a symphony of all the moments in her life she's been rejected, and then sing it to herself. And she does exactly this as she trudges on to her apartment, starting from Bryan and ending at the time in primary five when a boy named Justin had called her hard to look at. At home, she pulls out her phone from her coat's pocket. There's a text from Bryan: Hey! Can we talk about this? Call when you are home? She deletes the text, blocks his number. She arranges her best paintings, three canvases on which she'd painted fading brown ghosts, wanting so thoroughly to capture Bryan's unbelonging, to understand him in ways beyond words, to feel him, feel him deeply. She packs the canvases, hauls them down the stairs, and hurls them into the large brown trash bin. That night, she feels nothing, nothing of that acute soreness. It is as though the stone he'd thrown at her hit a part of her so thoroughly beaten it has lost its ability to feel. She crawls into Bayo's bed and falls asleep in his arms.

Amara, Nia, and Kayla all have different theories for what happened. Amara is certain that Bryan is gay. "Have you seen you?" she says to Sommy. "You are too fine. It's beyond me how anyone won't want to fuck you." Amara says this in her fake encouraging voice, the one she uses when making Instagram videos, where she stands in front of the mirror and affirms herself. "Bad bitch," she says. "Hottie, queen!"

Nia thinks it is all a game. She's certain Bryan wants to break her confidence, make her feel unworthy, and then have her work hard to earn her worthiness. "Men are scum," she says over the phone, breathless.

Kayla says that Sommy's being unreasonable. She can't believe that Sommy's let one moment, one vague moment, define two entire months of a relationship.

"You want me to have him confirm that he finds me disgusting? Two months and he's not attempted to touch me. Won't call me his girlfriend. What else can it be?"

"Girl," Kayla says. "You are wilding right now. Blowing shit out of proportion."

They are at a nail shop when Kayla says this. Sommy clicks her tongue so loudly that the nail technician drops the nail file on the table, throws her head backward, and laughs for a good minute. Kayla and Sommy watch, startled, speechless.

"Sorry," the nail technician says, after she's taken another minute to gather herself. "I no mean to laugh. It's just that you children let small things bother you, you know. Why not talk about things? Why assume, assume? Fight, fight? This your generation don't talk to each other."

Kayla smacks her lips and says to the nail technician that she's absolutely right. "Communication is a lost art."

After class one afternoon, three weeks after the incident, Sommy walks out of the department building to find Bryan waiting by the magnolia tree. He is pacing, hands in pockets, shoulders high up. He has on a variant of his many brown sweaters, this one chestnut-colored and round-necked. She sees him first and is certain that he's come for Melinda. She continues on her way, distraught. A few steps in, and he is running toward her, saying, "Hey."

"Hey," she says.

He searches her face. "Do you have a few minutes?"

"I don't want to be friends with you," she says.

"I know. Just, please, hear me out."

His face is swollen with purpose, and she peers at him, looking for cracks in the impenetrable way he holds himself up. Has her absence affected him the way his has affected her—chased sleep away, snuffed out his appetite, caused his hair to begin to fall out in clumps?

He wants them to talk in private, at his house, so they drive to his in silence. For the first time in weeks, she breathes steadily. She thinks now that she'll give up anything to be near him. She'll give up sex. She'll give up the safety of a defined relationship. She'll give up her friendship with Bayo. Anything, if she can be close to him this way.

At his apartment, he takes her into his bedroom. It's exactly as she'd expected—sparse, a chair, a desk, and a bed with a high, solid-wood frame.

Before he pulls her to him, he turns off the lights, draws closed the curtain blinds. The room goes pitch-black. He kisses her. He undresses her with nervous desperation. He fondles her breasts. He says, "I want you." She cannot say if he's trying to convince himself, or if he's trying to convince her. What she does know is that she wants him, she wants him dearly.

Soon, they are in bed. He's positioned her so that her face is pressed into the mattress, and he is behind her, on top, thrusting, panting. She's not bursting with pleasure. There's no tingling, no exhilaration. There's only a contentedness, and the fact that she's breathing steadily. They are no longer so far apart.

After he comes, he cradles her. The room is still pitch-black. All she sees is darkness. But she feels everything, her naked body cooped up in his, the smooth fabric of his inner shirt on her skin, the soft thumping of his heart, the soft thumping of hers.

"I'm sorry it took this long," he says, bringing a warm palm to her face. "I'm just sometimes nervous about sex. About underperforming."

She pulls his hand from her face and brings it to her chest. "You are perfect to me. Maybe if you are bad in bed, I won't feel all so undeserving of you."

She laughs and he laughs.

There's a bit of silence, and then he says, "Did you like it? The sex?"

"Yes. Very much." She shifts closer to him, certain that if she could melt into him, she would do it in an instant. She should tell him about Bayo now, promise to end things, but it feels too perfect a moment to ruin.

She knows that it's cowardice, her refusal to tell Bayo about Bryan. She cannot bear to witness his heartbreak. She cannot bear to bring into his consciousness the reality of what he's been to her, a bridge to her destination, and not her final stop. She makes up excuses, convinces herself that telling Bayo about Bryan so close to the end of the semester, with deadlines pressing in, is a cruel thing to do. She tells herself that she's hesitating because she worries about their friendship, and how they would continue to room together after he finds out. She tells herself that she cannot afford an apartment of her own, with the ridiculous security deposits and utility bills. These excuses cushion her, until she's in Bryan's arms, feeling so severely in love with him, and the haunting thought that he might be entertaining her the way she'd, all these months, entertained Bayo, sends her reeling toward the truth: that she'd used Bayo, deceived him, and she'll have to accept that she's capable of this sort of manipulation.

Sommy and Bryan start to go out like a couple, to spend less time at his place. They dine at the places he likes to eat, at an Italian restaurant that serves what he likes to call a "mean-ass Caesar salad," and the Indian restaurant at the sharp corner where Lexington and Burlington Avenues meet, at a yogurt shop on North Johnson, where Sommy always orders a bowl of vanilla-and-banana-flavored yogurt topped with granola and gummy bears, at the coffee shop of their first date.

He immerses her in culture. He takes her to an orchestra performance to watch a friend of his play the cello to a staging of Shakespeare's *As You Like it* and to a photographic exhibition titled *The Lives of Saints*. He takes her to an art showing, where she stands speechless as he discusses contemporary black artists reconfiguring the world's vision of what art should look like.

"This painting for instance," he says, "would have been deemed unrefined a few years ago, with its blend of strong colors, and its Africanist inspiration—you see what Ade is doing here with the yellow and these gentle black strokes?"

She doesn't see what Ade is doing. She thinks the painting ghastly, with its too vibrant colors, its anarchic undertone. But she nods nonetheless.

"Subverting classical aesthetics," Bryan continues. "It's what blackness does. Subversion."

She feels inadequate when he talks about cultural pieces she's unable to appreciate. It's the same way she feels about her response to his novel, which a few days ago he'd printed out and given to her. She'd begun reading it immediately but had been unable to go past page thirty. She did not get it. She found no momentum, nothing to pull her forward. Fifty pages in and the novel's protagonist is still taking a walk alone in nature, contemplating the beauty of trees and rocks and the great blue sky. There's not a moment's break from the character's awe. The tiniest mark of a tree branch is zoomed into and interrogated as if a miracle. She knows she must plunge on, that there's probably a reward at the end, when Will reconciles with his father. How can she say to him that she's unable to read his masterpiece?

Once, when he asks how she's doing with the novel, she says, "I'll give you my opinion when I'm done. Be patient." She says this with a fake, teasing smile, trying hard to mask her real feelings. He says he can tell she hates it, and it makes him feel safe that she wouldn't feign enthusiasm for something she dislikes. He loves that about her, her glass-like quality, easy to see through. She smiles uneasily at this compliment, tries to keep her composure. And it comes to mind that it might be a good time to tell him about Bayo, but she's still unable to imagine herself having that conversation to a conclusive end with Bayo, and she knows that Bryan will make her do it if she tells him.

The other day, while she sat on the dining chair, smacking at a blob of paint, Bayo had come up behind her.

"You are being very serious with the semester," he'd said with evident sarcasm.

Whenever he's asked her to hang out, she's come up with a school-related excuse.

"This semester is not smiling," she said, laughed gratingly. "These professors want to kill someone with work."

He frowned, sucked in his lips. "But you somehow have time to be painting these ugly things."

"Oga," she said sharply, "abeg, free me."

He stood, quiet, and she began beating the canvas, crazy, blind strokes, and there was this moment when she did not have a care in the world, and the words formed solidly in her mind—"I'm seriously seeing someone else, Bayo"—but when she raised her head, met the crumpled look of confusion on his face, her heart fell.

"I'm sorry," she said. "School is really stressing me."

"No wahala," he said, after which he walked to the kitchen, swung open the refrigerator door, and took out an orange.

She won't say anything to him about Bryan, she decides. She need not. She'll find him a new roommate when their lease expires in two months, and then move out, and he'll chalk up the loss of their relationship to a subtle and complicated drifting apart, and she'll be free of the burden of wounding him.

It's not a week after Sommy makes this decision that she runs into Bayo at the CVS downtown while with Bryan. They'd just finished celebrating their one-month dating anniversary at the sushi place by the mall, and had come to CVS to pick up a pack of condoms. Sommy then dragged Bryan to the skincare aisle, and was looking through the Neutrogena line, mocking his skincare routine—bodywash and water. No face wash. And most alarming to Sommy, no moisturizer. "Your white side is winning," she tells him, and he has his arm around her neck, pretend squeezing, laughing, and it is in this position Bayo finds them.

Bayo pauses, startled, and Sommy notices, in the quick flash of its occurrence, that he's almost let go of the pack of toilet paper rolls.

"My roommate," Sommy mutters to Bryan after a long minute.

Bryan peels away from her. "Hey, man." He reaches for a handshake.

Bayo takes the handshake, and while still clasping, turns to look at her. She cannot read his expression. Disbelief? Perplexity? He knows nothing concrete, she thinks. He could think Bryan simply a friend. She forces a smile, which Bayo doesn't return. Bryan comes back to her, throws his arm over her shoulders again.

When Bayo leaves, Bryan says, studying her face, "That was awkward."

"Is that a question?"

He raises his eyebrows. "Nope. I'm just saying."

She says nothing, continues browsing the aisle. The rest of their day is tinted with the murky air of this meeting, and they say very little to each other.

Later that night Bayo knocks on her door. She's leaned over on her desk, reading a book titled *The History of Twentieth-Century African Literatures*.

"We should thank the mosquitoes," she says to Bayo when he enters the room. Her voice is gay, an attempt to keep up the appearance of guiltlessness. "Our literature would be so different if white people had settled in Nigeria."

She notices then that he's red-eyed, drunk. She stands, straightens her wrinkled shorts.

"Are you okay?"

He sits on the bed. He funnels his palms between his legs, and stares at the ceiling, contemplative. Her father does this when he's too disappointed to speak.

"Come sit here," he says, tapping the mattress.

She does as he says. She's never seen him this drunk.

"Do you need water or something? You look dehydrated."

"I just want you to hold me," he says.

"Of course."

She brings his head to her shoulder. He rests it there for a while, and then heaves up, kisses her.

"Bayo—"

"Just this once," he says.

She opens her mouth, hesitant. He cups her breasts. His touch is rough, desperate. She wants to stop him, stop herself, but she owes him.

They fuck frantically. On the bed. On the carpet. He fucks her like he wants to take what's been denied him. Once, her phone lights up, and he stretches over her head, his armpit hovering near her nose, punches something on the phone screen. She cranes her head, watches mindlessly as he flips it over. He becomes even more frantic then, as if angered by the distraction. Harder thrusts. Louder pants. He wraps his fingers around her neck, a little more pressure than usual. Her breathing stills, as does the anxiety roving inside her. In the moment, she feels distended, as if full of air and light. Now she doesn't want him to stop, and she tells him, croaking.

When they are done, he doesn't lie beside her like he used to. He grabs his clothes, cradles them to his chest, and walks away, naked as a newborn.

She falls asleep right after, fatigued, feeling moist all over.

Sommy wakes up to twelve missed calls and three messages from Bryan. First message: Please answer your phone. Second: Wow. Third: Why would you make me listen to that? She's still hazy from sleep, and it's a few seconds before she realizes what's happening, what Bayo has done. She sits upright on the edge of her bed and stares out the window, which she'd forgotten to shut, at the drowsy morning sky and the dull-brown building opposite. She saw the road she should have taken, laid sprawled in front of her: spill everything to Bayo and Bryan, watch both relationships stagger and then maybe stand straight again. Round and round she went with her excuses about not wanting to hurt Bayo, or to infuse the air in their home with malice. Here's real life now, cornering her like a notorious loan shark who's ambushed their debtor. She grabs handfuls of her bedsheet, stills her breath, briefly observes the bipolarity of her insides, first mania and then a subsidence of fatigue, a depressing solemnity. Like clockwork, it goes, and she just sits, feeling like she's spinning, but unmoving still. She cannot leave her room, run into Bayo, and she cannot call Bryan and right what has happened. There's nothing to say. She's finished. She pulls out her phone and does a quick Google search for apartments to rent. She'll rent something, anything. She'll share an apartment with fourteen people if it comes to it. She soon finds herself on

Delta.com, searching for flights from Chicago to Lagos. She shouldn't have come to America at all. She shouldn't be in grad school at all. This wave she's riding is not one she created or craved. She'd absorbed the panic of everyone around her, her brother, her friends, her former co-workers. Everyone so bewilderedly frustrated by the country's economy. She saw it then, too, the dark slab above them all. Try as hard as one might, it was there, this unconquerable enigma of a decayed system. But she's never wanted to conquer anything. She's not a conqueror. Mezie is.

When she first learnt of his deportation, a few weeks after she'd gotten her admission letter to James Crowley, she'd told Amara that she wanted to defer her admission, reject it, even. It just seemed like the right thing to do, she'd said, to stay with Mezie, to refuse to chase a dream that was his. Amara, with that dramatic alarm of hers, had dropped the bread she was munching on, said, "Just think to yourself if this thing you just said makes one bit of sense. There's nothing here for you. Nothing here for anyone except you are Dangote's son." It was all she heard, in quiet and loud ways: that if America calls, one answers. There was no way around it. And it made sense—it made sense for the dreamers, the hustlers. Her? It didn't exactly make sense to her. She's never been interested in that quiet, determined unbraiding. Like Bayo. Like Mezie. That rigid focus of theirs. Their hunger. She's, however, followed the path, and she's become distended, tousling about like a traveler with no destination.

She massages her phone. The pain has settled in her chest and in a spot behind her ears, and there's this sensation in her body like she'll rip up her vocal cords if she tries to swallow spit. She swipes on her phone, reads through Bryan's text messages again. Each word is like a spike breaking her skin. And Bayo? How could he? She's blind with tears. She scrolls now to Mezie's chats. It's been six months since she last tried to reach out to him through Elin. She's filled the silence between them with Bayo, and then with Bryan, and now it jangles, loud, ferocious.

Hey, she types. How are you?

She watches the gray delivered marks turn blue. She waits for a reply, knowing it won't come. And when it doesn't come, she scoots deeper into the bed, folds up in a fetal position, and dead-stares the wall.

It's Kayla who comes to her first. They'd planned to meet that evening, and when Sommy doesn't show up, doesn't call or pick up, Kayla, panicked, shows up at her doorstep. Sommy lets her in. The house is quiet. Bayo loudly left hours ago, banging the doors, stomping the floors as if he imagined them to be her face. In Sommy's room now, Kayla pulls her work chair, sits, says, "Are you okay?"

Sommy reports everything with as much mechanical accuracy as she can. She wants Kayla to tell her what to do.

"That fucking Bayo dude," Kayla says. "That's an actual evil man right there."

"I hurt him," Sommy says.

"Oh please. Isn't what he did considered a kind of revenge porn?"

"I don't think so," Sommy says, turning slightly away. "It wasn't premeditated. It was Bryan who called, and I guess Bayo decided in the heat of the moment, out of sheer anger, to humiliate me like I humiliated him."

"I don't know why you are defending him."

"I'm not. I'm just telling you everything."

Sommy turns to Kayla, whose mouth is parted in withheld shock.

"What are you going to do about Bryan?" Kayla says.

Sommy's quiet. She'd wanted to lie to Bryan. That had been her first impulse when she thought of calling him. She wanted to tell him that Bayo had set her up, that what he heard was recorded a while ago when they had a brief fling during the winter break. A perfect lie. Erase the pain. Erase the shame. Make them happy again. She asks Kayla if this is a good idea.

"If I'm never going to do it again," Sommy says, "isn't it better to lie, to make it easier for the both of us? I really like him, K."

Kayla leans back into the chair, and her face forms what looks to Sommy like an expression of disappointment. "I know I fuck around a lot," she says. "But I'm serious right now. This is not the kind of shit you lie about when you like someone. You have to come clean, face the consequences, and then pray to God you guys survive it. You can't lie about this stuff. The truth will rear its head when you least expect it."

Sommy's silent for a while, and then says, "I'm ashamed of myself."

Kayla presses her lips together and says there's nothing wrong with feeling ashamed. It is signal that a person has higher expectations of themselves.

Sommy wants to cry, but she doesn't. She feels undeserving of even that.

Bayo becomes a ghost in the days after the incident, hardly in the apartment, and when around, quiet, locked in his room. Sommy wants to be angry at him. She wants to take whatever it was Kayla said about his actions being excessive and run with it, but she cannot sustain reasonable anger at him. They are even now. It is thoughts of Bryan that keep her up. He's not called, and she's not called, either. She imagines him pacing the breadth of his apartment, wracked with confusion. Or perhaps he's left Iowa. It's what she'd do if she were in his shoes and could afford to travel. She'd pack her bags and leave, scrub herself clean of the chaos.

She spends a few days subsumed in her sadness, believing this to be the end of their relationship, and the end of the self she'd formed with him and with Bayo, hopeful Sommy, wanting-to-do-better Sommy. She wraps herself in stoicism. If no one wants her, she says to herself, then she'll want no one. She'll be her friend and her lover, her mother and her father. When was the last time her mother called her, even? When was the last time her father sent her a WhatsApp message? And Amara, always with a complaint about her boss or her sister whenever she calls. Sommy declares herself to be done trying to have a relationship with the people in her life.

But a week later, wearied by the gloom, and slightly steady again in herself, she phones Bryan.

"Hello," he says quietly.

"It's me, Sommy," she says.

"I know."

A brief silence follows, and she feels it all pressing at the muscles of her throat, the web of lies that will keep her safe, keep the peace, but she says instead, "I'm sorry, Bryan."

He's silent, so she adds, "Can I see you? Just a twenty-minute meeting so I can explain everything. There's no defense, but I'd like for you to at least know how it came to this."

"I'm not sure what use that is," he says.

His voice is gentle, not raging as she'd expected, and she wishes it were, then she'd know that he's not resigned, done with her.

"Please," she says. "You don't have to change your mind. I just want you to have the full picture. To judge me according to my real sins."

She hears a voice in the background and a sinking feeling passes through her. Perhaps it's the group, Joel, Clark, Melinda. She imagines that he's told them about what she's done. Dear Lord, what they must think of her now.

"Please, Bryan," she whispers.

They meet at their usual café. Bryan arrives first, and he's seated at the table near the hallway leading to the restroom. Their usual spot is empty, and Sommy takes this as a bad sign. He's determined to distinguish this meeting, to enforce their separation.

"Sorry I'm late," Sommy says, though she's not late—Bryan is early.

He nods, folds his hands, and leans back. She sits with her purse on her lap and tries to hold his sad, unwavering gaze.

She opens her purse, pulls out a wrinkled sheet of paper. Before she spreads it, she takes a quick look around. There's a girl in a spandex top seated by the entrance, and the unsmiling barista behind the counter, and then Bryan and her. She's not certain she can keep from crying while reading the note, so she's grateful for the small audience.

"I want to make this right," she says. "So I wrote everything down here, and I revised myself to make sure I'm saying the whole truth."

The note is a page long. It had been four pages long, and she'd written that everything had come at her with the force of a torrent. She felt terrified that her choices could result in losing him, hurting Bayo, revealing herself as cruel, so she thoughtlessly made the easiest choices. When she reread the note, she knew that Bryan would call it dishonest, say that the choice to be unthinking is always a well-thought-out one. She began again. This time she wrote that she was a coward. Deep down, she didn't believe Bryan's love. *Look at you and look at me*, she wrote. *You are perfect and I am unremarkable.* Bayo was the one she believed would always be there. And while it's true that she did not want to hurt Bayo with the truth, the other truth she refused to acknowledge was that she hoped Bayo could be a place to return to if it all failed with Bryan.

When she's done reading the note, Bryan rubs his palms together, forms a fist atop which he rests his jaw, and says, "Okay."

"Okay?"

"You wanted me to hear you out and I did. So, okay."

She opens her mouth and closes it, and then says, "Bryan, please, I'm sorry."

He looks exasperatedly about. "I appreciate the note. The desire to be honest. But we are done, Sommy. Done-done."

She'd not expected her earnestness to bring about a swift change of mind, but "done-done"? Sickening.

"You don't think I'm worth it, right?" she says. "You don't think I'm worth fighting for?"

"That's the point. I don't want to have to fight for love."

She stares at him, feeling violently mad. "Oh please, Bryan. Enough with the self-righteous attitude, okay? It's not like you were forthcoming with the whole being exclusive thing. I literally had to beg you to ask me out properly. Yes, I should have broken it off with Bayo. But how about this?" She points a mean finger at him. "You should have made me feel more secure. How about fucking that."

She heaves into her chair, lost in the grid of her anger and self-pity, exhausted. Bryan's quiet, fiddling with a button on his sleeve. There's the look on his face like a man quarreling with himself.

After about a minute passes, he nods as if decided on the private conversation with himself, stands, and walks out. Sommy stands, but she doesn't leave. She buys a caramel latte and walks to the spot by the window they usually sit at. There, she sits looking at the cloud-stained sky shaded by a line of scant trees, and then drops her gaze to the bush of lilies below, and then slightly to the left, to the worn wooden stairs in the backyard of an old house, and up to the sky again, buttered by the trees, the image of which brings to mind the fragile, clear texture of lace, the kind she's sure her mother would sew into a blouse and wear with thick gold jewelry. Blue and green are her mother's favorite colors. And maybe purple, too. How come she's forgotten what it feels like to be near her mother? Why's she thinking about her mother? Why's she not dashing after Bryan?

The semester ends. The streets thin out. The green of the trees deepens. Profuse sunlight coats the city in the afternoons, and the air smells of baked sand. Kayla and Nia go home. Bayo, still with the silent treatment, packs a bag and leaves for an unknown place.

Sommy's alone.

She busies herself with reading, cooking, cleaning, the occasional pathetic attempt at painting. She wants to text Bryan again. Beg him again. Apologize for her outburst. But she also wants to do what a good person would do. Though she's unsure what that is. She distrusts herself now. She goes on YouTube to watch videos of women who have it figured out—Michelle Obama, Oprah Winfrey, Chimamanda Adichie—and they give some variation of the "Know yourself" advice. It drives her insane. From where is she to excavate a definition of herself? She who is constantly unsure of what to eat for dinner, what to wear, what books to read, what books to like. She who came to grad school because everyone, panicked about the country's economy, was going to grad school. She, always in need of something to be moored to. Wasn't that what Bayo was for her, and Bryan? And did it not all begin with Mezie? Had she not heard all her life that she could not spark wonder in the way that he did? That he was the light, and she the darkness surrounding, consumed by him, made irrelevant by him? And now she ought to define herself, know herself, be herself? Now she ought to be the light and she's never even learnt to flicker?

One evening she tweets about this feeling of severance.

Turning twenty-five in a few days, she tweets, and someone asked what I'd like for my birthday, and I looked at him and said, I'd like to be a stone, or one of the four legs of a chair, or one of those little spoons people forget inside a bowl of sugar. Lol.

No one had asked what she wanted for her birthday. She needed a story to lighten the tweet's desolate tone. Still self-conscious, she follows the tweet with a series of others about having backaches, being over-whelmed with paying bills—attempts at mimicking the tone of tweets of similar topic. Moral of the story, she tweets, turning twenty-five is a scam. If you are yet to turn twenty-five, don't do it. Lol.

The next day she sees that Mezie has liked her tweets. She's known vaguely that he has a Twitter account, but she'd thought it inactive. He never posts. Now she clicks on his profile. It's mostly retweets of foot-ball news. But there's one, a retweet from a person named @FierceViv: Nobody owes you a friggin thing. Not your friends or family. Know this and know peace. Learn to deal with your problems! It goes through her, clean and swift, leaves a majestic injury. It's here it hurts the most, in this knowledge that he's certain of their separateness. He's come into himself, sees his life as independent from hers, and she's still, like she always has been, hinged to him.

A few weeks into the summer break, a month after the meeting with Bryan, Sommy decides to reach out to Melinda. She types and retypes the message until she's satisfied. Hi, Mel. Sommy here. Writing because I'm worried about Bryan (re: the current circumstances of our breakup) and I just want to know that he's doing okay.

Melinda replies shortly after. No, he's not doing well.

Sommy imagines Melinda's tone to be acerbic, and she regrets sending the text. She's about to delete the messages, pretend it never happened, when Melinda texts again.

Call in an hour? Driving . . .

The call is brief. Melinda says she's just arrived in Des Moines to visit a friend who's newly birthed a baby girl, but would it be okay if she lets Sommy know when she's back in town so they can sit, talk?

Sommy's effusive with her response. Yes, please. That would be really, really great. Thanks. God bless.

Two days pass and when there's no text from Melinda, Sommy sends one, asks if she's back in Iowa City. Melinda replies, says she'll be back the next day, and asks if Sommy can visit on the Saturday of that week, say, noon?

When Sommy arrives at Melinda's, she's welcomed with a glass of red wine.

"It's terribly hot outside, isn't it?" Melinda says.

Sommy nods foolishly, slices through the thin hallway, feeling stripped, as if a slut shoved into the market square to be heckled. She cannot imagine what Melinda must think of her, Melinda with her certain sense of right and wrong. She wishes now, as she takes a seat on the couch, from where she can see Iowa City's glittery cutout, that her failure had some edge, a compelling complexity, was not something so banal, so cowardly as the fear of being alone.

Melinda crouches in front of Sommy, grabs a bowl of grapes from the table, balances it on her folded thighs, and begins to crunch. She asks if Sommy has been in Iowa all the while. She'd expected that she'd go back to Lagos for at least a part of the summer break. Sommy lies that she'd planned on it, but things came up.

Melinda says she might visit Des Moines again to spend more time with her friend, the new mother. She says the trip has got her questioning her choice to remain childfree. She's amazed at her friend's transformation, her new anxiety and selflessness. "Won't it be wonderful?" Melinda says. "To have a part of you just walking around in the real world. It will sure cure me of my self-obsessiveness."

Melinda does seem unbalanced and heady, trapped in the afterglow that follows an awe-inducing experience. Sommy—Sommy's problems, are inconveniencing afterthoughts for her, and Sommy's glad to be, even if slightly, experiencing something outside of her that is positively forceful. This feeling morphs into a dull irritation as Melinda continues on and on about holding the baby, feeling her tiny legs and hands, the vulnerability in her red eyelids. Sommy sits politely, quietly. She has no choice but to wait for Melinda to arrive at the point of their meeting. Melinda eventually does as the clock strikes one.

"I've known Bryan through three breakups, and this is something else," Melinda says, her tone still heavy with awe. It's as though she's finding a connection between her experience of this new birth and Bryan's misery. "He's lost. I can't quite explain it. He's not functioning, refuses to hang out, to reply to emails. Clark had a reading at Fossil, and he didn't show up for it. It's unthinkable. Bryan loves Clark. He's been wanting Clark to share his work. It's all really concerning."

Sommy says, "I'm sorry to hear this."

Melinda leans in on her bent legs, pinches her gold pendant, two glittering interlocked circles. There's a queer look on her face—suspicion, disappointment? And it brings to the fore of Sommy's mind the shame that had receded. She'd hoped for too much. She'd hoped that Melinda possessed magic answers. But what Melinda is offering now, this confusing look, as if she sees no better than Sommy sees, is devastating.

A long silence passes, and then Melinda says, "We are meeting here on Wednesday, me, Clark, Joel, and Bryan. Do with that what you will."

Melinda is kneeling now, sunlight blasting her red face, looking up to Sommy.

"It really was a mistake," Sommy says. "I care about Bryan. I promise."

"I know that you do. I know that he's not over you. Doesn't want to be over you. It's why I'm doing this."

When Sommy shows up to the ambush three days later, Bryan is standing by Melinda's window in brown corduroy pants and a black polo, gripping a plastic coffee cup. Bryan doesn't notice when Sommy walks in, doesn't notice when she drops her tote bag on the floor, only turns when he hears her say, "I'm really sorry."

His gaze first lands on Melinda, and then her, Sommy, and back at Melinda again, who whispers, while backing away, "Don't hate me."

They are alone in a second, and Sommy's shivering. She's embarrassed that she's shivering, that she feels fragile. She can hear Melinda whisper forcefully to Joel or Clark from behind the door.

Bryan walks toward and past her, takes a seat on the couch.

"I want you to give me another chance," she says before he's able to speak.

He stares at the lavender candle burning on the center table, elbows atop knees, fingers entwined.

"What's the point if I can't trust you?"

"The point is trying," she says. "The point is not giving up so early."

The moment is painful, and everything seems to be passing through some sort of burnisher, appearing on the other side as a thing too bright to be looked at, and therefore, to be understood.

After a short silence, he asks if she's in love with Bayo.

"I love Bayo," she says. "But I'm in love with you."

His gaze wanders all over her, sardonic, biting. "What's this, semantics gymnastics?"

"I want to be wholly honest with you, Bryan." She goes to sit next to him as she says this. "I won't say Bayo and I didn't have a connection. We did. When I first got here, I was so fucking lonely, especially with everything that happened with my brother. Bayo took care of me. He made my life here feel real. So, yes, I formed a kind of heart connection with him, which is partly why I couldn't break off things. But with you, it's different." She lowers her voice now. "I love you in an unreasonable, obsessive way, and being apart from you feels unnatural. Like I'm breathing through my fingernails or something."

He rubs his chin vigorously, as if confounded, and asks if it's something he did, if there's something he could have done better.

She places a cautious palm on his thigh. She's never known the people in her life to be this bare, especially the men. She's always had to read them, to understand them through a series of expressions beyond language. Gestures, movements. Sieve their words through the private machinery of her mind, her own intuition and superstitions, her past and present. And yet still arrive tentatively, fearfully, at somewhat of a conclusion. But Bryan's surface is also his depth. He often means what he says. He's quick to cut himself open for her, for his friends. It's how Melinda knows him: she can see him because he shows her who he is. It's a kind of trust in the world that before now Sommy would have scorned at, thought careless or naïve, only possible in people the world has been good to. And maybe the world has been good to Bryan, maybe he's often been made to feel safe. Or maybe not. But what a quality this is, how it coats him in this pristine, angelic lacquer.

"It's all me," she says to him. "I fucked everything up."

He says he needs time to process it all, and she says, "Sure, take all the time you need."

Later that evening, when he calls her and says he'll give them a chance if she'll move out, find another apartment, she's ready to jump, to say, "Yes, of course," but she hesitates first. She can't afford an apartment all by herself, and neither can Bayo. She'll have to wait for him to find a new roommate. Bryan's quiet when she tells him this, and Sommy's heart thumps madly in her chest. But then he says, "If you are serious about us, move in with me, and we can continue paying your part of the rent until Bayo finds someone else."

She hears nothing but "we," and her skin starts to feel like it's bleeding happiness, a million thrilling tingles. "Of course," she says. "Of course, Bryan, I'll move in with you."

It makes her feel awful all over, but she texts Bayo anyway, tells him she'd like to end the lease.

Great, he replies.

Great? she texts back.

I already told the landlord we were ending the lease. I thought it was obvious that we couldn't live together anymore.

Sommy: You could have informed me.

Bayo: How hypocritical . . .

Sommy: ?

She ripples at Bayo's resentment. It was not long ago that they were curled up in her bed, singing, watching YouTube videos. It was not long ago that his laughter boomed across their apartment. She misses him, but she's quick to wrap her loss in the shawl of her recommitment to Bryan. Sometimes, the shawl unwraps, like when she walks past a Kum & Go and it brings to mind Bayo's crude jokes, and she feels an urgent desire to lean on something solid for support.

Sommy takes her essentials to Bryan's at the end of the week. He had suggested this, that she move in slowly.

"You do have a lot of stuff," he says as he watches her hang her clothes in his cleared-out closet.

"I don't know how men can survive with just five T-shirts of slightly different colors."

He laughs. "I have more than five T-shirts."

He's moved his clothes, shoes, and books to his writing office. To give her space, he says. He's certain they'll heal quickly if they're forceful about their recommitment. Spend more time together. Give no space for doubt or distrust. Sommy's not opposed to his plan. She so direly wants to be near him, recoup lost time.

Sommy finds that Bryan spends most of his time in his writing room. In there, he's quiet, and often emerges drained, thoughtful. She feels most attracted to him in these moments and it stuns her that he believes himself bound to her. There's no question that he's out of her league, belonging to a world she's only ever known from afar. She wishes she can think of love as holy, untainted by selfishness, by the abstract systems of the world—class, beauty, status, race—but every day she's convinced of their power. There are times she brushes against the painful truth of the mournfulness Mezie's silence induces in her—that she'd passively weaved her identity into his because it was the easy thing to do, to hide, to allow someone to go in front of her. If even that, this love she considers to be rooted in the center of her being, is shaped by her selfishness, what about Bryan's love for her? This way he looks at her like she's oxygen. This question rings louder when she stumbles upon the Igbo paraphernalia Bryan collects—a red ichie hat, a hand fan made of faux tiger skin, a brittle chicken feather. When she brings it up with him, he says it's his attempt to run toward himself.

"I can't continue to pretend that this whole other part of me doesn't exist," he says. "I'm Igbo. It's in my blood whether or not I accept it."

Sommy imagines a phantom limb then, real only to whom it afflicts. To be Igbo by blood and nothing else, no language or tradition or land or human to act as a bridge is tenuous, and rings, to Sommy's mind, as a figment. Does an identity exist if it cannot be used as a site of difference and of community?

She wonders if she's part of his paraphernalia. If he's collected her, too. A bridge to his lost lineage.

On this rainy night, a few weeks after she's partly moved in, unable to sleep and overcome by the morbid thought that embedded here, in this desire to know his father, is the *why* of their relationship, Sommy asks Bryan if he's still thinking about finding his father.

She has her head on his chest, and she's not sure he's awake. But he stirs soon, says, "I do sometimes think about it."

The room is pitch-black. Bryan is unable to sleep with even the faintest light.

"Why don't you do something about it, then?" Sommy says. She doesn't want to be part of his paraphernalia, she thinks. She refuses to be a place of yearning.

There's a long silence, and then he says he did have a lead two years ago. He'd found a college classmate of his father's, the only other African student on the "Class of 1987" graduation list from the physics department at the University of Chicago, who sent him an old address of his father's.

"An address?"

He pulls away from her, and she can hear his palm beat around the bed. His phone light soon breaks the darkness, and he punches the keys, and then tilts it toward her. "Here," he says.

She studies the screen, his Facebook Messenger, a message. It's hardly an address. It's a description of how to get to a place. She, however, sees familiar names: *Amawbia Roundabout, Eke-Awka market*.

"I went to school near Amawbia," is all she can say. She can't believe he's kept this from her all the while.

"The man says he knew my father briefly. And he had the address only because he'd come to Nigeria sometime in the early nineties and had reached out to him. They never got to meet, though."

She sees how it consumes him, thoughts of his father, thoughts of fathers, thoughts of masculinity, the lack of it, the excess of it. Once, while they sat watching *The Odyssey* for what seemed like the millionth time, he jokingly referred to himself as Telemachus, and then followed with a pointed, longing silence. Sommy's hardly considered Telemachus, with his short, wavy hair and questioning eyes. It's Penelope's forbearance, anger, lust, and love that holds her attention.

"Why are you just telling me this?"

He locks the phone. "I don't think I'll do anything with the address."

"And why's that?"

"It's a very old address. I'm not sure I'll find anything there. I'm not sure I want to find anything." He sucks his teeth, a thing he does whenever he's nervous. "You think I should go look for him?"

"Oh, Bryan, of course you should go find him."

It's the sort of thing that hovers. When have we ever left the unknown alone?

"I don't know," he says.

"You do know," she wants to say, but she doesn't.

In mid-July, Sommy moves fully into Bryan's, and by the beginning of the new semester, her second year in grad school, their relationship matures into a solid routine. They eat dinner together. Take evening walks. When he goes grocery shopping, he buys her strawberry cheesecake and seltzer water. He learns how to take down her braids, to detangle her hair with water and conditioner. He sits with her while she watches nineties Nollywood, falls in love with Afrobeats—Wizkid becomes his new favorite artiste. Often, he begins their phone conversations with phrases he's picked up from Nigerian Twitter. Once, he greets her by saying, "Babe, how far?" and she careens with laughter. With the excited temperament of a child showing off their new skill, he then adds, "You have wahala too much."

"No, babe," she says, laughing. "The correct way to say it is 'Your wahala is too much,' meaning, 'Your trouble is too much.'"

He laughs, says, "There's no difference."

And she says, "True, there's no difference."

She's happy, but she's aware that they are both faint from holding each other too tightly. She sees it even clearer when Bryan insists on weekly meetings to strengthen communication between them. The first few meetings are lovely. He tells her stories that he'd shared with her when they first began dating. He tells her that he wore braces as a kid, thought himself ugly for a long time, and only grew into his features in high school. He tells her that he's always genuinely surprised when he's referred to as handsome, and she says, "Oh no," though she's a little skeptical. He often pauses to look at himself in the mirror, his back straightening briefly after, as if shot through with dopamine by what he's seen.

She learns also that the only person he's ever deeply loved romantically besides her was his first girlfriend, Chloe.

"She used to cut herself," he says. "I believed it was my life's mission to save her, and boy, did I try."

With his other partners, it was mostly intellectual attraction and the comfort people with congruent politics and values find in each other.

He told her of his stepfather, a decent man conquered by addiction, even though he hated that the man held himself a little away from him.

"He was always gauging the emotional and physical labor he poured into me. Always wondering if it was too much, as though he didn't want to overpay for something he'd been reluctant to buy in the first place."

A month into these weekly meetings, he said, in a tense moment of confession, that when his stepfather left, he felt relieved for a bit, believing himself to be now totally like his brothers. But he quickly learnt that it was different. His brothers' father had stayed for a good portion of their lives. Him? He could walk past his father on the street and not recognize him.

She listens to him keenly during these meetings, supportive with her pained expressions and gentle knee squeezes, and he soon begins to complain about what he terms her "emotional miserliness."

"You don't tell me much," he says. "I feel like I don't know enough of you."

"I just don't have your kind of interesting life," she says.

The accusation bothers her. She's told him everything. She's told him about growing up under Mezie's shadow. She's told him about her mother, a forceful energy of her childhood, and her father, his quiet, steady presence. She knows that his dissatisfaction is anxiety: he's searching for something to fix, to stave off another Bayo-like incident. They don't talk about what happened with Bayo, but it's a cumbrous presence in their relationship. It's there in the awkward sex they have, Bryan fumbling, overly self-conscious—"Do you like it?" "You want me to go faster? Slower?" "To pull your hair? Spank you?" It's there whenever her phone rings, and she notices him pause and listen to detect who's calling. But nowhere more than in these weekly meetings.

It's their eighth meeting now, and the fall chill has descended, turned the air crisp and hostile. A candle burns on the center table, next to a box of Walmart pastries. Through the window, she sees the blanket dark blueness of the sky. It's the last days before the fury of winter arrives, the snow, the slippery ice, the cold.

"Is your brother the reason you don't talk about going home?" He says, pulling her into an embrace, as if to soften the impact of his question.

"You know I don't have three thousand dollars for a flight ticket."

"And you know I'm willing to pay for the tickets."

She releases herself from his embrace. "You've never offered to pay for the tickets."

He squints, "You've never asked."

Her cardigan is suddenly prickly, and she sinks one hand into the sleeve, rubs her warm skin furiously. He's about to speak when, in a blind moment of defensiveness, she asks if he's focusing on her issues because he's escaping his. How is it possible, she says, that he often bloviates about honesty, transparency, but he doesn't tell her that he has what might be his father's address? When he does eventually tell her, he refuses to do anything with the address, refuses to even try. Is he comfortable simply with romanticizing this whole "Daddy" thing?

She cannot say if she's certain of these accusations. They are simply thoughts floating on the surface of her mind and she's arranged them into something competent and coherent, in truth, to divert the attack on her, and also because she's angry. She's angry he didn't tell her about the address. She's angry because the meetings are exhausting. She's angry because Bayo's presence is a vengeful ghost, permeating vital aspects of their relationship.

"You are right that I'm scared to pursue the information I have of my father," Bryan says. "But that doesn't make my question about your brother some sort of tactic." He crosses his legs, a protest move, and continues: "And it says a lot that you couldn't think of a better way to say this to me. You don't think it's the point of my insistence that we carve out time to talk in depth, with real language, saying things as they really are?"

She's quiet now, adequately reprimanded, remorseful.

"And bloviating?" he says bitterly. "Who bloviates? Me?"

"That wasn't the word I was going for."

"Bloviate," he mutters.

"I meant to say preach," she says.

He shakes his head. "I think we've had enough for today." He then stands and disappears into his writing room.

Later at night, Sommy sits on the edge of the bed, watching Bryan scour through a pile of books by the closet. He's just taken a shower: his hair is wet, and his skin is glistening from the shea butter she bought him from an online African store. The tension between them is apparent. Usually, while he scours the pile, he'll hold up a book and ask if she's read it, and he'll then tell her all about it. She's recently discovered his views to be iconoclastic. He's excited by the transgressive, defiant. It bothers her slightly that his appreciation of a thing is filtered through a set of values. "What about how it makes you feel in your body?" she often wants to ask. She doesn't, though. She knows he'll miss her point.

"Babe," she says now. "Do you mind sitting with me for a bit?"

He folds the book, comes to sit beside her.

She asks if he'd like to go to breakfast at Perkins tomorrow.

"Sure, we can do that."

She's silent for a moment, and then she tells him he's right—she's scared of going home. A year ago, she wanted nothing more, but that reality feels now like a furnace, burning wildly in wait for her. The things she doesn't want to learn, but she knows she must face when she goes home: the state of her brother's life, the truth of his feelings for her. She's seeing things too clearly, she tells him. Turning twenty-four a year ago had come with questions she didn't know one must ask of their life: What does it mean to own my life? Can I even own my life? Perhaps Mezie's attempt brought about this awareness. Perhaps it was leaving home. Perhaps it was the simple, quotidian fact of becoming older. But deep down, she's aware that no life will feel like real life if she has to do it without her brother, and she's afraid that home holds final and difficult answers on the matter.

Bryan moves closer to her. "I'm scared about these things, too," he says. "But the strange thing is that I'm brave for you, for the things that concern you, and if you need to, you can borrow my bravery."

"I'm brave for the things that concern you, too," she says.

She can see that he's alert to her, responsive, so she adds, as a gift, "You should go look up that address. It's a long journey, but I'll come with you."

His face lifts. Surprise and then calm. He takes her hand, squeezes. She's never felt closer to him. Never felt their love to be this pure. Not any weightier, but simply purer, like how diamonds of the same weight can have vastly different costs based on their clarity. Maybe for love to feel like love it must be good. In that former thing they had was the will to be good, but they were yet to bridge the gap between will and action. But here they are now, here she is now, bridging that gap, one difficult brick after another.

Part Two

S ommy and Bryan arrive in Lagos at exactly ten A.M. Outside the tiny oval window: a cloudy sky and shy rain, grass plains whipped into servitude by whirring airplane blades, luggage trucks, inside which sit men in glowing lemon jackets, gliding on the wet runway. In the far distance, airplanes, white, motionless, sublime like dead doves, and farther away, outside the airport, worn houses, shops, offices.

"We are here," Sommy says.

Bryan looks out the window. "It's beautiful."

She slides her hand into his. She thinks the word "beautiful" too dainty a word for Lagos. "Profound," maybe. "Grand," maybe. If life, she thinks, its surprises, the slices of deep joy contained, its ruggedness and impliability, its contradictions, the implosion of it, the nonsense of it, were a physical place, it would be Lagos.

The plane soon stops, and the commotion of alighting begins. Blankets are folded, bags are packed, phones are turned on. The once dark and quiet airplane sparks with phone conversations, the cracking of the overhead compartments, the cries of children spooked by the disarray.

Until now, time has moved slowly. At the airport in Chicago, while she and Bryan sat waiting for their flight, she'd amused herself by listening and watching the people about. The scenery was incredibly Nigerian; of course, it was incredibly Nigerian, the flight was headed to Lagos. It surprised her, the little details she noticed, and the delight she took from them—the woman who had on a black suit jacket atop an Ankara blouse; the little girl who roamed about the waiting area, asking people if they, too, were going to Lagos, and making sure to add that she was seeing her grandma soon; the man on the phone, speaking pidgin rapidly, laughing loudly; the elderly woman seated opposite her, hair covered with a bonnet, face squeezed, as if in a hurry to leave, to go back to the only place she really knows. On the plane ride, Sommy mostly slept, and then read some Jane Austen. She'd felt completely at peace, especially with Bryan being near her.

Now, as she alights the plane, she's toppled by anxiety. Her mother has just sent a WhatsApp message: Your brother is coming to pick you people up. It's better for you and your person to stay at his new flat. He will call your WhatsApp very soon. Mezie, whom she hasn't seen in two years, who has kept her walled off, suddenly offered to pick her up. She shows the text message to Bryan while they stand waiting to get on the airport shuttle.

"That's great," he says, absentminded, head bent toward the sky.

If it were possible, she would climb out of her skin. Stand in a corner and watch Mezie receive a body empty of a mind. She'd known that they were going to eventually meet, even if it was hard to imagine what he would say to her, what she would say to him. But this is too soon. She's unprepared for him to meet this new person she's become—the returnee, the one with a honey-glazed future. And there's the issue of Bryan. She's certain the men won't get along, Bryan with his shining Americanness, and Mezie, at least the Mezie she left two years ago, with this hapless arch in his soul, emitting constantly the pheromones of a doomed man.

Her anxiety stalls as she walks to the baggage reclaim area, and then to the immigration counter, where she stands in awe as a belligerent immigration officer pesters her to *find* him *something*, give him "small" dollars, while two men behind complain about the airport. *Imagine,* they say, *an international airport without functional Wi-Fi and proper air-conditioning. It is a disgrace.* Hasn't she missed it all, this stark display of foible. She's home.

While she stands on the slow-moving immigration line, Bryan waits for her on the other side of the counter, looking voraciously about. She can feel his nervous excitement, though he's tried to hide it from her, from himself, too. After they made travel plans to Nigeria, he began referring to the trip as "our summer travel," mentioning nothing of going to look up what might be his father's house. Sommy believes that he secretly nurtures the hope of a blissful reunion, which convinces her of the essential difference between them. With Mezie, she's certain of a warlike reunion.

Mezie's WhatsApp message comes in. He's in front of the parking lot, he says, waiting for her. Bryan doesn't notice her discomfort as they stand in front of the airport, next to the infinite traffic line, lost in the avalanche of people heading toward and away from them. All signs of the light rain have vanished. The sun is blasting. The heat is merciless. The noise is clattering—blaring horns, people conversing, taxi drivers competing for customers.

He looks at her now, distracted still, eyes bleary with feelings. "I can't believe it. It feels just like I imagined."

"It does?"

"Everyone is black. Everyone."

"Of course everyone is black, babe." What a juvenile declaration, she thinks.

"It's a homecoming," Bryan says. "That's what it feels like. Like I have arrived home."

"Ha," Sommy says, laughing. "This your poetry sha. You'll be speaking a different language in a few days, after you've sat in traffic for like three hours."

He throws an arm around her and presses her body into his, his eyes still wandering about. "We are here!"

They walk to the parking lot arm in arm, their luggage stuttering on the gravel-paved sidewalk.

Sommy sees Mezie before he sees her. He is by the entrance of the parking lot, near the boom barrier, punching his phone keys. She's not quite herself when she screams his name, flings her luggage, jerks away from Bryan, and runs toward him, buries her face in his shoulder.

"Big head," he says, jaw grinding gently on her shoulders. "Long time."

Sommy pulls away, inspects him ravenously. "Is this you?"

"No," he says, laughing. "It's my ghost."

She punches the side of his stomach, says, "Mumu."

He looks different, taller than she remembers, his eyes brighter, nothing of that darkness enshrined in the months before she left. Oh, how she's missed him. Oh, how she loves him. She throws an arm around him again. He leans into her embrace.

"I go love o!" someone from the security post screams. "Make una continue they do PDA!"

Sommy rolls her eyes. Mezie laughs. His laughter is like a light seeping out of him, sincere, boundless. It's easier than she'd anticipated, effortless, this reunion. Look how they settle into each other's presence like in the old days. Look how he holds her now, unthinkingly, a careless arm around her shoulders. Why then had he built this wall between them? Not one phone call when she needed it the most.

They walk up to Bryan, who stands now by the bag she'd flung. The men shake hands. Mezie, at six foot seven, hovers over Bryan, and it's the first thing Bryan points out.

"She didn't tell me you were basketballer height." His manner is effusive, desperate to please. "And she's told me so much about you."

Mezie looks at Sommy from under his eyes. "Hope she's not been bad-mouthing me."

"She adores you."

Sommy raises a hand. "Please o! Don't tell him that so his head doesn't get any bigger than it is." For emphasis, she tiptoes, shoves Mezie's head with a finger.

Mezie smiles weakly. He's dressed smartly, a light-blue shirt with navy-blue pants. Black belt. Black shoes. Freshly shaven. He'd prepared for this meeting, as though anxious about his effect on her. Or perhaps it's for Bryan he wants to put a good foot forward.

On the drive home, Bryan sits at the backseat, Sommy in the passenger seat. She cannot stop smiling, cannot stop pointing out things that had seemed mundane two years ago. *That billboard is still there! They've been building this road since I was in secondary school, and they've still not completed it? Traffic, traffic, traffic! Wait, did the churches multiply in two years? Why am I seeing churches everywhere? Remember Sade, Sade from Angel Kids, she used to live over there. Do you think she still lives there?* When they reach Egbeda bus stop, she turns to Bryan and says: "During my National Youth Service year I used to stand here and fight to get onto a bus that will take me to work!" He says he cannot imagine her fighting for anything. "Ah, in Lagos, we fight for everything." At a traffic light in Igando, she winds down the car window, and whistles at a woman hawking gala rolls and cold soft drinks. She buys four rolls and a bottle of Fanta. "You have to try it," she says to Bryan. "Gala has saved many Lagosians from dying of hunger in traffic."

"Calm down, madam," Mezie says. "You've just been gone for two years. You are acting like it's fifteen years."

"It feels like fifteen years, I swear."

Mezie's apartment is a new three-bedroom bungalow, which still carries the faint smell of paint. It is lightly furnished, in that masculine minimalist way Sommy finds boring. A black leather chair, a glass center table, a large television atop a taupe stand. The bungalow sits somewhere in the middle of Graceland Estate, three miles from Iba Estate, from where her parents are driving to join them.

When she walked in, hit by the cool air, the newness of the furniture, a sort of unwelcoming quality in its stiffly rendered spotlessness, she'd detected in his manner, and in the obvious arrangement of the room, a longing for acknowledgment, so she said to Mezie, "Nice one, man."

It's clear that he'd walled her off to build this glossy life, and now that he can show her that he belongs to the group of Lagosians who live in estates surrounded by beds of flowers, sporting children's parks and water fountains, show her that he hadn't really lost it all, that everything he'd gone to Norway to find, he'd found back home, he's letting her in. Letting her somewhat in. She cannot say how he reconciles the image he aims to project with the fact that their mother was the one who had done all of these things. She told Sommy over the phone that she rented and furnished the apartment. She bought him a second-hand Honda and put him on a one-hundred-thousand-naira-a-month salary. Every bit of profit their mother makes from her business, she funnels into Mezie. She says it's until he gets on his feet, and Sommy is grateful for it, but she's worried her mother will soon feel drained. She's worried, too, about Mezie's desperation to hold up this false image of a glossy life, saddened that he thinks her underserving of the true meat of his life.

Now she sits on the couch, beside Bryan, who is reclined, watching the news. She's surprised by his comfort, how effortlessly he's slipped into this new world. She places a hand on his thigh, and he covers it with his. Their plan is to spend a week in Lagos, and then travel to Amawbia, to the address. She'll buy their plane tickets this evening, when they are showered and ready for bed. In the moment, she's overwhelmed with a torrent of love for him, and she tells him, and he beams, leans in for a kiss, and she's struck anew by their reality—he's here, at home with her.

"Your brother seems nice," Bryan whispers. "And happy to see you."

Sommy shrugs. "I'm surprised."

Mezie walks into the room then, sets two glasses of orange juice on the wooden side stool beside Bryan, and sits on the smaller couch opposite her.

"So, how long are you guys staying?" he says.

Bryan looks at her, forehead scrunched, and then turns to Mezie, "Two months?"

"Yes," Sommy says. "Our return ticket is dated August twenty-fourth."

"Two months in Lagos," Mezie says. "Nice."

There's an unnatural sonance in Mezie's voice, a drawl in his speech, as if compelled by the wave of Bryan's accent. Sommy knows that Bryan can't notice this, but she feels embarrassed nonetheless. She hates to think of Mezie as a person capable of contorting himself to rise or descend to another person. At least, it is not the picture of him she's painted for Bryan. It's not the picture of him she has in her mind. In her mind, he is a formidable thing caught in a tempest. He might bend and break, but never without resistance.

Sommy asks Bryan to pass her a glass of orange juice. Mezie asks if it's Bryan's first time in Africa.

Africa? Sommy thinks. Had Mezie become one of those Africans who referred to Africa as though it were a country? Or had she become one of those people who read power imbalances in every interaction?

"First ever," Bryan says, handing Sommy the cold glass.

"What's your first impression?"

"I like the noise. I grew up in the suburbs, but I've always loved the hustle and bustle of city of life."

"You don't strike me as such," Mezie says.

"How do you mean?"

"You don't strike me as a city boy."

Sommy holds the glass to her mouth, and stares quizzically at Mezie. His expression is hard to read. Bryan is silent, flashing a strained smile. She can tell that he's trying to decipher the real meaning behind Mezie's accusation. Is it an accusation? It sounded like an accusation.

"Can you call Mummy?" Sommy says. "Let her know we are here."

Sommy's aching terribly now. A striking pain in her back from hours of sitting on the airplane.

Mezie excuses himself and goes on to execute the business of the phone call.

"Are you okay, babe?" Sommy asks Bryan.

"Tired."

"You want to go rest inside?"

"No, I'm good. I might just doze off once my head hits a bed, and I do not want to miss your parents."

"Okay, babe."

She can sense his discomfort. Something to do with the "city boy" comment, she's sure. She knows how easily he unspools at any statement or gesture indicating an absence of ruggedness in him. He's never told her this, but she knows that he's sore from years of being asked, "What are you?" Not white enough. Not black enough. A displacement enhanced by that other displacing force of his class. A mixed rich kid in the humanities. It doesn't get softer than that. He sometimes grumbles about the money factor, never about the mixed-kid factor, as if anxious about putting the thought in her consciousness should it have never occurred. She finds it sadly amusing that he believes she hasn't caught on to this anxiety of his. It is obvious. It propels him in ways he's unaware of. He performs blackness, a certain kind of blackness. He calls black people "my people." He does not like rap—she can tell because he hardly ever bops his head to the music, none of that fluidity of the body that a beat induces—but he knows the lyrics, is adept at philosophizing about it. He quotes Frantz Fanon and bell hooks and Aimé Césaire to her, never to Melinda, Joel, and Clark, all of whom are white, as if with them, he need not defend himself, showcase his blackness.

She looks to him now. A sweat stain the shape of a spoon crawls down the neck of his shirt, and she leans over and unbuttons the top buttons. She wants to kiss him. It is an irritating urge she gets whenever she assumes she's fallen short of his grace, a need for reassurance.

Mezie walks back in. He's changed into a singlet and a pair of tan baggy three-quarter shorts. Sommy's about to ask him to show her to their room when the gate jangles open, and then the wooden door, and her parents enter, her mother in a flowing flowery dress, an iridescent crepe scarf around her neck, her father in a simple black T-shirt and plain trousers, smelling of his everlasting signature scent, a harsh oily musk.

They are not a family keen on gestures of intimacy, and she's mildly surprised at the force of her mother's hug, the crying, the praying. Her father hugs her, too, gently. When he unclasps, she peers into his face, moved by how deeply he's been marked by age. "Daddy," she says, and it is all she can muster. There's then that fleeting, wounding thought that she's never known him, that the universe had never aligned in a way that made it possible for them to talk as adults who liked each other, and that it might never align, that one day he would be gone and all she would know of him is what he'd been to her—a father who'd provided, been there. But not a person, not a person with a past.

"Welcome, nne," her father says.

"Is this my son-in-law?" her mother says of Bryan.

Sommy's flustered by this, and she cannot hold Bryan's gaze. But Bryan is unmoved. He goes to her mother, asks if she doesn't mind a hug. He tells her that he's heard so many wonderful things about her, and it's an utmost pleasure to finally meet her. Her mother laughs, says she cannot understand his American *supri supri*. He should speak slowly. Bryan apologizes, drawing the words, like a broken machine. Her mother starts to laugh. "I am playing with you, my dear." She hits him lightly on the shoulder. "Be yourself, okay? And welcome. Welcome to Lagos."

Her father takes the seat beside Mezie. Bryan walks to him, and they exchange a brief, brusque handshake. "Nice to meet you, Mr. Nwachukwu," Bryan says.

Her father nods, says nothing. He sits with his legs crossed. She's struck again by how thin he's become. He has jowls now. If someone were to describe him, "old" would be one of the descriptors.

Her mother asks about their journey and Sommy begins to list all the inconveniences she's experienced since she boarded the flight in Iowa: the bad food they'd been served on the flight, the long immigration line at the airport, the immigration officer who kept pestering her for money, the terrible traffic from Ikeja to the apartment.

"That's Nigeria for you," her mother says. "Other countries are getting better, ours is getting worse." She turns to her father. "Have you seen a thing like that? A regressing country?"

Her father shakes his head disinterestedly. Sommy wonders if his disenchantment has something to do with Bryan. She's never discussed men with her father, never brought one home. It always seemed like a situation that would never arise. But with Bryan, it is different. She's certain about him: their love is forever. So certain, too, Bryan had been about them that he took her to a cousin's wedding in Miami a month ago, and introduced her to his brothers, Robert and Philip, and his mother, Catherine, as "Sommy, my partner." Sommy had not felt, in their presence, that which she often felt when the men she'd been with introduced her to family, like they'd brought her to be scrutinized, to receive confirmation that she possessed the abilities of a good wife. She'd, however, felt a deep disquiet at the whiteness of the wedding, herself and Bryan being the only black people in the large hall. She'd felt such tenderness toward him afterward and had gone days secretly nursing a small joy at her new understanding that she shared something with him that the people who loved him the most would never be able to access. She'd felt guilty about it soon enough. She liked Catherine. A pleasant, silver-haired woman. The kind people referred to as a "good woman." She endured—Sommy could immediately tell from the quickness of her actions: her unceasing smile, the way she held Sommy's hand, and said, "Please let me know if you need anything," and then three minutes later, walked back to repeat the statement. She had an insuppressible desire to make people comfortable. On a wealthy white woman, this behavior looked like gracefulness. On someone without the status, it would seem cloying. Still, Sommy liked her, was grateful for the warmth, and before she left, held her in a too-long hug.

His brothers, Robert and Philip, treated her like an ordinary guest. Civilly, coldly even. They were handsome, in what Sommy thought was a generic white boy way, slicked-back fade, ruler-straight face, square jawbones. They had light-brown eyes like Bryan. She thought the resemblance striking, and she thought, too, that race was a stupid thing. They all had the same face, their mother's face, and yet one was black, the others white, and in the eyes of many in the world, it was what mattered the most, their race.

Now her mother asks if they are hungry. She points to the cooler sitting on the floor. "I made jollof rice and goat meat."

"I'll eat, Mummy," Sommy says. "But not now."

Bryan says the same, and her mother smiles, says not to worry, there's time for tons of eating. She then tells him about the thanksgiving party she's planning. "The array of food will be second to none," she says. She wants it to be the party of the year. She wants to put Satan to shame.

Sommy and Mezie stifle giggles, just like in the old days, as their mother describes the largesse that will be on display on this day. They both understand that Satan has little to do with this party. It is the church women their mother wants to put on a display for, women who'd sniggered when Mezie came home.

"Mummy," Sommy says, laughing, "are you sure this is about thanking God?"

Her mother rolls her eyes. "What else will it be for?"

"You tell me," Sommy says. "Madam Stainless?"

"You better shut up there."

They all burst out laughing at the sharp retort, even her father joins, and when the raucous calms, her mother asks Mezie when Elin is arriving.

"In exactly two weeks," Mezie says.

"I didn't know she was coming," Sommy says, her gaze swinging between Mezie and her mother. "I didn't even know you guys were still together."

"Well, we are, and she'll be here for two months."

"Mezie wants to go back," her mother says. "If they get married, him and Elin, he can go back. Even though I don't know why he won't stay here and settle down."

Sommy, embarrassed that her mother is talking about marriage in this context in Bryan's presence, says she wants to go rest. It's late afternoon now, and the sun is pouring into the sitting room. Mezie has tuned the television to a music station, and P-Square's "No One Like You" is playing. The room is cool, and the air smells of fried meat and vanilla. It is as she's always wanted. To be home. To be near Mezie. Yet she can't fully slip into his staged act.

Inside the room, Bryan says it's exciting that Elin will be joining them soon.

"It is," Sommy replies, her voice tinged with doubt.

"Is it?"

She plops on the bed. "I just hope it does Mezie some good."

He sits beside her, places a comforting arm around her shoulders. "I think it will."

She turns to him, nods somberly.

He raises an uncertain eyebrow. "I see why you're worried about him. I can't quite place it, but I feel it. I might also be reading too much into this thing he does where he tries to throw me off for no reason."

"I'm sorry," she says.

"No, no, babe. Don't apologize. I know it has nothing to do with me. He's just going through whatever he's going through. I think he'll feel more relaxed when Elin gets here, though." He squeezes her shoulders. "I have a good feeling about this trip."

"You have a good feeling about everything," she says, pulling gently at his cheek.

The next day, Mezie drives Sommy to their parents'. Bryan stays back at the apartment, jet-lagged, asleep. Mezie is dressed in his NYSC uniform, white T-shirt tucked into khaki pants, a fat green belt cinching his waist. On his feet are ugly burnt-orange boots. When Mezie told her that he's participating in the National Youth Service, she'd been surprised. Around the time he'd graduated university, their mother urged him to apply to the program while he waited for school acceptances. He refused. What use was an NYSC completion certificate to someone who planned to work abroad? he asked. He did not budge when the rejection letters came from U.S. schools. He did not budge when he started looking for jobs after another season of rejections. The program took on a metaphorical meaning. If he accepted participation, he inadvertently accepted participation in a society he was eager to flee. Now here he is, uniform and all, headed soon to a CDS meeting.

They drive past Igando, and Sommy's reminded of Bayo. It's been a year since the incident. A few weeks ago, she texted him. She let him know she was spending the summer months in Lagos and asked if he'd like to send gifts back home for his sister and mum, but he replied, Enjoy your break. Nothing else. She'd expected time to blunt his rage. It was Bayo, after all, the same Bayo who mocked her broodiness, who unburdened himself quickly.

They drive into her childhood estate now. She stares at the identical blocks of flats, their peeling yellow paint holding maps of algae and watermarks, their rusted zinc roofs, the satellite dishes hanging from netted windows. There's no sign of change. The estate remains the same. The newspaper stand her father has visited every Saturday since she was a child still stands by the gate, its battered red umbrella sloping, the newspapers—the *Guardian, Vanguard, The Sun,* falling down the wooden table like a curtain, held in place by small gray stones. Her father always read *The Sun*, something to do with its decent representation of Igbo people. Oga Tunde, the vulcanizer who's been pumping her mother's tires since she bought her first car in the early 2000s, leans now on an electric pole, wiping sweat from his forehead with a curved finger. A little down the road, they come to Mama Dotun's kiosk, where she sells akara and moi-moi in the evenings. There were many nights when Sommy stood on the other side of the heavy frying pan, waiting for Seyi, Mama Dotun's first child, to fish out the newest batch of akara from the hot oil. Sommy always begged for the crust, tiny shapeless balls she liked to crack with her teeth.

They drive into Zone C. She spots Madam B's Grocery, a blue container with a table in front, atop which sit open cartons of biscuits and large bowls of dry rice, beans, garri. Madam B died two years before Sommy left for Iowa. As kids, whenever their father gave them money, Sommy and Mezie went to Madam B's shop to buy biscuits. They came to associate her shop with a sugar rush. They never walked there. They skipped. They ran. They somersaulted. There were months when things were particularly hard, and Sommy's mother had to collect foodstuff with a promise to pay soon. No specific date. Just soon. Madam B was happy to oblige. The first time Sommy saw her period, it was to Madam B she went. "I want to buy pad, ma," she said proudly, having waited for so long to finally be, as her mother called it, "a full woman."

Madam B's death was a shock. She seemed an invincible aspect of Sommy's world. Her shop opened at eight A.M. and closed at seven P.M. every weekday. She never missed a day, and then suddenly, she was no longer there walking sluggishly around the shop, tying and untying her wrapper. She was gone. It whipped the wind out of Sommy's lungs. That was her first brush with life's fragility, before Mezie's attempt.

Mezie parks the car by a gutter. Sommy stares at their own block of flats, in the middle of which sits her parents' apartment. The space between the gutter and the block holds three soakaways, one for each of the three blocks of flats surrounding it. There's a well from where, before their parents built in a water-pumping machine, Sommy and Mezie took weekly turns fetching water to fill the black baff in their kitchen. Clothes hangers sit in the middle of this space, and underneath them wild grasses spring. By one of the clothes hangers is a wooden storage shed slanting from old age. It's been there since Sommy was a child. It belonged to Aunty Rose, the sex worker who lived on the last floor of Block 229. In a short distance is what was once Fidelis's electricals shop, a red container that is now a hair salon covered with long packets of braiding hair, sporting a tall shampoo bowl. Beside the salon stands a barbershop. Sommy cut her hair there once, when she was nine, and Clifford the former shop owner, a short, bearded man, yellow-skinned like pineapple flesh, kissed her full on the mouth. She'd run out of the shop with her hair half cut. When her mother tried to persuade her to go back, Sommy told her everything. Her mother immediately changed into leggings and a bodysuit, grabbed a pestle, marched to the shop, and took the pestle to Clifford's mirror, chairs, drawers. When she was done, the shop looked like the site of a hurricane attack. All the while, Clifford stood in a corner, mouth buried in his palms.

After her mother was done, she turned to him. "If I see you near my daughter again, you are a dead man."

Sommy remembers the stunned crowd parting as her mother walked away. She remembered her pride, fluttering, as if a bird caged in her chest.

"This place never changes," she says now to Mezie, who's buckling his belt.

"Normal people live in a place for a while and then move on," he says. "Not Mummy and Daddy, though."

Her parents rented the flat in the last years of the nineties. Sommy was about five then, and Mezie seven. It was a cheap apartment, one of the low-cost housing estates built in the early eighties by a former Lagos state governor, Lateef Jakande. She'd been happy when they moved in. Before then, they'd lived in a one-bedroom apartment, where she had to share a flat mattress with Mezie. The mattress was rolled up in the mornings, and it took on the function of a cushion. The apartment did not come with a bathroom, so her parents shared one with their next-door neighbor. Sommy bathed outside, by the front door. Every morning, her mother filled an iron bucket halfway, stood her by a bench and scrubbed her clean. Mezie, too, bathed outside. Around the time Mezie turned six, he was allowed the privilege of using the bathroom with the adults. In this new flat, Sommy had her own room, her own mattress. The flat also came with a bathroom, and Sommy had her own little soap dish that sat on the windowsill, and this pleased her immensely. Over the years, while their mother's business grew, the estate wore into a dilapidated mess, as did the apartment. Mezie urged her to move.

"We live in the backwaters," he said often. "Let's at least move to Ikeja. Let's be close to where things are happening."

Their mother, averse to new experiences, shut him down. "Lagos is dangerous," she insisted. "Our estate has security. We are safe here."

By the time Sommy left for university in Awka, the apartment had become overridden by rats and cockroaches. The sitting room walls bore watermarks. The kitchen walls were blackened by smoke. Most of the floor tiles were off. The window had missing louvres. The doors wore holes, screeched as if wounded when opened. Yet her mother would neither move nor renovate. She seemed to be simulating the one-room home in which she and her sister, Clara, were raised. What use was repainting a wall? What use was a new curtain? Her mother could not stop being a poor person.

Sommy turns now to Mezie, who's rummaging in his bag, says, "So you'll come get me at four?"

"Just pray I don't jam traffic on my way back."

"Okay, please, try. I don't want Bryan to be alone for too long."

He looks mockingly at her. "Okay, Madam Wife."

"He's not used to here," she says, defensive.

"I didn't say anything o!"

She hangs her bag over her shoulder. "Sha come and get me at four."

"I don hear."

Upstairs, Florence, the new house girl, opens the door.

"Aunty, good afternoon, ma," Florence says, smiling shyly.

Sommy walks in. "Why are you shining your thirty-two?"

Florence looks about thirteen. She has on isi owu, and they fall down her small head like little sticks. She smiles even harder at Sommy's retort.

"Nothing, Aunty," she says, giggling.

"Where's my mum?"

"In the room, ma."

"Go and call her for me."

"Yes, Aunty."

Florence patters away. Sommy sits on the long couch by the wall, a few inches from the balcony, which looks out to Block 227. The sitting room looks the same as it did in the early 2000s. They've owned the same set of couches and curtains since they moved in. On the wall, beside the flat-screen television, the only new furniture in the room, hangs a picture of Mezie as a baby. In the picture, he sits atop a car, wearing a white singlet and red shorts, drooling. It was taken the day of his baptism. Beside that is a picture of Sommy. She looks about three. She's holding a lollipop, dressed in a long-sleeved blouse and ankle-length skirt made from purple-striped aso-oke material. Next to that is a picture of her mother and father on their wedding day. Her mother has on a cream-colored, off-the-shoulder wedding dress, her father, an oversized black suit. Sommy was nine when they got married. She'd been her mother's flower girl. She wore a lace dress, and her hair was slicked back in a telephone wire ponytail—"gel packing" as the hairstyle was called then.

"You are here," her mother says.

"Good afternoon, ma."

She has on a worn gray T-shirt and jeans. Her face is scrubbed clean, the slight pallor of one who's been swimming. She's just recently out of the shower.

"Where's Daddy?"

"I sent him to Alaba to help me look for a good DJ for my thanks-giving party."

"Mummy, Daddy is too old for you to be sending him on errands."

Her mother clicks her tongue. "If I don't send him anywhere, he'll sit here all day reading his newspaper. Is that better? You don't want him to move his body?"

Her mother takes the chair by the balcony door. Florence walks in carrying a glass of water. She places it on the stool beside Sommy.

"This girl," her mother says to Florence. "Your ears are obviously for decoration. How many times have I told you not to drop a cup on the bare table? Will you go and get a plate to place under before I seal your ears with a slap."

"Sorry, Mummy," Florence says, smiling, scurrying away.

"That girl makes me talk and talk," her mother says. "It's only God who will help me in this house."

Sommy sighs. It must be exhausting to be a person incapable of letting the smallest things go. As a child, Sommy loathed her mother's incessant nagging—"Why won't you close the toilet seat?" "Why didn't you rinse the plate twice?" "Why won't you spread open the curtains?" Everything not done in the exact way her mother would was met with ire or irritation, depending on her mood. It caused Sommy great anxiety, and she tried to create the perfect environment, one in which her mother's every need was met, so she never forgot to close the toilet seat, or rinse a plate twice, or throw open the curtains after sunrise. She soon figured out that she'd taken on an impossible task. Her mother conjured new irritations. It was hard to keep up. Sommy wished now that she hadn't tried. Perhaps it is from here her anxiety stems, this smoldering desire to fix anything seemingly crooked.

"Why didn't you come with Bryan?" her mother asks.

"He's very tired. Jet-lagged."

"He looks like someone who's always tired. Does he eat well?"

"Mummy, he eats well, and he's not always tired."

"I'm just saying that he's kind of slow. He's not alert. Can he survive in this Lagos?"

"Mummy—"

Her mother starts to laugh. "I am playing with you." She slaps the hand of the couch, an old habit. "O'maka, Bryan. He's a fine man."

Sommy fights back a laugh, but she cannot help it. Her mother's laughter draws out her own laughter. Sommy's always thought it beautiful, her mother's laughter, uninhibited, made intense by her large teeth, her dark gums.

"He's finer than your husband," Sommy teases.

"You don't know what you are talking about," her mother says. "If you had seen your father as a boy, you wouldn't be saying this nonsense.

Your father was a great footballer. He was tall and lean and very fast. Not like your slow boyfriend." She laughs again, this time so hard she's tearing up.

This poking is her mother's roundabout way of finally approving of Bryan. She'd bristled when Sommy told her about him. "What do you mean he does not know who his father is?" she'd asked after Sommy furnished her with Bryan's biography.

Sommy had reiterated that Bryan's father is Nigerian, Igbo precisely, that he'd left the United States when Bryan was a baby because his papers expired.

"What if there is madness in their family?" her mother said. "From the father's side? What if they are osu, outcasts? Somkelechukwu, mba. No."

"Mba, as in how?"

"Mba, as in look for someone else."

She'd not planned to tell her mother that they were coming to Nigeria to find Bryan's father. She did not want her mother's hopes raised and dashed. But faced with her mother's petulant resistance, Sommy blurted it out.

"You should have started with that information," her mother said, her voice quietening. "It's a good thing that he's the kind of man interested in tracing his roots."

Now Sommy watches the lines around her mother's mouth spread and shrink when she tells her that they plan to leave to Amawbia in a week to go find the address.

"What if Bryan's father is an important politician?" her mother says. "He can appoint me as a commissioner for something. Maybe Commissioner for Happiness. Didn't Governor Rochas Okorocha appoint his sister as Commissioner for Happiness?"

Sommy looks skeptically at her mother, who breaks into a long laughter.

"Nigerian politicians are clowns," her mother moans.

Florence walks in, places the plate and cup on the stool, and then stands in the corner, smiling. She's not stopped smiling since Sommy walked in. She has the shine of a child flush with serotonin after having discovered a new plaything. Sommy's the new plaything, "the aunty from America."

"Do you think he'll ask for your hand?" her mother says.

"Bryan?"

"Who else?"

"Please let's not put pressure on him."

"Who says anything about pressure?"

"I know how you are, Mummy."

"Please shut up there. You think it's wise to live with a man who's not your husband? Tell me, if you are already performing the duties of a wife, what's his motivation to marry you?"

"I am not performing any duties. Bryan is a feminist."

"Feminist, my foot. There's nothing like a feminist man. Every man wants to be served."

"Not Bryan."

"That one is your business. In my opinion, at your age, you should be thinking very hard about marriage."

Sommy rolls her eyes. "How come I'm the only one you have all these rules for? What about Mezie?"

"Ehnn? What about Mezie?"

"He's not married. He's older than me. Why do I get the heat and he doesn't?"

"He's a man?"

"So?"

"Men do not have the same rules as women. You do not see me asking about your plans after you graduate. I do not expect you to get a big job or anything like that."

"You obviously don't expect that from Mezie, either. You rented that apartment for him. You bought him his car."

"Mezie's own is different."

"Different, how?"

"I'm helping him get on his feet. You'll see, very soon he'll fly."

Sommy's silent. Mezie is her mother's impeccable son, incapable of failure. It's never been a bother to Sommy until now. "He'll fly," she says. How can he swing from death to aliveness? Such two extremes? And what's this with her mother and Mezie united in their performance of a good life? And for whom? For her, Somkele? Did they not know that she knows them? That she hears their unspoken words, sees through their actions. That two years isn't enough to make them unfathomable to her. She can see that an odd anxiety simmers under everything Mezie says. She can see that he has developed this new, closed-off slouch in his walk, that his face constantly holds the expression of someone arguing with himself, that when he smiles, his lips barely spread.

"Mezie needs to go therapy," Sommy says now. "He's not doing well."

Her mother's forehead crinkles. "What do you mean by that?"

"He has depression, Mummy."

"He has depression as in how? As in he's carrying it around in his pocket?"

"Mummy, people have depression. It's a normal thing. He can get medications for it. He can also do talk therapy."

Her mother sniggers, in the way she does when she wants to begin a conversation by pointing out how little Sommy knows, how a child cannot see what an elder sees while sitting on the floor even if the child climbs the tallest tree.

"He literally didn't speak to me for two years," Sommy says. "All my time in Iowa, I called and called and he didn't even find it in his heart to pick up or reach out. Now that I'm back, he's acting like nothing happened."

"If you went abroad," her mother says, "and you stayed there for six years, working different jobs, just looking for a small break, but the break doesn't come, and instead you get arrested and deported, won't you be depressed?"

"I would," Sommy says patiently.

"Now, that happened to your brother. He came home depressed, and, in that confusion, he did something stupid."

"Mummy, attempting suicide is not something stupid."

"Please, Somkelechukwu, let me finish."

"Okay, ma, I'm listening."

Her mother's face in the moment, furrowed brows, wild eyes, is still. She's holding her breath as she does when she's irritated. After a while, she sighs, as if nobly choosing to avoid raising her voice, and then says, "There's no soul in this entire world who would not be depressed if they experience what your brother has experienced." She swipes a finger back and forth, emphasizing the rarity of the scenario. "But that he was depressed for a time does not mean he's a depressed person. Me, I've been depressed before. It doesn't mean I'm a depressed person. It doesn't mean that I need treatment."

"I agree," Sommy says, shifting, bracing to absorb her mother's outburst. "But that's not Mezie's situation. Mezie is a depressed person. He was depressed before he went to Norway. He was depressed in Norway, and he's depressed now."

Her mother's eyes shrink, and a moment passes before she says, "God forbid. My child is not a depressed person."

"Mummy, people just don't attempt suicide because they feel like it."

"Somkelechukwu, you are saying a lot of rubbish, and it's as if you are delighting in it, too."

"I do not find joy in any of this," Sommy says. "I just want to let you know what we are dealing with. It wasn't clear to me, too, for a while. Or maybe I didn't want to see it. I don't know which one. But it's clear now, and I know, and you should know, too. That way, we can join hands and do the right thing."

"The right thing?"

"Yes," Sommy says. "Let's encourage him to go to therapy. Talk to someone. Or even talk to us. He's just carrying everything inside himself. He looks like he'll just explode one day. Also, can we just stop pretending like everything is fine? You didn't have to rent him a three-bedroom apartment. You could have rented a one-bedroom apartment. You also don't have to throw this pointless thanksgiving party. It's like you are trying to prove something to yourself."

Her mother stands, snatches the blanket splayed on the couch beside her. "Florence," she calls. "When this person leaves, lock my door." She then turns to Sommy. "When you have disciplined this your wayward mouth, then come and talk to me. Until then, please stay in your brother's house. Bye." She walks past Sommy, and into the corridor.

Sommy sits quietly for a while, massaging her rage.

Florence, who Sommy's forgotten has been standing in the corner, asks, "Aunty, do you want me to get you more water?"

"I'm fine, thank you."

It's about two P.M. She has two free hours before Mezie comes to get her. She'd call Bryan but she doesn't want to wake him up. He'd been tired when she left. She hopes that her father will return soon. She's done with her mother for the day.

"Aunty," Florence says, shifting from the corner of the room where she's tucked herself all the while. "I want to ask you a question."

"Okay?" Sommy says.

"Is it true that in America everyone is rich?"

"No, Florence, America has poor people, too."

"Okay," Florence says, her face squeezed, as though constipated by the answer.

"Can I ask one more question?" She raises a finger.

"All right?"

"Is it true that in America everyone has a gun?"

"No," Sommy says. "Some people do, some people don't."

"Okay," Florence says, looking studiously about. "One more question, Aunty—"

"This girl, leave me alone!"

Sommy knocks on Aunty Dera's door. Aunty Dera, their next-door neighbor, was twenty-three and newly married when she moved into the apartment. In her early teens, Sommy spent most of her free time on Aunty Dera's bed, scouring through her makeup bag, reading her morning devotionals, scribbling rubbish in her journals. Aunty Dera taught her about boys and menstruation and lipsticks. It was Aunty Dera who first bought Sommy shawarma when everyone except Sommy and Mezie had eaten shawarma in her secondary school. Their relationship fizzled out after Aunty Dera birthed her first kid, Victoria. Sommy was sad for a short while, after which Amara came in and filled the empty space.

The door creaks open now. Aunty Dera thrusts her head out, squints, stares for a while. "Somkele, is that you?"

"Yes, Aunty."

"It's a lie!" Aunty Dera exclaims, unlocking the gate.

"It's me o!" Somkele sings, laughing.

"Look at you!" Aunty Dera says. "My American baby."

She pulls Sommy into a hug, releases her, does a little dance of joy, and pulls her into another hug.

"When I woke up today, I said to myself, today is a good day. I don't know how it will be a good day, but it will be a good day. Now, look, my baby girl shows up."

"Aunty, I've missed you o!"

"I've missed you, too, my darling."

They are now seated on the biggest of the four couches in the sitting room. The curtains are closed, leaving the room dim. This is as much home as her parents' apartment. She and Mezie had jumped on the couches, run up and down the room. They'd watched *Blood Sisters* and *Karashika* in this room.

"Victoria is still in school?"

"Yes, she'll be back any minute."

"I'm sure she's now a big girl."

"My dear, that girl is bigger than me. The other day, I asked her to go and do the dishes. Do you know what she told me? She said that it is a waste of her brain matter, that she could be doing more important things, like thinking up the cure for cancer."

Sommy laughs. Victoria was about five when Sommy left for Awka. Though her birth had separated Sommy from Aunty Dera, university life made it worse. When Sommy came back home during school breaks, she rarely visited Aunty Dera. There was the sense that they had infinite time, that if they didn't catch up now, they would catch up later. Years have passed, and *later* hangs between them like an accusation.

Aunty Dera asks about her studies. She seems the only one interested in what Sommy is doing in America. Her mother and father hardly ever ask about schoolwork. Sommy says school is fine. Hard, but fine. Aunty Dera taught English in a public school a few miles from the estate, and she'd always been an advocate for education. If Sommy were to speak of this tremendous ennui that sits on her chest whenever she's doing schoolwork, Aunty Dera would swing into problem-solving mode, and Sommy knows there's no solution to this problem. She's simply unable to convince herself that it matters, her going to school, reading all of these books. It feels pointless. She's tried to persuade herself to believe that there's some goal, some good it does in the world, but good that isn't quantifiable isn't convincing enough for her.

"You finally saw what I always knew was there," Aunty Dera says.

"Aunty—"

"I'm serious, Somkele. I am happy that you are finally believing in yourself, pursuing your goals. I know it's not an easy thing. They ask us women to be selfless. To forget ourselves and put other people in the center. You are not doing that. You are doing your master's in America. You are building your foundation, and it's not for anyone else. It's for you."

"Thank you, Aunty," Sommy says, trying to hide her discomfort. She cannot see the Sommy Aunty Dera talks of. "What's happening with you? How are you?"

"My dear, I am how you left me." She laughs weakly now. "But we are alive. That's what we ask from God these days. Life."

A year before Sommy's graduation from Awka, Aunty Dera's husband, Nnamdi, who lived in South Africa, where he worked an unspecified job, came back to Nigeria paralyzed. There were rumors that he'd been arrested and jailed for drug trafficking, but when the cells became jam-packed, he was injected with a drug that induced paralysis, and released afterward, an agonizing life sentence. Aunty Dera took care of him with the devotion of a nun, and though her relationship with Aunty Dera remained depthless, Sommy often thought of her with great sadness. A confusing shift happened when, a few weeks before Nnamdi's death, a year before she left for Iowa, Sommy saw Aunty Dera kissing a man by the staircase of their block. Sommy watched them for a while. He was tall and broad shouldered, this man. Sommy did not like the way he ran his hands up Aunty Dera's skirt. She did not like that Aunty Dera wasn't doing much with her hands, just standing there, letting him feel her up. She'd understand that scene better, in the first months of her arrival in Iowa. She'd understand why Aunty Dera stood there, taking cold warmth. She'd understand that the arc in her neck was that of lone-liness. But back then, Sommy had felt betrayed, overcome by a blind self-righteousness, and she'd let the incident further widen the distance between them.

The lights go off now, and Aunty Dera mutters, "Stupid NEPA." She walks to the window and swipes the curtain open. Harsh white light pours in.

Sommy still remembers clearly twenty-three-year-old Aunty Dera, sprightly and hungry. She'd been to most of the Nigerian states, and her next plan was to travel Africa. She was teaching, saving up money. Her husband was going to help, too. That twenty-three-year-old is nothing like this woman who's taking a seat before her now, in a faded blue wrapper, her relaxed hair combed backward, sticking out like chicken feathers. Did life just make people weaker? Did it just throw curveball after curveball until a person quietens, becomes muted?

"I said I should come and greet you," Sommy says.

"Give me your number ehnn? I'll be disturbing you from now. I want to know everything going on with you."

"Okay, Aunty."

Back at her parents' apartment, Sommy feels wistful, wistful about Aunty Dera. Aunty Dera had once been a shooting star, and she'd had the will. She moved with force, wished with force, and yet it seems to Sommy that her dreams now lie beneath the debris that gathers after rain, and it's evening now—the sun has come and gone.

Mezie is stuck in traffic, so he asks Patrick to drop her off. Her mother protests on hearing this. She doesn't like Patrick, she says. He's bad company. She offers to drop Sommy off instead. Sommy refuses. She wants to catch up with Patrick, she says, an attempt to further irritate her mother. She hates that her mother blames Patrick for Mezie's shortcomings.

"It's unfortunate that you people don't listen to me," her mother says, resigned.

"Mummy, I'll see you tomorrow," Sommy says.

"I have heard."

Sommy's at the door when Florence appears from nowhere.

"Aunty," Florence says.

"What is it, madam?"

"Can I ask one last question?"

"Okay, what?"

"Is it true that Americans don't shit?"

"Don't shit?"

"As in poo-poo?"

"Florence, every human being shits. Shitting is a normal human function."

Florence nods, rubs her jaw thoughtfully. "Okay."

Downstairs, Sommy walks through the cleared path flanked by wild grasses. There's a child sticking their head from the gated window of the middle flat of Block 225. Her childhood friend Benita used to live there, used to stick out her head in the same way while all the other neighborhood kids played ten-ten and suwe, games Benita thrived at before her mother birthed Susan, the youngest, and spiraled into schizophrenic disorder. Sommy wonders where Benita is now. She last saw her during a long holiday her first year of university, and they had a brief conversation, during which Sommy learnt that Benita was training to be a nurse, and that her father had finally divorced her mother. It was with Benita that Sommy had first seen love and resentment so finely balanced. Benita suffered greatly under the weight of her mother's schizophrenia. It was a usual thing back then to hear Benita's desperate screams ring out of their flat as her mother rained blows. And yet, even as a child, Benita was quick to differentiate the two dimensions of her mother, "the mummy before Susan," and "the mummy after Susan." She never could forget the mummy before Susan, who had been full of love, patient, warm. Sommy makes a mental note to look up Benita on Facebook.

Patrick claps his hands dramatically when Sommy opens the car door.

"Somkele, you don become big madam," he teases. "How did you grow all that ass in two years?"

She laughs. "Patrick, you still don't have sense?"

"I swear, this America is good on your skin. You just dey shine."

Sommy beats his chest playfully with the back of her palms. She buckles the seat belt and wipes the map of dust on her black jeans.

"It's good to see you," she says, smiling, meaning it.

"Good to see you, too."

She studies the changes in his face. His skin looks somehow tougher, dry and blotchy. He'd always been sort of weird-looking, with a square-shaped head and large eyes that seem like they could fall off his head if pressed. But in secondary school, he pulled all the girls. He had an unshakeable cool about him. He could dance and sing. He was good at football. He had a way of getting out of trouble whenever caught, so no one had any memory of him getting flogged, a major addition to his cool factor. He also had a way of staying mysterious. He was from a single-mother home, and he had no siblings. No one could figure out what was happening in his life, and he never told. It was a rare thing at their school, especially because most of the students lived in the estate, and the homes in the estate had thin walls, and everyone knew everyone's business. Sommy guesses this is the reason her mother easily paints onto him whatever suits her. His life seems like a blank canvas, ready to absorb any color, any image.

Sommy wonders if Patrick and Mezie's friendship has thrived all these years because they both share this ability to lock up their thoughts in a mental box.

"Mezie told me you now work at the UBA in LASU?" she says.

"Yes," he says. "I left Oceanic Bank. Better pay here."

"Nice," she says. "That means you are packing money now."

"Packing money? I wish."

"But the pay isn't bad, right?"

"With the inflation now?" He shakes his head. "Have you checked the naira-to-dollar exchange rate? It's four times what it was when you left. I remember changing dollars for you naa. I'm telling you, Naija don spoil."

"Everybody keeps saying 'Naija don spoil' as if I did not just leave the other day. I did not leave for too long. I know."

"A lot has happened in two years," he says. "It's nothing like what you left."

His tone is subdued. It is the same tone Amara adopts whenever she complains about the country. Sommy hates it, the alarm, the resignation. What she hears whenever they launch into their complaints is that she can never return home, that there's nothing here for her. It had not bothered her as much until she left for Iowa. It's one thing to hope for a better life somewhere else, and another to arrive at the hoped-for place, and be disillusioned by it. Where else to go then if home is on fire, and abroad is so icy cold it's unhabitable? Whenever she tries to say this to Amara, to say that nowhere is better than home, Amara is quick to shut her up—"You are saying this because you can leave, because you left"—so Sommy doesn't even try to bring it up with Patrick.

They drive through the estate gate, onto the main road, thick now with traffic and hawkers and pedestrians thronging the sidewalk, crossing the road, shopping from wooden stalls arranged haphazardly by the roadside. If she looks hard enough, she can see herself in any one of these pedestrians, for she has done all of these things so many times, the walking, the shopping. Her life used to revolve around these daily routines, but it will never be so again. She'll never live with her parents. They won't send her on errands. She'll never walk these sidewalks this way or stand by the road to haggle with a tomato seller. That chapter of her life is closed. It now belongs to Florence, who, one day, might drive down this road and think these same thoughts. It is a sad realization, that time passes, seasons come and go, and worthy experiences, very few of which are conceived as such in the moments of their creation, are often irretrievable.

Patrick winds down the car window, shoots his head out, and gently says to the bus driver trying to cut into the lane: "My guy, you think sey you fit squeeze this big bus inside this small space? Check am now? How e go work?"

The bus driver waves a cutting hand at Patrick. Sommy laughs. She finds it amusing that Patrick is trying to have a logical conversation with a man driving a beat-up bus, a man who's probably done the route over twenty times that day, and has had to evade harassment from touts, fight with passengers who wouldn't pay the complete fare, stop once or twice to fix the overheated bus engine, escape a policeman trying to arrest him for breaking an ambiguous traffic rule.

"Lagos has too many mad people," Patrick says, winding up the car window.

"Does that man look like someone who has patience for your big grammar?"

Patrick shakes his head. "This is why Nigeria will remain a zoo. Nobody follows the rules. Zero patience."

"Calm down, Oga," she says. "Don't start talking like Mezie."

Patrick had been the optimistic one. He'd wanted to be a businessman. He did not specify what business exactly he wanted to do, but he always talked about making it in Nigeria. He had no desire to leave, was never under any illusion that it was better somewhere else. In this, he differed from Mezie. Over the years, his optimism crinkled. Job loss after job loss, bad boss after bad boss, and he has heaved on the usual pessimism of Nigerians.

They soon escape the traffic, and she asks him how Mezie is doing.

"The best he can do with what this stupid country has to offer," Patrick says.

"I'm talking about his emotions, Patrick," Sommy says. "I am not talking about jobs and stuff like that. I am talking about his feelings. How is he feeling? Do you guys even talk about stuff like that?"

Patrick glances at her, as if to gauge her seriousness, and then looks stonily at the road.

"You have to take it easy on him," he says.

"Why does everyone keep saying this? Why would I want to stress him? I'm just trying to understand and help him."

"You are trying to fix him as if he's broken. He can feel it."

He pushes out the flesh of his cheek with his tongue to show that he's said all he has to say on the topic.

"But he's broken, isn't he?" she presses. "You were there. You saw what he did to his body. Why is everyone acting like that didn't happen?"

"It's in the past," Patrick says, his voice heavy with finality.

Patrick's discomfort is similar to her mother's, and Sommy wonders if this is what they all do, a survival mechanism: bury the uncomfortable, keep on trudging.

A long silence passes before Patrick says, "Mezie says you brought an American boy home."

"Surprise, surprise," Sommy says, making sure to steep her voice in sarcasm, to let him know she's aware he's purposely changing the topic. "I can pull a man."

"It's not fair o! Me too, I want an American boo."

"You have to stop your ashawo lifestyle first."

"I'm a changed man. I'm looking for a wife now. No more games."

"Story for the gods."

It's a Thursday afternoon, two days after the visit to her parents'. Mezie offers to drive Sommy and Bryan to the beach to meet with Amara. Sommy's wearing jean shorts and a yellow crop top. She's seated at the back, and Bryan's in the passenger seat, next to Mezie. She's done this intentionally. She wants the men to get along. But now she regrets it. The silence unnerves her. Early on the drive, Bryan had tried to get Mezie to talk about his experience in Norway, to bond over their global black-masculine experience of racism and isolation. Mezie had told stories of being followed around in stores, being yelled at by strangers to go back to his country, but Bryan, she was sure, had noticed in these stories skeletal clichés, prepackaged untruths, and to loosen Mezie, had told him that America was no better than the countries in Europe in how it dealt with racism. America, he said, thought that talking about a problem was the same as solving the problem. At least Europe did not pretend to care. He said that his perspective on race was unique because he grew up with two white brothers. He then said that if he were to dismiss the instances of second-class treatment, how whenever he went to restaurants with them, the waiter looked straight to one of his brothers to start taking their orders, or how in their all-white high school, he was considered hot, but his brothers, with whom he shared exact features, except, of course, skin color, were considered extra hot, what could not be dismissed, at least for him, was the constant awareness of his blackness in all spaces. It didn't matter whether the people around him cared; he carried around this awareness like a pistol, as if for protection. He began saying something about Du Bois and double consciousness when Mezie coughed. It was a shallow cough, the kind people do to keep from laughing. As if trying to expand the injury, Mezie began humming. Bryan said nothing and had been quiet ever since.

Now Sommy pulls out her phone and texts Amara: How close are you? Amara replies: I dey Iyano Oba, so give or take, I'll be there in fifteen minutes. Sommy texts back: Okay, because I need you. Mezie and Bryan are being weird and it's stressing me the fuck out. They are nearing Agbara when Amara texts: I got you, babe.

At the beach, they settle in a cool spot shaded by a palm tree. Sommy spreads a blanket on the warm sand, and lays out pockets of snacks: puff

puff, Ritz Crackers, strawberries. Mezie and Bryan sit quietly, watching the beach crowd. It's Bryan's first outing in Lagos. They talked about this aspect of the trip for a long time, in what Sommy thought was an effort to avoid talking about the other aspect of the trip: traveling to Amawbia to find his father. They made plans to go clubbing, shopping, sightseeing. Sommy had painted an idealistic Lagos, one birthed from her homesickness and nostalgia. She's anxious now for it to live up to that image, but Mezie's messing up her plans. He's on his phone, distracted. Not seeming to care at all that he's spoilt the atmosphere.

Amara soon arrives, a large black bag in hand, wearing black leggings and a white T-shirt tied in a knot at the back. She has on huge gold hoops and a pair of white wired earbuds snakes down her neck and chest. She looks even more beautiful than Sommy remembers.

"How are you so thin?" Sommy says, holding her in a tight embrace.

"My dear, it's Lagos stress. Person no fit fat for this Lagos."

Sommy and Amara sit next to Bryan, who has on his usual strained smile. Opposite them sits Mezie, whose countenance is uneasy. He now has on his dark shades and is crunching on a cracker. He's only regarded Amara's presence with a head nod.

Amara and Bryan exchange a handshake.

"Nice to finally meet you in person," Bryan says.

"Same o!" Amara exclaims. "We finally have the opportunity to turn you into a Lagos boy."

"I so want to be a Lagos boy," Bryan says, laughing.

Amara and Bryan had formed a wispy sort of friendship over Facebook Messenger, exchanging pleasantries, sending each other memes.

Amara turns to Mezie, says, "Why is this one wearing shades?"

Mezie chuckles, takes off the shades. "How are you?"

"I dey o. We dey hustle am for this Lagos."

"Na so," Mezie says.

His discomfort is palpable now. It's no longer the mocking nonchalance he's had with Bryan all day, it's something else, something heavy and urgent. Sommy wonders why, if he knew he was going to sulk, he'd offered to come with them. He could have stayed home, allowed her this good time.

Amara sets the contents of her bag on the blanket: a bottle of red wine and three wineglasses, and a bunch of red grapes.

"So how have you guys been enjoying Lagos?" Amara says.

"We've not done much," Sommy replies. "We are trying to make plans. You know what I want to do, though?"

"What?"

"I want to go to Angel Kids."

"What are you going to do at that dead school?"

"I don't know. I've missed it."

Amara laughs, picks up the wine bottle, and traps it between her thighs. "Is it not just two years you spent in this America? Why are you behaving like someone who was exiled for twenty years? Reaching back to your past?"

"Leave me, abeg. I missed the school."

It's strange, Sommy thinks now, strange how longing creates its own queer map, a map alien even to the one who longs.

"Imagine." Amara laughs, tries to get an arm around Sommy, who's staring at her wildly, embarrassed. "Visiting places that hold *childhood memories*."

Sommy elbows Amara, and goes to work on the bunch of grapes Amara set before her.

"How was she?" Bryan asks now. "In high school."

A breeze raises his shirt slightly, exposing the smooth hair around his navel, and his pale skin, untanned by the sun.

"We say 'secondary school' here," Amara says. "You know this is a British colony. The Queen is our spiritual leader."

"God, you are embarrassing," Sommy says, faking exasperation.

"Okay," Bryan says, hands in the air, "secondary school. What was she like?"

"Always fighting," Amara says, and then throws a glance at Sommy.

"That's a bloody lie." Sommy places a hand on Bryan's knee. "Babe, do not listen to her."

Bryan laughs, mock judgment spreading across his face. Mezie sniggers.

"I was a good kid," Sommy says.

"She was a good kid," Amara says, drawing Sommy back into her embrace. "My best person. My partner in crime."

In secondary school, Sommy did not have many friends, and for so long, she did not care. She went to Aunty Dera's after school, and whatever longing for friends she had, Aunty Dera cured. And then Victoria, Aunty Dera's daughter, came into the picture, around the same time Mezie got with his first girlfriend, Chisom, inside whom he so completely disappeared, and Sommy was left feeling completely alone. She thinks now that this way of hers to secretly pine, to never speak out loud a want, to rage over the want until the desire burns away and all that is left is ash and smoke, shadows of dead yearnings, emanates from that period of her life, when she yearned to be looked at, even if for a little bit. And Amara had finally looked at her, liked her. She realizes, as she watches Bryan and Amara go back and forth about the different images of her they know well—Amara insisting that she's hotheaded, Bryan that he's never met a gentler person— that Bryan affects her in the same way Amara affects her. With him, she feels liked. Not just loved. Love, she feels with Mezie, with her mother and father. But liked, enjoyed. It is Amara and Bryan who give her that.

Evening sprints forward. About them, people are sinking feet into the white sand, throwing themselves into the ocean. Children run about half-clothed. A man walks up and down the shore with a tray of fake jewelry, another perches by a tree, giving fake tattoos to young women dipping their feet into rebellion. And groups, like theirs, sit in circles, beside coolers of food and drinks.

Sommy can't wait to have Amara alone, so she pulls her away, and they take a walk down the shoreline, barefooted.

"He's too fine," Amara says of Bryan. "How are you able to breathe around him?"

"I am not," Sommy says. "I can't even believe he likes me."

"Abeg, don't say that. You are a whole catch." Amara, just like Kayla, is quick to dish out compliments. It's a quality so rare amongst women, Sommy realized in university in Awka, where girls tore each other down with their tongues.

They stand by one of the identical green huts that serve as shade for beachgoers. Beside them a lanky man kneels, taking shots of the ocean. The sun is receding, sinking into the clear blue water, and the sky is a conglomeration of gold and blue and purple, radiating a gorgeous alchemic shimmer. Amara asks if Bryan has brought up marriage. Sommy is prepared to tell her that she feels he might. He knows she has one more year in the three-year program, which means her F-1 status will expire, and she'll need to leave the country. She's sure he would do it, even if to keep her near him. But Amara launches then into her usual complaints of hating her job, hating her sister's husband, his tiring exuberance, and hating being unable to live on her own, of wanting to flee it all, leave the country, go where she can earn enough money to rent an apartment of her own.

"You know my biggest dream now?" Amara says. "I want to keep my headphones on the table, go to work, and come home to find my headphones on the table. I'll give anything for that."

"I want that for you, too," Sommy says.

She stares at Amara, and something in her face, something inexplicably sad, causes everything to take on an intense mood. There's the deep murmur of the ocean, and the fresh smell of salt, and the gentleness of the breeze. There's also laughter and music from the green huts, and bright yellow bulbs hanging from wires, doing now the sun's job.

"What were you saying? About Bryan?"

"Nothing," Sommy says, smiling.

Amara stands akimbo, and Sommy inserts an arm into one of the lopsided triangles, and they walk back to meet Mezie and Bryan.

Later that night, back from the beach, Sommy knocks on Mezie's bedroom door.

"Ehnn," he says, "come in."

She pushes the door open to find him on the bed, his laptop on his lap shining metallic light all over his face.

"How far?" she says.

"Chilling."

She walks to the table by the window, leans on it. The room is slightly bigger than the guest room. The mattress is queen-sized, a plain dark-blue bedsheet over it. The curtains, too, are dark blue, and they contrast sharply with the light-cream-colored tiles. It's the first time she's truly taking in the room. Mezie closes his laptop and asks if she needs anything. She takes a deep breath. What she's come here to really ask him is why they've floated back into easy, depthless conversations, circling around what had really happened, his mental breakdown, his repression after-ward, as though the past has no bearing on the present, even when every-thing they do now, preparing for their mother's thanksgiving party, preparing for Elin's arrival, reeks of the past. This is what she wants to ask, but she says instead: "Why are you giving Bryan a hard time?"

He places his laptop beside him and smooths his yellow shorts. "Because he's annoying."

"And you can't pretend for my sake?"

"So you agree that he's annoying?"

"No. But you have a right to feel how you want to feel. You don't have to like him, but you have to at least try to make him comfortable."

"Okay, but will you tell him to stop trying to relate to me because I do not relate at all."

"Why are you so angry?"

"Oh, so now I'm angry?"

"Yes, you are angry."

"Because I don't want your rich white boyfriend to keep stressing me with his 'black people are the downtrodden' talk like he knows shit about what he's talking about? And why the fuck is he speaking academese to me? Du Bois? Double consciousness? What's that?"

"First, he is not white. Second, he is trying to connect with you."

"I don't care."

"You are being unreasonable."

He turns to look at the clock behind him, and then stands. "I have an early morning tomorrow."

"You know what?" she says, full-on vexed now. "Have it your way. We will go and stay with Mummy and Daddy."

"Fine," he glares

"Fine," she glares right back.

She bangs the door on her way out.

Back in the bedroom, Bryan is on the phone with his mom. He gives Sommy a conniving look when she walks in. Catherine is probably drilling into him one of her many facts about Nigeria. She'd tried to educate him before this trip, insistent that he not become an ignorant American expatriate. She'd read a lot of literature about the country, Catherine told him, especially when she'd first gotten with his father. Bryan of course did not tell her the real mission of the trip. She thinks it an ordinary summer vacation.

Sommy sits beside Bryan, rubs his shoulder.

"Catherine says hi," he says after he's ended the call.

"Aww."

"She wants me to buy her a sculpture of Oshun."

"The Yoruba goddess?"

"Yes."

"What for?"

"Something to do with this Ifa-worshipping thing her friend, Sharon, got her into."

Sommy laughs. "I just can't. Your mother is hilarious."

"She gets into the most ridiculous things."

He pulls her into an embrace now, buries his nose in her neck. They are both sweaty. She can feel the grittiness of beach sand on her skin.

"Did you have fun today?" she asks.

"Amara is fun. I like her."

Sommy reaches into the back of her top to fish out grains of sand. "She wants me to visit her office tomorrow so we can fully catch up."

"That sounds like fun."

"You'll come with me?"

"No, you girls should catch up."

"Maybe spend time with Mezie?"

"You know how I said before that his aggression has nothing to do with me? I don't think so anymore. I really think he hates me."

"He's being protective," she lies.

"I know the difference between a man marking his territory and a man just straight-out hating. He doesn't like me."

"I like you," Sommy says, curling her arms around his neck.

He slides his palms down her hips and jacks her up. She strings her legs around his waist, and heaves up a bit, so that she's looking down at him. She buries her mouth in his, a soft kiss. He drops her onto the bed and begins to unbutton his shirt rapidly. She doesn't undress. He likes to do the undressing, slowly. It's part of the foreplay, he says. He kisses her neck, her chest, her left boob. He slips her dress from her shoulders, waist, legs, and takes his finger between her legs. He rubs her clitoris, while biting a nipple. He does this until she expands and there's no more of her left. He then turns her to her back, slides his penis in, and starts to thrust. It's not too long before he comes. In the period after the Bayo incident, they would have long, nervy sex. Bryan would pull out multiple times, hold the head of his penis to keep from coming, bruising her on penetration. She hated it. But she couldn't complain, scared as she was to make him feel even the tiniest bit unsettled. Slowly, over the past months, he's relaxed into sex with her, and she's seeing that there's much to like about sex with him—the small, lovely size of his penis slides easily into her vagina, leaves her without bruises when he isn't trying too hard to last long, his grip on foreplay, his eagerness to use her vibrator when she asks. She does sometimes miss the kind of animal sex she and Bayo used to have. That endless, hungry pounding. With Bayo, she had not been eager to please, so she demanded things. *Choke me. Pull my hair.*

Bryan lies next to her now, facing the ceiling, a longing expression on his face, and he says, "I'm aware that I'm disarming. People like me because I look safe. But there are people who don't like me exactly because of that. They can see that it is unfair, the way people relax around me. I think your brother is one of them. He doesn't like me because I'm likable, and I think that's fair."

She takes her hand to his face, and he scoots closer to her, and places his head on her neck bone.

"I don't think it's fair," she says.

She's looking at the ceiling, but she can feel that he's smiling. He likes that she's on his side.

The style of Amara's office is typical of modern offices on the Island—white lights, white tiles, fancy décor like diffusers and flower-shaped table lamps, an overdone bourgeois air. It was the same way at Sommy's former office where she worked as a sales representative before her admission to James Crowley. Her boss, a bald man with a face that reminded one of a tortoise's—head so small, eyes so pinched, an alarmingly small nose that was mostly nostrils—had an irritating obsession with appearance. He penalized the gatemen for wearing rumpled uniforms. He mandated them to greet all the customers who walked in with an enthusiastic: "Welcome to Life Code Luxury. We appreciate your presence." Female members of staff had to have on makeup and high heels, even those who did not have contact with the customers. He did not bring this obsession to the quality of the perfumes they sold. He bragged often of the high profit margin. He believed that people bought the idea of a thing, and not the thing itself. Status mattered. She hated him, hated the starkness of his vanity. She hated that he excused the cruel ways he treated the members of his staff with quotes from Robert Greene's *48 Laws of Power*. In business, he said often, all is fair.

"Why didn't you bring Bryan?" Amara asks now.

They are seated in the lobby on a plush mauve sofa, facing a center table decorated with roses and stacks of Dior coffee-table books.

"He wanted me and you to have alone time."

Sommy can hear the rush of work life happening in the main office, the sound of chairs scraping against the floor, the droning of a printer, the measured voices of people engaged in officious conversations.

"We'll go inside soon," Amara says. "Please, just put on your posh girl vibes. I want them to know that you are an 'I Just Got Back.' I'm serious. Force an American accent if you must, please."

"You know you don't have sense, abi?"

Amara tilts her head, as if in defeat. "Insult me later. But please, for now, just do it."

Sommy laughed when Amara told her about the office drama in which she's currently embroiled. In a bid to climb up the office hierarchy, Sewa, the new girl on the accounting team, has started a beef with Amara. According to her, around their colleagues, Sewa is polite and civil, but when alone with Amara, she's cold, snobbish. Amara had been determined to ignore her, but Sewa has recently taken it a step further. She's begun inviting their colleagues for lunch, organizing pedi and mani dates, and she makes certain to exclude Amara. Now, the girls all share jokes and stories that Amara isn't privy to.

"She's trying to ostracize me and she's succeeding," Amara said on one of their phone calls.

Sommy's here as evidence that Amara is not desperate for friends—she has friends, and not just ordinary friends, but abroad friends, whom she doesn't need to buy over with food and mani dates.

The main office is an open space with rows of desks and chair. Sommy tries hard not to make eye contact with Amara's colleagues as she walks in, but she feels their eyes burrowing into her. When they reach Amara's desk, Amara makes a show of pulling out a seat.

"Welcome to my little office," she says.

Sommy smiles stiffly to keep from laughing. She finds the entire show both ridiculous and moving. She'd been here not too long ago, wanting to show off Kayla and Nia to her classmates, to the whole of Iowa, to announce that she's loved, liked, that she's cool. How desperately she envied some of the girls she saw at the café, or at the mall, girls who walked around with hordes of friends, all of them chattering, laughing. Sommy is thinking now, as Amara asks if she'd like a cup of coffee or tea, that a person exists only in relation to the people around them. Descartes had gotten it all wrong: "I think, therefore I am." No—people see me, people like me, therefore I am. She's also thinking this: that one can be a foreigner even when at home.

Amara leaves and returns soon with a cup of plain black coffee. She then asks very loudly if Sommy is still leaving for New York in two weeks. It's a few seconds before Sommy realizes that Amara has said New York and not Iowa because New York carries a stronger whiff of sophistication.

Sommy crosses her leg, says, in her thickest American accent, that she and Bryan might be going to New York first, and then Chicago later.

The statement elicits the right effect. There's the sound of shuffling, a throat being cleared. Sommy's eyes are fixed on Amara's forehead, but she knows that more and more people are turning to peek at her. She's glad that she's dressed for this, a white crop top, faded blue mom jeans, and white Adidas sneakers. On her head are the black Versace sunglasses Bryan gifted her on Valentine's Day. To her mind, she looks very American.

"My lunch break is in thirty minutes," Amara says, wheeling her chair closer to the Mac desktop computer. "I'll send a few receipts and then we will go do lunch."

Sommy nods, and blinks back tears of laughter. Amara's eyes stretch with glee. She, too, is trying to keep from laughing.

While Sommy waits, she takes in the office—an office of about fifteen, twelve women, two men. Each with their desk and computer. There's a door a few feet from Amara's desk with a gold nametag, MANAGING DIRECTOR OLUSEGUN SAMUELS, and right next to it, another leading to the restrooms. The office is quiet now, alive only with the clicking of keypads, someone occasionally rummaging a bag of chips, and the printer sizzling awake. Sommy hopes that Amara gets the opportunity to point Sewa out to her.

And the opportunity does come, as Amara clears her desk of paper and pens and phone cords. A girl, tall and thin, dark-skinned, walks to the desk, says, "Getting ready for lunch?"

In response, Amara forces a taut smile, and Sommy doesn't need to be told that it is Sewa standing in front of her.

Sewa smiles an equally taut smile, and then brings her gaze to Sommy, a very uncomfortable head-to-toe sweep. "Amara, introduce me to your friend naa."

"Oh," Amara says with indifference. "Meet Sommy."

Sommy nods and does a strange thing with her lips. She ought not to seem too friendly.

Sewa stretches her hand, and Sommy takes it.

"Nice to meet you," they say in unison.

Sewa takes her palm back slowly and cradles it in the other, and then says, "Nice shades."

"Thanks," Sommy replies, rippling with an ancient fear. Beautiful, affecting women who know that they are beautiful and affecting destabilize her. Sewa destabilizes her. Even more so because Sewa oozes a rugged sadness. She's the kind of woman who doesn't cry, who responds to pain with anger. She keeps the world at a distance, a towering wall between her and everything else. She's the kind of woman Sommy wants to be, controlled and injuring, and perhaps Amara does, too, which is why they both flutter uneasily now.

Another girl, as if spurred by Sewa, walks toward them. She's short, with a full, beautiful face. Sewa regards her with a quick nod, and the girl smiles coyly, and then turns to Amara says, "Is this the friend of yours doing her master's in America?"

Amara says, "Youp."

"Nice, nice."

Sewa asks what it is Sommy's studying. Sommy says, and Sewa says she, too, is applying to schools in the United States.

The short girl adds that she's applying, too.

"Everyone is trying to leave this country," Sewa says.

The short girl says, "You can say that again."

Sewa turns to Sommy, asks if she can get her number. She has questions about the application process. She's thinking about doing something tech-related. Tech is the future, but she'd like Sommy's input still.

Amara jerks up, says, "Unfortunately, Sommy is yet to get a Nigerian SIM card, and is currently not reachable."

Sewa says, "She can speak for herself, can't she?" She does this with a smile, that fake corporate smile that had filled Sommy's life at one point.

"Oh no," Sommy says. "She's allowed to speak for me."

Sewa's face straightens, and she stares right into Sommy's eyes for a few seconds before walking away.

The short girl purses her lips, begins to fiddle with a strand of her curly wig. Sommy imagines her narrating the details of this event to the other girls, embellishing, miming, suffusing their otherwise boring day with ripe gossip. Sommy's thinking now that it matters, the minutiae of office life, gossip, hierarchies that hold no real power, but are, for them, power. And how necessary this thing called power is, even in the briefest relations. Look at all of them jostling for it, bending, twisting, and folding.

Outside the gate, now out of character, Sommy begins to laugh. "Did you see her face? That was so mean. Oh dear—I can't believe how mean I was."

"Isn't she stupid? Like what did she expect? That you will give her your number?"

"Crazy," Sommy says.

"Crazy," Amara echoes, her eyes shining with victory.

Later that evening, aching with fatigue from sitting in a two-hour-long traffic jam, but still reeling with wicked joy from the drama with Amara and Sewa, Sommy relates it all to Bryan. She notices that he is distracted, but she keeps going, thinking it's his abiding irritation with Mezie's behavior. She's not told him that she'd threatened Mezie with moving out because she doesn't want to leave yet, and she's aware that Bryan wants to leave. He'd brought it up to her the other day, said: "Babe, we could actually stay in a hotel. It will be like a little sweet vacation." She'd not replied, and sensing her resistance, he dropped it. She holds out hope still that on this trip, she'll catch Mezie with his walls down, and they'll take a painful walk down memory lane, asking and answering questions that'll bring them a little closer to each other.

While she's still speaking, she notices that Bryan is packing. She pauses. "Did Mezie say something to you while I was gone?"

He turns to her, frowning. "No, why?"

She nods toward the open bag. He looks about confused, and then says, "Oh, yes, I'm packing for the trip."

It's in three days, the trip to Amawbia. Sort of too early to begin packing, Sommy thinks. "Feeling excited?"

"Excited?" he chuckles.

She's intuitively avoided talking to him about the impending trip. It's what has gotten them this far into this strange expedition, that they've both deftly shunned the reality that what stands between Bryan and a truth he's longed for all his life is a little bit of time.

"Nervous, then," she says.

"Definitely nervous."

She places a hand on his back, swipes it up and down. "You'll be okay. I'm here."

He smiles, gathers her hands, and brings her knuckles to his lips. He then continues folding shirts into the bag.

Later that night, he turns to her in the dark, groping. She yields to his caresses, and he soon abruptly stops.

"I'm sorry," he says, slumping onto the bed.

She wants to say something of great comfort, something wise, but she feels empty of words. She just lays there with him in silence, feeling his anxiety like a cord twisting between them.

The day before the trip, Sommy's mother calls, asks that she visits.

"For what, Mummy?" Sommy asks.

"I want to discuss something with you."

"Why don't you discuss it over the phone?"

Silence, and a sigh. "Stop being silly and do as I say."

Sommy knocks on Mezie's door and asks if she can use his car. He says he has somewhere to be with it later in the day. She asks that he drop her off then.

"Can't you call an Uber?" he says bitingly. "I'm busy."

Sommy stares furiously at the top of his head until he closes his laptop, says, "Fine, I'll drop you off."

On the drive, they are both silent, evidently angry. They've gotten past the glossy part of their reunion where he tries to keep on a mask of normalcy, and she, just like her mother, helps him hold the mask in place.

At their parents', smiling Florence opens the door. "Welcome, ma. Mummy is in the room."

Sommy pats her head fondly, and they walk to her mother's room.

Her mother is in front of a giant table, which functions as both a work desk and a vanity, fumbling through her beauty things, getting ready to leave for her shop.

"Ehen, you've come," she says, as Sommy shuts the door.

"Good morning," Sommy says, taking in the room. Bags hang on the wall by one of the only two windows. Clothes hang from nails in unexpected places, for her mother won't keep frequently used clothes in the wardrobe, says the enclosed space leaves an odor. There's the giant table, where her mother haphazardly arranges books and receipts on one side, and on the other, a hairbrush, makeup, a large Vaseline tub. By the bed are magazines, books, and pamphlets her mother wants to read but never gets around to, so they lie in a pile in the shape of a falling bridge. Sommy thinks the room overwhelming. For her mother, it is a sanctuary, over twenty years of moving toward her own sense of comfort.

"How are you preparing for the trip?" her mother says.

"I'm just escorting Bryan. I'm not doing any preparation."

"I think you should," her mother says. "Just in case you people truly find the man. You want to be prepared to impress. Remember he is your father-in-law."

"Mummy, I don't think so. The man doesn't matter. At least in my opinion. So there's no need to impress him."

"What do you mean he doesn't matter?"

"He can't just show up after twenty-eight years and start to have opinions about who Bryan is dating. I don't think impressing him is something I should worry about."

"A person's father is a person's father."

"Well, I don't think so."

Her mother is done tying her scarf. She turns to Sommy now, says, "Blood is blood. You can't argue that."

Sommy is quiet, listening for her father in the other room. She imagines that he is reclined on the bed, the day's newspaper spread in front of him like a curtain.

Her mother stands, peers into the mirror. "I like Bryan," she says. "I like him for you. I can see that he is a patient man and that he cares about you." She puts up a finger. "But what I appreciate most is that he can take care of you. You will not suffer if you marry him."

Sommy feels compelled to protest. "I don't care about his money."

"Biko, shut up. That is not what I said. I'm just saying that it is important that he has the money to take care of you. What is bad in saying that?" She raises her shoulders and brings them down forcefully in disdain. "This America has changed you. Any small thing now and you want to argue." She picks up her worn black handbag and hangs it over her shoulder. "Please come and be going so I can lock up my room."

"Why do you lock your room?"

"I don't want that Florence girl coming in here to do whatever she likes when I'm at the shop." She pauses, stares at Sommy. "Why are you still standing there? Biko, leave my room."

"Wait, is this why you called me? To tell me to impress Bryan's father?"

"Yes. That's my duty as a mother. I have to make sure you understand the importance of these things."

"You could have told me this over the phone," Sommy grumbles.

Her mother drops her off at Mezie's. She tiptoes into the room, where
Bryan is snoring softly. He's been sleeping an unusual amount, strained
from nervousness, and she wishes there was something she can do to
help him. She's about to take off her clothes when she hears a noise
coming from the balcony. She walks out of the room, stands in the
sitting room for a while, tries to piece together the voices. Perhaps it's
Patrick and Mezie, doing whatever it is men do when they get together.
She opens the net door, and before her is Chisom, Mezie's ex-girlfriend,
who she's not seen in three years. Her once chubby face is now almost
gaunt, in a way that makes Sommy think it'd been a deliberate weight
loss, and perhaps it was deliberate—she'd struggled with her weight
back then, counting calories, taking long walks.

Sommy nods at Mezie, says she'd heard voices and came out to check.
He is shirtless, with just shorts on. His legs are slightly apart, and his
hands hang lazily between them. He looks relaxed.

"Long time," Chisom says.

"Long time," Sommy says.

Sommy briefly turns to inspect the still night, the houses dotted with
light bulbs. She hadn't known that Mezie and Chisom were still in
touch. After he left for Norway, Chisom had disappeared. When she'd
asked about Chisom during a phone call with him, Mezie said vaguely
that it was complicated. Elin then came into the picture, and she needed
not ask anymore. It seemed quite clear. But now she's confused seeing
them this way.

"I'll be leaving," Chisom says, standing. "Good night, Somkele."

Sommy shoots her a rigid smile. It has always been this way with
them, tense, gritty with unspoken rebukes.

"I'll walk you," Mezie says, follows behind.

Sommy takes Chisom's seat and looks emptily into the night. The breeze, the dark sky, the silence, is comforting. Since her return, it's been impossible to find alone time, to just sit still in the dark, thinking useless thoughts.

The door soon creaks open and Mezie appears. He's holding a bottle of water, which he offers her now. She collects it, cracks it open, and takes a sip.

He stands still for a bit, contemplative, and then sits.

"Chisom?" she says.

He shrugs, takes the bottle from her, and gulps.

"Does she know about Elin? Does she know she's coming?"

"She understands," he says.

"Does she, though?"

"I have been totally honest with her."

There's silence, and then she says, "Is she hoping to be your Nigerian wife or what? Is this like a weird undying-love situation?"

"We are just friends."

Sommy chuckles. "Friends?"

"She understands me is all."

"Anyone can understand you if you explain yourself to them."

"I wish," Mezie says, and crosses his legs.

She wants to say, "Remember when I was the only one who understood you?"

"I think you should see a professional," she says now.

"Professional what?"

"Person to talk to."

She doesn't want to say the word "therapist," to make him feel indicted.

He cradles his jaw. "I don't have to talk to anyone."

"What happened—"

"What happened?" he says now, daring her. "What is it that happened?"

She stares at him. Of course, she cannot say it to him. She's entrapped in the same fear and illusion she accuses her mother and Patrick of. If a person has created a story that makes their pain fathomable, who is she to pull it apart?

He rubs his forehead and stares into the night, at the apartment beside theirs, from where, every morning since her return, she watches a woman walk two toddlers to a black jeep and wave until the car is out of sight. She thinks now that she should ask him if he's angry with her, angry that she'd seen him so terribly out of control, that she'd witnessed those years before he left for Norway, the hopeful cloud that hovered above him after his university graduation, hope that chipped, and then got mauled, year in and year out, as he walked the streets of Lagos and then Abuja and then Port Harcourt, looking for a job, and finding none—looking and finding nothing, the music of his life—those days of searing rage, of coming home drunk and lying on the floor of the sitting room, legs and hands thrust out in total defeat, days of darkness, for he'd done everything right, he'd applied for jobs, worn his good shirt to interviews, smiled his most impressive smile, all to futility; he'd done everything right and had failed, so he came home to them, the star boy no longer the star boy, and he stole money from their mother's purse, and drank to stupor in nearby beer parlors, as though wanting his degeneration documented by the same neighbors who had watched him walk to school in his polished black shoes and well-ironed uniform when he was nine, and thirteen, and sixteen, neighbors who had hailed him, who had called him "Brain" when he came home victorious after a state or national mathematics competition, and who had, with heads thrown back, an exaggerated look of surprise on their faces, said to him when he came home during school breaks and holidays while still a student at Awka, "Mezie, you are growing bigger and bigger. Don't forget us when you make it." Did he hate her for knowing this? For being amongst those who had thought of him as the light, a light that would someday burst and spread for everyone to bask in, an expectation that hung above him like a guillotine, a little sleep, a little slumber, and it comes crashing.

There's the time to ask him. This time of low energy, with the world asleep, and his face somber, as if in deep thought. There's the time to ask, and the time passes, and she doesn't ask.

On the flight to Enugu, Bryan and Sommy sit separately, and for this she's grateful. For the next hour, she can be alone with her thoughts. The woman beside her is mostly asleep. Halfway into the flight, the woman jerks awake, as though coming out of a nightmare. She stares at Sommy bewilderedly for a moment, before turning to the window and staring at the long, white wing of the plane. She does not speak to Sommy, and Sommy does not speak to her, but the silence isn't awkward. The woman seems to be one of those people attuned to the feelings of others. Sommy is certain of this when the woman turns to her as they alight, and says, with a small smile: "You look like Omotola Jalade." Sommy doesn't think that she looks like the actress, and from the lazy way the woman says this, she can sense that she doesn't think so, either, or doesn't care, that the woman says this now, at the end of their journey, to let Sommy know that she'd kept to herself during the flight because she'd gotten the feeling that Sommy wanted her to keep to herself.

The air in Enugu is clean, easily breathable, but they leave quickly to Awka, where the atmosphere is different: everything coated in red dust, the air thick, sliceable. On the ride, Bryan is engrossed in taking pictures with his Canon, which he'd not pulled out until this trip. He takes pictures of trees, and the small pockets of tables and kiosks where people splay bananas and pineapples and tubers of yams for sale. He takes pictures of an ashy old man riding a bicycle on the side of the road, and another of some herdsmen and the cows trailing beside and behind them.

"This is peculiar," he says to her. "These images. It is unique to here. And I'm thinking that if I hadn't come, I wouldn't have experienced it. Isn't that crazy and a little sad? Thinking of all the places and all the things we can't experience, won't experience."

She can see clearly that he's trying to hide his nervousness with the chattering and photographing, and she goes along with the act, agreeing, complimenting the pictures he takes. She's unable to let herself fully enter her nostalgia. It's been five years since she was last in Awka, and the place has hardly changed, still with its blistering heat, its congested bus stops, its mad drivers, its bright, bright food stalls of fresh fruits.

When they get to the hotel room, shower, and lie quietly side by side, she asks how he's feeling.

"Anxious, I suppose," he says.

She takes his hand in hers. "Babe, it will be fine."

He starts to say something, but swallows it, and nods instead.

Her heart breaks a little, and she moves closer to him. "What's the worst outcome you can think of?"

He slips a finger into her squeezed palm. "That he won't regret leaving me?"

"But you'll at least know, right? Be at peace? No longer continue to search?"

"I guess you are right," he says, burying his face in her chest, a gesture she thinks so, so epically sad.

Their driver, a man Amara had recommended, peppers them with questions about getting into college in America. He wants Bryan to mentor his son, Jidenna, who, according to him, is the best student in his school, getting all As in his WAEC, and even winning a statewide debate competition.

"The boy has potential," the driver says. "I don't want Nigeria to kill his dreams."

Sommy studies the man's face from the rearview mirror, dark and deeply wrinkled, a lived-in face.

Bryan asks the driver if he's thought about enrolling Jidenna in SAT lessons. He says that it is the first step to getting into an American college.

The driver nods, says he'll look into it, but he doesn't own a smartphone, although he is saving money to buy one for Jidenna. In the meantime, he says, he would be extremely grateful if Jidenna could contact Bryan for next steps.

Bryan says, sure, that Jidenna can call him anytime.

Sommy watches the two men quietly. She's the only one of the three of them who knows what applying to an American college as an international student entails, yet she's not asked a thing. She files it in her depository of things she plans to bring up to Bryan when he's happier, finally reunited with his father. She'll ask if he notices that whenever he's around her, she disappears to other people.

The house is a yellow duplex with white window frames. From outside, it seems the sort of house people who live in two-bedroom apartments in Lagos or Abuja save up money to build: a real village house with an unpainted, unfinished fence, surrounded by trees, the house next to it blocks away. A home big enough to house a family when everything goes awry in the city. It is neither extravagant nor plain. It is the sort of house Sommy's father had built a few years ago, after he'd been paid his pension in full, a few million naira. The exterior of her father's house is made to finish, but inside, the door handles are broken, the toilet bowl has no seat, the kitchen no windows, the staircase no rails.

They've hired the driver for the day, so he parks at the corner of the street, and says he's going to look for a place to pee.

Bryan, who's leaning on the car door, nods but doesn't move. There's no one about, and the sun is awfully bright, and everything is still, not even a leaf flutters. Sommy pulls out a sunscreen tube and applies it. She passes it to Bryan, but he takes it and mindlessly puts it in his jeans pocket. She looks keenly at him then, and she's taken aback by the fear on his face.

She takes his palm in hers. What to say to him that she hasn't already said?

"You want me to go in first?" she says.

He says yes in a barely audible voice.

"Okay. I'll tell whoever I see first that I'm here to see Dr. Chike Diobi?"

"Yes," he says.

"When I see him, I then come get you?"

He nods, wipes sweat from his forehead. "I'll be here."

As Sommy walks into the compound, she thinks briefly that she won't at all be surprised if she comes back for Bryan and he isn't there.

A boy of about ten opens the front door, shirtless and breathless.

"What?" the boy says angrily.

Sommy frowns. She wants to scold him, ask if he has no respect, but she remembers that her mission is an important one.

"Is there a grown-up I can talk to?" she says.

"What am I to you?" the boy says, standing fully now, his chest broader.

"A child," Sommy says. "A child who I can give a very painful knock on the head."

The boy squeezes his nose at her, says, "Wait here," and then scrambles away.

About five minutes pass before a woman comes to the door. She's middle-aged, heavy, but with youthful eyes.

"Yes," the woman says of Sommy's enquiries. "This is Dr. Diobi's house. Is there a problem?"

"We want to see him," Sommy says.

The woman leans forward, a hand on the door rail, her head poking out, looking for the other part of the "we."

"Myself and my friend," Sommy says, not thinking it appropriate to call Bryan her boyfriend in this instant.

"What for?" the woman says in a firm but kind voice.

Sommy sucks in spit. "To talk," she says. It's the only reply she can come up with.

The woman steps back and takes a sweeping look at Sommy. Sommy had tried to look as neutral as possible, as imperceivable as a plain sheet of paper, grudgingly heeding her mother's advice. She's wearing a black knee-length dress and flat sandals with gold buckles. Her braids are packed in a bun. Her face is bare, no makeup, small stud earrings for a little brightness. Her hope is that if she meets Bryan's father today, he'll be unable to read her, to have so little information with which to judge her.

"Talk about my research," Sommy says. "I'm a former student of his."

The lie is spontaneous, and when the woman moves to the side to let Sommy in, she feels a rush of fear. This is something Amara would do, she thinks. Lie effortlessly. Plunge into the unknown with bravery. This is not her.

She had thought wrongly. The house is not at all like her father's. The interior is rich and wooden, something out of a bougie late-nineties Nollywood movie. The sofa is gold-rimmed, and there are two golden statues of a leaping lion. The pillows are made of gold tassels, as are the curtains, which flow onto the white-tiled floor. Sommy stands humbly on the tiger-print center rug, onto which yellow lights from the chandelier pour.

"Sit," the woman says.

What is she to say when Dr. Diobi walks out? Is she to blurt out: "Sir, your son is outside waiting for you"?

The woman studies her quietly for a minute and then disappears through a door and comes back out in a short minute with a glass of water.

"When was the last time you heard from Dr. Diobi?" She says as she hands the glass of water to Sommy.

Sommy squints, trying hard to keep her act intact, but her heartbeat is rapid, and despite the cool air-conditioned air, she feels terribly hot. "I'm going to be honest with you, ma." She puts down the glass. "My friend who is outside waiting has sent me here to confirm that this is Dr. Diobi's house. He thinks that Dr. Diobi is his father. We are not sure about anything. We have a name and an address. But the details are complicated. We just want to ask Dr. Diobi a few questions."

The woman's hand finds the knot of her wrapper, a quick squeeze. Her face is blank. There's no way to tell what she's thinking.

"Why is he outside, this friend?" she says.

"He is nervous."

The woman nods, an understanding, gentle nod. And something about that nod relaxes Sommy. She feels immediately that she can trust this woman, so she says, "He is my boyfriend."

The woman doesn't seem moved by this confession. She asks Sommy to go bring Bryan in. She wants to see him.

Bryan is pacing when Sommy reaches him.

"Is he the one?" he says, eyes wide with fear.

She walks to him and pulls out the sunscreen from his pocket. She smears a blob on his face as she tells him, in slow, tepid words, that the woman, who she thinks is Mrs. Diobi, wants to see him.

He lifts her hand away from his face. "I think we should leave."

"Bryan—"

"I don't think I can do this."

"Bryan," she says, again. "Hey."

He is not listening to her. He gets into the car and starts speaking rapidly to the driver. Sommy is confused. Had all this been for nothing? She knocks on the car window, and Bryan winds it down.

"Babe," he says. "Please get in."

"You can leave," she says. "I'm going back in to find out."

His eyes dilate. Sommy looks away. She feels lacking, lacking in compassion and love for him in this moment. She cannot stand him this way, small and scared. She starts to walk away furiously, a kind of mad anger taking over. She swings open the gate. She hears footsteps behind her, but she doesn't look back. She's almost at the door when she feels Bryan's presence.

The woman is silent upon seeing Bryan. It is the silence of shock. Her eyes move from Bryan to the picture above the mantelpiece by the dining table, which Sommy hadn't noticed earlier. It is the picture of a man dressed in a black suit and a red bow tie. It is undeniable, the resemblance between the two men, the same wide head, the flat, impertinent nose, the charged eyes.

The woman asks them to sit. Bryan waits for Sommy to sit, and then sits beside her.

"So you say Chike is your father?" the woman says, a finger pressed to her lips.

"That's what I was told," Bryan says with a shaky voice, even shakier palms.

The woman is staring at him as though on his forehead lay the answer to a puzzle. "Who told you this?"

"My mother went to college with him in Chicago. He got her pregnant and left shortly after. I never met him. I just want to talk to him."

The woman looks at him, her eyes demure now, and says, "I'm his wife. He's never said anything about you. But you are clearly Chike's son."

Bryan bows his head. Time slows. Sommy watches the streak of light pouring through the window slit, leaving lines of shimmer on the center table. She thinks now that she's watching a marriage end, a marriage of twenty or ten or five years.

"Can I meet him?" Bryan says.

The woman clears her throat. Sommy looks up. The woman is hugging herself now, as if cold. Sommy had expected some sort of collapsing, screaming, expected her to march them out of her home, but she's only looking at them with firm eyes.

She tells them to come with her. They walk through a door, past a cold corridor, and into a dark room.

The woman turns on the light to reveal a man sitting on a chair by the window, his naked, frail back turned to them.

"Chike," the woman says. "Kedu?"

She goes over to him, places a gentle hand on his shoulder. He turns to her, smiles, covers her hand with his. It's a while before he turns to look at Sommy and Bryan. He's a shrunken version of the man in the picture, and of Bryan. It is more startling in person, the resemblance. Sommy thinks it a cruel trick of nature, to be so completely, visibly, connected to someone who has never claimed you. And she knows, from the vacuous quality of the man's eyes, that there will be no claiming happening today. She moves closer to Bryan and slips her hand in his.

The woman waves for Bryan to come over.

"Someone is here to see you," she says to the man. "Nwa gi. Your child."

The man continues to smile at Bryan. The words mean nothing, stir nothing. They are standing face-to-face now, father and son. Bryan's face is swollen and red and he's breathing noisily.

"You are a few months late," the woman says. "In January, he had weeks when he remembered some things."

"He never told you anything about me?"

The woman shakes her head. "Ten years together and a son, and he never said a thing."

Bryan sucks in his lower lip, says, "That's all right." And then starts to walk to the door.

He turns at the door, says to the woman, "Thanks for your time. Very kind of you to let us into your home. I am sorry that we just sort of sprung this on you and I hope that it doesn't soil whatever you both have. Had."

"He's a good man," the woman says. "I don't know what happened, but I'm sure if he could have, he would have wanted to be a good father."

Bryan opens his mouth, and then shuts it, and then says thank you again.

Outside, the sun has dimmed. The road is empty still. In the taxi they find the driver in a deep sleep, mouth parted slightly, head tilted helplessly to the side. Bryan sits, staring at the rearview mirror. Sommy does not know how to comfort him. How broken he looks, as if thrown at a wall again and again. She feels terribly guilty for her earlier insensitivity, overtaken as she was by fear that they'd leave without finding what they'd come to look for, and perhaps startled by his unbridled, unconscious display of fright.

"Are you okay?" she asks.

He folds his hands childishly on his thighs, and nods.

Sommy rubs his thigh. "Is there relief at all? Relief that you at least found him?"

"One question," he says. "That's all I wanted answered."

Sommy leans into the car seat. "You should ask then. Even if he's not quite capable of answering. But you'll at least know that you asked."

Bryan says that he wants to go back in, he wants to ask.

Sommy nods in agreement, and they leave the sleeping driver and walk toward the house.

The ten-year-old answers the door.

"You again," he says, and moves aside to let them in.

Bryan doesn't wait to be shown in. He plummets forward, into the corridor, and then the room. Sommy walks rapidly behind him, and when she gets to the room, Bryan and the man are standing face-to-face. The man is smiling, and Bryan's face is squished with pain. His mouth is open, but the words don't come out. Sommy stands by the door, one hand on the door rail, the other lightly on her chest.

"Do you know me?" Bryan says, finally.

The man's face is vacant, barren. Bryan lets out a sharp sob, and Sommy rushes over to him, but the man is quicker. He holds up Bryan and cups his head with a palm. With the other, he taps Bryan's back, gently, rhythmically, as if to the sound of a dirge.

They leave for Lagos the next day, under the thick glob of Bryan's sadness. Sommy's anxious about his silence, his sadness, and she finds herself touching him often, asking how he's doing. On the flight back, she leans toward him, and says, "You know I'll always be here for you.

Always." He replies with a murmur, and the sound goes through her like a stake of ice. The distancing has begun, she thinks. He'll do to her what Mezie did to her.

Her mother calls that evening, asks how their trip went. Sommy picks up the call while on the balcony, away from Bryan. She tells her mother everything. Her mother is silent for a bit, and then she says, "If you people are thinking of having kids, this is something you must consider. I know that illnesses like these—dementia, okwia?—can be passed down to kids."

"Mummy, why would you say that?"

"I'm just giving advice. If you like take it, if you like don't."

Sommy takes the phone away from her ear as her mother goes on about how her advice is for Sommy's good. When her mother is this way, stoic and cruel, she shuts her out. It is a reality so discombobulating, this cruel quality of her mother's, that absorbing it feels like chewing stone. Sommy cuts the call and switches her phone to Flight mode.

Mezie walks in then, a can of beer in hand. He's startled by her presence. She observes him briefly and then turns her gaze to the view outside. It's a cool night. The air feels easy on her skin.

He leans on the balcony rail, and before he asks, she tells him about the trip. Just as she'd narrated it to her mother. It's a story she wants to tell everyone. It's the kind of story that makes a person pause and ponder.

"How come his wife received it so well?" he asks.

"I don't know. Imagine living with someone for that long and not knowing something this serious about them."

He stands upright, looks into the dark night. She's struck by his great frame, and by this new realization that when people look at him, what they see is an adult male. She, on the other hand, doesn't only see the adult, she sees the child, too, sees the same person who she'd run around the carpark with, playing hide-and-seek, the same person she'd shared her snacks with. And perhaps, she thinks, this is the way to see people:

to see the child alongside the adult, because the child is always there, under all that fluff that comes with age.

"You know what I find interesting?" he asks.

"What?"

"He can't confront him or be mad at him. That's the absolute worst thing. The anger goes inward or is directed at someone else, who most likely doesn't deserve it."

His articulacy is odd as is his ability to identify these tendencies in others and not in himself. He leaves the rail, and comes to sit beside her, arms folded and propped on his slightly protruding stomach.

"He'll be fine," he says. "Bryan. He didn't find what he went looking for. But now he at least knows to stop looking."

"I hope so," Sommy says.

There's a moment of silence, and then he says, "I'll be nicer to him."

She chuckles. "That one is your own."

He laughs, places his palms at the back of his head, stretches. "It's good to have you back."

Her body slackens with glee. It's his first real acknowledgment of her. And she thinks now how ironic it is that as much as she wants to tear down this wall of his, she also admires it somewhat, this quality of a guarded private life.

"It's good to be back home," she says.

Bryan enters into himself. So quiet. So broody. To fill the silence between them, Sommy tells him stories from her childhood days, how when she was about eight, she'd come across a TV ad on HIV/AIDS. The virus was transmissible by blood, the ad said. In that same week, she learnt at school that malaria was transmissible by blood. And because she'd been sick with malaria once, she saw no reason why she couldn't be sick with HIV. She was paralyzed with fear, she told Bryan. She laid on the couch for days, afraid to get eaten by a mosquito. When she told Mezie what was happening inside her head, he hadn't explained it away like her mother had done. He'd slapped a mosquito dead and brought it to her.

"See?" Mezie said. "See the blood?" He then pulled up his trousers, revealing a grazed knee.

She did not expect that he would rub the smeared blood on his open wound.

"See?" he said again. "I don't have HIV."

She'd been puzzled. Then the thought came to her that he'd just transferred the virus to his open wound. She threw herself on the floor, weeping.

She tries hard to sustain an animated voice as she speaks. "My mother flogged the hell out of us," she says.

She tells him more, about her childhood dream of being a nun. "I was such a Mother Mary girl," she says.

None of her stories move him. He nods, murmurs, shifts.

"What about all the plans we made?" she says finally, four days after their return from Amawbia. "You plan to waste the holiday brooding over a man that did not have it in him to look for you?"

He's lying in bed, eyes to the ceiling, cradling his journal, which he now drops, face battered with hurt, and says, "That's an insensitive thing to say to me."

"I'm sorry," she says. "I'm just trying to help."

"If you want to help, you'll let me be."

"I'm sorry."

Sommy doesn't know how to handle it. This Bryan is peculiar—sullen, irritable, the Bryan after the Bayo incident.

"I feel useless," Sommy tells Kayla over the phone. "I want to help him, but I don't know how to."

"Give him space, girl. He's struggling."

Sommy tries to do just that. She spends time at her parents', with her father, with whom she has very little to discuss. The quiet, his quiet, is comforting. She spends a Saturday with Amara, who tells her all about her newly acquired respect in the office.

"We really shut that Sewa girl up," Amara says. "Now she know sey levels dey."

Each day, Sommy comes home to Bryan either journaling or punching away at his laptop.

"It's how I cope," he tells her one evening after they are done having sex and they lie side by side, breathing harshly. "I write stuff down."

"Can I read?" she asks, jokingly, but meaning it somewhat.

He says nothing, pulls away from her.

A few days pass. Then she wakes up to find him invigorated, pacing, his face infused with the ridiculous joy of having finally grasped what had once, and for a long while, been elusive. At first, she thinks that Elin has arrived. She ought to arrive today. Just in time for their mother's thanksgiving party. But Bryan says, "We have to go back there."

"Go back where?" Sommy yawns, blocks her face from the early morning light coming through the window.

"We didn't ask for his diagnosis. His detailed diagnosis. What if all he needs is the right doctor?"

"Bryan. What are you saying? Sit, please. Can you just sit?"

The house is quiet. On normal days, music floats in from the sitting room, something by Burna Boy or Wizkid. But today isn't a normal day. Elin arrives today.

"There's a chance he doesn't even have dementia," Bryan says. "We don't know. We don't know the kind of medical care he gets."

"I'm sure his wife would have found the best care for him. You need to calm down, babe. Have you talked to your mum?"

"How would they know to deal with a person like that?" Bryan says. "I'm sure they looked at him, an old man, kind of losing his mind, and they slapped a diagnosis on him."

"You are sure? How are you sure?"

He looks around, eyes open, hands sweeping the air as though he thinks the answer as obvious as both their bodies occupying this space in the moment. "Forgive me if I don't think he'll get the best health care in Amawbia."

He says "Amawbia" like it's the name of an illness, the word mutilated by his feathery accent.

"Bryan." She stands, gropes the duvet, clasps it to her chest. "What the fuck is wrong with you?"

He stands still now, his back to her. "I am going to take him with me to Iowa. I'm going to have him see Dr. Graber. He's a neurosurgeon at—"

"You are acting fucking crazy," Sommy says gently.

"He's a neurosurgeon at the university hospital," he says quietly. "I'll have him see my father."

Sommy sits back on the bed. Father? Too desperate to feel a void, he creates a patina, calls someone who doesn't know his name "Father."

"He is not your father," Sommy says. It is her duty to say this, to undo his delusions. It is her duty because she loves him, and when you love someone, you disassemble their untruths.

He sits next to her now, his back hunched, his hand holding up his head. "He needs to tell me that. To tell me that he isn't my father. He needs to look me in the eye and say it."

He tells her, with a tone of finality, that he'll go to Amawbia the coming Wednesday, the day after the thanksgiving party. As soon as he says this, he hugs her, kisses her hard on the forehead. He says, "I feel something and it's good, babe. It's good."

Sommy sits stiffly, watching him like he's a strange animal let out of its cage.

At exactly noon, the door rattles open, and the soft laughter of a woman follows. Sommy immediately takes a seat by the window. Something about meeting Elin standing makes her feel exposed. After their phone exchanges during her early days in Iowa, they'd not really conversed, only sometimes exchanging holiday pleasantries. She doesn't know what to expect.

Elin walks in, rolling a powder-blue suitcase. She pauses at the foyer, stands admiring the family portrait. She's taller than Sommy had expected, definitely above six feet, and her hair looks darker.

Bryan, hearing the light commotion, emerges from the bedroom, and joins Sommy on the couch. He puts his arm around her shoulders.

"Hi," Elin says from the foyer, not entering the sitting room yet.

Sommy waves, smiles.

Elin doesn't move until Mezie walks in front of her, leads her into the sitting room. Bryan stands and goes on to shake her hand. He is smiling, his usual impressive self. Sommy's always proud whenever she introduces him to people. She can see how people see him: polished, oozing the scent of a good life. She can see how their perception of him elevates her in their eyes.

Sommy doesn't stand, but she doesn't fold, either. It is Elin who walks up to her, and says, "I'm so glad to finally meet you in person." They exchange a handshake. It is not the meeting of people who immediately take to each other. In that handshake is a withholding of grace, and Sommy is aware that this withholding comes wholly from her, and she blames her stiffness on Bryan's sudden change. She cannot stop looking at him like he's gone mad.

Elin sits on the couch opposite Sommy and Bryan. She looks around the house and says that the apartment is gorgeous.

Mezie sits on the arm of the chair, looking down at her, and something in the way she looks back at him, with total adoration, tells Sommy that this is the metaphor of their relationship, Mezie on top and Elin below.

Elin rests an arm on Mezie's legs and relaxes into the couch. She is visibly tired, deep eyes, the hairs by her ears slightly matted. She is not beautiful in that easy, soft way, like Bryan or Melinda or Amara. One has to peer to see the softness around her eyes, and to dazzle, she has to smile, flash those healthy, well-aligned teeth of hers.

Mezie rolls Elin's bags into his room. He looks unlike himself, very stilted, performing every act with great effort. In his absence, Bryan tells Elin he traveled to Oslo the year he turned fourteen, a short trip with his mother who was delivering a speech at a medical conference. He says it is the most beautiful, most pristine place he's been to. He says he's not had a better skiing experience anywhere else. Sommy restrains herself from staring at him. He's never said anything about being in Norway at fourteen. But then again, he says very little about things he considers extravagant: holiday trips abroad, houses bought and sold, old jobs.

Elin says that the grass is perhaps always greener on the other side because she thinks New York the most beautiful place she's ever been. The air isn't pristine, she says, but the city is gorgeous, with an ancient, careworn appeal. And the arts and culture aspect of the city is "uber vibrant," she says, in the way that it isn't in Oslo.

Bryan nods along and says she has a point. Sommy notices that Elin possesses the same warmth as Chisom, a nurturer's air. The camaraderie between her and Bryan is unforced. Elin is paying attention to him as he gushes about his favorite Ibsen play, his genius. She doesn't seem trapped in her head, doesn't seem to be wondering whether he thinks her fat, unintelligent, the way she sits unrefined, her laughter too loud. Sommy's thinking about this, what it means that she's unable to spread open, that she's constantly vigilant. She's thinking about this perpetual feeling of being wrong, being below everything. She's thinking this, and half listening to Elin and Bryan's conversation, when the door swings open, and Chisom walks in, holding a plastic bag. She's dressed ostentatiously. Her dress, black and short, hugs her curves. She has on a well-oiled afro wig, and her makeup is glassy, radiant. Sommy knows what and who it is she's dressed for. Elin watches her quietly.

Sommy sits up straight, confused about how to introduce Chisom. But then Mezie hurries into the sitting room. There's the sense that he is holding back a scream in the forcefulness of his steps. He stretches a hand to Chisom, gesturing for the plastic bag, and says, "Thanks for bringing the food."

Chisom doesn't let go of the bag. She looks Mezie right in the eye, still smiling, a glowless smile. Mezie grabs the bag, tugs at it. It doesn't budge. He tugs again and Chisom slowly releases her grip. She then turns to a confused Elin.

"My name is Grace," Chisom says. "Welcome ehnn."

Elin stands, stretches her hand for a handshake. "Nice to meet you," she says softly.

The women stare at each other. The air grows threatening, a vicious silence. And then the uncomfortable squishing of the plastic bag: Mezie, getting the food cooler out. Sommy, desperate to relieve him of his pain, summons her brightest smile, and asks Elin if she wants to be shown to her room.

"Sure," Elin says. "I'll give anything to spread flat on a bed right now."

Mezie doesn't stop fiddling with the bag. He doesn't look up at them. Chisom takes the seat next to Bryan and tells him that their mother has hired her to make attires for the thanksgiving party. She says the fabric is a luminous cream color and would go well with his skin tone. Bryan says he's excited to try it on. Chisom brightens.

When they enter the room, Elin asks if Grace is a cousin.

"A longtime friend of ours," Sommy replies. "Almost like family."

"She is suspicious of me, which is no surprise. Mezie tells me you are a very close-knit family. Protective of each other. And I admire that very much."

Sommy wants to smile, but she cannot. She cannot believe how easily, reflexively, she'd just lied.

"Get some rest," Sommy says. "And let me know if you need anything Mezie can't provide. I am in the room right at the end of the hallway."

Elin thanks her, stretches, looks around satisfied.

She's twisting the doorknob, on her way out, when Elin says, "I'm glad that you and Mezie are good now. I know how hard it was for you."

Sommy sighs, turns, wrung out by Elin's earnestness. "Thank you, Elin."

Sommy finds a poem Bryan wrote on their way back from Enugu.

The Return
The city's landscape appears
bright lights

what greets me first
cutting through the thick of night clouds,
like a long-buried memory tugged awake, by a feather of pain.

She holds the paper to her chest. She's sometimes certain that she'll pass out from this ailment of love. It's smothering, at once painful and exhilarating, and often, she catches herself watching her father and her mother when they come over to see all four of them, seeing them anew. She'd always wanted to reshape their expression of love. Her mother's love is a wildfire, anxious, rushing through her, and her father's love is the opposite, calm, repressed, so that one sometimes wonders if it exists at all. She understands it now, that this sort of love overwhelms, and all a person can do is tame it how they know best. Her mother lets hers explode; her father sits on his, soothes the feeling until it's a quiet, disciplined thing.

She decides to support Bryan on his mission to return to Amawbia, to look for a second opinion on his father's health. When she tells him this, on their way to the ATM, in a car they'd rented to avoid asking Mezie for rides, he's quiet for a long time, and then he crumbles in a hail of tears. It's a strange thing to watch, the heaving and coughing. She drives carefully into the banking complex, and parks beside a beat-up bus.

"I'm sorry," he says, wiping tears and snot. "I'm feeling really stressed is all."

"Please don't apologize, babe."

He looks into the far distance, at the ATM, where there's a small line. It's evening, and the sky is dull, as if preparing for rain. She allows the quiet, though she wants to tell him to grieve this loss freely. He might not know it, she wants to say, but he is in mourning.

Two days before the thanksgiving party, Sommy and Elin drive to Trade Fair to meet her mother at Chisom's shop. The plan is to try out the dresses Chisom has sewn for the thanksgiving party.

"It's disgraceful," Sommy had said when her mother brought it up. "What Mezie is doing to Elin is disgraceful."

Her mother's reply was curt and nonchalant, her usual approach to any discussion regarding Mezie. "Let that boy breathe," she said. When Sommy pressed, her mother threatened to drive Elin to the shop herself. Sommy, afraid of what would come out of having her mother and Elin trapped in a car alone, relented, and said she'd do it.

Now Elin sits beside her with her white collared shirt buttoned all the way up. She has a queer sense of fashion, Sommy thinks. Everything all the way up to the neck and all the way down to the ankles. Sommy has often been tempted to ask if this is a church thing, the modesty, so she brings it up now, as they pass a broken streetlight. She skips the part about the modest fashion and asks instead if Elin is religious.

"No, no," Elin protests. "I grew up in an atheist family." She arranges her collar. Sommy admires, for the umpteenth time, the light blue of her gel polish. Clean and modest is how she'd describe Elin, and, perhaps, organized, the sort of person with a color-coordinated, compartmentalized brain.

"How was that?" Sommy says. "My parents are not super religious, but Mezie and I grew up in the church. They made sure we went, and I have mixed feelings about that experience. There was a lot of fear, fear of dying and going to hell, and at a point, fear of dying and going to heaven. Because no one wants to spend forever singing alleluia to the Almighty God. Especially eight-year-old me."

Elin laughs. "The Christian heaven does indeed sound painful. I have complicated feelings about being raised atheist also. I guess it made for an explorative childhood. None of that fear you talk about. But as an adult, I'm wishing more and more that I can genuinely turn to something bigger than myself. I envy people who have that. I think it's a wonderful thing to have—faith."

"Well," Sommy says. "I don't practice anymore, so you probably would have ended up right where you are, without the occasional fear that you might have crossed God or whatever. It's a fear that never quite leaves you."

Elin says, "I guess the grass is always greener on the other side." Same thing she'd said to Bryan during their first conversation, Sommy notices.

They drive through the sprawled Trade Fair gate. It's as Sommy remembers. In her undergrad years, she and Amara frequented the market to buy cheap clothes. Amara would take a bus from her sister's in Festac, and Sommy would take a bus from her parents' in Ojo, and they'd meet right here at the gate, and then board a motorcycle to the complex where secondhand clothes are sold. There were times when, to save money, they walked to the complex instead, the hot sun burning the backs of their necks, their feet covered with white sand. Life moves with speed, Sommy thinks, as she often does these days, a wind of melancholy sweeping through her.

At the shop, their mother pulls Elin into a hug. "Nne," she says. "Hope you guys didn't spend too much time in traffic." To Sommy, she says a simple, "Sit here."

The shop is a small red container, draped with an assortment of fabric. Sewing machines sit on both ends. At one of them sits Chisom peering down at the seams of a dress. She has on glasses. Sommy has never seen her with glasses.

"Welcome," Chisom says, raising her head, dragging the dress toward her.

"Thanks for having us," Elin says.

Chisom beams. "Of course. I can't wait to see you in your dress."

Elin brings her palms together and toward her chest in a gesture of excitement, and echoes, "I can't wait, too."

Sommy sits beside her mother, watching the women. She thinks it pitiful, Chisom's pretense, this folding of herself, and for what? A man. She wonders what Mezie must have told her about Elin. Perhaps that he is just with Elin for the papers? That she, Chisom, is his one true love? It has always vexed her, this relationship of theirs, Chisom's relentless pursuit of Mezie, and Mezie blousing along like a nylon caught in the wind. This passion is the root of her dislike for Chisom. She'd watched as Chisom chased Mezie, waiting for him every day after school at the shop where they stopped to buy zobo and biscuits, bearing love letters and gifts. Chisom bought him a Walkman with several CDs, a Walkman that before he went to bed, he plugged into his ears and listened to music with until he fell asleep. She remembers still Faze's "Need Somebody" cooing through the headphones. It was Chisom who had gone with Mezie to open his first bank account, and who had, the next day deposited her savings into the account, which she said belonged to him, since they were going to get married anyway. Sommy remembers now how, when she and Mezie left for university, Chisom visited every chance she got. She was as constant, as certain as Mezie's heartbeat. And it didn't matter that Mezie's friends called her an old woman because of her deep eyes and too-sharp cheekbones, and that when she laughed, she seemed to have not a single care in the world, hitting whatever was beside her, swinging her head here and there, totally unselfconscious, or that after writing and failing JAMB for the third time, she gave up trying to get into university and decided to sew women's dresses full time. It didn't matter to Mezie. He stayed with her. And when he'd begun seeing Fiona, a girl in Sommy's department, and Chisom had found out, she'd marched to Fiona's hostel, and according to Fiona, who narrated it all to Sommy in a fit of laughter, had been levelheaded, calm. "Please leave Mezie for me," was all she'd said. Even after that, their relationship stood, solid as a dying man's last words.

"This is your own dress," her mother says now. "Try it and let's see if you need any adjustment. Go to the back of that curtain."

Sommy tries on the dress at the covered corner behind the shop. It fits her, hugs her curves. The perfect length, the perfect V-neck that shows a bit of cleavage, but nothing risqué. She wants to find fault with the dress, but there's none. It somehow makes her angrier at Mezie, that he would reduce someone so talented to a toy that springs alive only to do his bidding.

"I like it," Sommy says, dress in hand.

Chisom smiles, and it's her first genuine expression since Sommy walked into the shop. It's the same kind of bright-eyed smile Bryan has on whenever he reads an excerpt of his fiction to her, and she says, "Wow, babe, I really like it." It strikes her then that she's known Chisom since she was thirteen. Over twelve years. It's the same amount of time Chisom has been in love with Mezie. She formed her person around his person. It's what sixteen-year-olds do. To untangle herself would perhaps require a loss of an identity. Usually, Sommy would discuss this sort of thing with Bryan, and he'd have a clever perspective, what he likes to call a "human" perspective. He'd reach into Chisom's childhood in search for a lack and find ways to tie it to her current impulses. But she fears that her "loss of identity" angle might strike a close emotional chord, for it is the same sort of crisis in which Bryan is enmeshed.

Elin tries on her dress, and it fits perfectly. She runs her palms down the dress. It's the same style as Sommy's, V-neck, long, grazing the concrete floor.

"I look like a mermaid," Elin says, turning here and there, eyes radiant with admiration.

"You look really beautiful," Sommy says, and she means it, Elin does look like a mermaid. It's not just the fitting, it's the color of the fabric, the warm lemon against her whey-colored skin.

"Imaka, nne," her mother says, smiling.

"Thank you," Elin says.

Chisom, too, has on a smile, but Sommy can tell from the quiver in her fingers as she unspools a roll of thread that she's working hard to hide an internal battle. Still, Sommy thinks the moment tender, with her mother staring at Elin, and Elin staring at herself in the mirror, dazzled at the transformative magic of a good dress.

Elin changes back into her collared shirt and black pants, still flushed, still beaming. She tells Chisom that she's gotten herself a lifetime customer. She says she wants Chisom to make dresses for her mother and for her best friend, a Lucy who lives in London now. She says that Chisom could compete with the best in the world.

"Ahhh," Chisom says coyly. "You are exaggerating, ma."

"I am not," Elin says. "You are very good."

A woman walks in then, carrying a tray of jewelry. Tall and thin, with competent wrinkly hands.

"Abigail," Chisom says, standing. "Can I help you?"

"Madam," Abigail says. "Good evening o!" She sweeps the room, gives the same exaggerated "Good evening o!" to everyone.

"Can I help you?" Chisom asks again, eyes feral with suspicion.

Abigail laughs. "We dey fight? I just come to show oyibo my jewelry. She might want to buy." She turns to Elin. "Madam, you will like my necklaces. They are original gold." She drops the tray on the floor and pulls a thin chain from the bunch. "See this one? It's your color."

"Abigail," Chisom says. "She doesn't want to buy."

"Oh no, no," Elin says. "I'll check them out."

Chisom crinkles, stepping back, an ocean receding. Elin does buy a silver neck chain. No one says a thing when Abigail adds about an extra thousand naira to the original price, and as they drive home, and Elin chatters about how nice and talented Chisom is, how nice everyone is, Sommy is perplexed by the details Elin is oblivious to. She neither noticed Abigail's mischief, nor Chisom's moping after Elin had gone ahead and entertained Abigail. Nor does she notice the wedge her mother has inserted between them, even though she pulls her in a hug every time. Sommy thinks now that at every point we exist in the realm of the spoken and the unspoken. To be an outsider is to have the tools to participate only in the realm of the spoken, and to flounder in the realm of the unspoken. She, Sommy, would know this more than anyone.

On the morning of the thanksgiving party, Sommy wakes up to the sound of rain pelting the window. There are several missed calls from her mother. Bryan is asleep beside her. The room is a mournful gray. No bright sunlight pouring in. There's a noiselessness outside, as though the morning is reluctant to breathe. Sommy takes a while to roll stealthily off the bed, walk into the sitting room, and plop herself by the couch, near the slightly open window, from where a chill breeze wanders in.

She dials her mother. She picks up on the first ring.

"The devil has it out for me," her mother says, panicked. "I should have rented the hall by the church."

"Maybe it will stop raining," Sommy says. "Let's give it some time."

"The ground will be messy. The canopies are supposed to arrive in exactly one hour and the boys are supposed to put it up soon, so that the decoration lady will start decorating. Now I probably have to start looking for an indoor venue. I am so tired. What is all this?"

Sommy is silent. Her mother is not asking for suggestions—to give one would be tantamount to talking to a stone. Her decision is already made. She's only letting out her rage, and perhaps her nervousness, nervousness that this might all go bad, this long-planned thanksgiving party, in which she's supposed to showcase a patina of her own, a patina of successful children, a happy marriage, a good life.

"Don't worry," her mother says. "You people should just get ready to come here at nine thirty. Make sure the boys don't forget their ichie caps. You, when you come here, I'll help you and tie your scarf. And Elin, too. I'll tie her scarf for her. But I want all of you here at nine thirty on the dot. Please, don't let me call you to ask where you are. Biko."

"Mummy, I've heard."

"That's what you will say now, but by nine thirty I'll call, and you will still be drawing on your eyebrows."

"Mummy—"

"Don't 'Mummy' me. Just be here on time."

Bryan looks comical in his ichie cap. Sommy tells him this and they have a good laugh. The laughter loosens her somehow, and she wants to kiss him, press her body into his, and have a warm fuck. But it's nine, and they have to be at her mother's soon. She focuses on preening in the mirror. The dress is even more beautiful now, with her braids grazing her shoulders, her face slightly made-up, a loose powder and glossy nude lipstick.

Bryan comes from behind her and puts an arm around her waist. She looks at his reflection in the mirror, his eyes flattened with desire.

"You look amazing, babe," he says.

She turns to him, leans in to kiss his forehead. "I'd say you look amazing yourself, but this cap—it's just funny."

"It's good for something," he says.

"What?"

"Making you laugh."

She laughs. "You are so corny. It kills me."

"I'm also horny."

"Oh Jesus, babe, cringe."

He brings his mouth to hers, and they both begin to undress each other. They have to pause to get the dress off Sommy's hips, but after that, everything happens quickly, and in a flash of passion, Bryan holding her head to the wall, Sommy clutching her boobs. He fucks her for longer than usual. By the time they are done, she is pleasantly sore, and Bryan is sweating, his face a painting of content.

The church is an uncompleted bungalow. Palm trees and gnarled lemon trees surround it. A small shop stands by its makeshift gate, a table in front, on top of which biscuits and sweets are arranged. She looks about for an ice-cream man, a fixture of her childhood church memories. There's none.

Father Gibson is in the thick of a sermon about forgiveness when they enter the church. They settle into the pew at the back, to the consternation of the usher standing by the door, who arranges the sash of authority, on which the words ST JUDE'S CATHOLIC CHURCH are boldly printed, hanging around her shoulder.

"See? We are late because of you people," her mother says. "I said nine thirty. You showed up at ten. Now Father will be looking at us like we are unserious people. How do you want to thank God, but then you arrive late to mass?"

No one responds. Not Sommy. Not Mezie. Bryan and Elin, who are seated together on the other end of the pew, smile piously, but say nothing. Her father bows his head as if in prayer.

Sommy notices people throw glances at Bryan and Elin, and then at her mother, who is pompously dressed, a sequined maxi-length dress with high puff sleeves, a gele high as a lighthouse, her silver necklace heavy around her neck. Next to her, Sommy's father looks forlorn, washed out in his Ankara up-and-down. It is something to look at, Sommy thinks.

Right before the first offering, Chisom walks in. She's dressed exactly as Sommy and Elin, down to the silver shoes with their crafted glittering flowers. Sommy tries to meet Mezie's gaze, but he isn't looking at her. His face spurts a playlist of emotions: fear, irritation, resignation.

Chisom bends now to greet her mother, who throws an arm around her.

"You made us all look beautiful," her mother whispers, scoots closer to the arm of the pew, taps their father's lap, and, with a stiff palm pushing air away from her, signals for him to shift. Chisom sits between them, smiling. Sommy is too embarrassed to look at Elin. She stares instead at the altar, as Father Gibson glides through the eucharistic rites, raising the white bread, kissing the golden cup, carefully reciting the prayers—"Blessed is he who comes in the name of the Lord. Hosanna in the highest"—his green chasuble glinting in the yellow glow of the light pouring through the window.

Their thanksgiving song is "Anya Oma ne Ele." Her mother and father lead the procession, Sommy and Mezie follow behind, Bryan and Elin follow next, and then a long array of church members, including Madam Stainless and her cohort, all of them dancing and singing praises. A group of boys carries the offerings to the altar.

Her mother shimmers. She'd given Mezie and Bryan wads of cash to throw at her as she dances, and they do so, Mezie rigid with embarrassment, Bryan delighting in the dramatic display.

After mass, they stand outside. Aside the deep greenness of the leaves, there's hardly a sign that it had rained earlier that morning. The air is ablaze with heat, and the sky is a bright white. Her mother exchanges greetings with people who come up to congratulate her for a successful thanksgiving offering, and to remind her that they will be at the reception.

To each person her mother says, "You remember Somkele? My daughter. The one doing her master's in America?" She pulls Sommy by the hand. "That's her fiancé." She points to a flushed Bryan. "They both came back for visitation. And Mezie, my son. He was in Norway. But he came back to settle down, start his own thing."

They exclaim, "Wow, what beautiful children!" "All grown!" "Isn't this what every mother prays for? That all the hard work and love they pour into their children amount to something?" Those who knew them as kids shift back, falsely flummoxed. "Is this not Sommy of the other day? Sommy who used to sneak out during mass to go and buy ice cream? Look how big she is. Doing her master's in America! What can our God not do? He is indeed capable of everything. A giving God!" Sommy's particularly irritated by Mrs. Umeh, who seems to have conveniently forgotten how cruel she'd been to Sommy during lector meetings, and who now hugs her enthusiastically, asks how she's doing. Sommy wants to say, "Were you not the one who kept calling me a 'dirty girl' during lector meetings for no reason?" Sommy ignores Mrs. Umeh's question, stiffens in her embrace, and moves away hastily afterward.

Before they leave, their mother insists that they see Father Gibson for a private prayer. They walk to his office, where he stands, greeting members of the congregation. Father Gibson is a handsome man, with a well-defined face shape, all its angles proportional in a way that feels slightly cloying to Sommy, like a too-sweet thing. He's taken off most of his regalia, and now has on a black long-sleeved shirt, two buttons open, the collar skewed in the endearing manner of an important person who does not take himself too seriously. Unlike everyone around them, he doesn't pin his gaze on Bryan or Elin. He addresses her mother and father. He thanks them for giving to the church, and says a quick prayer of mercy—"Be there for your people in their time of great need, Lord."

Mezie and Bryan drive together to the reception venue, while Sommy drives with her parents and Elin. Her mother spends the entire car ride talking about how dashing everyone had been. Of course, except Madam Stainless and her minions. Did Sommy see how shriveled Madam Stainless looked? she asks. The woman can't stand happiness that isn't hers. Sommy nods, says, yes, she did see that Madam Stainless looked shriveled. In truth, Sommy did not pay much attention to Madam Stainless, but she wants her mother to get all that she seeks, to feel deeply satisfied by the day's grand performance, so that she can finally let go of the grudge.

When they arrive to the reception, the canopies are already up. Underneath them are tables and chairs covered in white-and-blue cloth. On the tables are fake flowers in wooden vases, gold-rimmed plates with silver utensils lined beside them, and a menu printed on A4 paper. Sommy is impressed by the attention to detail, and she tells her mother this. They are standing under a canopy. Her mother is inspecting the cutlery on the table beside her. No one has arrived yet.

"Okwia?" her mother says. "It's beautiful. Everything is beautiful."

"It is," Sommy says.

In the far distance a car zooms past, leaving a trail of dust behind. A shoemaker walks down the side of the road, jingling his workbox.

Her mother picks up a napkin and stares at it for a while and then says, "They said my children are losers. That my Mezie is a failure. That is what Madam Stainless said to me. That my child is a failure." Her voice is languorous, and Sommy's caught off guard by the intensity of emotion. Her mother, who at the hospital, after Mezie's overdose, had stood on her tiptoes, looked the doctor in the face, and said, "You better save my son."

"It is okay, Mummy," Sommy says, and she thinks, for the first time, that their wounds are identical, her mother's even more blistering. She almost lost a son. He was almost gone. And all of this, the dresses and canopies and chairs with blue ribbons sticking out of their backs, is an attempt to convince herself that their realities have changed, that he is still with them. Alive. Breathing. Sane. She thinks now that she ought to be kinder to her, more understanding.

Her mother gathers herself and continues inspecting the tables. Sommy excuses herself to go meet Elin, who's sitting on a chair under an empty canopy, punching her phone keys rapidly. She's halfway to Elin when she notices Chisom walking slowly toward Mezie and Bryan. Mezie is scratching his head, evidently nervous. Sommy turns and walks toward the trio.

"Hey, babe," Sommy says to Bryan.

She turns to Chisom, says, "Good afternoon."

Chisom takes a step back, dragging her dangling bag strap to her shoulder.

"I didn't know that you sewed the same dress for the three of us," Sommy says, her voice fierce with accusation.

"I liked the style," Chisom says brittlely.

"Can I speak to you in private?" Sommy says to Mezie. He looks at her with raised eyebrows, and she adds, "Money stuff."

They walk toward the DJ's corner and stand by a riot of wires.

"Are you fucking Chisom?" Sommy says.

"What kind of question is that?" He shoves a hand her way.

"Why is she acting like your bride?"

"Why don't you ask her? Why are you asking me?"

"You are sweating."

He takes a quick look at the sweat marks around his armpits.

"The fuck you mean by 'I am sweating.' Of course, I am sweating. It's hot. You are sweating, too."

Sommy's always believed Mezie's recklessness to be circumstantial, like how she'd straddled Bayo and Bryan in a haze of confusion. But this, this flagrant nonchalance, is tumbling everything she knows about him.

"What are you doing, Mezie? What is all this?"

"Remove your hand from my neck, Somkele. Please. Leave me alone."

He stomps away, his long back hunched. He knows he's hot coal that she will continue to hold delicately no matter how searing the burn. Just like Elin and Chisom do. Just like their mother does.

The caterers arrive in a jaunty yellow bus and set up behind the canopies. The MC arrives. Soon the party is full and alive. There are all the staples of a Nigerian party: a chairman, Uncle Osondu, who before the party starts, scolds Sommy for not calling him from America; a family dance during which her mother staggers majestically, singing and shaking her buttocks here and there as Mezie and Bryan plaster naira notes to her forehead; a couple's dance, her mother and father holding each other, swaying, an air of relief around them. The servers dish out jollof rice and chicken, eguisi and okro soups with garri and pounded yam. On tables and on the ground, beside plastic chair legs, are open bottles of Malta Guinness, Star Beer, Guinness small stout. The music, from Osadebe to Flavour, a sonic composition of Igbo music from the late eighties to date.

Sommy is seated next to her mother, whom she often catches watching the flamboyantly dressed church women, all of them in sequined white blouses and lace wrappers, their necks decorated with red beads and pearls. They've been assigned a designated canopy. Until they are called to dance, the women do not stand. They dance in their seats, shaking their bodies with strained elegance. Some of them hold tiny electric fans, some hand fans, which from time to time they bring to their faces and necks. They often lean to each other to whisper and then slowly, as if with much effort, take their previous positions, and continue to look on like judges presiding over a trial.

Sommy wishes Amara, who had to show up at work, were here. She'd like to have someone to gossip with about the women's mean-girl energy, and how ironic it all is since her mother, who seems now the object of disdain, will, in a heartbeat, join the group to do the same to another. She could have said this to Bryan, said to him that she finds it a little sad that the women, although aware that the group thrives on targeted disdain, and that they could someday be the target, continue to fuel the engine. But Bryan is walking around now, his camera hung around his neck, taking pictures. Since she'd agreed to go back to Amawbia with him, he's been happier, taking more photographs, journaling less. Once she opened his laptop and found search histories for *best brain surgeon in the world, symptoms of dementia, is dementia curable?* She can't wait for this period of his life to be over.

She sights Patrick standing with Mezie by the DJ stand, both clutching bottles of Star Beer. Surely Patrick had known about the Elin and Chisom triangle when he dropped her off at Mezie's the other day but had refused to say. Did the world work for men in this way: They did whatever they pleased, and everyone *understood*, explained it away? How different this scenario would be if she were in Mezie's shoes, stringing two men along and everyone was aware of it.

The sun pours a glorious light all over now. The sound of laughter and music and people requesting that their plates be refilled and their drinks replaced infuses the air, Sommy thinks, with a kind of magic. She observes their neighbors now, many of whom she'd not had a proper conversation with since she left for university in Awka. They are the mothers and fathers of kids she once played with, kids now gone, scattered across Lagos, across the world. She especially notices Benita's father, with his long gray beard. He sits quietly on his own, eating jollof rice. Before his wife began suffering from the disorder, he'd read to Benita and Sommy. It was from him Sommy had first heard about Achebe's *Things Fall Apart*, and it was because of him that she'd decided to study literature in university. She'd admired his passion for books, loved how he mellowed as he told her about Okonkwo and Ikemefuna's relationship. "Okonkwo killed his son," he'd said then, melancholic, as though Okonkwo were a real person. She wonders if he still feels the passion, or if, just like Aunty Dera who sits not too far from him now, bent toward Victoria, it's been wrung out of him. Perhaps she'll ask him about Benita and Susan later.

Outside the canopies are the uninvited, shirtless children, ashy and wiry, dancing, scrambling for food and drinks, beggars now without the sloping in their shoulders, so that they assume the respectability associated with those invited and aren't shooed away. Elin stands to dance at intervals. She grips a cold bottle of water and flaps a fan in her face. Florence, who hadn't attended the mass with them, swaggers from canopy to canopy now with her group of friends, girls her age, about five of them, angling under the weight of their almost-maturity, with their too-bright lip glosses and over-gelled baby hairs. Her father walks around the canopies asking guests if they need more drinks. Often, Sommy catches Bryan in a courteous conversation with a guest, and she does her best to sit still. She hates that people fawn over him and Elin, ask them for money, and though they are both polite, sometimes even pressing a few hundred naira notes into hands, and Bryan sometimes giving out his phone number, she feels ashamed, as though she's let strangers into an untidy house.

Bryan walks up to her now and smiles. Sweat beads roll down his forehead. He points to the DJ corner, where Mezie and Chisom stand speaking intensely to each other. Patrick stands a little away from them, watching, too.

"Is there some kind of problem?" Bryan says.

"Huh?" Sommy says, glancing at Elin to be certain she isn't watching the argument.

"Something is going on with Mez and Chisom. It's obvious he doesn't want her here."

"I'm sure it has something to do with the food or drinks. Mezie is sort of a control freak with these things."

Bryan shrugs, and then pauses, squints, brings his camera to his face. Chisom is walking away now, headed to the catering stand.

"A moment, babe, okay?" Sommy says, and gives him a quick kiss. She walks a straight line to Chisom, who's speaking to a caterer.

"What are you doing?" Sommy says. "Mezie doesn't want you here. Why not go?"

Chisom sweeps her with a severe look, and then turns to the caterer, and continues passing along her message. She tells the caterer to make certain that two small coolers of rice remain for guests who might come to the house later.

When she's done with the caterer, Chisom turns to Sommy, says, "Ehen, you were saying?"

"I was saying that you should go home," Sommy says. "Mezie's real girlfriend is here. Don't spoil this for him. When she leaves, you both can continue whatever tragic, codependent relationship you guys have."

Chisom stares at Sommy, bored. "Are you done? Because I'm busy."

Sommy feels a light tremble run through her, and for a minute, she's black all over from anger. "He doesn't love you. He is using you."

Chisom flinches, forms a fist. "Are you done?"

"He's fucking using you," she says, and walks quickly away, to the car, to hide her falling apart.

On her way, she sees Bryan walking toward a crowd of children calling out to him, "Oyibo, oyibo, abeg take my picture, take my picture."

The fury inside her bubbles and swirls and then stills, gives way to a chill. When she reaches the car, she remembers she doesn't have the key, so she walks to the other side, which faces an unplastered wall. There, she stands, leans on the hot metal car, feeling deep sorrow. It's a minute before her father appears, his face crinkled with concern.

"Nne, are you okay?" he says.

Sommy forces a smile. "Yes, Daddy."

"Come back to the party, nnu?"

She walks back with him. It is hard to sit and watch Chisom as she continues to prance around, directing the servers, and Elin, who's absorbed in dancing and punching away on her phone, and who often leans toward Mezie to share a laugh. The children staring at Elin from afar have dispersed, her once surprising presence now ordinary, boring.

Evening comes. The DJ shifts from highlife to R & B. A quiet air replaces the chaos from earlier. Bryan is still taking pictures, and Sommy finds this unsettling now, his ogling, his persistent overanalyzing of everything, an anthropological impulse. He seems to have decided that it is the best way to experience the moment. To see it in stasis, capture it in a motionless picture, clipping away everything that comes before and after. She hates it.

When the DJ has packed up, and the canopies have been rolled up, her mother, tired but still with energy, asks that they all meet at home for a private family dinner.

"This could not have gone any better," she says to Sommy, her voice awash with joy.

Soon all of them are driving to her parent's home. Bryan still rides with Mezie, and Sommy with Elin and her parents. Chisom rides behind them, with Florence in her backseat, clutching the cooler of rice.

At her parents', they all sit around and listen as her mother chatters on about the successful party. Her father sits quietly, watching his wife with mild adoration. Sommy thinks that he has always liked in her that which he doesn't possess: a boisterous liveliness. She wonders if this is the same for her and Bryan. She turns to him, watches him eagerly, waiting for a slight opening in his collapsed posture so she can sneak in a touch. She hates that she's thought such vile thoughts about him. She hates it even more knowing that he's just been recently re-hurt by the starkness of his fatherlessness, that now he will have to lay to rest a wound as old as his first memory, and give space for all the other wounds that have lain trembling underneath. What a terrible burden to carry, she thinks.

On the other side of the table, she notices Mezie watch Chisom like she's prey. Elin is chatting with their mother. She laughs affably, wanting as always to please, to receive their mother's blessing. The other day, while Sommy and Elin were in the kitchen at Mezie's making dinner, Elin's best friend, Lucy, had called. Elin picked up and they went on and on in Norwegian, a language that sounded very much like Efik, throaty and watery. After Elin finished the call, she told Sommy that Lucy wants to come to Nigeria with her during her next visit, and Sommy had been taken aback that Elin was planning a next visit, that she truly was devoted to Mezie. She felt then that she could drown in the pool of her guilt. She feels it even more intensely now, the guilt, and she wants everything to end, the dinner, her mother's chattering, Elin's terrible demureness. She wants to get Bryan in a room, to get her legs around him, and fuck him until she feels forgiven. She wants them to go to Amawbia and be back already. Frankly, she's done with it all. She wants to go back to Iowa.

Her mother leans over the table to pierce a fork into a piece of meat. "Chisom, you made us all look beautiful. We blinded everyone with our beauty."

It's on Sommy that Elin's gaze first lands, her face tight with realization.

"Chisom?" Elin asks. She turns to Mezie. "Is this Chisom?"

Mezie lowers his head to the table.

Elin turns again to Sommy. "You said she's a family friend."

Mezie breathes forcefully. Sommy stands. It's a thoughtless move. Something will fall is all she knows, and she'll need to pick it up, so she stands. It takes a minute for everyone in the room to reach the same understanding, especially Bryan, who now looks at Sommy with something like pain on his face.

Elin turns to Sommy and then to Chisom, her eyes wide with shock. She's noticing that all three of them are wearing identical dresses.

"Your Chisom?" Elin says to Mezie, and heaves, a disbelieving heave, an "Even you?" heave, a "But you promised" heave. She pushes back the chair and walks out.

Shame roots Sommy in one position.

Mezie takes a bottle of vodka and gulps it senselessly. Her mother stretches and stabs at another piece of meat. Sommy looks at her, as though for the first time. Had she left the country and come back to find a different family? Mock actors and actresses? And why does her father sit inert? Why won't he call everyone to order?

Mezie stands, goes after Elin. Sommy turns to find Bryan staring at her still. On his face is the look of heartbreak, a caving in, shutting down.

Chisom begins to clear the table. Florence stands to help her. The only sound now is that of ceramic scraping ceramic. A few minutes pass, and Mezie doesn't come back with Elin, so Sommy calls him.

"I can't find her," he says. "I don't know why she'd just storm out."

"You don't know why she'd just storm out?" Sommy says, her voice steely.

"Please, Somkele, not now. Can you come meet me downstairs with the car key? Let's drive around and look for her."

Sommy picks the car key from the center table and announces that she's going to meet Mezie downstairs.

"I'll come with you," Bryan says.

Sommy is surprised that he says goodbye to her parents and to Chisom. Is she to read this as hope?

They meet Mezie downstairs, and Sommy hands the key to him. He gets into the driver's seat, she the passenger seat, and Bryan in the back.

"Do you know anywhere she might be?" Mezie asks.

"I should be asking you that. You are her boyfriend or partner or whatever. You should know."

"Please," Mezie says. "Just please."

Sommy rolls her eyes and looks out the window. It is dark now. The dim streetlights barely illuminate the streets. They drive toward the estate gate, Bryan looking to the left, Sommy to the right, Mezie forward.

Sommy soon begins to feel full panic. A white woman, out in the streets of Ojo at night, alone. Had she not thought of the consequences?

Did she not read all the warnings about kidnappers and armed robbers in Nigeria on the embassy's website?

"And she left her phone," she says to break the silence in the car, and to drown her panic.

She'll be fine, Sommy thinks. It is the obvious thing, Elin getting kidnapped, getting harmed. But rarely does the obvious happen. They have driven onto the main road now. She peeks at Bryan through the rearview mirror, and wonders if he's looking through the film of their relationship and thinking that there's not a scene with truth in it. She had not meant to lie about Mezie and Chisom, of course. The truth of that matter had revealed itself piece by piece, and in a bewildering manner. And there's also the matter of the strangeness of her family, how distant they seem now to her: her mother quick to dish out cruelty, and Mezie with his dangerous ability to, in a muted way, unleash pain on women. Or is it that they've always been this way, and she sees it now because she sees them through Bryan's eyes?

"I don't think she would have gotten this far," Sommy says.

Mezie doesn't reply. She notices that he is shaking, as if cold, and gripping the steering wheel tight. She bends toward him, looks into his eyes. They are wide with fear.

"Mezie, park the car," Sommy says. "I'll drive."

Mezie accelerates even harder. "Why the fuck would she just storm out?" he says.

Raw fear. She can feel it in his voice. She wants to grab his hand, but she's afraid that the car will swerve. She grabs her seat belt and tries to breathe through her panic.

"Bryan," she says, "please talk to this idiot. Tell him to fucking slow down."

Bryan leans forward then, holds the headrest of the driver's seat, says in a contained voice, "You lied to me. Several times. With a straight face. And I trusted you, even after that shit with Bayo."

"So we are going to talk about Bayo now?"

"Yes, we are going to talk about Bayo because you continue to lie. It's an intrinsic characteristic."

"Intrinsic characteristic? Fuck you, Bryan! Fucking fuck you!"

"I should have known," Bryan says, over her screaming. "People don't just change. I can't love you into a better version of yourself. My love can't change you."

"Bryan—" The car feels light under her now. "Please tell Mezie to pull over. Mezie, please, pull over."

"I really just—"

"Mezie!" Sommy screams, and it is through that, her voice, that she hears the thud, the jerking of the car, the screeching. The car comes to a halt. Then silence. She holds her head and screams as if to dislodge something deeply embedded. She looks blankly at the dark sky, and then at Mezie's frozen face. She unbuckles her seat belt and opens the door. She pauses, clenches her fist. She sees the shapeless mass immediately, shaded from the streetlight by a lone tree, and then Bryan, in front of her, speeding toward it. She walks slowly behind.

"What the fuck?" Bryan wails as he presses an ear to the body.

Sommy's stooping now, touching the woman's woolen hair. She looks around. They are alone. The woman is bleeding from her head, and her eyes are closed. Her lips are slightly parted. Her skirt, red and knee-length, is smeared with sand and mud and blood.

"She isn't breathing," Bryan says, his voice panicked. "Dial nine-one-one."

"We're in fucking Nigeria," Sommy cries.

"Dial something, then!" he screams. "Dial whatever it is you guys dial in this fucking dead-ass country!"

Sommy's crying fully now, wide mouth, contracting nose. "I don't know what we dial. I don't know."

She runs to the car, to Mezie, still seated on the driver's seat, transfixed. She grabs her phone. She dials the number of the one person she knows to dial.

"Mummy," Sommy says. "Mezie has killed somebody."

"Isii gi ni?"

"He hit her with the car," Sommy says.

There's silence, heavy breathing. Bryan comes behind her and says to Mezie, "Dude, you need to fucking snap out of this shit, and get the fuck out of the car. You just fucking hit a woman. We need to get her to a hospital."

Mezie doesn't move. He sits, trembling.

Sommy listens as her mother dishes out instruction: "Get her in the car. Drive to Graceland Hospital. I'll call Dr. Okoye. I'll meet you people there. Do not panic. The best way to spoil things is to panic."

Sommy yanks open the glove compartment and takes out a pair of scissors. She rips her dress from the knee and signals to Bryan that she's ready. There's a sensation of disappearing that overwhelms her as she walks to the body, like she's becoming multiple smaller, anesthetized persons. On reaching her, she sinks her hands into the bloodied, muddied skirt, grabs the woman's legs. Bryan folds his arms into her underarms. They stagger to the car. Bryan places the woman's bleeding head on the seat, and runs to the opposite door, scampers onto the backseat, and grabs her underarms again. Gravity is on Sommy's side. It is Bryan who does all the pulling. She focuses on gripping the bony legs.

The woman is frail but tall, and her entire frame fills the backseat.

"I can't sit in there," Bryan says, after they've folded the woman into back of the car.

"You are the one with the most blood of the three of us," Sommy says. "And you don't know the way to the hospital, and apparently Mezie can't drive. You have to sit at the back."

Sommy pushes the ripped piece of her dress at him, says, "Clean your hands."

She opens the door to the driver's seat, leans over to unbuckle Mezie's seat belt, and tells him to step out. He does so in slow motion. She walks with him to the other side of the car. When she's certain he's fastened in, she shuts the door.

It's terribly dark now. The street is still empty. Cars drive past occasionally, but no one stops. She's grateful for the dark, for the quiet. It's all she can think about, that no one has seen them.

At the hospital, a team of nurses meet them at the entrance. The woman is lifted onto a stretcher and rolled into the building. A nurse, face swollen with sleep, says Dr. Okoye is on his way. She asks them to wait in the reception area.

Mezie, released from shock, is pacing. Bryan stands by the window, looking as if through a camera lens, with a precise quietude.

The nurse behind the reception desk walks to Sommy. She's holding a form.

"Did you find anything on her? A wallet, an ID?"

Sommy says she didn't.

"Did she say anything to you? Anything that will help us locate her family."

"No. She lost consciousness immediately."

The nurse adjusts the pink clip holding the bun of her silky weave. "Your mother said the person who did this didn't even stop for a second. Just drove away. Why would someone do that?" She shakes her head. "Just hit another human being and run away? Even if it's a dog, you stop and help them. Life is not nothing."

Sommy takes a hand to her chest and presses to still the hammering. The nurse walks to Mezie, who is pacing still.

"Sit, sir," she says. "I'll get you something to help relax you. Just try and breathe through it."

The nurse disappears through a door.

Sommy walks to Bryan. "Are you okay?"

He gives her a bewildered look, head so awkwardly bent, as if reorienting both body and soul to understand her. She looks away, looks now to Mezie, who's seated, head lowered toward the floor. She leaves Bryan and walks toward him. When she reaches him, she leans forward, whispers stiffly, "You, get yourself together. Mummy has taken care of it. No one knows anything. Just, please, behave."

He doesn't seem to be hearing her. "I hit her," he says. "She might die."

"No. The car in front of us hit her and sped away. We stopped. We stopped because we are good people. We helped her."

Mezie raises his head.

"We helped her," Sommy says again, with a nod.

Mezie breathes. "We helped her."

"We helped her."

Bryan walks over, holding the bloodied rag she'd pressed into his chest. His eyes are unusually clear, and she sees them now as if for the first time, a soft snail brown. She takes his hand and pulls him to the corner. "Just follow my lead. I beg you. Please."

She doesn't want to imagine how he sees her in this moment. She wants a warm bed, and darkness. She wants to sleep and wake up to a life blanched of this stain.

Her mother and Dr. Okoye arrive at the same time. Elin is still nowhere to be found. Sommy's father is out looking for her. It is exactly midnight now. Three hours since Elin walked out of the house. They all sit quietly in the reception. Not a word is said.

Dr. Okoye walks in, tells them that the woman is alive, but in a coma. There's a head injury, and a head scan is in progress. He tells them to go home. The hospital will take care of her. He thanks them again for stopping, for helping, and says that the incident will be reported to the police later in the day.

Her mother tells Dr. Okoye to call immediately if the woman wakes up. She would like to come and see her. She wouldn't want the woman to feel alone, especially seeing that it might take a while for her to get ID'd. Dr. Okoye says he will. He encourages them all to try to get enough sleep.

———

Sommy rides alone with Bryan in the bloodied car. They do not speak to each other. Sommy thinks that if there is a hell, it is this, this in perpetuity.

When they arrive at her mother's, Elin is seated with their father. She'd walked back herself. She tells everyone she'd gone to a hotel bar near the estate gate. She says this while staring at their blood-stained clothes. Her eyes are scared, seeking. Their father has told her about the accident, that they'd come upon a woman hit by car and left to die.

"Are you okay?" she says to Mezie, touching his elbow.

"I am fine." He leans on the wall by the door.

Bryan slumps onto the couch and covers his face with his palms. Sommy stares at his soft curly hair. How she wishes she could see through it, into the movie of his mind.

Her mother doesn't think it safe that they go back home. She wants all of them together. They take turns in the shower. Mezie and Bryan change into her father's clothes. Her mother hands Sommy and Elin each a wrapper to tie. No one sleeps. Even little Florence. They sit in the sitting room, watching the window, waiting for the sun to rise.

The next morning, as they leave, her mother instructs them to keep their phones' ringers on, and to get some sleep, and to Sommy in particular, in a quick conversation by the door, she says: "Keep an eye on your brother."

When they arrive at Mezie's, everyone disappears into their rooms, but Sommy stays back in the sitting room, nervous about being alone with Bryan. Elin walks into the room shortly after, and says she wants to make everyone breakfast. She perceives them as saviors now, pities them. Chisom's matter is inconsequential. Sommy dozes off for a bit, and when she stirs awake, Elin is setting the table. She's fried eggs and toasted slices of wheat bread.

"Can you get Bryan?" Elin says.

"Sure."

Sommy's fear feels palpable as she pushes open the door. Bryan is lying on the bed, face down on the mattress.

"Babe, breakfast?" She shuts the door quietly behind her.

He half rises, turns slightly to her. "I am good."

"Babe."

He rises fully now. He's shirtless and she can see the pink welts of mosquito bites from last night on his arm. He walks to the wardrobe, throws it open, and begins to pull his clothes from the hangers.

"I'll move to the guest room," he says, without looking at her. "I need to be alone."

"You don't need to move. I'll move. I'll leave you alone. I promise."

He pauses and turns to look at her. It's a long stare. She quickly busies herself with packing some clothes, her makeup and skin-care products arranged carelessly on the plastic table by the window.

At the guest room, Sommy collapses on the floor. There's an acute moment when she has the urge to walk back into the room and speak diplomatically to Bryan, furnish him with the horror stories she's heard of prison. Men jam-packed in tiny rooms, shitting and pissing on each other, feasts for mosquitoes and ants. Tell him about Awkuzu Police Station, where officers kill old inmates en masse, throwing their bodies into dumps to create space for the constant overflow of new inmates. Ask him if she ought to fold her arms and watch her brother become a victim of the system in a much more vicious way than he already is. Ask him if he was here with them when Mezie came home from the airport that day, with that washed sallowness of the dead, and said to her that he feels finished. Ask him if he'd joined them on their rounds of suicide watch after the attempt. If he knew what it meant to them that Mezie's, after all these years, risen from the depression and humiliation of imprisonment and deportation. Ask him if she's expected, knowing all that she knows, having seen all that she's seen, to facilitate his return to those dark depths. The decision had been as clear to her as day and night, as it had been to her mother.

The day goes by in slow motion. Sommy lets Elin know that Bryan wants to be left alone, and Elin says she understands, that

Mezie is also very quiet when he isn't asleep, and barely ate breakfast that morning.

"It must have been traumatic," Elin says.

"It was," Sommy replies.

Around evening, Sommy goes to ask Bryan if he'd like to pack for his trip to Amawbia the next day. He says no. And that's it: "No." She doesn't know what it means, if it means he doesn't want to pack yet, or if it means he's canceled the trip. She doesn't ask for fear that he might begin to answer other unasked questions.

Her mother calls to give updates about the woman. She tells Sommy that the woman is still in a coma, and that no one has come to claim her. She says, too, that the police have called, inviting them for questioning. She says there's nothing to worry about, that the DPO is a customer of hers. She's known him for years. He'll be kind to them.

"But what if the woman wakes up?" Sommy says, holding back tears.

"What about that?"

"What if she knows what car hit her?"

"How will she know? And if she insists, it will be her word against ours. Just get Bryan and Mezie to have their stories straight. Okay?"

Sommy begins to cry. "Mummy, this is so fucked up."

Her mother sighs. "There will be time for crying, but now isn't it. Okay?"

"I can't," Sommy says, snorting.

"I know, nwa'm. I know. Please, for your brother's sake. For my sake. Okay? Biko. Just get it together. Don't let Mezie see you like this."

"What is Daddy saying?"

"I didn't tell him anything," her mother says. "You know how he is. He will start panicking. Do we want that?"

"Mummy—"

"I'll tell him later. He knows the real story."

"The real story?"

"Yes. The real story."

To feel something other than misery, Sommy calls Amara. Amara is stuck in traffic and has a bad connection. She calls Kayla and listens as she narrates her adventures with her new Chicago boo, an R & B artiste, who Kayla's convinced will one day be a superstar. She calls Nia afterward. They spend long minutes talking about the nutrition and fitness certification Nia's taking to become a fitness instructor. Sommy laughs and laughs at her friends' sunshine stories. It's a strange sound, her laughter, and once, while on the phone with Kayla, she stops, pulls up her skirt, and traces the birthmark between her thighs, searching for evidence that she's still the Somkele Nwachukwu whom all of this had indeed happened to in real life, and not in a dream. She, who had at last found love. She, for whom life had finally opened for. Look how easily the wind blew everything away.

Sommy had imagined that the days after the incident would come with roaring destabilization. She imagined arrests, flying accusations, screaming matches. She imagined more blood. Everything falling apart. But the days pass languidly, with everyone so cautious, so suspicious, as if relearning how to be human.

Sommy is unable to talk to Mezie alone. Elin clings to him like she's his shell, and he her soft animal body. It is a role Elin seems to have been waiting for, the caregiver, the healer. It is in this role she looks most like herself—vibrant, assertive. She wants to coax him back to life with small touches and warm food. Through the thin wall of the bedrooms, Sommy can hear her say to Mezie: "Babe, you should eat." "You should go out and take some sunshine." "Would you at least drink a glass of water?" It's the opposite of Sommy's interactions with Bryan, which are stilted and occur only when she goes to ask if he'd like to eat. Sometimes he says yes, and she brings him Elin's meatball stew or salmon pasta. Sometimes he says an abrupt no. Other times, he meets her with silence. She wishes fiercely that like Elin, Bryan had not witnessed the accident.

All four of them only seem capable of cooking and eating. Real words fail them. It is as though they cannot skip past what has happened and continue on with their future plans: all of the places they had planned to explore when Elin arrived, Bryan's plan to go back to Amawbia to see his father. They've decided to stay transfixed in the present. Not acknowledging the past and not acknowledging the future, for to leave the apartment, to talk about leaving the apartment, would disrupt the present, and kickstart the after, an after heavy with foreboding.

It's around this period, when days blend into days, and morning and night seem the same in Sommy's mind, that Chisom knocks on the door.

"What?" Sommy says, blocking the doorframe.

"Mezie hasn't been picking up my call. I need to know how he's doing."

Chisom looks delirious, as if from sleep or sorrow. Her braids are messily packed in a high bun, and her nails are chipped.

"He's doing fine," Sommy says sternly.

"Can you just go in and tell him I'm here?"

Sommy steps out and closes the door behind her. "Are you obtuse or what? He doesn't want to speak to you, or he would have picked up your call."

Chisom bites her lips and takes in a deep breath. "He won't pick up my call if she's there. If you just find a way to tell him I'm here, he'll come meet me outside. She doesn't have to know I'm here."

Chisom avoids eye contact as she speaks, and Sommy can tell that it's taking something grand and bottomless for her to say what she's saying, that without the history she has with Mezie, these words would seem unbelievable even to her, and it softens Sommy.

"What do you hope to get out of this?" Sommy says. "You think he will leave her for you?"

"It's none of your business, Somkele."

Sommy laughs, a small, snide laugh, and says, "I know you think he's with her because of the papers. He's told you that he plans to apply for another visa in five years. That she's his ticket out of this fucked-up country. That it's you he really loves. That when he gets his papers, he will come back for you. Right? Am I lying?" She waves a hand, shifts her weight to one hip. "But isn't it what he told you when he left the first time? Did he come back for you? Was he not forced back? And when he got back, what happened? You were here, waiting for him. He slipped into you like you are an old abandoned cloth, and you let him. You let him because you can't imagine your life without him. You've just never been able to." She pinches back the snort dripping from her nose. "It all starts in the imagination." She drums a finger on the side of her forehead. "You have to reimagine your life, Chisom. Imagine a life without Mezie in it, and then start to live. He is my brother, and I'll die for him if it comes to it. But you don't have to. You can find someone better. I can't find a better brother. He is it for me. It's not the same for you. You can walk away."

Chisom looks at her with shrunken eyes. "Somkele, with you, there are no surprises. How can I take advice from you about loving? You people did this to Mezie. You people caused his depression. You and your mother. You people forced him to go to that stupid Norway. 'Buy me this, buy me that. Make money. Hustle hard o!' That's all he hears from you people. That's all you people care about." She shakes her head, stares boldly at Sommy. "One week after your brother tried to kill himself, what did you do? You carried your bag and went to America. And you say you love him? I was the one here for him. When he was having panic attacks, I was the one who held him." She beats her chest with her fingers. "With these hands." She raises her hands and then stretches them toward Sommy. "For days. I held him. I did not sleep until he slept. I did not eat until he ate. Do not tell me anything about loving someone." She breathes hard. "Just respect yourself and tell Mezie I came."

Chisom starts to walk away, but she turns back, gets very close to Sommy so that their noses almost brush, and says: "Never ever in your life give me advice like you care about me. I only take advice from people who have shown me love, and you've never even liked me. You've always looked at me with disgust."

For a minute, they stand, silent, staring, both of them now carcasses, having direly devastated each other. Chisom then wafts away, as if a ghost, leaving Sommy standing there by the door, wishing for an apocalypse.

Sommy feels an urgent need to check Bryan's phone. Something tells her he's trying to rebook his ticket to the United States, bring his departure date closer, abandon her here with her murderous family. She doesn't know how to tell him that he might get questioned by the police, and how to tell him that if it happens, he must stick to the real story, the story they've all agreed upon. The thought of losing him feels like strangulation, a total absence of air. It distorts her insides. She understands that he needs time. It's his one request from her: "Leave me alone." And she's tried to give him that in the past week. Yet, she thinks that he of all people should understand the pain of uncertainty, that peculiar, burning position of not knowing. It is where he's left her, just as Mezie had done during her first months in Iowa.

It's a Tuesday morning in late June, and Sommy, Mezie, and their mother are on their way to the police station. Their mother is the driver. Mezie sits in the passenger seat. Sommy sits watching them from the backseat. Mezie is nodding as their mother tells of a squabble she had with a customer a few days ago. It's the first time all three of them are alone since the incident. The last time was the morning of the party, when her mother called her and Mezie into her room for a quick prayer. It's been a little over a week since the thanksgiving party, and they have become different people. They have grown and shrunk at once, Sommy thinks, and it took mere seconds, this event that has shifted everything.

As they pull into the police station, their mother preps them for questioning. She says that the questions will be brief. The police have no witnesses, and they aren't looking, she says, and the hospital says no one has come to claim the woman.

"She's like a nobody," her mother says. "Like she fell out of the sky." She makes eye contact with Sommy in the rearview mirror, and then turns quicky to Mezie. "Both of you, don't worry, nnugo?"

"Okay, ma," they say in unison, suddenly like children looking for safety under the wings of their mother.

The police station is a squat bungalow, painted leaf green. A stripe of white paint goes around the building like a ribbon. At the compound in the middle of which it sits, there are dusty cars and dusty trees, and a few people standing about, on their phones, or in tyrannical conversations with policemen who have something they need. The atmosphere feels oppressive, and there's this moment, as they walk into the station, though it passes swiftly, when Sommy wants to bolt. Run and not stop until she's tucked safely under a blanket in her and Bryan's shared Iowa apartment.

Inside, it is stuffy. A lone, cobwebbed bulb shines a meek yellow all over. A fan turns lazily, squeaking, blowing more heat than breeze. On the bench by the counter is a man in a round cap, palms pressed to his face, legs shaking. He doesn't look up at them. Sommy and Mezie stand by the man, while their mother walks to the officers behind the counter and tells them they've been invited.

"Mrs. Nwachukwu?" The officer says, looking down at a large notebook.

"Yes, Mrs. Nwachukwu," her mother says.

He raises his head for a quick inspection, after which he calls for an officer, who scuttles in from a door behind the desk.

"Take our friends to DPO office," he says.

"Yes, sir!"

They walk through a dark hallway, past open offices that smell of sweat and harbor piles of paper, corked water bottles, half-eaten dishes. Before they near the rows of cells down the hallway, from which hoarse voices float—men begging for food and mercy in broken English—they are ushered into an office where three officers sit, eating boli and groundnut.

The DPO, an athletic man, middle-aged, newly graying, leans back upon seeing them. "Madam, madam," he hails.

He could be older, but his sprightliness gives him the appearance of a man at his peak.

"Oga DPO," her mother says, smiling. "You invited us and we've come."

"I would have sent my officers to your house, madam. But you didn't give us transport money."

Her mother waves a hand, laughing. "Abi, we are now here." She takes the cracked leather seat by the window, and gestures for Sommy and Mezie to sit beside her. "This your office is too hot. Is your air conditioner bad?" She smiles. "And you know my children—my daughter, Somkele, my son, Mezie—they've lived abroad for so long. They don't like the heat."

"Ahhh," the DPO turns to them. "Sorry o! Abroad children! Officer Dele, oya go to the other room and bring that standing fan. These are my special guests."

Her mother laughs. "Abeg, don't worry yourself too much. Let's just do the questioning fast and finish."

The DPO picks up the old, soaked newspaper that had formerly housed the now eaten boli. He squeezes it as he runs the tip of his tongue through his teeth, and then hands it to Officer Dele, who collects it with a bow. He gulps a bottle of water, sucking until the bottle contracts, makes a cracking sound. Satisfied, he launches into the questions. The questions: What time did the accident happen? What was the color of the car that hit the woman? Did they catch a glimpse of the plate number? Was there anyone else around? Why did they stop to help? Why didn't they drive off? Did they find anything on the woman? Anything that can help them identify the woman?

Sommy answers it all. She's not surprised at how unflinchingly, convincingly, she speaks, how detached from herself she feels, as though possessed by someone both strange and familiar. She's had enough practice now, and she's glad Bryan didn't have to come along, to see her this way. Their mother said it was best that he did not come, and when Sommy told him this, he said, "Good, because this whole thing is a circus show, and I can't partake in it anymore."

"Madam Nwachukwu," the DPO says. "You have raised premium children, good citizens. Many people would not have stopped to help that poor woman."

Her mother sighs. "It's not my doing, Oga DPO. It's God's doing, and we thank Him."

Sommy has avoided looking at Mezie for fear that she might absorb his evident weakness, but she finds herself turning now, inspecting. His head is bowed, his elbows rest on his knees, and his hands are clasped. It is a wonder what they've all become, Sommy thinks, killers and liars. It is a wonder how she and her mother sashay through it all with the grace of peacocks.

Before they leave, her mother hands the DPO an envelope. "For a new air conditioner for the station."

The DPO thanks her profusely. Oga Dele says he'll stop by the bar later that evening. The third officer, Officer Chukwu, sits quietly, watching them with what Sommy suspects is judgment.

Her mother drops them off at Mezie's, and Sommy and Mezie alight without saying a word to her. They climb up the apartment staircase. At the landing, Sommy grips the railing and Mezie fishes for the keys in the pockets of his black pants. Through the hexagonally cut holes in the wall, Sommy can see her mother's silver jeep parked by a blue water tank branded GEEPEE.

"You are not going to say anything?" Sommy says.

Mezie turns to her slowly, jangling the keys. "About what?"

The railing feels cold in her palm. She releases her grip and grips instead the strap of her tote bag. "I'm just wondering if you think that when you don't talk about stuff it disappears."

"What do you want me to say?"

"You are doing the same thing that you did when I left for Iowa."

He turns his back to her, and ruffles through the bunch of keys. She can see her mother drive off now, leaving a cloud of dust behind.

"You are shutting me out," she says.

He pauses. The apartment key is in the door hole and the rest of the bunch fall, a shower of steel.

"It's because I don't know what to say to you."

"Are you going to tell Elin the truth?"

He looks at her, horrified.

"I mean about Chisom. I'm sure you lied. It's why she's still here."

His face calms. "There's nothing to tell."

"You know she came visiting, right? Chisom?"

"She texted me."

They stand in silence for a short while. Mezie clicks the key in the lock and opens the door. He holds it for her to walk through. She doesn't move. She feels glued to the ground by the heft of her sadness.

"I don't know you anymore," she says.

He stares at her angrily, and she can feel him argue with himself before he releases his hold, and the door, as if pushed by a gust of wind, slams shut in her face.

Inside, Bryan sits on the bed, alert. He has on blue shorts but no shirt. His journal is open. Sommy squints to see if she can catch a few words. He notices and closes it.

"How did it go?" he says.

"It went fine."

There's silence, so she rummages through the wardrobe, where she's hung her T-shirts, singlets, blouses. She pulls a light-yellow cotton singlet from the cloth hanger and lays it on her shoulder. She's refused to move all her things to the guest room. She wants every opportunity she can get to see him.

"Fine. That's all? This is about me, too, Sommy."

"I am sorry. I didn't know you wanted details. They asked us questions, but they weren't really interested in the answers. It's not a real case for them. No one knows who the woman is. There's no one on her side."

"Why can't they identify her?"

Sommy shoves her hand inside her shirt and unclips her bra. "I don't know. That's how it works here."

He tucks his palms into his lap. "I want to leave."

Sommy holds a breath and releases it. She then nods meekly, understandingly, and says, after a moment of painful, turbulent emotions, "Bryan, I am a good person."

He turns to her fully, and his face is cold, naked. He's perhaps thinking that everyone believes themselves beacons of goodness, attributing their ugliness to the circumstances of life. Twisted and bent by life, so they twist and bend other people. The cycle of pain.

"Do you believe that?" he says.

"I'm sorry that you had to see that, and that you have to carry this. That you had to see me that way. I am sorry."

"No, answer the question. Do you believe that you are a good person?"

"Yes."

There's a long melancholic stare out the window, and then he turns to her. "Then tell Elin. She's there right now with him, which means he also lied about his relationship with Chisom. Go tell her the truth."

"It's not my place—"

"Fucking bullshit."

"Bryan—"

"I can't do this. I'm literally shaking right now. I've been shaking all week. I need to get out of here."

"Just wait a week and we can leave together."

"I'm done with your family's mad drama, the lies and deceit. It's beyond me."

"Bryan—"

"And don't tell me that's how it works here like I'm some fucking expat fool. This is common decency we are talking about. And common decency is universal. I am no fool."

There's a knock on the door, and then Elin's head peeking into the room. "Is everything fine?"

Bryan stands, presses his palms together. "We are good."

Elin turns to Sommy, raises a brow.

"We are good," Sommy says, her gaze fixed on Bryan, his gaze fixed on her.

Elin is silent for a moment, and then she says, "You two be good."

When she shuts the door, Bryan collapses onto the bed. Sommy walks to him and sits. In that instant, the sky brightens, a shattering surge of light illuminates the room: Bryan's tired face, his Moleskin journal pimpled with pen marks, a teacup and a small potted plant, the sole occupants of the table where Sommy had once lined her skin-care products.

"One week," she says. "Please."

She's able to ask this now because she knows something she did not know before, that he's become bound to her, that they are ruined tree branches now fused. He could have left for Iowa. He could have said something to Elin. He can afford to do both. But he is here. He's inherited her fears and burdens, and what greater love is there? Falling to the deepest depths and rising to the highest heights together.

He picks up his journal, holds it to his chin, and then tells her that he'll only stay if they can go to the scene of the accident and ask around about the woman. Someone might know something, he says, and he hates that she lies there alone, still in a coma, unclaimed. Sommy says she's been thinking of doing just that. She makes to hold his hand, but he moves it, a slight move, almost imperceptible. But she perceives it. She's awake to his corporeality in a way that she never was.

They spend the next few days around the scene of the incident, going from house to house, shop to shop, asking if anyone knows of someone looking for a missing person. On the fourth day, back from searching, and still with no leads, they sit quietly in the room. Their optimism has waned, and their daily journey feels the more like penance, a useless suffering.

Bryan develops a new containment. He smiles and chats with Elin. With Mezie, he is distant but cordial. Sommy is suspicious of this. She thought he'd at the very least insist that they move to a hotel while Sommy prepares for them to leave. The money he'd transferred to her Nigerian bank account was enough to pay a whole year's rent for an apartment. He's also not brought up his father, the visit they planned, the treatments he'd suggested to her. It's as though that pain had to give way for this new one.

She's suspicious, too, of the new spring in Mezie's steps. He's laughing again now and making plans with Elin. They will go to a resort in Abeokuta the next week, and then to Abuja to see a friend of Elin's, whom she met on Facebook. They might go to Ghana, just to explore. To see new places. Sommy thinks she ought to be grateful. There's a sense of normalcy back in their lives. What she'd thought completely broken is standing, albeit on one leg. But she's not grateful. Try as she might, she cannot allow sunlight in. There's a dreadful gravelly gray mist in the air. Inside her.

She invites Amara over, an attempt to clear the mist. And as always, Amara arrives with the energy of an airplane taking off.

"This Lagos traffic no go kill person," Amara says in that high-pitched voice of hers. She sits with her feet folded under her butt. Her bright blue eyeliner gives a lovely shine to her face, and Sommy thinks she's never seen her this beautiful.

Sommy asks if she wants a drink, and Amara requests a Diet Coke.

She's opening the can when Amara says, "You don't want to show me your brother's oyibo girlfriend?"

"They went swimming," Sommy says of Mezie and Elin.

"Bryan nko?"

"Sleeping," Sommy says.

"Ahhh. This house is boring. Let's go out, abeg."

Soon they are in an Uber, heading to the Island, and trading pains—Sommy, a lank version of the story of what's happening with Bryan, that he's seen her too closely and is now retreating; Amara, of a constant feeling of hopelessness.

"I am tired," Amara says. "My target is to bring in a million naira into the company every month, or my salary gets slashed. One million, Somkele, and because I couldn't meet my target last month, my fucking boss cut twenty K from my salary. After all my hard work, I looked at the end-of-month bank alert, and I cried. When I complained, the stupid man told me to resign if I can't work hard. That there are many people looking for jobs." She sighs. "Sometimes I feel like my life is on standstill."

"You'll write TOEFL," Sommy says. "And you will leave this country. Leave that stupid job. Okay?"

Sommy thinks that being with Amara this way after a long time apart feels like returning to a childhood home. She knows this place. Her fingerprints are stamped on the walls of every room. But she left, and time changes things. The pots are no longer in the bottom drawer in the kitchen. The spoons are now fewer than five. And the stove? Maybe it's no longer a kerosene stove. Maybe the new owner has replaced it with an electric stove. It is the house she knows, but it isn't.

"I hope I don't kill myself before then," Amara says, and laughs.

Sommy hits her shoulder. "Stop that, abeg."

Throughout the ride, Sommy sneaks glances Amara's way. She thinks how suddenly adulthood sprang upon them. Not long ago, they had been undergrads, and the things they wanted seemed possible, simple things, a nice job in a bank or an advertising company, a well-off husband, nice clothes and nice shoes, kids sometime down the line. They'd never been girls with big dreams. Their dreams were compact and safe. They could pull them out of their pockets and show them off, and no one would look quizzically at them. Their dreams had been shells for their desperate need for ease. Ease. In their undergrad days, they did not have ease. This was before Sommy's mother's business began booming. Before, when her father was the sole breadwinner, with his meager civil-service salary that barely kept their home running. Most of the dates she and Amara went on then, they went on so they could eat. They went days without money in either of their accounts. They had hope, though, hope that either Sommy's father or Amara's sister would send them money. Their hostel had no running water, so they had to draw it from the well in the next compound. Their room had no air conditioner, and the ceiling fan broke often, and they sweated and sweated. But it was all fine. It was all fine because they believed it would get better. They would graduate and get jobs and have their own money. Simple money. Money for a car and a house with running water. They would marry well. They would have husbands whose responsibility it was to take care of them. Their lives would be ones of ease. They had not believed otherwise. They had not known life then. Sommy had not known that life was a tangled mass, and she would always be in a state of untangling it. That there would be many days it will all feel like eating rubber, a kind of pointless, unfeeling gnawing. That there was no being okay, no ease. Being okay for a while, a few days, maybe, a few weeks, maybe. But never for too long. And looking at Amara now, her face turned to the window, Sommy's glad that she had not known. She's glad that they had been so full of hope, that they had gone on those dates with men they did not like, spent many laughing hours coming up with ways to escape these dates unscathed, glad that they had used their infrequent feeding money to buy nice secondhand dresses, dresses they wore clubbing, and to their fake dates, glad that they had found every opportunity to dance and to laugh and to dream. She's glad that she had not known true loss then, had not felt the vast, obliterating pain that settled in after Mezie's attempt. She's glad that she could breathe then, and her entire body received air gracefully. No stops. No holding back. She's glad. She stretches her hand now to Amara, and Amara takes it in hers, but she does not stop looking out the window.

When they arrive on the Island, it is night, and the air is chill. The Uber drops them at Cuba Lounge, and they stand outside for a while, taking selfies. Sommy feels then, with Amara's face pressed to hers, a sudden burst of profound love for the night, the musical arrangement of the streetlights, which, from where she stands, seem to be scraping the dark sky. She feels love for the buildings, tall and brightly lit, with a spryness to them, colorful and seeking, unlike the stoic, assured colors of the buildings in Iowa, gray and light gray, brown and deep brown. She loves the palm fronds that peek into the road like elegant Igbo masquerades. They remind her of the beach, that she is close to water, on an Island. She loves the cars moving slowly on the other side of the road, loud music banging from their stereos, the red of their taillights like angry eyes; she loves them, the cars, the people in them. They are doing what people do to get going in life: go out drinking, dancing, touch each other with an intimacy reserved for night, an intimacy that in daylight would mean something else, something invasive and encroaching. She loves the night hawkers glittering under the street-lights, their trays of chewing gum and sweets and cigarettes balanced on their heads, their thighs. She loves the agile men controlling the traffic, directing cars into tight parking spaces for change. She's glad for this feeling, and she wishes that Bryan could be here, the Bryan before the incident, the glass-eyed, touristy-eyed Bryan, the Bryan for whom this scenery would have felt like a kind of homecoming.

Inside the club, Davido booms from the speakers. The darkness is occasionally shattered by thin lines of varicolored lights, which illuminate the people on the dance floor. Sommy and Amara sit by the bar. Sommy says she wants a cocktail, but Amara says, "Cocktail ke? In a club on the Island? You don miss road be that." She laughs, continues, "They sell things in bottles here. A bottle of wine or a bottle of Hennessey. Gone are the good old days of ordering a glass of cocktail."

They decide on wine.

"Oyibo man wife," Amara hails as Sommy hands her card to the waiter. There's a slash of sarcasm in her voice, which Sommy in the moment decides to ignore.

Beside them are three drunken girls. They are dancing atop a table, hands swaying, their long golden braids whipping the air. Sommy watches them for a while, amused at how similar they look: tall, heavy backsides, thin waists, light skin. They seem to have risen from the sea, beautiful in the way of unnaturally cultivated things—sandpapered, too clean. It is painfully obvious that their display is packaged for the table of six men opposite them. Men who, in what Sommy thinks is a clever contrivance of nature, look similar also, all of them showing the onset of a potbelly, their necks adorned with gold chains, their wrists with expensive watches. They are not old men. They look to be in their midforties, the age around which men, noticing the loss of their youth and eager to make up for what seems to them like a lack, turn to the glamour money can buy—jewelry, designer T-shirts, shoes.

"Why are you smiling?" Amara says. She's bopping her head to the music.

Sommy tells her, over the loud music, that there's something inexplicably right about being amongst people whose gestures, ticks, movements are accessible to her, so that she can sit here and understand their sociality, even if in a limited way. It is a way of being she'd missed while away, a thing of constant frustration while in Iowa, her inability to read people.

Amara says that Sommy sounds a little racist, and Sommy says that it is an easy conclusion to make. The truth, she says, is that we are all drawn to the familiar, whether or not we like it.

"What if a white person or an Asian person says this?" Amara says lightly. It is obvious now that the conversation is aimless, a slightly drunken one, for they are now relaxing into the night, enjoying themselves.

"It's okay to yearn for the familiar, but we are also complex beings. We can, and must, transcend this limited way of being."

It is in Bryan's voice Sommy speaks. It is the sort of conversation they'd have. The thought of him spikes something in her, and she fills her glass with wine and takes a big gulp. She'd left him a text to let him know she'd be back late, but she'd not said where she was going. In some sick, desperate way, she'd hoped that withholding this information would make him worry about her, and perhaps make him a little jealous. She takes another big gulp.

"Easy girl," Amara says.

"Let's buy Hennessey," Sommy says, feeling suddenly the urge to drown thoughts of Bryan.

They get a bottle of Hennessey this time. The waiter, a smallish man, reluctantly uncorks a bottle and places it before them. Sommy suspects that he's the type of man who despises serving young women, and she wants to tell him that she's paying as much as the men around whom he flaps gratefully. But she isn't drunk enough.

"You are a big woman now o!" Amara says. "Look at you buying Hennessey in the club."

"It's Bryan's money," Sommy says. "I might wake tomorrow, and he would ask me to give him his money back."

"Never. He is so taken by you."

As if scorning Sommy, a couple walks past them then. The girl is holding the boy from behind, hands around his waist, her face pressed into his back. The sight of them causes Sommy to sigh. She's raw with misery. She knows that Bryan is still caught in the shock of what has happened. She knows that he would arrive soon at the inevitable decision to end their relationship.

"Are you okay?" Amara says. She touches her gently on the shoulder, and Sommy caves quickly. She tells Amara everything. She can't tell what Amara hears, what is swallowed by the music, and what is clipped by her crying and snorting.

"I feel like if the woman dies, she'll haunt me," Sommy says. "She can't just go like that. Don't you think? People don't get away with things like this. One way or the other, we will pay."

"But Mezie didn't know," Amara says, unsure. "It was dark, abi?"

"He was drunk. I knew he was drunk. But I wasn't thinking about that. I wasn't expecting that he'd hit anyone. I didn't even know we would drive that long. I thought we would find Elin nearby."

"That Elin sef," Amara says. "Why would she just walk out of the house in the night? Does she think this place is Norway?"

Amara is taking it too well, too casually, so Sommy brings to the fore what is most pressing.

"Bryan saw everything," she says. "He witnessed us, me and my mum, lying to the doctor. He knows we lied to the police."

Amara is quiet. She takes a sip of drink. The music switches to 2face's "African Queen." The atmosphere changes, goes from a frenzied jerking of bodies to soothing back-and-forth movements.

"It will be okay," Amara says finally.

It will be okay—what people say when the only option is to hope for the best of an utterly irredeemable situation.

The bottle of Hennessey is halfway done. Sommy's sorrow is mixed now with recklessness. She tells Amara that she wants to go to the hospital, that she senses that the woman would die soon, and she wants to ask forgiveness from the living, and not the dead. Who knows what happens after death? Who knows what could become of a restless spirit?

"Are you sure?" Amara asks.

Sommy says she is, and Amara, who seems less drunk, orders an Uber. Their Uber arrives immediately, and they make their way to the exit, where they are approached by two men who ask if they'd like to join their table.

"Please get away," Amara replies snidely.

One of the men, startled, vexed, screams, "Frog-faced bitch!"

Amara turns around, stretches her hand, widens her fingers. "Waka! Your mother, frog-faced bitch."

They hurry into the Uber and drive away.

The drive to the hospital is short. The road is clear, few cars, fewer people about. The driver tries to make small talk. He says that he wishes Lagos roads were this free all day. He says that earlier that evening, he'd spent three hours in a standstill traffic at Third Mainland Bridge. He says that he is thinking of relocating to Abuja. Lagos life is too hectic. He soon stops talking when he notices their laconic replies.

They knock at the hospital gate for a while before a sleepy man shows up, pointing a flashlight at them.

"Oga," Amara says, hands on her waist. "If someone is dying and we are bringing them here for treatment, they would be dead by now."

"How may I help you?" the man says, grudgingly, as if to unruly children throwing a tantrum.

Amara stares at Sommy, and Sommy who had thought they'd easily slip into the hospital, says she wants to see her mother, who's a patient at the hospital.

The man observes them for a minute and then steps aside.

The nurse on duty immediately recognizes Sommy. She'd been part of the team of nurses who had come to meet them at the hospital entrance when they brought in the woman.

When Sommy tells her she's come to see the woman, the nurse turns to the white clock hanging at the other end of the room, and says, "Is it not too late, my dear?"

"Please, ma, I want to pray for her."

The nurse looks at Sommy sadly, like she knows something of this kind of madness. She then turns to Amara, says, "And you are?"

"A friend," Amara says, pulling down the edges of her miniskirt.

The nurse says to follow her. They walk through a hallway, heavy with the smell of Dettol, and past rooms covered with flimsy blue curtains, with lines of rolling beds. In one room, a patient is slouched, vomiting into a plastic bucket. In another, a patient is seated on the bed, legs dangling, humming a familiar gospel tune. A nurse walks past, holding a tray of syringes.

The woman's room is at the end of the hallway. Sommy wonders if this is where the hospital keeps the hopeless, in the rooms at the end of the hallway. She pauses, stares at Amara. Amara holds her hand, and nods, and together they walk in.

The woman's small, dark body is covered in an oversized blue hospital gown. Sommy moves closer. She realizes now that she hadn't looked the woman in the face, that the face she'd seen in her dreams had been another face, an imagined face. This face is big-jawed and small-lipped.

No one has come to claim her, but Sommy's sure that someone is out there looking for her. There's no one without people, without a person. Or perhaps not. Perhaps the woman is alone in the world. Sommy makes to touch her, but she stops midway.

"Someone would come for her, right?" Sommy whispers to Amara.

"I don't know," Amara says, studying the woman as if attempting to inscribe her every feature into memory. "You know what I'm thinking?"

"What?"

"It's inappropriate somehow, but I'm thinking it."

"What?"

"This kind of rubbish disaster doesn't happen to beautiful people or rich people. Like, if this woman were fine or rich, there will be people here for her. Does that make sense?"

"No, it does not make any sense at all." Her voice is surprisingly resentful.

"Seriously," Amara says now in a whisper. "When we were coming here, I kept thinking that this is a thing that happens to only ugly people and poor people, and then I came here, and found out that I was right to think so. I am not calling her ugly. But—"

There's the urge to throw up, and Sommy cannot tell if it's the effects of the alcohol, or if it's the sharp knife of the truth twisting itself in her. It says something about her position in the world in relation to this woman that her mother could make this go away, that Mezie isn't in prison right now, that her mother and father aren't skittering in pain, trying to find a way to get him out, and that she, Somkele Nwachukwu, is breathing well, that she hasn't turned into ashes. Ashes because if she ever goes even an inch near the pain she'd felt when she'd believe Mezie gone, she's certain that she'll dry up and crumble. But that isn't happening. What's happening is that this woman is lying here alone, lying here small, lying here wounded, lying here abandoned, and it is Mezie's fault, Mezie who, at the moment, is asleep, wrapped in Elin's warmth. It is his fault, and it is her fault, and it is her mother's fault.

"Maybe someone would come for her," Amara says

Sommy drags a stool and positions it near the bed, by the woman's head, sits and leans close. She's afraid that the woman might jerk awake and clutch her hand, but she stays still. She says to the woman that she's sorry. It's at first a whisper, then her voice grows louder. She says that this will be the last severely unkind thing she'll do in her life. She says that she'll always carry her in her conscience. She says that she's beautiful. She says that she feels deep regret. She says that it is hard for her to do this. She says that she chose, and she had to choose the only person in the world she would die for. She says, "I don't know if you'll understand. I don't know if you had this kind of love in your family, this kind of love that feels primal and primordial, love that existed before you were born, love that just has always been, love that you can't walk away from because it is inside you. It is in your blood. It's in your flesh." She holds the woman's cold hand. "I hope you understand this kind of love, and I hope you understand why I'm doing this. I truly do."

While they are in the Uber heading to Mezie's, Sommy thanks Amara for heaving on the burden of her lies.

"The thing you said about primordial love," Amara says. "It entered my heart because that's how I feel about you, as if we are destiny friends. Friends from before."

Sommy is taken aback by the sincerity, let free this early in the morning, with the sky covered in darkness and the world quiet, so that it feels as though they are the only ones alive.

"That's how I feel about you, too," she says, and it takes everything in her not to buckle onto the car mat and cry.

Sommy doesn't tell Bryan that she went to see the woman until the Monday of that week, when he walks into the guest room to tell her that he is leaving. The apartment is suffocating, he says, and everything feels strange and icky, and he needs space to think. And he's tried, he adds. He's been waiting for the missing piece of the puzzle, a new understanding, something, anything that will help him move on with what they have. The truth—his voice is emphatic now—is that he's looking for redemption where there's none.

Sommy clatters up from the bed and tells him that she and Amara had gone to visit the woman. It's a desperate plea, a show of her goodness, a virtue he thinks her now incapable of.

"Did you tell Amara the real truth or your version of the truth?"

"I told her Mezie hit the woman," she says. "I said the truth."

He's all dressed, striped short-sleeved shirt with black jeans, light-brown sunglasses sitting on his head.

"I don't believe that you did that," he says. "I don't believe that you told her the truth."

The thing is, she's seen them, her and Bryan, in her mind's eyes, taking a morning walk. Both of them sixty in this daydream, graying, stooping slightly now, holding hands, just taking a simple walk in their neighborhood on an ordinary spring day. She's seen herself handing him a jug of water and then pausing to watch him drink from it. She's seen them stopping to sit on a bench by the sidewalk, under the grandeur of a blossoming tree. She's seen herself pulling out a fresh tangerine and peeling it slowly, cutting it in half, and handing a portion to him. She's seen them sit in silence, a balmy air between them, their bodies easy with each other in the way of people welded together by years of waking up side by side. It's a film so vivid in her mind.

"I need you, Bryan," she says.

He heaves, sags, and his face now bears a quiet sadness. "I need you, too, Som, but I don't know you."

"It's still me, but in a bad situation."

"The person I know would say the truth."

"I didn't have a choice."

"You did. You had a choice."

She stares, seeking mercy. There's no right response and she doesn't care for one. Yes, she'll admit to being the perpetual wrongdoer, the coverer of crimes, the conjurer of woes, if it means he'll stay. He moves back, leans on the wall, as if too fatigued to hold himself up.

"I'll find a hotel," he says. "I'll stay there, alone, until we leave."

The woman dies the Sunday after Sommy's visit.

Sommy and Mezie sit around a Guinness-branded table outside their mother's bar. The cold bottles of malt and bowls of pepper soup served by one of the barmaids remain untouched. Their mother is on the phone inside the shop. It's late afternoon and the bar is empty. In a few hours, people will begin to walk in, and the speaker will start to blast highlife music. Glasses will hold beer foam, and bowls will hold soups. The air will be infused with joviality. There will be shy kisses here and there. Laughter erupting from the tables. Someone will probably spill beer and call for the barmaid to bring a rag. Someone will probably ask that they change the music and put on Flavour, and that someone might stand and sing along to the music. But now, it is quiet, and the air smells of pepper-soup spice, and it's just Sommy and Mezie seated, solemn.

Done with her phone call, their mother ambles to the table, and takes the white plastic chair beside Sommy. She waits for a while, as if catching her breath, and then turns to Mezie and asks how he's doing.

"Fine," he says.

She leans forward, touches his lap, says, "I di sure?"

"Mummy, I'm okay," he says, frowning. "What are we doing here by the way?"

Sommy's legs fidget. She squeezes her arms around her belly to suppress the urge to lash out at him. "What are we doing here? You committed manslaughter," she wants to say. "And we are here because we need to talk about it."

"Dr. Okoye called me," her mother says. "The woman's sister showed up and they've taken her body to the mortuary."

"She has a sister?" Sommy asks.

Her mother nods. Sommy squeezes her belly even tighter. From the small bush in the corner, a rat races by, disturbing the calm grasses.

"I told him to give my number to the sister. I want us to help with the burial."

Mezie's face is vacant. The urge to slap him, slap him until he crumples, fills her. *Idiot, idiot,* she says in her head over and over.

Unable to restrain herself, she drops her crossbody bag noisily on the table and says, "Why don't you ever have anything to say?"

He takes a mindless hand to his collar, exposing his throbbing jugular veins. "What do you want from me, Somkele? Why do you always think I owe you an explanation?"

Sommy's silent, roiling.

"No, please, tell me," he continues. "Because your own is getting too much. And I want to know what is giving you this power you think you have. Is it your white boyfriend blowing up your head, so that you think you are now in charge, and everyone should bow to you?"

He's sitting on the edge of his seat, jaw pressed toward his neck, and he's really asking her these questions. They aren't merely rhetorical, spur-of-the-moment insults. They are deliberate, chewed-upon questions.

She turns to her mother, who now has on her "I'm washing my hands of this" look: puckered lips, wide eyes, head slightly turned away from them.

"You think I'm Chisom or Elin?" she says to Mezie. "You think you'll just shout with your bass voice and I'll start to run around scared? Or you think this is two years ago, when I still thought you had a heart? Let me tell you—I have gotten to the point where I can tell you this: go and die. Mezie, go and die. I don't bloody care."

At this, her mother stands forcefully, "My son will not die, Somkele."

"Mummy, abeg, sit down and leave me alone! How long are we going to keep coddling this boy? After everything we've done—"

"This is what is scattering my head," Mezie says. "What is this everything you've done? Why are you always trying to make my life about you?"

"Mezie—"

"You think we are still thirteen and sixteen. We are adults now, Somkele, and whatever we have is transactional. That means, I give you what you give me."

Sommy chuckles. "Strong man, strong man, but you can't be straightforward. Open your mouth and say what you really want to say. Say you hate me because I left and you are stuck here. Say it."

"I hate you because you are a fucking hypocrite," he says, something monstrous breaking through his otherwise soft features. "You say, 'Mezie, I'm here for you,' and in the same damn minute you are packing your bag, getting on an airplane. And then what? You blow up my phone looking for me to make you feel better about your decision as if my life is about you, as if everything is about you. Listen, it's yourself you are deceiving, not me."

"What would you rather I'd done? Give up my spot in the program?"

"What I would rather you do now is stop acting like the kind of person who would do that. Stop acting like we have that type of relationship."

"I just buried a crime for you."

"You buried it so that your boyfriend will remain spotless."

Sommy draws back. "Mummy, look at what this boy is saying."

"Biko, lower your voice," her mother says. "People are passing by."

She turns now to Mezie. "Even you don't believe that I did it for Bryan. You are a liar and a manipulator. But you are not a fool."

Mezie slumps into the chair, spreads his long, gangly legs, and looks up at the sky, a posture of defeat.

"After everything I've done," he says, in the tone one uses to speak to themselves or to their God.

It rises in her now, just like it had risen and spilled from him—*What is this everything you've done?*—but she doesn't spill it. She knows that he'd left for Norway to give them a better life, that he believed himself to be their savior. Chisom had seen it. She, Sommy, did not see it. This private burden of his. His anger with her isn't that she left him when he needed her; it is that she unwittingly refused the role of the saved. Now he walks around purposeless, empty. But who doesn't have their own private burden? For whom is it well?

"You know what he's been through," her mother says now, near tears.

"What about me?" Sommy says quietly. "What about what I've been through?"

"What have you been through? Look at you—you are doing your master's. You have your American boyfriend. Your life is good."

Sommy starts to laugh. *Your life is good.* Her laughter dissolves into quiet sobs. She looks at Mezie. His eyes shine with withheld tears. He is not the boy she used to know. Along the way to here, something essential broke, and he walks around now, half human, half acid, burning everything in his way. She knows this and yet she cannot sink her hand into her chest and wrench out this bulbous, chafed love and lay it at his feet, and say, "Here, take your shit." What does she do with love bent on ruining her?

Her eyes are closed so she doesn't see Mezie stand and walk away, but she hears the crunch of his shoes on the sand, and his smell, his specific Mezie smell, indescribable but one she can tell apart in her sleep, fading away.

The woman's sister visits the day before Sommy and Bryan are to leave for Iowa. Their mother's house is the venue. Everyone except Bryan, who's taken residence in a guesthouse a few miles away from Mezie's, is present. Earlier, she'd texted him about the visit, and he'd replied simply, "Good luck." She did not know what she was expecting, but it wasn't a bland idiom.

She sits now at her parents' house without Bryan, next to Mezie, who has Elin's dark hair on his shoulder, and right opposite the woman's sister, who says her name is Judith. Sommy's father stands by the door, trying to fix the broken air conditioner.

Judith is eating jollof rice slowly but with a frequency that speaks of suppressed passion. Sommy recognizes this kind of slow eating. She'd had enough free meals in university from strange men while grappling with hunger-mangled dignity to recognize the same now in Judith. It occurs to her that she was once Judith, but she isn't any longer. Her family was poor for so long, but they aren't now. They climbed quietly out of poverty, and into a tenuous but thriving middle class. Still, she's not able to drop the anxiety of not having, perhaps because she's aware of the fragility of their status. One misfortune, and they could sink back into where they came.

Her mother is telling Judith now that she'd like to help with the funeral arrangements. "Just let me know how many crates of drinks you people will need. I'll provide it free of charge. Malt, small stout, Coke, Fanta. Anything. Just let me know."

Judith gathers the last grains of rice on her plate. "Thank you, ma. I'll let you know through text in one week."

She looks to be about forty, Judith. She's frail like her sister, with the same broad brows. Her facial expressions are contained, as if appearing only after careful deliberation.

Their mother asks if there's an estimated number of people who will attend the burial.

Judith, done with her food, tilts her head toward the ceiling fan. "We don't have people like that. Our neighbors will come. So, maybe, like, twenty."

Their mother sighs. "What about church people?"

"Christie did not like church," Judith says.

"That's unfortunate. You mean she won't have a Christian burial?"

Judith shakes her head in the negative.

Their mother adjusts her scarf, and says, "I'll arrange for a priest or a pastor to come and bury her."

Mezie shifts uneasily. "Maybe we shouldn't do that."

Their mother turns slowly to him. "Do what?"

"If the woman did not like going to church while alive, why should we impose a Christian burial on her?"

Their mother flashes him a sharp, derisive look.

Elin squeezes his hand, a gentle, nonverbal "Calm down, babe."

Sommy has thought often about the after of dying, obsessed as she is over Mezie one day successfully facilitating his own. She's pondered the absolute powerlessness of it. Everything, once so intimately yours, becomes another's to touch, to decide over. The body, a person's most owned possession, becomes the property of whatever family is left. She thinks of the fate of the woman's other possessions, her phone, her clothes, her shoes, her toothbrush, her hairbrush, her keyholder, and she wonders about the spaces the woman had carved as hers, the side of the sitting room couch no one else sits on, the side of the bed no one else sleeps on, the chair at the dining table no one else sits on. She thinks about those spaces, filled now with nothing but air, and her heart breaks all over again. When she'd thought Mezie dead, it was this gap she could not deal with, the thought that there would always be a space in the world carved by him and for him, and he would no longer be here to occupy it, and try as anyone might to fit into this space, they simply never would because it was his specific space.

Their father sits beside Sommy, screwdriver in hand. The air conditioner hums in the background. Her mother insists that she hasn't told her father the real story, and he acts like he isn't aware. But Sommy finds it hard to believe. How can't he sense it? It sits in the air between them like a loathsome ghost.

Their mother relents about the matter of the priest and says that she'll, alongside the drinks, donate one hundred thousand naira for other expenses that might accrue.

"Thank you," Judith says, with a peculiar expression of gratitude, somewhere between sincerity and coldness. "God bless your family."

"Amen, my dear, Amen," her mother says, as she hands Judith two thousand naira for transport fare.

One hundred and two thousand naira and a few crates of drinks is the price of a woman's life. Sommy is glad that Bryan isn't witnessing the transaction.

There is the sense that it has ended. Mezie is in the clear. Her family is in the clear. They have gotten away with it. And it is unbearable, the knowledge that she, Somkele Nwachukwu, a nobody, an always nobody, has rewritten reality, that she spoke a string of words and it became. It is unbearable. She offers to drive the woman home. She wants to prolong this chapter.

Their drive is silent. Judith is lost in thought. It feels sacrilegious to intrude, so Sommy sticks with the silence, though she wants to ask questions. She wants to know if Judith can smell the rancid odor of lies and pretense. She wants to know what her relationship with Christie had been like. She wants to whiplash herself with knowledge. She wants the face that comes to her in her nightmares to be Christie's face, the real thing. She wants her penance, brutal, once and for all. She wants to scourge herself of this blustering guilt.

They arrive at a bungalow, in front of which sits a bench, on top of which sits an old man, chewing a stick, his brightly colored aso oke cap sloping on his head like a small vibrant flower. There's a baby on the ground beside the old man, naked except for his diapers, his body slathered with mucus and sand.

"Thanks for the ride, sister," Judith says as she unbuckles her belt.

Sommy doesn't want her to leave, but she doesn't know what to say to stop her. She turns off the car and alights as Judith alights.

Judith is looking at her quizzically, and Sommy blurts out: "Can I use your restroom?" There's silence before Judith shrugs, says, "Okay."

They walk past the baby and the old man, and into a dark hallway littered with stoves and pots and foot mats, and into an even darker room. Judith gropes for the light switch, and it's a short while before she finds it, before the room comes alive. Neat, well arranged, the sitting room, even with the clutter. It is brown-themed: a carpet, two plastic chairs, one couch covered with a stretch of Ankara fabric. There's a circle of drums at the corner, right beside a tall heap of old newspapers.

The house is quiet, terribly quiet, as though aware that Christie is dead, and silently mourning in its own unalive way. Judith disappears into a door and returns after a few seconds to say the restroom is ready for Sommy's use. Sommy enters, but she doesn't use it. She mopes around, taking in the peeling, water-stained wall, the small rusting mirror, and the toilet bowl, old and cracked but like everything in the house, neat, scrubbed clean.

When she walks back into the sitting room, Judith is standing.

"So it was just you and Christie living here?" Sommy says.

Judith nods. "And our dog. One-Eyed Dickson. He is outside now, doing God knows what."

"I imagine that this is very painful for you," Sommy says.

She wants to pry open Judith's private life. It makes her uneasy, how closed-off Judith is. Judith must know something, she thinks, and is simply refusing to act for her own strange, Judith reasons. She wonders what Judith would do if she knew the real story. Would she have Mezie locked up? She doesn't seem like the sort of person to want a pound of flesh. But Sommy doesn't really know what sort of person Judith is. For a long time, she'd thought that the single criterion for knowing people was being a person. That all of human inclinations stemmed from the same source, and everyone was connected to that source. She'd thought that because she couldn't bring herself to commit an act, then it was simply an unhuman thing to do. But she's learnt that isn't true. There's evil in the world, evil that makes no sense, evil alien to her. She wonders now if someone else would think this of what they've done, herself, Mezie, and her mother, think that this thing they've done to Christie and Judith is unhuman. Not a mere evil act but an alien evil one, impossible to comprehend.

Judith is saying now that God knows best. She is standing with her legs spread apart. In the gesture, Sommy reads that Judith wants her to leave, she isn't interested in sharing. Sommy doesn't want to leave. She's still not ready to put this chapter behind her.

"You and Christie," Sommy says, "were you guys close?"

Judith shifts her weight on one foot, as if resigning to Sommy's persistence.

"We were close," Judith says, and nothing else. Just silence, cut through occasionally by the squeaking of the ceiling fan.

"I am sorry if I'm being intrusive," Sommy says. Better to acknowledge the obvious, even if she's going to plunge on notwithstanding Judith's resistance. "I just want to be sure you are okay before I leave."

Judith looks at Sommy now, straight in the eye. "Ms. Nwachukwu, you and your family have done enough."

You and your family have done enough. Her chest swells with panic. Judith knows something. It is not possible that this incident will die the quiet death of passing time, with no ruffles, no challenge, the truth perfectly imperceptible.

"I am sorry," Sommy says to fill the silence.

"Don't be sorry," Judith says. The low timbre of her voice suggests that it is not indictment—*You and your family have done enough*—it is gratitude. A gray feeling comes over Sommy now, and she brings her palms together in front of her. Judith continues: "I am no stranger to death. I have lost my parents. I have lost a son, my only child. I have lost friends, too. Uncles and aunties and distant relatives. Neighbors. Death is not new to me. Death is everywhere. Do you read the news?" She gestures to the heap of newspapers. "Every day, everywhere in the world, people drop dead like flies. It is not a new thing." She stomps a roach crawling toward her. "I will mourn Christie. I will think about her every day. I will look at everything in this room, her chair. This one." She lightly kicks one of the identical brown plastic chairs. "This television that she was always watching. Her drums." Her eyes linger on the drums, a trio of drums, wrapped intricately with colorful ropes. "If Christie was not watching TV, she was playing the drum. This ugly curtain that she sewed with her bare hands. I will look at them and my heart will twist with pain. But then one day, I will look at them and I'll only see them for what they are, drum, television, curtain. I will not remember Christie. I will then remember that I have not remembered her for a while, and I will cry. But I will not cry for the whole day like I do now. I will cry small. I will clean my eyes and I will continue. You know why?" Judith takes a step toward the door. "The living must continue to live."

Sommy crosses both hands against her chest. She cannot understand this concept of loss. Death is not simply final, she thinks. It is the meridian of finality, the most irretrievable of all losses. How does one accept it with such grace?

"It's my greatest fear," Sommy says. "Not for myself. I don't mind dying a quick death. Then I won't know, you know? I'll be dead. I won't feel anything. But I can't bear to be alive without the people I love."

Judith smiles coolly, and then says, "Death is everywhere, and it is a must. Everyone will die. The earlier you accept that, the better."

She wants to pierce through Judith's steeliness, draw out something unreasonable, wild with grief, but she's aware that she's burdening the already burdened, so she says instead, "It will be well."

"It will," Judith says.

Sommy thinks now, as she studies Judith's crestfallen face, that her own fear is the catalyst of this tragedy. Somehow, a transference has happened. For her to gain a life, Judith had to lose one. It is the character of fear. It builds a home in a tiny corner of the heart, a small seed of intimate feeling, that slice of pain, and then grows, explodes, makes you destructive.

"Thanks for your time," Sommy says finally.

Sunset flames the windowpanes, a bright golden hue.

"I'll walk you out."

Outside, Sommy watches as One-Eyed Dickson wobbles toward them. She had not thought that he was a literal manifestation of his name—a one-eyed dog. Judith bends to him and he walks straight into her open arms.

"Good boy," she says, stroking his back. "Good boy."

Part Three

In her first weeks back in Iowa, Sommy is plagued by the loss of a place for which to pine. She had gone home, and home did not feel like home. The concept of home had become warped. Is it a place? A memory? An idea? The therapists on social media say "Home is wherever love is." In *Omeros*, Derek Walcott, says of house (home), "I do not live in you, I bear my house inside me, everywhere.".

If home is wherever love is, and Bryan, whom she loves with all of her, has shut his doors, does that make her homeless? Since their return, he's moved into his study. He sleeps now on his reading couch, and leaves only to eat, and sometimes, at night, delirious with fatigue and sleep, to have dry, uncomfortable sex with her. He is in "the state," he tells her. He is creating, writing, manic with ideas. His flow cannot be broken. Sommy wants to believe that this is the truth, but she knows better. She knows that if he is in any "state" at all, it is one of deliberation. He will come out of this state clear with understanding, definite with his decision to leave her.

Walcott: "I do not live in you, I bear my house inside me, everywhere."

Inside.

She ponders this rigorously, what it means to carry one's home inside them. Does this mean self-love? Walcott had written a poem on the subject after all: "Love after Love." "Feast on your life," he writes. When Mezie had made his attempt, hadn't it been, for him, a matter of self-preservation, a matter of self-love? What were suicidal thoughts after all (I am tired, I can't fight anymore, I need to rest) if not self-preservation? He'd told her, days after his attempt, that he was staying for them, for her, their mother and father. That was love, his staying. Real love. Sacrificial love. Sacrificing love. Wired in him already was the urgent need to free himself from his pain. He had to work up this real love, and every day, he pays for it, like a due owed.

She practices self-preservation when she, in between classes, in the middle of the night, during a commercial break, takes a few minutes to masturbate, and to then cry afterward, a purging. She practices it when she spends countless hours scrolling through Instagram videos, watching animals do human things, children do adult things. She practices it when, to stop from barging into Bryan's study and demanding that he make a decision about them, she buries herself in her thesis on black women's travel narratives, reading sad books about women on journeys, women learning new places (Buchi Emecheta's *The Joys of Motherhood*, Nella Larsen's *Quicksand*, Octavia Butler's *Kindred*). It feels like a kind of worship, the reading of these books and the writing of her thesis, which, when she started out, had been about the false dichotomies of modern love and traditional love, and which has now drastically morphed into an exploration of travel as survival, of what it means to leave home not for the mere adventure of it.

It is not quite accurate to say that she buries herself in her thesis. She does not get lost in it. The problems of her life are at the forefront of her philosophizing, and in a much more concrete way, her thesis, the writing of it, signals the end of this era of her life. In a few months, she will have completed her three-year program. She will no longer have the status to continue to stay in the United States. She could apply for an OPT and then a PhD, extend her stay in the United States. She could afterward get a job teaching postcolonial literature in a small private college, fill up the representation quota, the plump African woman with an afro and an accent to go with it. But she thinks: For what? If Bryan ends it, what will all the hassle be for? To remain love-less in a foreign land? To swivel mindlessly about, searching for the good life, while real life quietly passes her by?

A month after their return, with Bryan still in his "state," Sommy visits a shisha place on North Milwaukee Avenue with Kayla and Nia. They'd not hung out since Sommy's return, though Kayla had tried, sending messages and voice notes, wanting them to "do something sometime."

Their reunion is filled with loud "Oh my god girl, I've missed you" type of greetings, hugs, kisses, and the stilted air that settles after a long absence. They sit in a booth in the corner. The stereo blasts reggae. They order chicken and fries and glasses of mojito and bob their heads to loud music.

Outside, it's a cool fall night and Sommy, having spent the whole day sleeping, feels immense energy in her bones. She misses Lagos a bit, sitting here, half listening to the girls argue. Kayla's shared with the table that there's a handsome boy on the dance floor she likes, and she wishes he'd come up to them. Nia replies that Kayla ought to be more discreet, and perhaps engage in other activities that did not pertain to a male person or several.

Sommy's not quite in the bar with Kayla and Nia. Earlier that day, she'd spoken with her mother on the phone, who had told her that she and Mezie had just dropped off Elin at the airport and were stopping at the market to pick up Chisom and take her to a doctor's appoint-ment. "The girl isn't feeling well," her mother said, with a kind of glee, and in it Sommy heard that her mother is hoping that Chisom is pregnant. She knows her mother well enough to come to this conclu-sion. Sommy of course doesn't care about Elin. Whatever pity Sommy felt for her had waned and died in the week after the incident. She cannot seem to forgive Elin for being the only one left unscathed, for having intact whatever false, coruscating life she's dreamt up with Mezie. She knows Elin's own shattering will come, that eventually she'll learn about Chisom, and those weeks she spent in Lagos will take on a new, painful meaning, but she can't bring herself to care. For Mezie, she feels now an unrestrained anger. Every time Bryan steels when she touches him, coughs when she says "I love you," hastens off when she meets him in the kitchen eating breakfast, she flashes back to the image of Mezie sitting at the steering wheel, stupefied, while she rushes out of the car to the bleeding woman, and she feels the love she'd thought infrangible disintegrate. She feels, too, a strange kind of exhaustion, an awareness of the chaos being around him brings, and she wants to keep as much distance between them as possible.

Now Sommy tries to start a conversation with Nia to get her out of her dreary mood, but her answers are curt. She soon gives up and continues to bob her head to the music.

"We should dance," Kayla says and laughs, throwing her head back, obviously tipsy. She grabs Sommy's hand, pulls her to the corner of the table. She snaps her fingers, twists her shoulders, and Sommy, though with a little more effort than Kayla, flings her hands in the air, and then starts to laugh. She starts to laugh because she didn't know that she had it in her to dance.

Nia doesn't join them, she sits, her face heavy with disdain.

"Your energy is so negative!" Kayla yells to Nia at one point. "Anyone can feel it from a mile away!"

Nia says nothing, looks the other way. The club is getting fuller, and the room darker. The dance floor is covered with bodies screaming along to the music, dancing and jumping and grinding. Occasionally, the lights come on in a flash, and a loud siren sound follows, the disco lights dance, and fog is released into the air. It is atmospheric, the first bubble of happiness Sommy has experienced since her return, and she hates Nia a little for killing the vibe.

Kayla struts to the bar to get a drink. Sommy's glass is almost empty but she's not sure about another drink. Kayla returns with three shot glasses, which she gulps back-to-back.

"Jeez, babe, take it easy," Sommy says.

Kayla throws her arms around Sommy's neck. She smells of some-thing chemical and floral. Sommy rubs her back affectionately. They both dance for a while before Kayla stops abruptly and turns to Nia, and says: "Why are you always so fucking mean to me? I can't do a single thing without your judgment."

"I'm sorry," Nia says, though she doesn't sound sorry. She sounds spiteful.

"What do you want from me?" Kayla says. "Why are you always on my neck?"

"She's drunk," Nia says to Sommy. "We should take her home."

"Talk to me," Kayla says. "What do you fucking want from me?"

"I was joking. I didn't mean to make you this mad. We say things like that to each other."

"No, you say things like that to me. You come for me. All the damn time."

Sommy can feel the gaze of the girls beside them and she wants to shush Kayla, clasp her mouth shut.

"Let me just take you home," Nia says. "We'll talk about this tomorrow morning."

"We fucked once," Kayla says. "Once. That doesn't give you any fucking right to police me. I can talk about sex anytime I want to. I can have sex with whomever I please."

"You've gone fucking crazy," Nia says, brazen now with vexation.

"I'll take crazy," Kayla says. "Better that than being a fucking repressed bitch." The words leave her mouth with such staggering preci-sion, Sommy's certain that it's been practiced, that she's looked in the mirror several times and said these same words to an imaginary Nia.

The lights come on then, illuminating Nia's hardened face.

"Will you make sure she gets home?" Nia says to Sommy. "I need to leave."

"Sure thing," Sommy replies.

"Fucking coward!" Kayla screams at Nia.

When Nia disappears into the dancing crowd, Sommy lowers Kayla into a seat, brings Kayla's head to her chest.

"Please calm down," Sommy says.

Sommy orders a ride, and soon she's walking a rambling, crying Kayla to the Uber.

The laughter comes after Sommy has laid Kayla to bed, and she's in an Uber home. The driver, an old white man, startled at first by the suddenness of her laughs, soon relaxes, and starts to laugh with her. When he drops her in front of the building, he doesn't ask why she's laughing. He says to her that her laughter sounds like a baby's, the kind that draws out other people's laughter, and she says, "I get it from my mother."

Inside, she finds Bryan leaning on the kitchen counter. She stands by the door for a while, adjusting to the room's temperature, to Bryan's temperature. She then steps forward, says a quiet, "Hey."

Bryan moves from the counter, slowly, and walks toward her, says, "Hey," and turns for his study.

He's grown out his hair since their return, and in the dark room, it looks like a sleeping tortoise, a carefully molded round thing.

"Bryan," she says disconcertedly. "It's your home. You don't have to run away whenever I show up."

"Run away?" He turns to her. "I was waiting for you to get back, and you are back now. That's all."

Had he been panicked by her absence? Worried about her? Hope, the warm blanket of hope, cocoons her.

"Thank you," she says.

"I want you to be safe." He says it like he's insulted that she's assumed otherwise.

"Thank you."

"Stop saying that."

"Saying what?"

"Thank you."

"Oh."

She pauses for a minute before asking if she can turn on the lights.

"Sure," he says.

She doesn't move immediately. She stands for a bit, in the dim glow of the kitchen-sink light, feeling the slight breeze floating in through the half-shuttered window, feeling, from where she stands, ten inches away, the beating of his heart, and feeling, through some weird machinations of this phenomena called love, his feelings like they are hers. She then flicks on the switch, enshrouding the sitting room in white fluorescent light.

Bryan stands now by the large television, his shadow slant on the wall. She moves close to him, says in a voice wavy with indecision. "I just want to tell you about my night."

He stands up straight. She'd not realized he was slouching. "What about it?" he says.

She pauses for a bit, tumbles the texture of his voice in her mind. Does she hear genuine curiosity?

"This thing happened between Nia and Kayla." She's looking away, fiddling with the seams of her long-sleeved shirt. "It was funny. I mean, afterward, it was funny. When Kayla went big crazy for a minute, no one was laughing, though."

"Sounds intense."

She takes her gaze to him. There's slight amusement on his face, and also slight fatigue, and the combination is a brutal handsomeness. What she would give now to run a hand up his cheek.

She tells him that Kayla and Nia have been fucking and she'd been unaware of it all the while.

"Kayla and Nia?"

"Right?" she says, eyes wide, a hand pointed his way. "There aren't two people in the world more different."

He walks to the couch but doesn't sit. He instead places a palm on the head rest. She wants to ask if he's sleeping well. The lines on his face have deepened.

"You think they'll be fine?" he asks.

"I don't." Sommy says. "Kayla said really mean things to Nia. I don't see how they'll come back from that."

There's a bit of silence, and then she says she isn't upset they'd kept her in the dark. She's always felt a simmering tension between the girls.

He sits now, and Sommy goes to sit beside him. They haven't sat this closely since the incident. Once, after sex, he'd dozed off in her arms, and the next morning had sprung back up and left. But this sitting and talking and smiling at each other like they used to do is a new development, and she's very aware of his body next to her, in the way she always is when she's had a little too much to drink.

"Have you been well?" she says.

It's a strange question to ask a person you live with but theirs is a strange situation.

"I got an offer," he says. "For my book."

"Oh wow, that's wonderful."

"It's a good offer."

"You must be relieved," she says. "Finally. It's happening. Everyone gets to know your genius."

He begins to massage his knee. "You didn't read the book. How would you know it's genius?"

She swallows a gasp. "I—"

He raises half his face toward her. "I know you hated it. I liked that you didn't pretend otherwise. But now you are. You are lying."

She takes her hands to her bun and unties the scrunchie. It's easy effort for him to make her so deeply uncomfortable. She hadn't even called his book genius. She had been referring to him, his mind. Not that any of it matters at all. He'd splice apart anything she says, looking to indict her somehow for lying. Lying, her singular identity. "Will it ever be different?" she wants to ask. Will he bruise and batter her, and when there's nothing else left to bruise and batter, leave her? She doesn't ask this. She instead says, and with a sprinkling of humor in her tone: "I have poor taste in books is what it is."

"You actually do," he says, chuckling.

She laughs because she knows he's thinking about her collection of old books, which he'd stumbled upon at her parents', romance novels with what he'd called "cringe romance tropes." She remembers telling him about a book she'd read as a teenager, about a woman who falls in love with her deceased son's best friend. She told him that she'd thought the relationship inappropriate and had been so affected by the book that she flung it across the room. He'd stared at her, eyes warm with admiration, and said, "I hate very much that there's all these many years of your life that I wasn't part of and can't ever be part of." He then pulled her gently to him, pressed a kiss on her forehead. She'd thought it very sweet.

Now, they sit in silence for a while. He looks to be in deep thought. She has a feeling that he's about to say something that will profoundly affect her coming days, and she wonders whether to intercept it, to remind him first that she loves him dearly.

"I have been thinking about us," he says. Pauses. "I want us to start couple's therapy."

"Therapy?"

He turns to her, nods. It's hard to see him this unkempt, his hair wildly grown, beard tufting about. But therapy?

"Okay," she says, trying to hide her hesitation.

"Is that a yes?"

"You think we can't talk this over ourselves?"

"We need therapy, Somkele."

He now calls her Somkele, her full name. Not babe. Not Sommy. Not Som. How distressing.

"I am in," she says, nodding vigorously, convincing herself, and after a short while adds: "We must celebrate your book deal."

He looks at her dryly, unenthused, and the thought that she's sucked his life of joy stabs her chest. When did she last hear him laugh? See him truly happy?

That night, they sleep in her bed together. They do not have sex, but when she wakes up, she finds him lying beside her.

The matter of going to therapy is a tenuous one. Sommy can see Bryan unravel in front of some judgmental therapist, confessing, indicting herself and Mezie. She imagines the therapist's shock, their insistence that they are mandated to report a crime. She imagines their arrest, news articles with the headline: FAMILY OF FOUR ARRESTED FOR MANSLAUGHTER. Most of it, she's certain, is her anxious imagination. The layers of possibilities in this ruin she's conjured creates resistance, so when Bryan informs her that their first appointment with the therapist is in three days, she says she has a meeting with her advisor.

"Let's do next Wednesday?" she says.

"I'll let the therapist know, see if she can reschedule."

When next Wednesday comes, Sommy begs Kayla to feign an emergency.

"Kayla is having really terrible cramps," Sommy says to Bryan when Kayla calls. "I think we might have to go to the ER."

"That sucks," Bryan says. "You need a ride?"

Sommy rejects the ride, says she doesn't want to get in the way of his novel edits. "Just focus on work, babe."

At Kayla's, they watch *Game of Thrones* and eat popcorn. They avoid talking about Nia, who keeps ignoring Sommy's messages. It is, of course, impossible to tell Kayla about the incident. She instead tells her that Bryan wants them to go to therapy. "To strengthen our relationship," she says.

"I need therapy myself," Kayla replies with a sigh.

Kayla doesn't press any further, and when they exchange hugs at the door later, Kayla says, "I'm here for you, anytime," and it means more than Sommy can vocalize, so she just squeezes her tight.

If Bryan notices that she's avoiding therapy, he doesn't show it. Since their agreement to go to therapy, there's been an obvious change in his treatment of her. He's touching her more and more—tenderly, not the quick, abrasive touches that had been the entirety of their intimacy these past months. He's resumed giving her forehead kisses. They now watch TV shows together and go on walks and have dinner. Once, he takes her to the African hair salon in Coralville that smells of peppermint, and sits with her while she gets her hair braided, and that almost convinces her that they are fine, that they have surmounted. Often, she catches herself asking what he's thinking. She's desperate for certainty.

When Catherine visits to celebrate his book deal and takes them to eat arepas at a Venezuelan restaurant downtown, and asks in that shy, affectionate way of hers, if they've given any thought to having kids, he smiles brightly at her, and says, "Yes, we are thinking two. Two girls." And Sommy, because they've never discussed kids, and she'd, after Mezie's attempt, decided not to have any—unable to fathom having a part of her walking around the world, open to danger—chokes on her Sprite and says, "Yes, two."

She runs out of excuses one day and tells Bryan plainly, "I don't want to go to therapy."

He looks at her, speechless. "Why not?" he says finally, with a steeliness that frightens her. If he had a cane, she's certain he'd bring it down on her in this moment.

"I'm not ready, Bryan."

"We are talking about the survival of our relationship. That's what we are talking about here."

"Can't we just, you know, talk to ourselves?"

"This is ridiculous," he says, hands up in defeat. "Fucking ridiculous."

"Just hear me out, please. I don't think that just any therapist will understand us."

"Why not attend a meeting first and then conclude?"

She's silent. She could tell him the exact reason she's refused to attend, but they've been acting like Lagos did not happen. He's not brought up the incident, nor has he brought up his father. Nothing has been said, yet everything bubbles up in the surface of mundane conversations.

"I'll try," Sommy says finally.

Bryan scoffs, murmurs, "Ridiculous."

It is their first meeting with the therapist and Sommy is unable to breathe. Bryan is doing most of the talking. He tells the therapist that there is a constant heaviness in his head, like someone has clasped his brain in their palm, and is pressing down forcefully.

"And why do you think that is?" the therapist asks.

She's a black woman, late twenties at the most, soft-spoken but with a sternness that women in her business must possess, especially one so young and so small-framed and so dark-skinned.

"I met my father this summer."

He tells her the story, his inability to accept that he will never know why his father really left.

"I feel unworthy of love," he says. "And I think that I'll continue to feel unworthy unless he tells me that he fought for me somehow. I know it's stupid. I know that I shouldn't feel this way, but I do."

Sommy wants to reach out, hold his hand, but she cannot breathe.

"It's not stupid to feel that way," the therapist says. "It is in fact perfectly reasonable."

She asks of his relationship with his mother, his brothers. "Splendid," he says. "We are as close as flower petals." She then spends a long minute jotting, before hinging her fingers together and saying, "And your wife? How is it between the both of you?" She says this staring at Sommy.

Sommy, frazzled, says, "Excuse me. Pee." She doesn't look at Bryan as she bolts to the restroom. Safely locked in, she looks at her reflection in the mirror, and mouths mockingly, "Excuse me. Pee." How silly of her, how childish. She fake shudders. Takes a deep breath. The whole thing is stupid, she thinks, and that therapist, sitting there listening to Bryan like she's God. Who but a narcissist decides that their day job will be to give advice about life? Everyone gets to do life once, and yet some people walk around thinking themselves experts. Except one who has lived, died, and been resurrected, Sommy thinks, a person does not have the adequate experience to give anyone advice. It's absurd, she thinks, that not too long ago she'd coaxed Mezie to go to see a therapist, as though it were a magical solution. She turns on the tap, flushes the toilet, spends a few minutes pacing, and then emerges with a smile.

"Sorry," she says, as she sits. "I'm doing this thing where I try to drink three liters of water a day. Trying to take better care of my skin."

The therapist smiles. "That's fine," she says, and then turns to Bryan. "You were about to say?"

"Sommy and I are not in the best place right now."

"And why is that?"

"We don't have honest conversations," he says.

"Why do you think that is?"

"Fundamentally?" Bryan says. "I think it's a lack of trust on my side."

The therapist leans into her seat. "Somkele? What do you think?"

"I trust him," she says. "So I guess we are here to fix him." She laughs dryly.

"She's not even taking this seriously," Bryan says, staring right at the therapist.

"I swear I am," Sommy says. "Forgive me." She turns to the therapist. "This is new to me."

The therapist tells her that there is no need to apologize, everyone has their own process, and in their next appointment, they'll spend more time with Sommy talking. She adds that unlike Bryan, Sommy does need more prodding to feel safe enough to speak her mind. Perhaps that could be part of the communication problem they have as a couple.

"Totally down for that," Sommy says.

In the car, before turning on the engine, Bryan sits still, his hands on the steering wheel, his head turned toward her. He stares and stares, and after a while, shakes his head, and looks away.

They do not go back to therapy. Bryan doesn't bring it up and Sommy feels more relief every week that passes.

"I think we are getting over it," she tells Amara over the phone.

"The man is crazy about you," Amara says. "I'm sure you guys will be fine."

Sommy wants to believe her, but she catches herself watching Bryan keenly, searching for signs. She surprises herself when, one Saturday, while Bryan is out playing golf, she goes into his study and turns on his laptop. She opens his emails with Joel, Melinda, and Clark. She finds nothing that deepens her suspicions, only conversations about their manuscripts and the weather, links to articles and their opinions on them. She's looking to atone, it's clear. She's looking to suffer because she deserves it, but he's not making her suffer anymore—no forcing therapy on her, no cold shoulders, no talks about breaking up. He moves around the house now like a raindrop on a glass pane, with ease, gentle with her. His old self again. She feels a vague sense of something left unfinished. Perhaps what she needs is a different perspective—to acknowledge how terribly she's suffered these past months, and to accept that she's done her penance somehow.

On this fall day, while they lie naked in the room after sex, Sommy asks Bryan what he's thinking.

He smiles tiredly. "Nothing."

She takes a quick peep at her belly and runs a palm down to her navel, tracing the faint soft hair.

"Thank you," she says.

"For what?" He turns to her.

"For loving me."

They are silent for a while, and then she says, "Everything that has happened—"

"We are working past it, and we are doing well."

"Why does it feel like we are burying it instead?"

"I'm learning to move on, Som. To let go. That's what you wanted, right?"

She stares at him thoughtfully and then says, "I'm glad that we are moving forward."

He looks away but reaches for her hand.

Weeks pass, and months pass, and one afternoon, after a meeting with her thesis supervisor, Sommy comes home to find Bryan pacing the sitting room.

"I'm ready," he tells her.

He's wearing a blue shirt with the buttons open down to his lower chest. She's told him once that she likes when he has his buttons open this way. It gives an air of carelessness, and something about that makes her wild for him.

"Ready for what?" They've talked briefly about vacationing in Puerto Rico, and she thinks that's it.

He takes her hands, and just stares at her.

"What, babe?"

"Let's do it."

"Bryan," she says, realizing what he's asking.

"Let's get married, baby," he says.

"Like husband and wife?"

"Yes, like husband and wife."

For the first time, she understands in a physical way the expression "My heart is bursting." Her heart is bursting, beating hard in her chest. All of that searching, the whirling and tumbling, and it is this arrival she's been waiting for.

"Are you sure?" she says, still in disbelief.

"I think I am," he says, holding her hands. "We need this. I'm positive we need this."

They exchange vows at the Johnson County courthouse, and take pictures afterward in front of the building, which looks to Sommy like a mock Catholic church. Catherine, Philip, and Robert are present. Joel, Melinda, and Clark are, too. Kayla is, but Nia isn't. The sky is sea blue.

The air is light. Melinda has appointed herself photographer, and she positions Sommy and Bryan by a bush of roses and moves them later to a slab dotted with rocks dedicated to Abraham Lincoln.

After the picture-taking, they go to dinner at an Italian restaurant with wooden ceilings and hanging yellow lights. Bryan takes off his jacket and tie, and unbuttons his shirt, looking beautifully wrecked with tiredness. He's not stopped smiling at her, and now they are holding hands.

"Don't they look smashing together?" Catherine says, pressing her folded knuckles to her chest.

Melinda says they do. Joel smiles mischievously, and Clark says their love is one for the books. Philip and Robert are talking to each other as though alone. They still regard Sommy civilly. Bryan says they are being protective, that it's nothing to do with her.

Catherine asks Bryan if they've picked a date for the big wedding in Nigeria, and Bryan, with a plain face, says they might shoot for a date during the winter break.

"Perfect, perfect," Catherine says.

Sommy imagines her mother sitting side by side with Catherine at an event. They will get along, she's sure, Catherine with her fear of offending, and her mother with her endless capacity to offend.

"Is there a need for two weddings?" Robert says, adjusting his tie, shifting uneasily in his seat.

Sommy's mother had insisted that they do a wedding in Lagos also. She said it is unacceptable that her daughter is having a thirty-minute wedding with no proper celebration, no guests bloated from over-feeding. Sommy had agreed to a wedding at the end of the year, though she's certain that she'll never go back home with Bryan, scared that it might peel open the scabs of old wounds. She tells Robert this, the part about her mother wanting a proper celebration.

"And she couldn't have attended today's celebration?" Robert says. He's looking at her from under his glasses.

"Her visa application was rejected," Sommy says.

"Oh," Robert says, and pushes his glasses up his nose.

Bryan squeezes her hand, and she squeezes it right back. He's smiling. He knows her mother had not applied for a visa, and she's said otherwise to make Robert uncomfortable.

Their food arrives—two waiters, with unbreaking smiles, eagerly asking, "Everything okay, ma'am?"

They are all having pasta dishes, except Melinda, who's having a quinoa salad. Catherine has ordered two bottles of wine for the "new couple." Kayla sits watching all of them with a dull smile. It's the first time she's meeting Bryan's family, and Sommy's eager for her to be impressed by them, though Robert is being such a bad representative with his overall dourness.

Midway into their meals, Catherine stands for a toast. "To two of the kindest people I know, Bryan, my baby, and Sommy, my other baby. May your love grow. May it withstand tough times. May you continue to need each other. I love you."

"Aww," Melinda croons as glasses clink.

"Thank you," Sommy mouths.

Catherine comes over to give Sommy a hug, and then Bryan. Sommy feels disassociated from the group. It doesn't feel like her wedding. The white satin dress sits on her like someone else's. Kayla is the only person on her side, seated right in the middle of this blitz of Bryan-ness. She wishes her father were here. She wishes Amara were here.

Sommy's about to stuff her mouth with a roll of pasta, when Catherine hands her an envelope.

Sommy opens the envelope slowly. It takes a while for her to figure out that it is a deed of sale for a condo.

"It has the best view," Catherine says, reaching out to touch Sommy's hand. "You can see the Chicago River from the patio. And there's this bakery right down the road. The best croissant. You are going to love it."

"Mom!" Bryan exclaims. "Really?" He stands, wraps her in a hug.

"Catherine, this is so nice of you," Melinda says.

Kayla mouths a "What the fuck?"

"I don't know what to say," Sommy says. "Thank you, Catherine."

"You know you can call me 'Mom,' too," she says, smiling.

Sommy laughs, stands, and gives her a hug.

Later, alone in their apartment, Sommy asks Bryan how Catherine knows they've been talking about moving to Chicago after they both graduate in May.

"I told her we were thinking about it."

Sommy nods, speechless.

"I can't tell if you are underwhelmed or in shock," Bryan says.

"I am happy," Sommy says. "It's a condo. A condo as a gift."

Bryan hugs her, but she doesn't feel it. She's numb. This is not a thing that happens in her world. A person doesn't casually get a condo as a gift. But it's a thing that happens in the world of others, and it grates her to experience it so nakedly. One woman dies unjustly, and another receives a condo. She thinks that the world is quite reckless in its unfairness, and she hates that she'll meet all her new outlandish privileges with this guilt, this sadness, and there's the feeling that it isn't worth it, to have all of this and to feel still like she's walking around with cold rocks in her stomach.

When she tells Amara this the next day, Amara says curtly, "I don't want to hear it."

Sommy is silent, hurt.

"Your guilt is becoming self-indulgent and a little irritating."

"Are you mad at me about something?"

"Will you move into the condo? Yes. So what's all of this 'Life isn't fair' nonsense?"

"I'm telling you how I'm feeling. I'm not saying it is the right thing to feel. I'm just letting you know how it's doing me."

"Do you stop to think how it makes me feel?" Amara says.

"Makes you feel?"

"Sommy, you've escaped. You've escaped this life and I'm trapped in it. Yet all you do is complain. Complain about your new condo, your new husband, your new rich in-laws, your classmates. I am here, in this fucking country, working a fucking stupid job. I can't even have a boyfriend because I'm exhausted and angry all the time. But I keep lying to myself that the reason is because I'm planning to leave the country anyway, so why enter a relationship that will end eventually? But deep down, I know. I know it is because I'm too angry and I hate myself and I cannot love anyone like this."

Sommy blinks back a tear. "I'm sorry that I make you feel that way."

"I'm sorry, too," Amara says in a voice not at all sorry.

When the call ends, Sommy wonders how she can be surrounded by abundance like its ocean water, and yet, like ocean water, every time she sinks her hand in and tries to grab some, it goes through her fingers.

In May, Sommy and Bryan graduate. Catherine comes to watch them both walk across the stage. A few weeks later, they leave Iowa for Chicago. Bryan begins a second round of book edits. Sommy, having nothing to do, is restless from boredom. She wants to apply for high school teaching jobs, but she's not in status yet. Bryan has hired an immigration lawyer to help with her green card application, but the process is slow. The lawyer says she might have to wait six months. Bryan suggests she takes painting classes. She has raw talent, he says. A bit of technique and she could produce masterpieces. She doesn't want to take painting classes. She doesn't want to do anything that requires a stillness of mind, going inside herself, searching, probing. She wants to be out in the world, away from their condo.

She starts to take walks up and down the lakefront. She watches the people in their activewear, running, walking, standing. She watches the blue lake, its surface made a silky silver by the sun. She sometimes stops at the breakfast place on the corner of their high-rise for a cup of red nectar tea and a croissant. She sits by the window, eating, sipping, looking out to the gray streets, watching the coiffed people in their baseball hats and sneakers. Back at the condo, she retreats into the bedroom to read Tolstoy's *War and Peace*. She finds it cinematic, a good book to disappear into. She finds, too, that she cares very little to follow the plot. She's content simply to go from sentence to sentence, moment to moment, so she reads it nonlinearly. There's the scene after Countess Rostova, distressed by Anna Mikhaylovna's financial plight, asks the count for some money on Anna's behalf. When the countess hands the money over to the hesitant and grateful Anna, Tolstoy writes: "They wept because they were friends, and because they were kindhearted, and because they—friends from childhood—had to think about such a base thing as money, and because their youth was over . . . But those tears were pleasant to them both." She cries a little after reading this, thinking how piercingly it reminds her of Amara. It's been two months since their fight. Amara apologized after a week, said she was feeling stressed, and she had no right to take it out on her. Sommy accepted the apology, but she knew that something had forever shifted between them. Amara no longer liked her. She perhaps still loved her, but she did not like her. Sommy has become the kind of person that Amara does not like, that Mezie does not like, and the knowledge of this is a heartbreak that consumes her. She of course knows that Amara would not end their friendship, just like Mezie can't do anything about being her sibling; that Amara will continue to carry her on like deadweight, so she's created the distance herself, calling only a few times in the past months. She calls Kayla often, as if to replace Amara's absence, and Kayla chirps on the phone about schoolwork and dating and the movies she's seeing. Whenever Nia comes up, Kayla mellows. Once, she outright said, "Please can we not bring her up ever again?"

Sometimes she spends all day in bed, watching *Grey's Anatomy*. This, she follows linearly. She likes its melodrama. She cries often while watching. People love easily there. There's a sense of justice. It is a world where good people win, and people say "I love you" to those they love. It inspires in her the feeling that there's good in the world.

Most evenings, Bryan makes them dinner. He sears salmon and greens beans, which he serves with white rice. He sometimes makes chickpea curry and quinoa. On days when he emerges from his study too tired, they order in Chinese. They eat on the patio, from where they can see the lake, and the city's glorious, metallic skyline, the slashing polychromatic lights, the sky, a calm dusky blue.

Their conversations revolve around Bryan's book edits. He says often that he feels like he's self-mutilating, cutting too close to the heart of the book. He wonders if he's being too trusting of his editor. He's anxious about the book's reception. He's considering opening social media accounts. He thinks he might need them for publicity. It's strange, he tells her, this part of the book process, where everything is outside one's control. He'd, for so long, been alone with the world of his novel, where he's lord and master. This part, he says, always with a hand forked in his hair, feels like a disembowelment, all of one's insides out in public.

"It's a deeply intimate thing," he says once, "writing a book, mining your failures, your anxieties, your joys, your hope, your vision of the world, and having it out there for all and sundry."

The pages of the book she's read did not seem like they'd provoke strong feelings from readers, and she thinks there's nothing to worry about, but she, of course, says nothing about this. She murmurs simple words of encouragement.

After their conversations, most days, they resign to the bedroom, she with a glass of cabernet sauvignon, he with a can of Budweiser. They make love, slowly, and then fast, desperately.

"Do you love me?" Sommy asks, clammy with passion.

"Yes," he says, breathing into her face.

"Say it."

"I love you."

"Again."

He says it, each "you" colliding with a thrust, and then dozes off soon after. And she stays up always, wondering why she feels so alone. How he could be so close to her, so close she could feel the hair on his skin, and yet feel as though she were abandoned on an empty street on a cold night, naked and shivering. Why, with her new wealth, this ease she'd desperately yearned for, with him, his love, so grounding, so giving, does she feel rootless, violently yanked off from the source of her life? Why does she feel so full of unspoken words? Unable to breathe fully, freely? Like a lone animal in a cruel, anarchial world?

Nia comes to visit Sommy. They sit next to each other on the patio, fumbling around like lovers who have forgotten how to please each other, and must now relearn by trial and error.

"I'm sorry I disappeared," Nia says finally.

The apology immediately irons out the awkwardness, and Nia springs into talking about the new online fitness business she plans to launch in a few months. She says she's anxious. She doesn't want to fail. When she notices that Sommy is quiet, she asks if everything is okay.

"You and Bryan are good?" Nia says.

Sommy contemplates this for a bit before replying that they are good.

Bryan cranks open the door then, beetles in, all smiles and glad gestures, hugs, pleasantries, small talk. They've always liked each other, Nia and Bryan, in the way people who are alike gravitate toward each other.

Later, Bryan back in his writing room, the sun setting, Nia says, "This is the life."

She's looking out at the lake, bright-eyed, as she says this, and in that moment, she appears to Sommy to be very much like Amara, the round, soft face, the susceptivity to awe. It's something Amara would say, "This is the life."

Sommy thinks now that she knows the root cause of her ennui. She knows why everything feels like lead, dark and sticky and heavy. She can't, of course, tell Nia that she covered up a manslaughter and it had been as easy as yawning. She can't say that Christie's face comes to her in her dreams. She cannot say she thinks often of Judith, and One-Eyed Dickson, and that home of theirs, marred now by emptiness in places that used to be full. She can't say that she's beginning to understand something of the passive nature of her brother's cruelty, his slipping into quiet despair, surrendering to apathy. Too tired to try to be good.

She can't tell Nia that she feels herself nearing it, too, the end of her goodness odyssey, that the pain is in the refusal to surrender.

Nia asks if Sommy's heard from Kayla. When Sommy told Kayla that Nia was visiting, Kayla had grunted disapprovingly. "I hope you all have a good time," she said. When Sommy pressed, asked if she was okay with it, Kayla said, "Nia hurt me. All that verbal abuse triggered me, and I realized that after the fact." Sommy said she was sorry, that she wouldn't meet with Nia if it so triggers Kayla, and Kayla said, "No, no, meet with her. I hate her but I love her. I want her to do well and be happy and whatever but fuck her."

Sommy doesn't say all this to Nia. She says instead that she does hear from Kayla. Kayla is good.

"Sweet," Nia says with a sad, quiet tenor.

Sommy looks out at the lake. She sees them together in her mind's eyes, Nia and Kayla, clasping each other in a dark room, breathing. Just breathing. A beautiful, stupid feeling rises in her then, and she wants to say to Nia: "Why can't we all love each other? Why?"

The next morning, Nia emerges from the guest room, well rested, with the vibrancy of a person who has newly laid down a burden.

"I'm glad we did this," Nia says as they walk to the parking lot.

"Me too," Sommy says.

They hug for a long time. No one wants to let go first.

It's a windy night, a few weeks after Nia's visit. Bryan's dusting cumin into a pot of boiling chickpea curry. Sommy's wiping the dining table. From where she stands, through the tall glass window she can see darkness gathering in the sky.

Bryan's phone rings. His palms are wet, so he motions for her to pick up the phone. It's Melinda. Sommy puts the phone on loudspeaker and places it beside him.

"It's searing." Melinda's voice bursts through.

"Thank you," Bryan leans into the phone.

"I was literally shaking afterward. You are so talented, and so incisive. How do you do that?"

"You are too kind."

"Oh, please stop being modest, dearest Bryan. You are a damn genius. And oh, Lagos! I was certain you were having fun. You seemed so happy when we spoke. And goodness gracious, that poor woman. Are you doing okay?"

He's now at the sink, rinsing quinoa in a large sieve. Sommy's staring hard at the phone, so hard she can see the reflection of the glass cup she's holding on the phone screen.

"I'm brilliant, Mel, and thanks for calling. You should come visit Sommy and I."

"I will. I'm working real hard on my novel. I'll be at this residency until I'm done with a first draft. You lit a fire up our asses, Bryan. A book deal, and now you are getting essays into the *Claim*? But I'll come visit immediately I'm done. I'll bring you a copy of my draft. You know that your feedback means everything to me."

"I'll read you, Mel," he says. "Anytime."

There's a short silence, and Melinda says, "I'm curious about Sommy's reaction. Did she okay the piece?"

Bryan places the lid on the pot. He's standing right under the kitchen bulb, golden from the lights.

"Can I call you later?" Bryan says. "I'm making dinner."

"Sure," Melinda says.

Bryan taps the End button, leaving a minuscule sea of water on the screen. It's the only thing Sommy can focus on in the moment, that and the unusually loud sound of the boiling curry.

"I wrote a thing," Bryan says after a while. "It got published earlier today. I've been meaning to talk to you about it. You should read it first."

He wipes his hands on one of the microfiber towels, picks up his phone, punches, raises his head, says, "I sent you the link."

Her phone is in the bedroom, but she can't make her legs work. The memory of a dream comes to her then. In the dream, she's running. She can't see what's chasing her, but she feels it, its perilous presence, and she feels, too, that she's been running for a long time, and that she's forever stuck in this pointless forward motion. It comes to her now, this dream. Perhaps because she's feeling exactly how she'd felt when she woke up that morning, scared, like she's trapped in a dark corridor without doors, nowhere to go, and yet feeling deeply the sensation of movement.

In the bedroom, she watches her phone for a long time before picking it up. Back to the sitting room, she sits on their sectional, legs folded, and steadies her breath as the link loads.

Notes from a Strange Land
Bryan Harris

I was a fatherless child. It was the second piece of intimate information I understood about myself. The first was the clear fact of my difference: a black child growing up with a white mother and two white brothers. Literature about the difficulty of this condition abounds, stories of the confusion and shame, belonging everywhere and nowhere. This essay isn't necessarily preoccupied with these matters, but it behooves me to mention them, for I believe them to be the genesis.

My mother did not speak about my father. In short, she often scorned the topic. But she did mention that he's Igbo. It was no surprise then that when I met my wife, an Igbo woman, in a small Midwestern city, I felt an instant kinship, certain that she was planted there for me. This became even clearer when, upon hearing that I had what might be my father's address, she pressed that I go find him.

This is how I came to be standing on the pavement of the Murtala Muhammed airport in Lagos on that April day, watching the hordes of black overheating bodies stride up and down the sidewalks, and feeling forgiveness toward my father. For the first time, even if fleetingly, I understood the pull he had felt, the pull to go home, to be with his kind.

Lagos created in me a voracious need to see. I was like a photographer losing his vision, a terminally ill person nearing his end. I wanted to be everywhere, to see everything, and there was much to see. My now-wife had the same enthusiasm. At the time, she'd been away from home for two years and was sore from homesickness.

A brief geographical description: Lagos is divided into two parts, the Mainland and the Island. The Mainland is home to the poorest Lagosians, and the Island is mostly occupied by the upper-middle class and the upper class. My wife's family lives in a small, battered estate on the Mainland, and about us was a lot of poverty. I found myself often stunned speechless, wondering: People live this way? Live and die this way? The traffic and noise, the air thick with the pollution of exhaust fumes, dust, smoke, stunned me. But it is the people that held my attention, the incredible number of human bodies laboring under Lagos's sweltering heat. Bus conductors, construction workers, market women, child hawkers, teenage prostitutes, all of them with offices on the streets. Unlike the poverty and homelessness crisis in American cities, Lagos's punctuates every part of its city. Everywhere one turns, there it stands, screaming for attention. There's also the emblem of the Nigerian condition: policemen in black uniforms sitting in black vans, or standing by the roadside, blackening in the heat, terrorizing road users. Once, on our way home from a local arts shop, my wife and I happened upon police officers carting away the petty goods of a roadside seller. I watched as the woman threw herself on the ground, screaming vituperations toward heaven. She seemed to believe that her squabble wasn't with the policemen, but with Fate. I pondered these moments for long days, and by the end of my trip, I understood why for every mile I drove in Lagos, I spotted over seven churches. In the face of powerlessness and hope, an illusion of power, is the second-best thing. And where best to seek hope than in the promise of a just God?

I experienced Lagos on a very intricate level when, a few weeks into my stay, I watched a woman get wounded in a hit-and-run accident, and then die weeks later from the injuries sustained. I will, for the sake of the privacy of all involved, leave out certain details of this woman's tragic fate. But here are the details pertinent to understanding the ethos of my essay: those responsible for this woman's death did not own up, those responsible for bringing her killers to justice did not do their jobs, and in the end, she not only lost her life, but she also lost the story of the end of her life.

"If she's dead, what does the story of the end matter?" you might ask. In French writer Édouard Levé's novel *Suicide*, I found the answer that I'd known intuitively but could not, even with my experience putting the abstract into words, asseverate.

"The way in which you quit [life] rewrote the story of
your life in a negative form. Those who knew you
reread each of your acts in the light of your last.
Henceforth, the shadow of this tall black tree hides the
forest that was your life. When you are spoken of, it
begins with recounting your death, before going back
to explain it. Isn't it peculiar how this final gesture
inverts your biography?"

I've thought of this often, how the story of the woman's death reverts the story of her life. It no longer starts from her birth or from any of the numerous significant moments in her life, a graduation, a forward-moving tragedy, even, the kind that doesn't end with the chaotic finality of death, the kind people refer to when they say, *What doesn't kill you makes you stronger.* No—the story of her life begins with her death. I often imagine family members recounting the woman's death, and it brings to mind this Nigerian phrase that aptly captures the atmosphere conjured by a death so casually dehumanizing: "She died just like that." This phrase I'd

heard from a taxi driver, who had, in the manner of the few Lagosians I met on my trip, begun to lament the state of the country.
He'd used this phrase while retelling the death of a woman who,
while on her way to work, fell into a large hole filled with rain-
water. Her body was discovered in the puddle a few days later.

My wife and I got married a few months after our return from
Lagos. In the months before our marriage, I underwent what felt
like an exorcism. On the matter of the hit-and-run, my wife and
I had different stances. She, after all, is a product of that society.
She understood it, accepted it, in the way one familiar with chaos
stands irresolute. I, the uninitiated, faltered. It had been to me a
simple matter of morality. Good and evil. Right and wrong. Actions
equaling consequences. I had brought unto this society (I mean my
wife's society) the ways of my own country. In a society where
people die "just like that," I had demanded from my wife a specific
kind of morality. I had wanted her to take a stance that is impossible when seen through her worldview. And to understand this,
to understand what happens to morality under fiery heat, I had to
go to fiction. It is through fiction, and not the law, or religion, or
philosophy, that I gained understanding of an incomprehensible
situation.

I would also need to lean on the strengths of fiction after I met
my father, after I learnt that he could provide no answers to long-
life questions: Was it a hard decision to leave? Do you regret
leaving? Do you have the slightest idea of all the ways your absence
made me suffer? Do you know how I suffer, Father? When I would
meet him, he would be there physically, but gone in every other
way. He would be suffering from dementia. I would leave feeling
as hollow as I'd arrived.

Who but a storyteller is expert at constructing something from
nothing? Who but the desperate, the brutalized, the traumatized,
is capable of the magical thinking and imagination that are the
very ingredients of fiction? When there is the rare meeting of both,

the perfect storyteller is born. The perfect storyteller, this is how I think of my child self, who, desperate and wounded, created fantastical tales to explain my father's absence. My favorite: my father as a village chief who was summoned back home to save his people from an evil dictator. He had, of course, left unwillingly.

After I met my father, in the face of nothingness and desperation, I burnished the storytelling skills of my childhood. I said to myself that, had I left with my father back to Nigeria, I would not have the privileges that make my life valuable, more valuable than the woman whose petty goods were carted away by the police, and the woman whose unjust death was overlooked, and the woman left to rot away in a mud puddle. Time and chance and the culmination of a series of random decisions, and I could have been in the condition of these women, a person whose life is without value. Oh, the comfort this story brought me, and then afterward, the shame, the ugliness. In the face of this powerlessness, I'd adopted the Nigerian defense of illusory hope, clamoring for any sort of relief. Isn't this utterly human, this psychosis? Isn't that why fiction exists? To scour through the inexplicable, the shameful, the ugly, with great humility and a thorough lack of judgment? It is in this realm that I processed my own shame, and the question of morality that had threatened my marriage. To forgive myself and to forgive my wife, I had to be okay with the shameful and the ugly. I had to say to myself: we are, after all, humans.

Sommy takes her hand to her navel, where she feels a painful knot forming.

"What do you think?" Bryan says calmly.

She holds the phone away from her like its poison.

"Is this what you think of me?" she says speedily, as if afraid the words will dry up.

He frowns. "Think of you? I barely wrote a thing about you."

"A product of an uncivilized society?"

"I didn't mean it that way. Don't say it that way."

"How did you mean it?"

He is silent. She wipes the snot streaking down her mouth. The cramping in her navel intensifies. He sinks his hands into his pockets, stands slanted backward. She waits impatiently, panting loudly like a wounded animal.

"This is how I know to process stuff, Som. Writing. I have to write my way into a kind of psychological resolution. After what happened, I'm sure you can understand why I needed that."

"You are punishing me? This is us being even?"

"This isn't punishment. What are you talking about?"

She stands and walks to him. She can smell curry on his skin. "You said everything was okay. That it was fine. That we were fine."

"And I meant it."

"But this is how you see me? I take you to my home, to my family, to experience my deepest nostalgias, and this is what you write?"

This is what he'd been doing in his study all those weeks after their return, writing about her, parsing her world through sentences, compressing everything about her into paragraphs.

"Som, stop acting clueless. Please, stop. I experienced gory fucking things. Callous fucking things. I had to process it somehow."

She briefly entertains the thought that it is a joke. He's set this all up to make her laugh, a joke gone bad. But it's not a joke. Look how tight his eyes are, how stiffly he holds himself.

"You said it was fine," she says, slumping internally with fatigue.

He walks to the kitchen. She follows him. He is at the stove, stirring the curry. She stands in the corner by the fridge and watches as he turns off the stove and walks to the cupboard. He pulls out two bowls, wedding gifts from Joel. He dishes the curry, which he sets on the dining table. He does the same with the quinoa. He sets the table—two flat plates, two bowls, two gold-plated forks, and two silver spoons. He sits at the head of the table, watching her. The room feels suddenly cold, comfortless. She looks around. She owns nothing in the entire room, not the couch, not the television, not the purple drapes, not the gold-plated forks. She owns nothing, and he knows it. He's always known it. He thinks her helpless. He thinks her a nobody. For him, she'll always be the one who he can immediately point to and say, "At least I'm not her." That has to have always been her appeal, because they did not make sense. They never did make sense. What else could she offer than a life poorly lived, one so prosaic in its tragedy that it elicits easy pity, makes people like him feel better about the mediocrity of their inner lives?

"You should eat," he says.

She doesn't move, and he starts to eat. After a few spoonsful, he stands, disturbed, and walks to the sitting room, where he flicks the light switch, turning the room into a canvas of dissolving light. He walks back to the dining table and continues with his food. Her heart is expanding, bursting, swallowing her. She'd known that this day would come. Like a horror movie, the danger had been set up from the start. It was only a matter of the manner of its unfolding. Still, the pain zips through her. She wants to break him. She wants to crawl into his tenderest place and put a strong fist to it. She wants to hurt him, desperately, viciously.

"You wouldn't understand," she says. "What I did for my brother. You wouldn't understand. You don't know what it means to have a real family. You will always be an abandoned child. Whether or not you spend your entire lifetime comparing yourself to people you believe to be in worse conditions won't change the fact that you are beyond fucked up, that your daddy did not love you enough to stay. You will forever remain Bryan, the unloved."

He stops eating, and drops his hand forcefully on the table, and the sound of his wristwatch hitting the glass sends a current through the space between them. Sommy braces.

"Somkele," he says with a maniacal snigger. "I know what is wrong with me. I have daddy issues. I don't feel like I belong anywhere. Whatever you say. Bryan—the unloved. I'm honest with myself about that, and now with the world." He gestures to the phone. "But you, Som, you don't know why you feel sad and desperate. Do you?" His voice is low, calm.

"You would die for your brother. And if we are together long enough, you would die for me, too. Look what happened with Bayo. You weren't even in love with him, but you almost threw our relationship away for whatever nonsense you said you shared with him. Because, alone, you don't think anything of yourself. You have no dreams, no ambitions. I beg you to take painting classes. Just to get you to want something. You hated every minute of schoolwork. I can't talk to you about books or movies or anything. Always nonchalant about every fucking thing that is connected to your self-improvement. But you'll cover a crime for your brother, lose your marriage for him. You are a spectator. The stage scares you. The stage has always scared you." He pauses, waits till their eyes lock. "You are right. My love for you is mired in pity."

There's nothing in his face she recognizes now, and yet it is his realest face, all its corners sharp, pronounced, unconstrained by the control he's quick to apply in moments of turbulence between them. For the first time, he's told her the whole truth. "I know you now," she wants to say. "I can see you clearly."

He drops his eyes to the glass table, and she drops hers to the marble floor, and they spend a moment in silent contemplation before she raises her head and he raises his head, and in both their gazes is the quiet sense that it is over.

The Return

Sommy is back. It is surprising how little she's packed, how little is needed, how much can be replaced. She rolls her travel bag to meet her mother, who stands waiting by the KFC at the arrival terminal.

"You look well," her mother says.

They walk in silence through the urgent crowd, arms strung together, a silence that doesn't unspool until they come upon a woman by the exit, clutching a sign: WELCOME HOME HUBBY. Beside the woman are three kids holding balloons, hollering, running chaotically about.

"She looks like she hasn't slept in weeks," her mother whispers about the woman, an attempt to make easy conversation, but Sommy wants quiet, so she says nothing.

It's this way as they drive home, the silence, and as they walk up the staircase to the flat, and as they sit for dinner with her father later that evening.

It's this way the entire week she spends with her parents. She stays in her former room. She has moments of déjà vu, when she catches herself doing things she used to do as a child, like reading under the table, and licking tomato paste out of the can.

She soon moves into a three-bedroom duplex in Agbara. She'd purchased it with part of her share of the money from the sale of the condo. She felt an instant connection when she saw the bright magenta bougainvillea vines curling up the yellow wall of the compound. A fortress made of beautiful things, she'd thought.

This new house is in a quiet area. The houses about have an antique quality. Most mornings, from her balcony, she watches the graying couple who live in the house opposite her. They sit on their own balcony, reading the news and sipping tea. They are always alone, and well dressed, the old man in a buttoned-up T-shirt and severely ironed plaid pants, the old woman in a floral mid-length dress. She imagines that this is how they dressed when they still had offices to go to. She imagines that their teachers at university had been class-mates with Achebe and Soyinka and Okigbo. She imagines that they'd left university bright-eyed, tottering in their acquired British manners, heavy with the mandate of making something of their new country. She imagines that they'd gotten jobs in the civil service afterward, that they'd done good. She knows they are Igbo. There is something in the fullness of their faces, and in the assured way the woman straightens the creases of the man's trousers, zealous about fixing things that he has, over the years of her fixing them for him, become blind to. She imagines that they'd lost family and properties in the war, and maybe lost hope, that bright-eyedness. Perhaps she'll ask them, she says to herself each time. They remind her of what she and Bryan could have been. Each day, the loss feels even more vast, and yet she seems to have space for it. She's not sinking as she had been a few weeks ago.

Once, her father brings Bryan up at dinner. He says to her, in a comforting voice, that he knew that Bryan wasn't "the one." She's surprised by her reflexive defense of him, that she wants to say that in another time, Bryan could have been.

She thought then of the apology email he'd sent a week after the fight.

> Somkele: I'm sorry I dragged us here. We were over in Lagos. I held on because I couldn't bear to lose you after losing this imaginary father I'd built in my head. I had to keep something, and I kept you, and that essay was my attempt at making sense of it all. You brought me closer to myself. If it means anything, my love for you remains intact. My respect might have wavered, but my love never did.
>
> All my love,
> Bryan
>
> P.S. Dr. Diobi (I remember how much you hated it when I called him Father) passed. I was informed by his wife, with whom I'm still in contact.
>
> P.P.S. Nia forgot to pack your copy of *Anna Karenina*. Did you want it mailed to you? Let me know.

Her reply:

> Keep the book, Bryan.

She'd been caustic with anger then. Their whole life together had spun into a yarn of deceit, dark with lies and betrayal. He disgusted her, and she disgusted herself. It was long weeks before she could look at herself in the mirror, before she could find a memory of them together not colored by her anger: in this particular one, she and Bryan are taking an evening walk down Brown Street when he stops and says, "You know, I won't ever let you go." He'd said it with such force. She knew that he meant it. Whatever he'd said and whatever she'd said during their fight is unable to color that memory. The energy of it remains vivid, bursting.

She's only recently brought herself to reread the essay. She finds that it is not as disparaging as she'd first believed. What she'd been reacting to, she realizes now, wasn't what he wrote about her, but that he had written about her at all, that while they slept on the same bed, he'd been plotting, armed with the knowledge that he'd share intimate parts of her with the world, and yet said not a thing. There's also something about the starkness of the revelation that there are parts of her he finds confounding and strange; that she's someone for whom he must make great leaps to know and understand. But she sees clearly her own fault in it. She should have let him go after the incident. She didn't have the capacity to mend him, mend them. Rarely does the person who does the wounding heal the wound.

She's made plans with the rest of her half of the money from the sale of the condo. She'll build an all-girls school. Her ambition has the neatness of a straight line. She wants to give herself to something. Bryan had been right—she's always needed something outside of herself. She'd given all of herself to Mezie, and then to Bryan, and she'd wanted in return for them to make her feel like she was living with purpose. She thinks, if Robert Frost is right, and "Home is the place where, when you have to go there, they have to take you in," perhaps her thereness, her simple presence, will feel like home to some of the girls in this school she wants to build. They'll have English teachers, math teachers, biology teachers, and maybe she'll be the teacher who's there for them when life happens. She'll tell them about boys, girls, love, tell them it's okay for things to come and go, and when there's that rupturing for them, the point of a permanent life change, she'll tell them that that's okay, too. "You'll get back all you've lost," she'll say. Perhaps she can feel purpose, a sense of home in this small space of meeting a simple need.

A few weeks after her arrival in Lagos, she goes to the Ministry of Education office, and says to the woman at the front office, who's sucking on a mango, catching its juice with a napkin, that she wants to build a school. The woman pauses, and stares at her for quite a while, before pointing her to an office where Sommy meets another woman, who hands her a pile of documents, walks her through the accreditation process. There's a competence to this woman, with her kitten-heeled shoes and thick-rimmed glasses, that reminds Sommy of Amara.

When Sommy gets home that evening, she calls Amara for the first time in three months.

"I'm home," she says.

"What happened?" Amara asks.

"I don't know where to start from."

"But you are good? Everything is okay?"

"Everything is okay."

They plan a meeting and when, before they end the call, Amara says, "No shaking, you hear? I dey your back," Sommy knows that they will eventually be fine.

Due to the time difference between Lagos and Iowa, Sommy doesn't speak to Nia and Kayla as much as they used to, but whenever they do speak, time collapses, and they chatter like nothing new has passed in their lives. Sommy had stayed with Nia at an Airbnb a few minutes from the condo in Chicago before she left for Lagos. Nia was the middleman between Sommy and Bryan. She'd brought up the matter of selling the condo, splitting the money between them. She facilitated the meeting with a divorce lawyer. While Sommy cried and moaned, Nia, with almost cold efficiency, packed Sommy's clothes, books, immigration documents, degree certificate. She booked Sommy's flight. She made certain that Sommy ate twice a day. Forced her to take vitamin supplements. Bought her a SAD lamp and placed it beside the bed. She said often, "Did you pee? Have you peed? You should pee." At the airport on the day of her trip, Sommy, crying, said to Nia, "You are such a mum. I love you."

Nia replied, "Show me. Passport? Boarding passes? Cash? Phone charger?"

Sommy flashed each one.

Satisfied, Nia said, "Good. Now get on with it."

Sommy's father helps with buying the land for her dream school. He finds an architect, who finds building contractors. He works closely with the architect and visits the site often. Some days, after a site inspection, they go to the eatery by the estate gate to buy ice cream. Her father gets the strawberry flavor, and she, the chocolate. They sit in a booth by the ice dispenser and talk about the project, the hassle of getting accredited, the rising cost of building materials, and the country, the ever-falling-apart country. He says that Nigeria is a rusted machine, and money is its oil. One only needs to say, "Oga, take this one use hold body," and what was once impossible becomes possible. There's usually a quiet resignation in her father's voice when he speaks, an "It is the way it is" feeling. She's surprised whenever she sees him working with the builders, sees how quickly he switches from a roaring lion to a tame sheep depending on which gets him what he wants. She knows he cannot understand why she left America for this. Everyone is leaving Nigeria, looking for a better life elsewhere. She'd had it, and she'd let it go.

When Patrick came to her house to help her move furniture, he'd said, "I really can't believe you've decided to settle in Naija." He shook his head. "It's those millions in your account giving you mind, sha. Nigeria is not it at all."

She'd said to him that she's aware of the challenges of living in Nigeria, but her rage for its brokenness is tampered now, for she has left, and she can say that there is no paradise, that the Earth is full of places with no warmth, and that at least in her own country, she need not earn her presence—they have to take her in. She told him, too, that she cannot accept this sort of exile. "People go home," she'd said. "When one has gone everywhere, they go home."

He'd looked at her with pity, and said again, "You have money, that's why you are saying this."

She'd laughed, said, "True, true."

Sommy learns from Bayo's tweets that he now lives in California and works at Google. His life has panned out the way he'd planned. There's this picture of him she pauses at: he's wearing a black-and-white-striped shirt and black pants, standing right in front of the Google office, his hands raised to the sky in that goofy way of his. He looks happy. She knows that even without Bryan as an obstacle, she and Bayo would never have been. In different simulations of their lives, she would always leave.

Now, over their ice cream, her father is quiet for a while, and then he says he's proud of her, what's she's doing, what she's done. She's taken aback. He's never said this to her. She'd not realized this, that he'd never said this to her, because she'd always felt it. She'd felt it in the most seemingly insignificant moments, like the time she won a spelling bee in primary school and she'd looked across the crowd and saw etched on his face, clear as seawater, his deep pride. He's always regarded her as whole and had never needed her to earn it, and she wonders where this desire Bryan speaks of originates, this desire of hers to hinge herself to someone.

She waits for him to talk about Mezie, but he doesn't. She thinks he knows the real story of Christie's death. She thinks that perhaps for them family is also about what is not said. This is not the case for her mother, who brings up Mezie at every turn. Once, they are watching a Nollywood movie in Sommy's sitting room. She is watching absently. She knows vaguely that it's a film about two sisters planning a heist. Her mother turns to her as the credits begin, and says, "Enyi akaro nwanne." She's silent, as she always is whenever talks of Mezie come up. They've stayed away from each other since her return. It helps that she now lives in Agbara, an hour from his estate.

But she sees him one Sunday, when she goes to get her father to drive him to mass. She watches as he walks toward the block of flats, in his thoroughly pressed white up-and-down, and she's shocked at her impulse to open the window and wave at him, to say, "Mezie, wait for me, let's go upstairs together," just like she used to do as a child. Yet she doesn't move, doesn't call out to him. Watches as he disappears into the block of flats. After, she rests an arm on the steering wheel. Her forehead on the arm. She then weeps. She weeps not only for the things she's lost, but also because, flayed of the scales she believed to be protection—Bayo, Mezie, Bryan, the illusion of a good life home and abroad—she lives still. Wakes up every morning with a pain she knows she can bear. She weeps because in her recent dreams, she watches herself cut through a thick bush, as if clearing out a path for hope.

ACKNOWLEDGMENTS

A first novel is a life's journey, so it's only appropriate that I begin my thanks from the genesis: Mummy—thanks for your belief in me, for the pile of books you furnished our home with, for your no-nonsense guidance. Daddy, thank you, for the bright glow that is your heart, for fighting for this life I have with so little. Muko, Nemenwa, Junior: What would I know about love if it weren't for the three of you? Chinedu, Aunty Amaka, Brother Okey—thank you for the million small sacrifices.

Nneoma, my human memory card—that I could withstand the years it took to finish this book is nothing short of a miracle made possible by your constant cheerleading. Ukamaka, confidante, best reader, so solid—I can't possibly tell you how much you mean to me. Lucia, Lulu, remember that life-changing conversation many years ago, where you drew back and said, "You should apply for an MFA. It's free." And it's been that way ever since: you, expanding my world, guiding me. I'm indebted. Yeli, you nourish me—thank you for listening to long sections of this novel with patience and enthusiasm.

This book began in Iowa because Lan Samantha Chang put that Iowa Writers' Workshop acceptance call through in 2018, and because I was so dearly held by fellow explorers, American newbies, and room-mates, Arinze, Dubem, and Gbenga (a brilliant poet, from whose poem I borrowed the title of this novel), and by my community: Ife, incisive reader, steady and sturdy human; Siyanda, superb thinker, spa date partner; Alonzo, truth-teller; Angela, warm, always with a listening ear. Thank you all.

The novel saw a new kind of beginning at Florida State University because of Elizabeth Stuckey-French's novel-writing workshop, where I met the best readers: Vince, Alyssa, Marcie, Sarah, Laura. Thank you for giving me your brains and time! Dr. Okonkwo, I'm grateful for your serious, luxuriant engagement with my work. Gbenga Adesina, you know the whole story, thanks for your witnessing. Hera, Li, and Brye: thanks for making the cold days warm.

Alexa Stark, thank you for believing in this book. Amber Oliver, champion editor—you've made this process a dream, thank you. The Bloomsbury U.S. team, thank you for validating not only this novel, but also my lifelong dream of telling stories.

Many thanks to the institutions that have provided me with the time and resources to write: the Farafina Trust Creative Writing Workshop, the Elizabeth George Foundation, Torch Literary Arts, and the Iowa Writers' Workshop.

A NOTE ON THE AUTHOR

Esther Ifesinachi Okonkwo is an assistant professor of creative writing at the University of Michigan-Dearborn. She received an MFA from the Iowa Writers' Workshop and a PhD from Florida State University. Her fiction has appeared in *Isele Magazine*, *Guernica*, and *Catapult*. She's a recipient of a 2021 Elizabeth George Foundation Grant. Home for her is Lagos, Nigeria. She lives in Detroit, Michigan.